DIANN THORNLEY

DOMINION'S REACH

TOR®

A TOM DOHERTY ASSOCIATES BOOK
NEW YORK

This is a work of fiction. All the characters and events portrayed in this book are either products of the author's imagination or are used fictitiously.

DOMINION'S REACH

Copyright © 1997 by Diann Thornley

Edited by David G. Hartwell
Map by Ellisa Mitchell

A Tor Book
Published by Tom Doherty Associates, Inc.
175 Fifth Avenue
New York, NY 10010

Tor Books on the World Wide Web:
http://www.tor.com

Tor® is a registered trademark of Tom Doherty Associates, Inc.

ISBN: 0-812-55098-6
Library of Congress Card Catalog Number: 96-30644

First edition: March 1997
First mass market edition: March 1999

Printed in the United States of America

0 9 8 7 6 5 4 3 2 1

GANWOLD'S CHILD

"Grips and holds from the first chapter—a *good* read!"
—C. J. Cherryh

"Good, hard, quick, no-nonsense reading. . . . Lots of far-future gunpowder gets shot in this promising first volume of a projected series."
—Los Angeles *Daily News*

"A very good first novel."
—Orson Scott Card, *The Magazine of Fantasy & Science Fiction*

"A boy raised by savages comes of age in the midst of interstellar war—fast action and characters you can care about."
—David Drake

"Thornley melds diplomatic intrigue, anthropological speculation, and military derring-do into an effective yarn."
—*Publishers Weekly*

"Smoothly written and appealingly told."
—*Cleveland Plain Dealer*

ECHOES OF ISSEL

"With writing that's clear and expressive, and characters that start out strong and gain depth, this proves to be a spaceworthy sequel."
—*Publishers Weekly*

"*Echoes of Issel* proves that Diann Thornley's excellent first novel was not a fluke."
—Mike Resnick

"Thornley's deft rendering of alien culture, battle strategy, and the subtle relations between the main characters should further her popularity with fans of military SF."
—*Booklist*

"*Echoes of Issel* is a terrific book on many levels. Thornley handles action-adventure scenes with that rare mixture of poise and authority, grace and grittiness, which leaves a reader breathless, heart pounding, wholly caught up in the story."
—Elizabeth Moon

Tor Books by Diann Thornley

Ganwold's Child
Echoes of Issel
Dominion's Reach

Fear not, I am with thee; oh, be not dismayed,
For I am thy God and will still give thee aid.
I'll strengthen thee, help thee, and cause thee to stand,
Upheld by my righteous, omnipotent hand.

The soul that on Jesus hath leaned for repose
I will not, I cannot, desert to his foes;
That soul, though all hell should endeavor to shake,
I'll never, no never, no never forsake!

Attributed to Robert Keen, ca. 1787

ACKNOWLEDGMENTS

This has been the most research-intensive book I've taken on so far, and therefore in many ways it's been the most exciting, at least to me. I've gained quite an education along the way, and I owe a great deal of thanks to those who were willing to answer my endless questions and then read various segments of the manuscript to make sure I'd done it right.

In the medical areas those include Dr. William C. Breuer, Director; Dr. Merle Barnett; Dr. Elizabeth Boswell; Tina McDonald, OTR/L; Karen Smoots, OTR/L; Melissa Jouskey, RD; and the support staff of the Sports & Performance Rehabilitation Facility in Louisville, Kentucky; Kareen A. Jones, RRT at Greene Memorial Hospital in Xenia, Ohio; Lieutenant Commander John Rossi, U.S. Navy; and Thomas C. Lolan and Dr. Robert G. Glaser, audiologists, Dayton, Ohio.

For keeping my E-mailbox full of answers to all my technical questions, I want to thank Lieutenant Colonel Max D. Remley (Ret.), Major John Connolly (Ret.), Captain Gary Watson, and Captain Dave Pilot, all U.S. Air Force; John T. Curtis; and Lieutenant Commander Warren Jederberg, U.S. Navy.

And for providing editorial advice, moral support, and sometimes even free meals, I'm indebted to John and Lucie Connolly, Lana Martin, Warren and Mary Jederberg and the members of the Dayton area SF writing group, the Exophiles (in alphabetical order): Peter Ahlstrom, Rand Blackburn, Rosemarie Connolly, Phil Conrad, Helen E. Davis, Jeff Jacobs, Lorna Simmons, Jessica Washer, and Cheryl Whitmore; and of course, I owe deep thanks to my family for all of their prayers and encouragement.

MYTHOS

SJENLUND

JONICA

Unified
Worlds

KALEO

SOSTIS

TOPAWA

YAN

BUHLIG

NA SHIV

ISSEL

SAEDE/OGATA

TOHH

Issel Sector

ADRIAT

— distance of 1 standard
days travel using
faster-than-light drives

Entire star system
(not just its main
habitable planets)

GANWOLD

ENACH

Bacal
Belt

E. Mitchell 1995

PROLOGUE

There was pain again, dull and persistent but bearable. The same pain Lujan remembered from the times he'd awakened before, except that this time it had localized: It throbbed at the back of his neck, between his nape and the base of his skull.

A stiff neck. A strained muscle, probably. He tried to tip his head forward and back, to turn it slowly from side to side, to loosen the taut muscles.

His head wouldn't move.

He lay very still for a moment, puzzled at that. And he became aware of the silence.

He listened. Listened for voices, for footsteps. For the sounds of equipment. For the background whoosh of air circulation. For *anything*.

The silence was total. Profoundly so.

He tried to open his eyes.

They wouldn't.

He would have to *feel* out where he was, feel his way out of the darkness, out of the silence.

He seemed to be sprawled facedown on a floor, arms outstretched before him. Except that he couldn't feel the floor under his elbows, under his belly and legs—

Was he falling?

He tried to flail, tried to seize hold of—anything.

His arms didn't respond. He couldn't even feel that they were there. Couldn't feel any of his limbs, in fact. Or his torso. Or heat or cold. Or pressure.

Only the ache at the back of his neck.

He broke out in a sweat. He could feel that, cold across his brow.

I'm dreaming, he thought. *It's just a very real dream; it'll end in a few minutes. I'll wake up. . . .*

But he had thought the same thing when the pain had roused him every time before.

ONE

"**Admiral Serege is fully out of the coma now,**" neurosurgeon Berron Gavril said, and pointed at the three-dimensional electroencephalogram tracings that filled the holoscreen on the wall behind his desk. The zigzag patterns charted electrical activity in various locations of his patient's brain. "We made this EEG earlier this morning. It shows nearly normal levels of activity throughout the cerebrum."

Scrutinizing the graphs, Darcie Dartmuth acknowledged the statement with only a nod. As a former combat surgeon, she recognized the EEG's positive indications.

"Show cervical vertebrae," Gavril said.

With a flicker, the display in the holoscreen changed to an image of several vertebrae attached to a skull. Clearly visible on either side of the cervical spine, anchored to the base of the skull with bone epoxy, were a pair of internal immobilization rods.

"Magnify by ten," said Gavril.

Even with the image magnified, Darcie had to lean forward and look hard to make out the fracture lines in the fourth cervical vertebra. It had taken thirteen hours of intricate surgery to position and laser-fuse the bone fragments in her mate's fractured neck and then implant the biopolymer immobilizing rods. Aided by the application of bone morphogens, the crushed vertebra was already mending. By the time it finished healing, the biopolymer rods would be completely absorbed into the surrounding tissues.

"The fracture's knitting well," Gavril said.

"Yes." Sitting with her chin resting in one hand, Darcie nodded again. "The morphogens seem to be very effective."

"Delete skeletal structures and show spinal cord with injury bracketed," said the surgeon.

The holoscreen flickered once more, to show the spinal cord extending from the brain stem. A small box appeared around an irregular portion of the cord, and Gavril said, "Magnify inset one thousand times."

At that level of magnification, the damage to the cord was plainly visible. Darcie drew herself up in her chair.

"Split screen," the surgeon said, "and show presurgical diagnostic scan."

With that comparison, the amount of healing that had occurred in the nine days since the injury also became apparent.

"Due to Admiral Serege's allergy, we weren't able to use neural cell culture implants," Gavril said. "In spite of that, the spinal cord is healing quite well." He swiveled his chair back around to face Darcie. "Thankfully, he isn't allergic to the regen drugs he's receiving. If the healing continues at this rate, he should have most sensation and limited gross motor control back in about a month's time."

"Thank Heaven." The words were a sigh of relief. But when Darcie thought of her mate's other injuries, her hands knotted back into fists in her lap. "Have you been able to determine anything yet about damage to the cranial nerves?" she asked.

Dr. Gavril released a full breath and leaned forward

against his desk. He lowered his gaze to his hands as he interlaced them on its top. "Dr. Moses and I conducted a series of tests after we ran the EEG," he said, and his voice was quieter than it had been a moment before. He looked up again, looked her in the face. "The results were unequivocal: Loss of vision and hearing are total. The protective reflexes—blink and gag and swallow—are intact, but he's lost all motor control and sensation in his lower face—though there's some sensation remaining in his upper face and scalp. But there was no response to any kind of stimuli below the shoulders. That's the result of the C-four fracture, of course."

"Of course," Darcie said, and let her head droop. She swallowed against a sudden tightness in her throat and the pang through her heart.

The news shouldn't have been a shock, she thought. She had known from her first look at the presurgical holoscans what the probable outcome would be, and she'd been bracing herself for it ever since—in spite of a faint hope she'd refused to let go of.

She wouldn't let go of it now, either, she resolved. Swallowing again to relax her throat enough to speak, she met Gavril's gaze. "It's been over twenty-five years since I last cared for combat casualties, Doctor," she said, "but I know there were a number of good prosthetics even then for the ones who lost their sight or hearing. I would think Lujan should be a good candidate for that kind of rehabilitation."

"Dr. Moses and I have discussed it." Gavril kept his hands together on the desk. "We'll have to conduct further tests, of course, to determine the most suitable alternatives, but in the admiral's case it's likely to mean artificial sensory replacements and complete cranial nerve bypasses.

"Once the best procedure has been determined, scheduling the surgeries will depend on how quickly the intracranial pressure returns to normal and how well the internal healing progresses." Gavril looked her in the eye once more.

"Of course," Darcie said.

"And you realize that even the most advanced procedures are limited as to how much of a patient's vision and hearing they can restore."

Darcie's hands curled tight in her lap again. "Yes," she said. "But even partial restoration would be better than what he has now."

"That's true," Gavril said. As if, finally, recognizing her inner ache, he added, "I'm sorry about all of this. We're doing everything we can."

Darcie's hands were still clenched when she started down the corridor to the lift. Clenched so hard that they hurt. She made herself flex and extend them, flex and extend, until the stiffness left her fingers.

"Neurology," she said as she stepped into the lift, and its doors sighed shut behind her.

She drew in a steadying breath as she stepped out on the neurosurgical floor. Two military policemen, stationed there behind a transparent shield barrier, nodded recognition. Returning their nods, and that of the woman at the med techs' station, she turned up the corridor.

Admiral Lujan Serege lay in the critical care unit at the end of the hall. Under ordinary circumstances a patient would be transferred to a standard room once doctors had determined his condition to be stable and were satisfied that he wouldn't lapse back into a coma. But Lujan's case was far from ordinary.

The decision to keep him in critical care was based more on security concerns than on the severity of his injuries, and not only because of his rank and position. Several of the protest groups that shouted and marched through the streets of Ramiscal City had openly declared their intent to complete what the would-be assassin had muddled. The activity around the VIP suite where he might have recovered was only a decoy.

Another pair of military policemen stood outside the door of the CCU. Darcie placed her hand on the infrared scan plate one of them produced, and only when it had confirmed her identification did they move aside to let her pass.

Every member on the team of caregivers assigned to Lujan submitted to the same procedure each time they entered his room.

A med tech was with him at the moment, replacing the splints that kept his wrists and hands from curling in contractures. She looked up as Darcie came in. "Good morning, ma'am," she said. "I wasn't sure how long your meeting with Dr. Gavril would last so I went ahead with the electro-stim and range-of-motion exercises. I just finished bathing him."

Darcie had received permission to provide such personal nursing care herself, but in her absence . . . "That's fine, Hanada," she said. "Is there anything I should be aware of?"

Turning toward the screen above the head of the bed, the young woman touched a button to display the patient record. "Vital signs are stable, pain readings are minimal, and intracranial pressure is continuing to decrease," she said. "Dr. Moses noted bowel sounds during her examination this morning, so they removed the nasogastric tube and started him on ice chips." She added then, "He's awake right now."

"Thank you," Darcie said.

The tech excused herself and slipped away, and Darcie drew up beside the fluid suspension bed.

Her mate lay motionless on his back. He wore no brace or traction device about his neck—none was needed with the internal rods in place—but his silver-gray hair had been spot-shaved to accommodate an intracranial pressure probe and a brain-wave monitor's electrodes, held in place by a plastic band.

His eyes, ice blue and piercing as twin lasers, had been unbandaged since the blink reflex was assured, but tiny sensors had been placed at their corners to monitor his blink rate. Looking into his eyes, she found it hard to believe they were blind.

At least *they* appeared normal. The muscles and flesh of his lower face seemed about to slide off their framework of bone, and his mouth sagged slightly open. Though the nasogastric tube was gone, the ventilator's hose still emerged from a tracheostomy. His chest was dotted with cardiopulmonary sensors, and an IV line ran from the hemomanagement system on the wall to the subclavian vein beneath his collarbone. Bedcovers concealed the catheter, but not the fact that he'd lost weight in the nine days he'd lain here.

"Lujan?" Darcie said. She knew he couldn't hear any more than he could see, but she couldn't bear not speaking to him. She wiped away a trickle of saliva from the corner of his mouth and started to pick up his nearest hand in its splint—then remembered that he had no sensation in his hands. She reached out to his forehead instead and began to stroke back his hair with her fingertips.

He blinked twice at her touch—a response so deliberate it almost startled her. As if he wanted to make certain it wouldn't be mistaken for reflex, she thought. It was an attempt to communicate in the only way he had left.

She drew her fingers across his brow in reply, back and

forth, to offer reassurance. "I'm here, love," she whispered. "I'm here."

As the creases in his forehead relaxed, a mild curiosity crept up from the back of her mind. How much could she make him understand besides the comfort of her presence? How well could she communicate with him by touch?

With one finger, she sketched a string of characters across his brow, spelling out, "It's Darcie."

His forehead puckered at that, his eyebrows drawing together as if with a question.

He hadn't understood.

Most likely, she thought, her attempt to write to him had felt like meaningless doodles on his face.

Biting her lip, she started over.

He wrinkled his brow again before she'd half finished. She could sense frustration in that partial expression, as if he knew she was trying to communicate but just couldn't make out the words. It was almost as if he were straining to do so.

"Don't, Luj." Glancing at the intracranial pressure monitor, she stroked his forehead as she had before. "Just relax," she said. "It's all right. We'll try again later." And, despite the band of electrodes about his head, she began to run her fingers through his hair as she did in their intimate moments.

His eyebrows arched at that, and then he swallowed convulsively, as Darcie had seen him swallow only on those rare occasions when emotion made it hard for him to speak. There was no mistaking his recognition of whose touch it was.

"Yes, love, it's me," she said, and felt her own throat tighten. She kissed his brow and whispered, "I won't let you go through this alone."

It was the only promise she could make him right now—the only one she could keep, at least. If the days dragged on for her, sitting here beside him, how must each *hour* seem to him, cut off from sight and sound and sensation? It would be so easy for him to feel he'd been forgotten, left alone to lie here in his helplessness.

She refused to let him feel that. She stroked his face and hair and spoke to him until his sightless eyes closed and the brain waves on the monitor showed he had drifted back to sleep. Then she removed the splint from his nearest hand and turned it to examine his fingers.

The bandages had been removed two days ago. Faint scars still showed where the electromagnetic pulse had left its exit burns. She took his hand between her own and began to manipulate and massage it.

His hands were slim but rugged, large enough to envelop her own. They were callused and tanned from years of outdoor labor, but Darcie had seen their gentleness each time he'd held their infant son. She'd seen their dexterity, too, as he cleaned and replaced the myriad gears of a windpump head, and their strength as he wielded a razor-edged *katana* through a series of *iaijutsu* drills.

His hand lay limp between hers now, but she could remember how it had felt when he'd placed it over hers and asked her to attend the treaty ceremony with him.

"I'm uncomfortable about this one," he had said.

Had he suspected something even then?

He'd been uneasy about the Isselan Assistance Agreement from the beginning, actually, and she knew there was good cause for that. By the age of fifty-one he'd spent over thirty years in the military, defending the Unified Worlds against threats from the Issel Sector.

"Takes some kind of nerve, doesn't it?" he'd said when he first learned of the proposal. "Two months ago they were launching a full-scale assault against us. Now they're requesting military assistance to help them put down the masuk threat!".

As commander-in-chief of the Spherzah, the Unified Worlds' special forces, Lujan had been at the forefront of repelling that full-scale Isselan assault.

"But I've heard you say a hundred times that you'd rather deal with the masuki in the Issel Sector than wait until they move into Unified space," Darcie said.

"I would," he replied, and began to pace the width of their bedroom. "But I don't want to do it in an alliance with the Isselans. I don't trust them."

In the end, it was the masuk slaving raids against innocent Isselan civilians, and the rekindled memories of his own anguish when Darcie and their son, Tristan, had been taken by masuki years before, that had caused his change of heart. Then, with other members of the Unified Worlds Defense Directorate, he had taken an active role in negotiating and drafting the agreement.

The greatest opposition had come from groups of veterans who, like Lujan, had spent their military careers deterring Isselan aggression. When the Unified Worlds officials were denounced as traitors and death threats were received, participants on both sides of the treaty were assigned bodyguards.

All of the antiterrorist precautions hadn't been enough. Darcie shuddered at the memory of how the signing ceremony had been disrupted by an expatriate of the Issel Sector world Na Shiv. By the time he'd been disarmed, the Isselan ambassador, the Isselan minister of interplanetary relations, and one member of the Triune, the three presidents of the Unified Worlds Assembly, were dead on the floor. The Isselan minister of planetary defense had survived only because Lujan shoved him out of the field of fire.

That minister had sealed the Assistance Agreement

three days later, in a ceremony witnessed only by a handful of officials gathered in his hospital room.

That had been six days ago.

Six days and fifteen hours ago, Darcie thought as she glanced at a timepanel on the wall. It was almost 2300. She passed the guards at their post and entered the lift, thinking that those six days already felt like six weeks.

A pair of newsnetters stood in the main floor's lobby when she emerged, one carrying a holocorder, the other a voice pickup. She froze upon spotting them, backed up a step and started to turn around—she could access the pedestrian tunnel by another lift at the far end of the hall, she knew—but they had already seen her.

Annoyance tightened her jaw and narrowed her eyes as the newsnetters crossed toward her. Annoyance and sudden wariness. The man who had nearly taken Lujan's life had been dressed in a newsnet blazer and armed with an electromagnetic weapon concealed inside his newsnet holocorder.

She glowered at the man who extended the voice pickup toward her. "The medical center spokesperson's name is Alyssa Danzl," she said before he could open his mouth to start questioning her. "Her office is in the administration building, on the second floor. She can tell you everything you need to know."

"But as Admiral Serege's mate, Captain Dartmuth," the man said, "surely you have some feelings on this. We know that he's out of the coma now, and that you've been with him all day—"

"—and I'm tired," she said. Firmly. "Go talk to the spokesperson." She brushed past him and strode toward the lobby's lift without a glance back.

As it began its descent, she realized that her hands were clenched once more and her body trembled with contained irritation.

That had passed by the time she reached her room in the medical center's family quarters; her hand was steady when she raised it to the scan lock. But she paused first to check the room's security monitor.

Satisfied that there had been no tampering or intrusions, she palmed the lock. The door slid open.

She started to say, "Lights on" as she stepped over the threshold, but the dark suddenly seemed like a refuge. "Cancel that," she countered. The door closed behind her and she sagged back against it, too weary to stand without support.

Too weary to fight back the emotions that welled up inside her.

She wouldn't allow herself to cry in Lujan's presence, even though she knew he couldn't see or hear her. Whenever she felt her throat tighten or her eyes begin to burn as she exercised him, bathed him, or watched him struggle to communicate, she gripped his nearest hand and prayed. *Grant him strength. Grant him calm in thy love. Help him rest. Help him heal.*

She couldn't hold back the flood any longer. She pulled the clasps out of her hair and shook it loose about her shoulders and down her back, until it wrapped her like a veil. Then she leaned against the door and sobbed quietly, letting the tears roll unchecked down her face.

She leaned there for several minutes even after she finished weeping, feeling drained but unburdened, as if a mounting pressure had been released.

Wiping her eyes and looking up at last, she saw the mail light blinking on the comms terminal across the room; in fact, the QUEUE FULL light was blinking—as it had been when she'd come in last night, and the night before that, and . . . More messages of concern and support for Lujan, she knew.

"Lights up, thirty percent," she said, and moved to

the terminal. "Voice off. Dump mail queue to the printer, compact font, print both sides." Someday, she thought, she'd read these messages to Lujan. Someday after the auditory rehabilitation, when he'd be able to hear them.

By the dim light she spotted a new bundle of prayer ribbons on the table, undoubtedly delivered by the housekeeper.

The ribbons were still a curiosity to her, in spite of the number that had been sent by the people of Ramiscal City since the incident. Each was five centimeters wide and twenty-five long with a cord at one end and a prayer embroidered down its length in curly script. Most of the ribbons were red, invoking the local deity of healers and healing, but some were amber, to petition the protector of warriors. They were supposed to be tied up in the patient's room, she knew, preferably where ventilation or an opening door would make them flutter, to attract the deity to whom they were addressed.

The ribbons that had arrived over the past nine days would completely cover the walls of three rooms the size of her quarters, she guessed.

Picking up the new bundle, she sank into the nearest chair and began to read the requests stitched on them:

Touch Admiral Serege with your hand, most Compassionate One, and let him return to us well and strong.

And another:

Pour your healing balm upon Admiral Lujan Serege, that his wounds will be healed and he will be restored.

Darcie didn't offer her own prayers to the local pan-
theon, but the urgency and feeling of those wishes caught
at her heart. Perhaps, she thought, the universal God
whom she and Lujan worshiped would recognize their
pleas.

She was still reading the ribbons, still curled in the
chair with her legs tucked up under her and her hair
spilling loose about her, when the door's call buzzed. She
actually jumped, then glanced at the timepiece on the
table. It was nearly midnight. Brow furrowing, she
slipped silently up from the chair and peered at the monitor beside the door.

Lujan's executive officer, Captain Jiron, and his mate,
Heazel, stood outside. Heazel balanced a square container in her hands.

Darcie thought of them almost as family. They had
been here for her every day since the treaty incident.
"Open," she said.

The homey aroma of a hot meal followed the couple
inside. Heazel came straight to the table and set down her
container. "I'm sorry we're so late," she said first. "Every
time I called the desk, the tech said you were with the admiral, and I wondered if you'd had anything to eat."

Not since early afternoon, over ten standard hours before, Darcie realized with dim surprise. Even that had
been more of a snack than a meal. "I—I haven't," she
said. And then, "Please, sit down."

"Oh, we shouldn't stay," Heazel said. "You need to get
your rest. . . ."

Exactly what Dr. Libby Moses had said an hour earlier
when she'd found Darcie nodding off in the chair beside
Lujan's bed, still holding his hand: "Crikey, Darcie,
you've been in here since oh-seven-hundred this morning—"

"Oh-eight-hundred," Darcie corrected. "I had that meeting with Gavril first."

"Whatever." Libby had made a resigned gesture. "Lujan's not going anywhere. Go get some sleep."

At the edge of her awareness, Heazel was asking, "How is he?"

"Hmm?" Darcie realized she'd been drifting. She drew a deep breath. "He's out of the coma now," she said, "but"—she looked from Jiron to Heazel and back to Jiron—"I think his real battle is just beginning."

TWO

"**At least the invaders didn't ravage the** whole planet this time," Minister Edde Weirmac mused aloud as he gazed out of the government skimcraft. "The hostages still have a world to come home to."

Seated across from Weirmac, Chief Cabinet Minister Seulemont Remarq acknowledged the comment with the arching of a sparse eyebrow and turned his attention forward to the Capital Spaceport. It was mainly by his own efforts that the first group of abducted citizens was about to be reunited with families and friends. He would be there to witness it but his name and role would not be mentioned when credit was given for securing their release.

It was just as well, he reflected. Working behind the scenes allowed him a freedom of movement lost to his high-profile colleagues. Like the director of a drama production, he could orchestrate his script without being seen.

Disembarking from the skimcraft a few minutes later, on the platform reserved for the World Governor, he paused to adjust the gold bandolier of office on his counterpart's shoulders, as if he himself were a mere aide. "You know what to do, what to say," he murmured.

"Of course, my lord." Weirmac made a slight nod.

"Very well." Remarq stepped back.

A handful of security troops encircled them both as they entered the lift to the main terminal.

They emerged in a broad concourse that had gates to a number of shuttle bays. The concourse was already filled with anxious relatives and personnel from the news services. Remarq, shorter and deliberately inconspicuous in his simple dark coat, dropped behind the other minister.

Newsnet holocorders turned in Weirmac's direction as he approached, and Remarq slipped out of his shadow as the shuffling and shifting of the crowd subsided.

"My lord Minister of Public Health and Safety." A woman in the burgundy uniform of a major newsnet made a half bow as she extended a voice pickup toward the cabinet minister. "What are your feelings on this occasion?"

Tawny-haired and handsome, Weirmac gazed around at the circle of holocorders and the cluster of voice pickups thrust close to his face and offered a compassionate smile.

He was a natural, Remarq considered, watching him. A fine actor. A fine tool. As were all the others he had approved for positions in Issel's cabinet.

"I'm grateful," Weirmac said, "for the courage all Isselans have displayed, and for the confidence you've expressed in your world leaders during this time of catastrophe. It's been a most painful time for all of us. Perhaps now, as we're reunited with our loved ones, we can finally place this unfortunate part of our history in the past."

With the briefest of glances in Remarq's direction he added, "I'm also grateful to the Unified Worlds for the role that they've played in helping us to liberate ourselves from the alien invaders. I hope this will herald a new era of cooperation and peace among all of our worlds."

Weirmac's remarks were answered with light applause from members of the crowd nearest him, but the collective attention was fixed on the gates behind him—particularly with the distant roar of shuttle engines now building to a thunderous crescendo outside the terminal. Faces taut with anticipation, the people pressed up to the barriers.

Outside, the roar of landing thrusts receded. Uniformed spaceport personnel crossed to one of the gates, released its latches, flung its doors open. Making a split-second eye contact with Remarq, Weirmac positioned himself in front of it.

From the primitive prison mines on Issel's second moon, all rescuees were being evacuated to waiting hospital ships for rest, decontamination, and medical care as needed before being shuttled to the surface. Those with serious illnesses or injuries were to be transferred directly to hospitals in their home regions once they were stabilized. A steady stream of shuttles were on their way; this would be only the first of many such homecomings all over the planet in the week or more to come.

The people who appeared at the far end of the passage all wore simple beige tunics and trousers stamped with MYS GOOD HOPE, and expressions as anxious as those of their waiting relatives. Weirmac clasped the hands of bone-thin men, kissed the hollow cheeks of gaunt women, patted the heads of teary children, and wished them "Welcome home" before steering them into the embraces of their loved ones. The weaker ones came supported on the arms of hospital corpsmen, and Weirmac pressed the corpsmen's hands, too, and told them, "Thank you, thank you!"

A touching set of pictures, Remarq assessed, watching from the press of the crowd, to be forwarded to the newsnets of the Unified Worlds.

Still, he was grateful when it was over, when Weirmac finally extricated himself from the mob and turned back toward the shuttle platform. Remarq sank into the deep leather-upholstered seat of the skimcraft as it lifted away from the spaceport. "Well done," he told the other, and then turned his attention to the countryside sliding by below.

Today it was carpeted with the variegated greens of crops. When the Dominion had seized Issel almost thirty years before, during the War of Resistance, nothing had been left untouched. Industrial centers and agricultural areas alike had been torched—mostly as an example to the rest of the worlds in this sector of the galaxy, for their recalcitrant attitudes toward inclusion in the Dominion.

The Unified Worlds, a fledgling confederation then, had managed to drive the Dominion's hordes back to the galactic core from which they had ventured. Remarq had not fled with them when the rout came. He'd stayed to watch and work quietly, always behind the scenes, during the ensuing years that Issel had spent in rebuilding.

This most recent threat, from a string of stars called the Bacal Belt, which lay near the galaxy's outer rim, had sought resources of a different kind. Not the wealth of whole worlds and their cultures this time. The masuki wanted only human slaves.

In a series of five raids, conducted with the methodical swiftness of long practice, they had carried off men, women, and children. They had caused almost no physical damage, and there had been very few deaths or injuries. But close to two hundred thousand Isselan citizens had vanished from cities all over the planet.

The masuki hadn't started out as a threat—not to the mind of the late World Governor Mordan Renier, at least. They were humanoid, but barely so. Over two meters tall, with ursine eyes and thick black body hair, masuki resembled the wolfmen of ancient folktales. Despite all advice against it, Governor Renier had hired them as mercenaries to assist in reclaiming his own homeworld, Sostis.

When that bid failed—as Remarq had warned him it would—the masuki had returned to Issel to collect their promised payment. With Issel's space fleet decimated and Renier dead by suicide, Remarq had been left with no recourse but to seek help from the Unified Worlds—which were headquartered on Sostis.

It had taken a great deal of effort—a profusion of official apologies to the Unified Worlds for Renier's adventurism against them, a number of dramatic news reports shot at the scenes of masuk slaving raids, and a carefully worded plea for help—to persuade Issel's recent enemy to become involved. But then, Remarq was a master of persuasion.

It was the Dominion's loss that his overlords in its highest circles hadn't recognized that.

When the skimcraft touched down again, on the Governor's platform of the World Government Building in the heart of the city of Sanabria, an aide was waiting for him. He dismissed Weirmac with a curt nod as he stepped out of the skimcraft and said, "Yes, Corita?"

"General Varuska of the space fleet is set up in the Defense Ministry's conference room, my lord," she said. "He has the update you requested on the status of military operations."

"Thank you." He turned toward the doors but then paused. "I would like to see the rest of the day's concerns following the briefing."

The conference room was large enough to seat the complete Isselan cabinet, but Remarq was the only one in attendance at this briefing. He crossed to the chair at the table's head nonetheless, and addressed the waiting officer: "You may proceed."

General Ronado Varuska, commander-in-chief of Isselan Space Fleets, relaxed from his brace. "This briefing has a classification of secret, my lord," he said. "Information is current as of oh-nine-forty local time."

Remarq nodded, and the general touched a button on his podium. The holotank behind him rippled as if a curtain were opening and displayed a view from space. Issel, veiled in clouds, rotated at its center.

"By zero-two-hundred local time yesterday," said Varuska, "all combat vessels of the Unified Worlds had withdrawn from Issel's planetary defense zone to assume defense-in-depth positions throughout the star system. All confirmed and possible lightskip exit points are currently under Unified surveillance and control, and Unified and Isselan patrol craft are searching the system for any masuk-controlled vessels that may have escaped from the battle." The world in the holotank was replaced by a schematic of the star system, with arrows marking the locations of the Unified defense groups.

"Mop-up within Issel's planetary defense zone is ongoing at this time," Varuska said. "Isselan salvage crews, with Unified assistance, have been working continuously for the past fifty-two standard hours to clear debris from our major shipping lanes." The holotank switched to a view of several space tugs maneuvering a carbon-scored hulk that had once been part of a ship. "They expect it will require another sixty hours at the minimum to complete the task.

"In addition, my lord, Unified Worlds salvage crews are accompanying our personnel aboard the Isselan vessels that were under masuk command. Their assistance in locating and rescuing survivors aboard those ships has proven to be extremely valuable. However, they are also dismantling and removing all high-powered weapon systems from those ships and taking them into custody." Varuska's tone of voice and facial expression both darkened. "Furthermore, their pressure suits are equipped with sensors that our analysts have assessed to be a variety of intelligence-collection instruments. If they are correct, the Unified Worlds are acquiring immeasurable amounts of data on our shipboard technology with every salvage mission." His look fixed on Remarq's.

Remarq dismissed it with a wave of his hand. "It's of little consequence," he said. "The technology in those ships is at least three decades old. It may be to our advantage to let the Unified Worlds believe we have nothing more modern."

Varuska studied him for a long moment before he said, "Very well, my lord." Then he shifted behind his podium and returned his attention to the text displayed there. "General Ande Pitesson, commander of the Unified Worlds forces, has also stated his intent to remove all remaining Isselan combat vessels to Yan for repair and secure storage."

Remarq shook his head a little at that. "Still so distrustful of us," he sighed. "But perhaps this issue can be negotiated. We can claim that those ships would serve us as armed freighters." After a moment's consideration, he motioned at the general. "Go on, please."

Varuska shifted again, then said, "Rescue and evacuation operations are continuing on Issel II. As of zero-nine-forty local time today, approximately fifty-one thousand people had been evacuated from the moon to hospital ships. The numbers of seriously ill and injured are surprisingly low so far, but all of those evacuated exhibit symptoms of malnutrition or starvation, and all have tested positive for a variety of viruses and bacteria from the prison mines. General Pitesson expects the rescue operations to take at least a standard week to complete."

Varuska looked up from his podium at last. "That is all I have at this time, my lord. Do you have any questions?"

Remarq pressed his gnarled fingertips together like a steeple and contemplated the information for several seconds. "No," he said at last. And then: "Our patrols with the Unified ships will continue until the last of them have left our star system, General. There will be no aggressive flight maneuvers or formations that might cause the Unified Worlds any concern or delay their departure."

Varuska gave a stiff nod. "Understood, my lord."

Corita was waiting in the corridor, microwriter in hand, when Remarq emerged from the conference room. "I've just received a communiqué from Minister Nioro Borith," she said. "He's accomplished the arrangements for transporting the bodies of Minister Istvan and Ambassador Pegaush home from Sostis, and he plans to escort them here. However, shipping service into the Issel system will not resume until a statement guaranteeing operational safety has been issued by this government."

"That's a matter for the Ministry of Intersystem Transportation," Remarq said. He turned and started up the hallway. "Minister Tibor will need to confer with the space fleet on the status of the in-system shipping lanes."

Following him, the woman gave a quick nod and tapped notes into her microwriter with jeweled fingernails. "The cabinet has also submitted a list of nominees to fill Minister Istvan's post," she continued. "You'll find the recommendation proposals under 'Nominees' in the Immediate Action file."

"Finally," Remarq snorted. Moments later he added, "While we're on the subject of Istvan and Pegaush, please contact the Protocol Office in regard to their memorials. There must be full honors, of course. If there are any questions, they're to be directed to me."

"Yes, my lord." Glittering fingers flew over the miniature keypad.

The massive double doors to the World Governor's office slid apart as they approached. The woman finished relaying the day's itinerary and slipped away, but Remarq crossed toward the vast expanse of the Governor's desk and seated himself in its high-backed chair. *"Capital Courier,* morning edition," he said to the terminal on the desk.

Its monitor lit up with the headlines, text, and a couple of hologram images. Remarq opted for the voice synthesizer, to have the text read aloud while he poured himself a cup of tea from the dispenser on the desk and sat back to sip at it.

The lead story was the homecoming of the hostages that he had attended earlier. There were images of people in beige tunics weeping and hugging their relatives, and a holocorded clip of Weirmac's speech. That story was followed by two or three related ones, and then there was a series of biographic sketches on the nominees for minister of interplanetary relations. There were a number of editorial pieces, too, debating whether or not Istvan's and Pegaush's assassin should be extradited to stand trial on Issel—particularly since he was a disgruntled former citizen of the Issel Sector world Na Shiv. Remarq listened to those with interest. But it was a short out-system report that drew him forward in his chair, mouth pursed with concentration as he took a sip from his teacup.

"Trosvig Accepts Seat on Triune," the electronic voice announced, and then continued, "On the sixth day of the twelfth standard month, the Honorable Seamus Trosvig of Mythos was installed as a member of the Unified Worlds Triune in Ramiscal City on Sostis. Trosvig fills the seat left vacant by the recent untimely death of Pite Hanesson, the first Mythosian ever to hold that position. As the former head of the Mythosian delegation to the Unified Worlds Assembly, Trosvig brings over twenty years of experience to this appointment. . . ."

"Trosvig." Remarq arched his eyebrows. "Well, well, our old friend! How wonderful for you! Who would have ever thought . . ." He let his voice trail off, the sentence unfinished as he tapped the intercom button on the desk. When the image of his aide appeared on its small screen, he said, "Corita, please send a message out to Ramiscal City, Sostis, at once. Address it to the Honorable Seamus Trosvig of the Unified Worlds Triune, and let it read 'Congratulations on your new appointment. May success surround you as we two work together to build a better future for our worlds.' "

"Right away, my lord," the woman said.

"Thank you." Remarq gave a curt nod as he released the intercom button, and pressed another button, which opened the desk's bottom drawer. The object he sought was in the back corner: a small box, three or four decades old, with a synthe leather cover. He brought it out, placed it on the desktop before him, and lifted its hinged lid.

It contained a military medal, a Mythosian Combat Crescent on a rich orange-and-green ribbon. It had been presented to Colonel Kosko Trosvig, Seamus's father, during the War of Resistance; the elder Trosvig's name was engraved on the back of the crescent. Remarq had received it from the younger Trosvig twenty-two years ago as the closure of an agreement between them. The time to return it had arrived at last.

He tapped the intercom again. "Corita, there's also a small congratulatory gift that I would like to have sent out with that message," he said. "Would you kindly see to its shipment?"

"Of course, my lord."

When Corita's image vanished from the intercom screen once more, Remarq carefully removed the medal from its case and held it up to the desk's illuminant to study the details of the crescent.

"How wonderful for you, my old friend Seamus," he said again, mostly to himself. ". . . And how very convenient for me. Perhaps this would be a good time to petition for reentry into the Unified Worlds after all, while Issel is still perceived as weak, while there's still goodwill between our worlds, and while I have someone in a position where I can use him."

THREE

There were hands again, at his head and shoulders. Lujan could tell by the shifting of their hold, by the pressure of palms and fingers, that they were turning him. But there was no sense of his position changing, no shift in his equilibrium. It puzzled him.

Fingers brushed the left side of his forehead and ran down his left temple: Darcie's fingers, telling him she was there. He knew her touch—was grateful for it. It anchored him in the silent darkness, relieved the almost uncontrollable urge to let go his sanity, to scream until his throat was raw just to be able to hear *something!* He could hold on to that touch, if only in thought—hold on to it in his memory even when it wasn't there.

He had no idea how long he'd lain this way. Had it been days? Weeks? Months? He tried to measure by the number of times the hands shifted him or worked on him and the length of the intervals in between, but he lost track when he slept. The regular turning always startled him awake. He would open his eyes—

He always blinked two or three times.

He could *feel* that he was blinking. There seemed to be tiny weights adhered to the outer corners of each eye; he could feel their pull at his eyelids with every flicker. He *knew* his eyes were open, but all he could see was impenetrable blackness.

From time to time a hand slipped a tube into his mouth and offered him something to drink. He wanted to suck at the tube, to pull in the liquid in starving gulps—but his mouth wouldn't work. So the liquid dribbled over his tongue instead, a little at a time, and he swallowed. That was pure reflex, he knew, the reflex that kept him from choking.

At least he could taste the liquid. Sometimes it was cool and had a vague fruit flavor; sometimes it was warm, more like a broth. It was always bland, and it never fully satisfied his hunger. Still, it was an improvement over the ice chips he'd been given so sparingly at first.

He slept a great deal, and when he slept he dreamed. Of Darcie, of running his hands through her thigh-length hair and returning her touches and holding her tight in his arms. Of Tristan, tall as himself now and filling out with the musculature of young manhood, hiking beside him across the red desert of Anchenko and trying to catch a fish bare-handed in a stream swollen with spring rains.

Once he dreamed of a man in the robes of an Isselan cabinet minister, an urgent man with ebony skin. That dream stayed with him, perplexed him when he woke again: He knew the man's face but he couldn't remember his name.

During the periods when his mind seemed most lucid he tried to remember what had happened, what had put him here. At first there were only dream images mingled with memories that twisted themselves into terrifying abstractions, like the hallucinations he'd once suffered during a serious illness. Two or three days passed—he estimated—before he could focus on some fragment and tell himself with any certainty, "I remember that."

He remembered slipping through jungle growth on a world called Saede, searching the shadows through his helmet's nightvisor as voices, quiet but clear, rattled through his headset. The underground facility was now in the control of Unified forces, the voices said. The masuki were committing suicide rather than surrendering; there were a number of wounded. . . .

That was where he'd discovered Darcie and Tristan, after all those years of thinking he'd lost them to the masuki forever. He remembered finding Tristan deep in the cavern, a bloodied knife in his hand, a dying masuk warrior at his feet—even remembered catching his son when, wounded and weary, the youth collapsed.

He remembered leaving Saede, too. Remembered bringing his family home to Anchenko, on his native world, Topawa—

No, there had been time on Sostis first. He remembered taking Darcie and Tristan to his admiral's quarters in Ramiscal City. He remembered their reaction to Kazak, his dog, and how Tristan stripped the bed in his room, preferring to sleep on the floor.

He remembered Tristan's nightmares, too, and Dr. Moses telling him, "Take him home to Topawa and just spend as much time with him as you can. It may be his only hope for recovery."

They had arrived on Topawa in the middle of the Anchenko Region's rainy season. He remembered how they had spent three days cooped up together in the old family homestead, watching the rain. He had passed time by repairing a windpump's head on the kitchen table.

What I wouldn't give for a windpump to work on now! he thought—and hands that could take it apart, and feel the sharp teeth of the gears and the places where they were worn. . . .

When there was a break in the weather, he'd taken

Tristan camping. He remembered his son's skepticism, his silent stubbornness; he'd lost count of how many times the youth had said, "Mum and I didn't do it that way when we lived on Ganwold!"

They had gone camping again after summer set in, he remembered, out at Lost Prospector Canyon. They spent that night in a shallow cave overlooking the river—and the barriers had finally come down. He and Tristan had spent a good part of that night talking. *Really* talking, from the heart.

The next morning they had joined the Anchenko Spherzah Detachment at its training exercises. They were practicing rappelling.

He remembered how Tristan stayed well back from the edge of the cliff at first, until a few of the younger troops offered to teach him how to do it. Lujan had held the belay line himself; he could remember its tautness in his glove, its tightness around his body.

He remembered Tristan's smile when his feet touched the ground at the base of the cliff. Remembered throwing an arm about the youth's shoulders and saying with a grin, "Well done, son!"

Late in the afternoon they had done a drop at the same time, from rappel points a few meters apart. He remembered sitting back in his seat sling and glancing across at Tristan just before he pushed off—

He couldn't remember anything else.

He couldn't even remember reaching the floor of the canyon. There was—nothing.

He swallowed, a reflexive convulsion of his throat.

There must have been an accident, he thought. Perhaps the rappel anchor, a horn of rock near the lip of the cliff, had broken loose. Perhaps the lines had failed. But he'd checked the anchor and ropes before he'd snapped himself on; he could remember *that!*

Another thought turned him cold: *What about Tristan?* Had he fallen, too? Who had been on his belay that time? Lujan strained to remember, and couldn't. All he could remember was Tristan's face, his jaw set with determination to beat his old man to the bottom.

If this had happened to Tristan, too . . .

He broke out in a sweat.

His dreams, when sleep overcame him the next time, were nightmares. Over and over he watched Tristan's lines snap, watched as his son hurtled to the floor of the canyon—and his own body was paralyzed, useless. He couldn't even shout the youth's name.

The dreams haunted him when he woke, roused by hands moving him again. The memory of the dreams broke fresh beads of sweat across his brow.

He had to know, had to find some way to ask.

The hands were exercising him. Darcie's hands. He knew by the way one paused to stroke his forehead, by the kiss she pressed there. He could feel some pressure as she flexed and stretched and worked his limbs, could feel that his arm or leg was being moved, but he couldn't determine its position, whether it was being raised or lowered, whether it was bent or straight.

He could feel the effects of the electrical stimulation, too: pulses that made whole muscle groups contract and relax, contract and relax.

He was hungry by the time it was over. He could feel his stomach growl under his ribs, as it always had by the end of his early morning workouts, and found himself oddly reassured at knowing *something* still worked!

He blinked to get Darcie's attention when she put the drinking tube to his mouth. She stroked his forehead in response and wrote "I love you" with her fingertip. She drew it slowly, distinctly, one word at a time, and he understood, though learning to do so had taken two or three days.

Warm liquid, slightly sweet, spilled into his mouth in spurts. It took his concentration from the questions he ached to ask and forced him to focus on swallowing.

A random memory slipped through his mind, one that he lingered over for some moments before he realized it was his solution.

He had taught Darcie the universal dot code soon after they were joined. It had started out as a joke between them but before long it had become their private means of communicating in public: tapping with fingers on the arm of a chair, quick squeezes of each other's hands. Once, years before when they were both junior officers, they had attended a military dinner with an exceptionally boring guest speaker. Halfway through the remarks Lujan had reached under the tablecloth and tapped out "Yawn" on Darcie's knee. She had almost giggled out loud.

He couldn't tap this time. Couldn't squeeze her hand. All he could do was blink. He hoped she still remembered the dot code.

She cleaned his teeth and washed out his mouth after feeding him. She'd bathe him next, he knew, and she'd start with his head, with the spots that felt like a ring of bruises around his skull; she was always very thorough, very careful about those.

He waited until she began to wash one tender spot high on his forehead, dabbing at it in circular strokes with something cool. Then he began to blink, "Where is Tris? How is Tris? Where is Tris?" The dot code even included a symbol for the interrogative.

Her hand paused in its washing, as if she had stopped to read his query. Then the cool pad drew away and her damp finger began to move across his forehead. He stopped blinking to read her response.

"Again," she wrote. "Slowly."

He started over, blinking slowly, deliberately, with a pause between each word.

She stroked his temple, and he sensed an excitement in her touch, as if she recognized what he was doing, as if she were trying to encourage him; but there was frustration in it, too. "Once more," she wrote.

"Where is Tris?" he blinked. "How is Tris?"

Her hand paused at his temple, and he read her mounting urgency in it. It lingered even after he stopped blinking. And then she began to write again, shaping each character carefully: "Wait. I don't remember dot code. I'll call someone."

She paused, then added, "Relax, Luj."

He couldn't relax. The nightmares swirled in his mind once more: nightmares of Tristan falling.

FOUR

Nothing the Spherzah intelligence officer
had said in the premission briefing had prepared Tristan
for what they found at the first masuk prison they freed.
Crouched in a dark cavern with his laser-rifle balanced
over his knees, he shuddered at the images that came
back, clear as holograms, through his mind. Images of
skeleton-thin people cowering in the corners of the wire
mesh cell block, dazed eyes staring out of their hunger-
gaunt faces. They were children and elderly mostly, the
ones who lacked size or strength to fight for the limited
rations.

There were images of women, too, with torn clothing,
bruised bodies, distraught eyes, cringing away from his
outstretched gloved hands, some weeping, others actually
trying to fight him off, all afraid of being raped again.

There were images of an old man with gangrenous ul-
cers on his legs; of two small boys with tear-streaked
faces, their skin and hair crusted with grime, who clung
to him tightly as he carried them out to an evacuation
shuttle; of a woman they found cradling her days-dead
child in her arms, who screamed, "Don't take away my
baby!" when two pressure-suited shapes reached down to
lift her to her feet.

There were images of the criminals, mostly men, who

had been sentenced to hard labor in the mines of Issel's moon long before the masuki began to use them as holding areas for their slaves. They leered while they were frisked and locked into restraints under the leveled rifles of Spherzah guards. Their hardened eyes and their bodies, gaunt from lack of food, were more telling than their colorless uniform coveralls.

Hardest of all to dispel were the images of the people who hadn't survived, the ones Tristan had helped to place in body bags. Youngsters who had been trampled in rushes to get rations, or succumbed to disease in the filthy enclosure. Victims of starvation or their fellow prisoners' brutality.

Tristan opened his eyes to force their nameless faces from his mind and tipped his head back against the rough stone wall.

The situation had been the same at the second mine, and at the third, and at the fourth. Like recurring nightmares, he thought, except that the faces were different.

And then they had reached Thrax Port.

The only way in was by the same stairs and through the same shield door that Tristan had sealed with a laser-rifle burst days before. They had taken out the mine complex's utility plant then, an action that had drawn masuk guards away from the lead Spherzah team's advance on the Issel II command post.

There had been no covering compressor noise from the utility plant the second time. The combat team crept up the flight of metal stairs one wary step at a time.

Espino's body still lay on the platform where Tristan and his team leader had been forced to leave it days before. Tristan swallowed, seeing it there.

They'd had to rebuild the shield door's control box, splicing in wires and soldering new connections to make the door operational.

"It'll probably come open with a bang," the chief petty officer cautioned when he finished.

"Right." Team leader Lieutenant Thirup nodded. "Sensors?"

"I've got seven lifeforms in the room," came the response. "Probable masuki."

"Looks like they know we're here." Thirup detached a concussion grenade from his belt. "Riflemen, to your positions; everybody else take cover. Okay, Ryoko, *now!*"

The chief pressed his switch; the shield door slammed open.

Red energy lanced across the room, shot through the doorway. One of the riflemen went down in front of Tristan. He returned fire as Thirup rose up enough to hurl his grenade. They all ducked—

The blast shook the stair platform. "Move!" Thirup shouted.

They lunged forward into the room, into the smoke. Infrared sights picked out masuki slumped in the corners; quick rifle bursts finished them off.

"There're more on the way, sir!" shouted Comms.

Bootfalls thundered along the passage. Palm lights cut wild swaths through its dark.

"Take cover!" said Thirup.

The masuki didn't come into the utility office; they took positions outside its door and fired into the settling smoke. Pressed up to one wall, Tristan heard one of his teammates yell, saw him crumple—saw the team's medic drop down beside him.

"Need another grenade!" Thirup said.

Tristan yanked one off his own belt, slapped it into his team leader's gloved hand. Thirup pulled its pin with his teeth, pitched it out into the passage.

Its blast stopped the shooting. Thirup led them into the passage, riddling the stunned shapes on the floor with

· rifle fire. "Let's go," he said. "Sensors, up front; there'll probably be more of them. Stay sharp, everybody!"

The explosion Espino had created days before appeared to have shut off every light in the complex; the whole place was cave black. "Nightvisors on," Thirup said. "Rifle maglights only—and only for shooting."

They moved swiftly through the tunnels, rifles trained on every shadow that could shelter an enemy. Twice they exchanged fire with snipers, and the second time Sensors was hit.

"It's not dangerous," the medic said when he'd tended to the wound and the firefight was over, "but he won't be walking out of here. He took the burst in the thigh."

Thirup slapped the lifeform detector into his palm a couple of times—then handed it to Tristan. "Take over, Scout," he said.

"Yes sir," said Tristan. His mouth went suddenly dry.

At nineteen, he was at least five years younger than the rawest Spherzah troops. He wasn't a Spherzah himself. Not yet. He had been recruited to act as the elite force's civilian scout because he knew the cave systems of Issel II. He'd been held hostage here himself, less than a year before.

He took the point position with his heart racing hard. His hand shook, wrapped around the lifeform sensor.

The shield door at the bottom of the passage had a manual control. Thirup motioned his team to take cover and ready their maglights before he punched the door's trigger.

The shield doors grated open.

"Sensors?" said Thirup.

The display in Tristan's hand should have lit up with readings from hundreds of humans, all crowded close together. Instead, it stayed blank.

"Something's wrong," he said. "I'm not getting any readings at all."

"Are we in the right place?" Thirup asked. "Try the area sensor."

He did. The natural chamber they faced was over one hundred meters across, nearly fifty wide and thirty high, and the wire mesh cell block itself stood out plainly in its center.

"We're in the right place," Tristan said, "but—there's nobody here. No masuki—no humans."

Thirup hesitated, considering. Then he said, "Palm lights on, but hold them wide. Let's have a look—but stay on your guard!"

They spread out. Advanced warily, rifles leveled. The lifeform sensor stayed blank.

Palm lights played through the mesh barrier of the cell block.

A few meters to Tristan's left and a little ahead of the rest, one of his teammates suddenly froze. "They're all *dead,*" he said. "Three or four days, I'd say."

Everyone stopped and stared.

They appeared to have been mowed down by their captors: men, women, youths, children. All lay sprawled on the stone floor and over each other in a tangle of twisted limbs. Their bodies were marked with energy burns; their faces still bore expressions of terror, of panic.

It was several seconds before someone even whispered a profanity. Tristan turned his head away from the sight, swallowing down the gorge that rose in his throat.

The Spherzah had loaded 1,225 body bags into the evacuation shuttles. When they were finished, Thirup had said, "Two hours until the troop shuttle gets here. Take a rest break, team."

Tristan had gone off to a dark, quiet corner in the underground prison, tugged off the helmet of his armored pressure suit, and heaved until he was strengthless.

"Scout!" Thirup's voice reached him from an outer chamber of the underground complex. "Troop shuttle's setting down! It's chow time!"

Tristan sighed deeply and shoved himself to his feet, grimacing at the stiffness in his legs and back. He stretched a little, trying to relieve it, and made his way out to the shuttle loading area.

The launch bay door was sliding open when he entered the loading area; the first troops were ducking under it and striding toward them. Lieutenant Thirup, also shed of his pressure suit, returned the other team leader's wave and said, "Hey, you guys, what's the word from topside?"

The new lieutenant grinned behind his faceplate. "The word is, you're running the logistics folks ragged! Every available shuttle is flying. They've got two shuttles grounded for engine replacements, and maintenance crews working nonstop. . . ."

Tristan turned away from the talk when another pressure-suited figure approached him, carrying an extra pack. Kersce, he knew, even before he could make out her face inside her helmet. He felt mild surprise at realizing how much he'd been anticipating her arrival.

Kersce was the one who had persuaded him to try rappelling the day he and his father observed the Anchenko Detachment in training. And when he was selected for the scout position and reported aboard the transport ship *Shadow,* she had taken him aside and drilled enough shipboard protocol into him to keep him from getting his head knocked off by one or another of the veterans.

"I know how it feels to be a 'raw egg,' " she had said.

Operation Liberation was only her second Spherzah mission.

Kersce set down the spare pack at his feet and looked him up and down. "It's a good thing this is just about finished," she said. "You and Lieutenant Thirup look almost as bad as the people we're trying to rescue!"

He was about to protest when he glimpsed himself reflected in her helmet's faceplate. He barely recognized his own blue eyes, hollow and reddened and circled from too little sleep, or his haggard features, etchèd with the lines of exhaustion and scruffy with eleven days of sand-colored whiskers. Still, there was no comparison with the images that rose unbidden in his mind. "I don't look *that* bad," he said seriously.

Kersce just smiled. She caught his arm and squeezed it with her awkward gloved hand. "Come on," she said. "I brought your provisions. You can eat while I replenish your pressure suit."

He let her steer him away from the loading area, where the new team was assembling, but only after he'd shouldered the provision pack himself.

Dinner consisted of combat rations: high-protein low-fiber food bars that tasted like the plastic they'd been packaged in—the only thing Tristan had had to eat for the past eleven days. He sat on a desk in the mine controller's darkened office, dangling his legs and chewing slowly and watching Kersce work over his suit on the floor.

She had green eyes and close-cropped dark hair, and she was so petite that Tristan thought certain her armored suit must weigh more than she did. In spite of her gloves, she replaced his nearly empty water flasks and oxygen canisters with filled ones and the urine reservoir with an empty one in a couple of minutes. "It's ready to go," she said, standing up, and placed a fresh powercell on the desktop beside him. "There's some new ammo, too."

"Thank you." Tristan reached for his laser-rifle, ejected the spent powercell, shoved the new one into its slot.

Kersce watched him, head cocked. "Why so quiet?" she asked.

He only shook his head and shrugged. But he knew what it was.

He had been seriously ill from the injuries he'd received under torture when he'd come through this part of the Issel II cave system months before. He'd been barely conscious most of the way. There were more bad memories, more dark images for him here than just the things he had seen in the prisons.

Climbing back into his pressure suit a few minutes later, he found that his hands were quivering.

Only one mine left, he reminded himself.

FIVE

In the news clip, two members of the Isselan cabinet placed the bicolored ribbon of the Order of Xintaras Medal about the neck of General Ande Pitesson, Commander-in-Chief of Unified Worlds Forces in the Issel system. The Xintaras Medal was Issel's highest military honor, awarded only by the direct decree of the World Governor or the unanimous decision of the cabinet. Most presentations were posthumous.

It was, perhaps, a bit extreme, Remarq thought. The Order of Xintaras Medal had never even been awarded to a citizen of another Issel Sector world, such as Adriat or Na Shiv. To decorate the chest of an officer of the *Unified Worlds* with it—

Remarq turned away from his monitor with a cringe, despite the fact that he had ordered it himself.

Mordan Renier's ashes must be smoking in their urn, he thought.

The cabinet had been appalled, of course. Some of its members had protested. Others had simply stared at him in shock. He had stilled the vocal ones with a sharp motion of one hand, and when they fell silent in midsyllable, he said, "It's a small price to pay for the benefits our motherworld may ultimately receive through cultivating a friendlier relationship with the Unified Worlds." He had selected the ministers of planetary defense and historical documents to make the actual presentation and had instructed them, "Be certain that the unprecedented significance of this tribute is not lost on the recipients."

The presentation speeches had been almost too emphatic, he thought. Even Pitesson, standing on the platform, appeared more uncomfortable than moved or flattered by it. His acceptance speech was short and distracted.

The newsnet moved on to provide details about the recent completion of the rescue and evacuation operations, the number of Isselan citizens who had been brought home, the number of Unified personnel who had been involved. Remarq breezed through that and then exited the program. The incoming mail beeper had been sounding from his terminal for some time.

At least a dozen messages were listed in the Official queue. One of them was from Ramiscal City on Sostis. He arched an eyebrow and called that one up first.

When the routing string appeared at the top of the monitor, he smiled. He had guessed correctly. "Ah, Seamus," he murmured. "So how does it feel to sit in the Triune's chair?"

He switched on the original voice recording along with the printed transcript, to listen to Trosvig's own rendition of his message. An individual's inflection and mannerisms often contained more information than did his actual words.

Trosvig's presentation was obsequious almost to the point of groveling, and the hint of strain in his voice suggested intimidation. "My lord Remarq, Chief Cabinet Minister of the World Government of Issel," he began, "I accept your recent congratulatory gift and message with the deepest humility. This appointment was a most unexpected honor, and I feel deeply inadequate in accepting

it—particularly in attempting to fill the seat of my colleague, Pite Hanesson. His death was a terrible tragedy—
as were the deaths of Minister Hampton Istvan and
Ambassador Gunh-Salminen Pegaush. I offer my condolences both to the World Government of Issel and to the
families of the deceased."

Remarq had never met Trosvig face-to-face, had only
seen pictures of him in news clips and political documents; but he could imagine the stocky middle-aged man,
with his thinning hair and bulbous nose, shifting his
weight uneasily from foot to foot and keeping his head
bent over his text as if in a perpetual bow from the neck.

"In light of the recent success of the combined efforts
of our two governments," Trosvig's voice continued, "I
anticipate increased cooperation between our worlds in a
variety of enterprises. I am eager to promote and encourage such activities, my lord, and I look forward to working with you to bring them about.

"I am, as always, your humble servant, Seamus
Trosvig."

Remarq sat back in his chair and considered that last
line on the monitor. *Your humble servant,* he thought, and
allowed himself a smile.

Trosvig hadn't been so humble when Remarq's recruiter first contacted him. He'd even become indignant
when he finally recognized the political web he'd woven
himself into. But by then it was too late to disentangle
himself; he had far too much to lose.

He'd doubtless been humble ever since.

Remarq smiled once more. He had had nothing to do
with the assassination on Sostis—fate alone could take
credit for that—but the personnel changes it had forced at
the highest levels of the Unified Worlds couldn't have
been more propitious if he had planned it himself. He
would never have a greater opportunity than he did now

to use this sleeper he had planted within the Unified Worlds years before.

He wondered briefly if Trosvig believed he *had* arranged the assassination—not that he felt it was necessary to set the record straight. As long as Trosvig had cause to wonder, as long as he remembered how easily a seat on the Triune could change occupants, Trosvig would remain compliant.

Remarq also had to give some of the credit to the Unified Worlds's laws of succession, especially those laws regarding members of the Triune who died in office. Trosvig would never have attained his new position of power otherwise, despite years of subtle maneuvering by Isselan agents.

Trosvig was in a position now to move on Remarq's orders, and he doubtless expected to do so at once. His recruiter's reports had characterized him as an impatient, urgent man. It had been that impatience, in fact—impatience to rise through the political ranks—that had first lured him into the recruiter's snare.

Trosvig wasn't the only one. Mordan Renier had been impatient, too. And there were handfuls of others scattered throughout the Unified Worlds, all willing to sell their political souls for a faster ascent or a higher position in the governing circles.

But Remarq hadn't survived in politics through the past seven decades by riding a swift lift to the top. He preferred the progress of the glacier: imperceptible, almost immeasurable, and yet inexorable, gradually grinding and crushing and covering all that lay in its path.

His patience had cost him his position of influence in the Dominion—had made one of his more eager subordinates his successor. But Remarq had crushed and covered a number of less patient men in his time. He had seen his successor's fall. And now he could see the Dominion's reach waning even as his own extended. One day, he mused, the Dominion would find itself subsumed, absorbed by the Issel Sector.

"Compose response," he said. The monitor lit up with routing blocks, and he directed, "Address it to the Honorable Seamus Trosvig and send it to the headquarters of the Mythosian delegation to the Unified Worlds Assembly, via the Isselan embassy on Mythos. Send it encrypted, for decryption by Seamus Trosvig only, with self-erasure after reading. Authenticator code will be Kilo Alpha, and there will be no copies."

Characters filled the routing blocks, and Remarq straightened in his chair. "Begin dictation," he said. And then: "My good friend Seamus, I trust that you are well and settling comfortably into your seat on the Triune by now."

As his words appeared on the screen, like text entered from a keyboard, Remarq leaned back in his chair. "I assure you that I, too, would welcome increased cooperation between our worlds in the months and years to come. I believe that our successful joint military effort has proved conclusively that such cooperation is both possible and mutually beneficial. I feel this is an ideal time to begin exploring new possibilities for exchange in education, agriculture, and industry as well as in trade.

"I feel it is also an appropriate time to begin to tear down the political barriers of distrust and suspicion that have grown between our peoples over the past few decades—particularly since those individuals and reasons that separated Issel from the Unified Worlds no longer exist. I believe we should take advantage of the current show of goodwill between our peoples to move toward reuniting them.

"The first steps have already been taken with the accomplishment of the Assistance Agreement. It may be beneficial to point that out to those you select to develop this proposal."

Remarq paused. "Dictation off," he said. "Return to top of text for review."

He didn't spend much time on the first paragraph; it was only an acknowledgment of Trosvig's statement of cooperation. The second paragraph he read more slowly, savoring the subtlety of his instructions, his suggestions. Trosvig was a reasonably astute man, according to the recruiter. He would understand and know how to proceed.

"Continue dictation," he said at last, and picked up where he'd left off: "In the meantime, you have a responsibility to help shape the top circles of leadership and thus consolidate support for the recommendations you will be making in the near future. I expect that your first opportunity will be in the selection of a new commander-in-chief of the Spherzah, if Admiral Serege's injuries are truly as grave as the news reports lead us to believe."

He hesitated, then went on in a thoughtful tone, "I find it truly remarkable how the unfortunate incident at the sealing of the Assistance Agreement is proving to be such a boon in terms of our long view: We no longer have to concern ourselves with removing Serege from his commandership at some point in the future, when his intractability toward the Issel Sector would threaten the accomplishment of our mutual goals of peace and cooperation."

He paused for a moment, then continued, "In fact, I would like to offer a recommendation for Serege's successor, if I may, Seamus. I believe you will find Vice Admiral Tolmich Oleszek of Sjenlund to be the perfect candidate. He is, at present, the commander of the Spherzah's Advanced Training Center on Jonica, where I understand he has cultivated the loyalties of many of the best and the brightest in the rising officer corps.

"But more useful, perhaps, than even his natural charisma is the fact that while *his* service record is sterling, the university record of his second daughter is not." Remarq arched a sparse eyebrow. "Where Oleszek's political naïveté ends, the possibility of that rather embarrassing occurrence at the University of Candiff being exhumed will certainly persuade him to continue his cooperation with us.

"I will be pleased to send you a complete dossier for his recommendation package if you wish."

There could be no mistaking the meaning of that last statement. Remarq paused once more to give it added weight.

"I look forward to hearing from you very soon, Seamus," he said at last—and added to himself, *My humble servant Trosvig.* "I believe we can accomplish a great deal together." And he smiled, an expression laden more with wordless message than with mirth.

Shutting off the recording, he said, "Execute message self-erasure upon computer decoding. Confirm with authenticator code Echo Victor." Then he sat back once more in his high-backed chair and interlaced his fingers. The messages that would survive would do so by his personal selection. Every move he made in this ponderous political chess game must appear to have its origins within the Unified Worlds.

SIX

Nighttime was the worst. When sleep didn't come there was nothing to keep him from thinking, nothing to distract him from the questions in his mind. Nothing to distract him from the depression.

It had been twenty days since he'd wakened from the coma. *Only* twenty days, Lujan thought. It seemed more like half an eternity.

There had been progress in those twenty days. Some of it had been minute, barely measurable; some had been dramatic.

He'd learned to mark the days by their predictable pattern of liquid meals and rest periods and therapies. Endless, exhaustive therapies. One caregiver even worked his facial muscles, the hands manipulating his jaw and cheek muscles through the motions of chewing and swallowing. The constant curriculum should have left him unable to do anything *but* sleep by the time day passed to night.

His body, as much of it as had sensation now, felt tight, his muscles bunched and knotted. Sometimes he felt them twitch or jerk—a momentary flexion of a thigh muscle, a flicker through his upper arm—as their nerves began to revive. He wanted to stretch, to pull at the sinews of his back and limbs and shoulders until they burned, until they quivered. But there was no control. He couldn't raise a hand to rub away the itch at the corner of his eye—couldn't even feel that he *had* a hand!

There was still so far to go.

Especially after yesterday's setback.

He forced the memory of those moments from his mind, pushed back the confusion of the blank out.

Drawing on discipline developed through years of martial arts training, he cleared his mind completely. Focused his thoughts on his source of peace. Tried, for what seemed the thousandth time since early that afternoon, to pray.

All he could shape in his mind were the same questions that had surfaced each time before: *Why this, God? Help me to understand why.*

Still weary but no longer able to sleep, he let his mind wander back.

"Try this," Darcie wrote with her finger on his forehead, and pressed to it something smooth and cold.

He felt several seconds' high-frequency vibration, and then—he *heard* her voice:

". . . hear me, Luj?" she said. "Blink twice if you can hear me."

He blinked twice, startled by it.

It was definitely Darcie's voice—the first sound he'd heard since waking from the coma. But he couldn't localize it, couldn't determine whether it came from beside or in front or behind him; it seemed to originate from within his head. "How?" he blinked.

"Dr. Gavril, sir," said a man's voice. "We're using an electromechanical sound transmitter. It uses an impedance cable and a skin contact to temporarily turn any part of your body into a substitute eardrum. Sound waves are focused on neural receptors in the skin through the contact. Because of their high frequency, the auditory centers of the brain interpret the impulses as sound."

Lujan understood the principle; it was similar to the direct sensory input instruments he'd used as a combat pilot.

"We've also reprogrammed your blink monitor to translate dot code into Standard," Gavril's voice continued as a finger touched the weights at the corners of his eyes, "so we can read what you're telling us."

"Thank you," Lujan blinked, and repeated the questions he'd asked of Darcie earlier: "How is Tris? Where is Tris?"

"Tristan's fine, love." Darcie's voice again. She stroked his temple. "He's not here; he's still away on the Spherzah mission. He'll be home in a few weeks."

Tristan on a Spherzah mission? What Spherzah mission? Lujan's stomach tightened.

Something in his skull tightened, too, causing a pinpoint of pain behind his eyes. He ignored it, trying instead to sort the sudden stream of questions racing through his mind:

The Spherzah have been sent out? Where? To do what? And why?

Who sent them? Who's in command?

And how long has Tristan been one of them?

He suddenly wondered how long he'd been unconscious.

"What is date?" he blinked.

"It's the twelfth day of the twelfth month, standard year 3308."

He counted back in his memory. Little more than five months since the field exercises, the rappelling drills in Lost Prospector Canyon. Tristan couldn't possibly have become a Spherzah in that time! Basic indoctrination alone took at least six months, and that was only after a lengthy selection process.

He blinked, "Can't be right."

"What can't be right?" Darcie asked.

"Tris a Spherzah."

It demanded his whole focus, creating each character with blinks and pauses. He forced back the pain behind his eyes.

"He isn't a Spherzah," Darcie said when he finished. "He went as a civilian scout. Don't you remember?"

He didn't. Bewildered, he blinked, "No."

After a moment he asked, "How long was I . . ."

And he couldn't remember "unconscious." Words whirled in his mind, none of them right, and the pain behind his eyes swelled with his frustration. All he could think of was "uncommon." At a loss, he blinked it out.

There was silence for the space of several heartbeats.

". . . suggests a word-finding deficit," he heard Gavril murmur as if from inside his head.

"Lujan." That was Dr. Moses. "Do you mean how long you were in the coma?"

In a coma? I was in a coma? Somehow that seemed more serious than "unconscious."

He hesitated. Swallowed. "Yes," he blinked.

"Nine days," she said.

Only nine days? Then why can't I remember anything about the last five months?

Disconcerted, he blinked, "What happened?"

There was another pause. Then Gavril said, "You don't remember, sir?"

No, blast it! he raged in his mind. *If I could remember, I wouldn't have to ask!*

He blinked only, "No."

Yet another pause. An ominously long one. And then

Darcie said, "There was an assassination attempt at the treaty sealing—a man with an electromagnetic weapon hidden in a newsnet holocorder. You saved Minister Borith's life."

Treaty sealing? What treaty? And who is Minister Borith? He strained to remember. The pain behind his eyes pulsed.

Several moments of searching his memory brought only fragments to the surface, like scattered pieces of a puzzle.

There were faces. Several of them, angry and earnest. He knew those faces, yet most of the names escaped him.

And documents. Paper copies, with SECRET stamped in red at top and bottom.

Some faint memory from a trip he'd made to Sostis shortly before the rappelling exercises in the canyon drifted to the forefront of his mind. He had been helping to negotiate . . .

"Issel Agreement?" he blinked.

"Yes, that's right." Darcie sounded hopeful.

He couldn't remember any of it. Nothing after his return to Topawa, anyway, and very little before. It was as if a portion of his mind had been wiped. Deleted.

That turned him cold, from the core of his soul to his skin. It left him nauseous—or maybe that was from the pain, pounding against the inside of his skull with every pulsebeat.

How much of my mind am I missing? he wondered.

"Luj?" Darcie said. Her voice held a note of concern.

He actually started at her touch on his face. But he had to know the truth. "How bad hurt?" he blinked.

She began stroking his cheek as if to offer comfort—as if to brace him for the news. "You were hit with an EM pulse that burned through several cranial nerves, including the ones to your eyes and ears and lower face," she said. "When you fell, your head hit the edge of the treaty table. It—snapped your head back and crushed a vertebra in your neck."

His neck was broken.

He'd known that was so from the first, at some basic gut level. But that foreknowledge didn't lessen the shock of actually hearing it. It only forced him to face what he'd been refusing to accept.

—And his skull seemed about to explode!

"His intracranial pressure has shot up!" Dr. Moses said just then. "The vibrations are focusing in his skull—"

Gavril cut her off with a curse. A hand scrabbled at Lujan's forehead, peeled off the contact—

The pain subsided almost immediately. Reflex made him try to gasp with relief, but the ventilator finished the breath for him. He drifted in a half swoon, in thick silence, his mind tumbling in a tempest of unanswered questions.

His caregivers had begun, almost from the day he regained consciousness, to elevate his head by tilting up the bed.

"Why?" he blinked to Dr. Moses.

They had placed a tactile pad on his forehead after the failed attempt with the sound transmitter. Now his caregivers tapped messages on a keyboard, and the pad pressed the characters to his skin.

Libby typed. Because of the spinal cord injury, his circulatory system wasn't compensating for position changes by dilating and constricting, as it normally would. Elevating him by small increments would, over time, restore its ability to pump vertically. He couldn't go on to more advanced therapy until he could sit upright.

Being tilted was like flying high-G aerobatic maneuvers without a G suit. He'd actually done that once, under "orders" from a group of upperclass cadets for his initiation into the Sostis Aerospace Institute. Getting caught would have cost him his student billet—if the flight itself didn't cost him his life. He'd vowed afterward he'd never do it again. Remembering, he thought, *I was an idiot to do it at all!*

The rush of blood from head to legs was as unnerving now as it had been then. The dizziness and nausea, crashing over his consciousness like a collapsing wall, were even worse. He remembered how his vision had tunneled, shrinking to a mere point of red light; he could *feel* blackness closing in—

They must have returned him to full horizontal in time; he didn't quite pass out. But he lay in a sweat for long minutes afterward.

It's like the centrifuge tests during pilot training, he told himself. *I survived those; I can survive this, too.*

The process left him exhausted, more spent than he'd ever been after combat, even when he'd flown two or three missions in one day. But by his twelfth day of consciousness he could tolerate an elevation of 38 degrees for twenty minutes.

They had already upgraded his diet.

"High protein, high fiber, high calorie," Dr. Moses spelled out for him. "Takes energy to heal."

The liquids Darcie squeezed into his mouth were thicker now: strained cereals, cream soups, custards, strained fruits and vegetables. Most were practically flavorless.

"Baby food," he blinked to her once. "Know now why Tris used to spit it out!"

She waited for him to blink out the whole sentence. Then she patted his face and kissed his nose—and he could imagine her chuckling.

* * *

Independence from the ventilator was the next major step.

"Diaphragm function and blood gases improving," the respiratory therapist typed out on his fifteenth day of consciousness. "Want to start weaning, sir."

He was going to conduct some tests first, he wrote. Lujan caught, "Going to disconnect . . ." but not what was being disconnected. *Surely not the ventilator hose!* he thought.

Apparently so. The push of air into his lungs suddenly ceased.

His gasp for breath was pure reflex. It was as if he were drowning on dry land, as if someone had placed a weight on his chest to keep his lungs from filling. He concentrated on drawing air—had to do it with his diaphragm alone.

Two breaths were enough to tire him. His pulse rate had accelerated; he could feel it throbbing in his head. Gathering his flagging strength, he started to inhale—

—the ventilator filled his lungs with a rush. He relaxed, more relieved than he cared to admit.

The therapist clapped his shoulder. "Good, sir," he typed. "Sufficient tidal volume. Will proceed."

The ventilator had been supporting him at sixteen breaths per minute, the therapist explained. To begin weaning, the rate would be reduced to twelve breaths per minute; he could take as many as he needed between them. As his strength increased, the ventilations would continue to be cut back. He should expect some soreness at first, as drawing his own breaths would be laborious for a time.

By evening the ventilator had been dropped to nine breaths per minute. Lujan woke in the night with his rib cage feeling crushed.

I've hurt worse than this, he reminded himself.

He'd been involved in a flying accident while he was stationed at a polar outpost on Tohh during the War of Resistance. Ejected from his crippled fighter, he'd found himself descending toward a glacier, steep and broken and dusted with falling snow. His boots shot out from under him on contact; the left one caught in a crack, twisting his fall onto his side.

He began to slide as his paraglider settled over him—slid sideways, half-tangled in suspension lines. He scrambled, clawing for a handhold, but the ice evaded his grasp as his momentum increased.

The ice pack slowed his sliding as it grew rougher, but it pummeled his chest and belly like fists. He grasped at chunks of ice to stop himself, but some split off to tumble with him and others were torn from his grip. He was still clawing, still flailing when he slid into a fissure.

Its walls were craggy, irregular, pocked with silt and gravel, and they kept him from falling very far. But he could barely breathe. His body was jammed in between the ice wall and his egress pack—and the rim was just beyond his fingertips. He strained with both arms first, then one, to reach it—and felt the egress pack shift. Felt himself settle, so the pressure on his chest increased. Fragments rolled down on his shoulder and head; a block the size of his helmet pinned his left arm to his side. He tried once to free it—and succeeded only in slipping farther down, where there was no room to breathe—barely enough room even to gasp. . . .

He'd been unconscious, close to death from hypothermia by the time the rescue ship tracked his locator beacon. He'd spent some time in the hospital recovering from that and the rib separations caused by compression in the fissure.

That had hurt worse. They'd had to apply neural clips

to several spinal nerves to block the pain. *I survived that,* he told himself. *I'll survive this.*

By Lujan's nineteenth day out of the coma, the ventilator's breaths had been reduced to five per minute and he could turn his head a little. Most important, he could tolerate an elevation of 72 degrees for over half an hour. Good enough to start allowing him out of bed for short periods, Dr. Moses had said.

When Darcie arrived, kissed his forehead, and typed out, "Good morning, love," he blinked back, "Show you something."

And he raised his left shoulder.

The movement wouldn't have qualified even as a shrug, and he couldn't hold it there, but Darcie threw her arms around him. Too excited to type, she kissed him again and again and ruffled his hair.

And then he'd had the seizure.

He'd just finished an afternoon physiotherapy session and his therapists were applying cooling wraps to his limbs when he lost all awareness of where he was. Confused and suddenly apprehensive, he tried to call out—as every muscle in his body began twitching and jerking, and consciousness collapsed on itself.

He had no idea how long he was unconscious before he came to retching. He was weak with exhaustion, wet with sweat, and every muscle in his body felt wrung out. He was only briefly aware of hands caring for him before he sank into a sleep so heavy it might have been drugged.

He remembered waking two or three more times after that, only briefly, before lapsing back into sleep. He was too drained even to dream.

He'd wakened the next day at Darcie washing his face with a cool cloth. Her hands were steady but her kisses, when he opened his eyes and she saw he was awake, were just gentle touches on his forehead and temples, over and over. "How do you feel, love?" she typed out.

"Tired," he blinked. "Sore all over. What happened?" Even blinking fatigued him.

She smoothed his brow. Kissed him again before she wrote, "Seizure," and added, "It's all right now."

A seizure? How could *that* be all right? His gut knotted under his ribs; his blood turned to ice water.

A seizure. The word echoed in his head, and he shuddered at it. If there had been one, there would probably be more, perhaps for the rest of his life. How would they affect his recovery? Could he ever hope now to regain what he'd lost?

It was afternoon, Darcie typed when he asked the time. But for brief breaks, she hadn't left his side since the seizure on the previous day. She stayed on through late afternoon and into the evening, massaging soreness from his body and printing scriptures, verses from *The Law of the Prophets,* on his forehead with the tactile pad. Finally she wrote, "Libby says I have to go." And she rubbed his shoulder briefly and kissed his cheek—and was gone.

Still awake, hours later, he couldn't remember ever feeling so alone.

Why, God? he prayed. The words poured from the depth of his heart. *Aren't the blindness and deafness and paralysis enough? Help me to understand why.*

Impressions from the tactile pad startled him out of his prayer. "Pain, sir?" they spelled.

There was no physical pain, and whatever the med tech would have given him for it wouldn't help the emotional torment. "No," he blinked.

"Can't sleep?" the tech typed.

He blinked, "Yes."

"Can give sleep patches."

"Please."

The tech applied one to each temple, then slipped away. He let his eyes close, waiting for it to take effect.

Why, God? he prayed again. *Please help me to understand why.*

Perhaps it was the sedative, peeling away the layers of anxiety to reach the calm at his core, but he thought not. Words came to his mind, one of the verses Darcie had spelled out to him earlier:

"There is strength to be gained from struggle; there is wisdom to be gained in suffering. There is no trial that does not have its purpose."

SEVEN

Seamus Trosvig wiped sweaty hands together on a pocket towel as he settled himself into the high-backed chair behind his desk. His hands had been abnormally damp for three weeks now, ever since he'd received Seulemont Remarq's "congratulatory gift." It had been twenty-two years since he'd given up his father's war medal. He knew only too well what it meant.

At the time, he'd been only an aide to Lewin Guchee Aguilar, head of the Mythosian delegation to the Unified Worlds Assembly. But even then he'd had aspirations of one day heading the Mythosian delegation himself.

Aguilar had also been chair of the Joint Committee on Isselan Relations and, as his aide, Seamus's duties had frequently taken him to the Isselan embassy. His counterpart there, the Isselan ambassador's aide, was an equally ambitious young man named Kaunas Eidsness.

There was also Jolenta Merkat, the assistant cultural attaché at the Isselan embassy. She was as witty as she was attractive, with her flaming red hair and lively blue eyes, and Seamus had found himself wanting her almost from the moment he met her. It was Kaunas who had introduced them.

The three of them had shared more lunches together than he'd bothered to count, at one or another of the posh restaurants that catered to the governing elite. Seamus still remembered trading anecdotes and laughter over glasses of wine. He'd actually felt more at ease in their company than he had with many of his fellow aides.

Jolenta plainly enjoyed his company, too. Within the year she'd given up her post at the embassy, and her Isselan citizenship, to accept Seamus as her mate and Mythos as her homeworld. Kaunas had received the news, over lunch, with no more display of surprise than an arching of his eyebrows. But he'd given it several moments' consideration before he proposed a toast: "To young love. May it never grow old!"

They had only been joined a few months when Seamus made his first bid for a seat in the Assembly. His experience on Aguilar's staff gave him credibility, but behind-the-scenes work didn't provide name recognition against incumbent opponents. "I don't have the funding they do!" he complained to Kaunas one evening over drinks in their favorite pub.

Kaunas studied him, brow furrowed. "This means a great deal to you, doesn't it, Seamus?"

"It's my life's dream!" he said. "I've known since I was a schoolboy that I was meant to take part in government! And I've known since the day I began working for Aguilar that someday I wanted to head the Mythosian delegation—maybe even win a seat on the Triune! Every assignment I've ever taken has been with that end in mind. But without the funds to conduct a campaign, all that study and experience will be wasted."

Kaunas nodded thoughtfully at that. Squinted into his tankard for several minutes. Screwed up his mouth into a serious expression. "Perhaps I can assist you," he said at last, and clapped a hand onto Seamus's shoulder. "After all, what are friends for? I'm sure you would do the same for me if our positions were reversed."

That was the point where his recruitment had begun, but he hadn't realized it until later—when it was too late. The offer of assistance had come with a catch: Someday, when he was in a position to do so, he would be called upon to return the favor. It might not be for fifteen or twenty years, but eventually that day would come.

Fifteen or twenty years. Seamus mentally wrestled with the idea. It was a long time—a good part of a lifetime! A great deal could happen in fifteen or twenty years, both in interstellar politics and in individual lives. But nothing would ever happen in his own political career without Kaunas's proffered financial help.

In the end, he'd given Kaunas his father's Combat Crescent to seal the agreement. It was one of only one thousand such medals cast, and engraved with an identifying number besides the late Colonel Trosvig's name. The fact that it couldn't be duplicated was vital, according to Kaunas, so both he and Seamus would know it was authentic. "When the medal is returned to you," he said, "you will know you have been activated, and the person from whom you receive it will be your control."

Seamus only nodded acknowledgment, too dry-mouthed to reply.

He'd never even told Jolenta what he'd done.

A few months later, funds and support began to appear from other delegates he hardly knew, and he won his first seat in the Mythosian delegation to the Assembly. But the message he'd received from Kaunas then had seemed more like a warning than a wish for success: "Remember me when you're the most powerful assemblyman in the Unified Worlds!"

Twenty years had come and gone, and he'd begun to hope, desperately, that the Isselans had forgotten about him. Perhaps the chief cabinet minister to whom Kaunas answered had died, considering his great age even at the time

Seamus was recruited and the fact that he'd since been dismissed from his post by Isselan governor Renier. Since such recruitment and activation files were known to so few individuals, even within the Isselan Intelligence Service, perhaps his had been lost. Perhaps the debt he had incurred to fulfill his young ambition might never come due.

He should have known better.

He must be an exceptionally valuable agent to have Remarq himself as his control, he thought.

That offered no consolation.

The devil never forgets, he told himself ruefully, and then added, *The devil never dies.*

He reached out to switch on his desk terminal and picked up the pocket towel once more. "Early edition news," he said as the menu appeared, and leaned back in his chair, wiping at his hands.

The lead headline, accompanied by a file holo of Admiral Lujan Serege in service uniform, brought him straight up in the chair again:

ADMIRAL SEREGE'S RECOVERY SET BACK BY SEIZURE

Trosvig pulled the screen closer and began to read, brow furrowed.

Admiral Lujan Serege's recovery from injuries received in the terrorist attack at the sealing ceremony for the Issel Assistance Agreement on 12/1 suffered a serious setback early yesterday afternoon when he suffered a seizure, according to officials at Winthancom Military Medical Center.

According to medical center spokesperson Alyssa Danzl, Serege had been undergoing physiotherapy when the seizure began. "There were no indications whatsoever that a seizure was imminent," said physiotherapist Sablon Meles. "It just started without any warning." He and physiotherapist

Pilita Elon took measures to prevent further injury to the admiral and then summoned his doctors. Meles and Elon reported that the seizure lasted approximately one minute.

The account continued with a holorecorded statement by neurosurgeon Berron Gavril, the admiral's attending physician, who confirmed that Serge had suffered a tonic-clonic seizure and explained that it was almost certainly a result of the head injuries he had sustained in the assassination attempt. Such a complication wasn't uncommon in cases of severe head trauma, the surgeon said, but it would necessitate a reassessment of and possible adjustments to Serege's rehabilitation program. Gavril also stated that it would be necessary to postpone rehabilitative surgeries until the seizure disorder had been brought under control.

Trosvig viewed the whole piece in detail, playing some segments back two or three times to be certain of their content, before he finally said, "Save document to chip in unit two."

Then he rang his aide in the outer office.

"Sir?" the young man's voice came back through the intercom.

"Talbot," he said, "I need to meet with the other members of the Triune and the chairman of the Defense Directorate at the earliest opportunity. Tell them that it concerns Admiral Serege. Please schedule the conference for today, if at all possible."

"Of course, sir."

"And, Talbot?"

"Sir?"

"Please also contact the Winthancom Military Medical Center and request the attendance of Doctors Berron Gavril and Libby Moses."

"Yes sir," said Talbot.

Trosvig leaned back in his chair, pleased with himself for spotting such an opportunity. A seizure. How convenient. It made his task so much easier. It might be all the ammunition he'd need to place Minister Remarq's recommendations on the Triune's table.

Especially if he had the support of one or two key members of the Defense Directorate. He reached for the visiphone.

He had just completed his calls when a sudden thought gathered the corners of his mouth back from their slow expansion into a smile. This seizure was almost *too* convenient—especially its timing. He began to wonder at the number of drugs that might induce seizures, and if Remarq might have an agent at the Winthancom Military Medical Center.

Wadding the pocket towel between damp hands, he rubbed at it hard.

Two chairs remained empty at one side of the conference-room table when Kun Reng-Tan of Kaleo and Alois Ashforth of Jonica, his colleagues in the Triune, and the membership of the Unified Worlds Defense Directorate in its entirety had taken their places. Trosvig shifted in his own chair and cleared his throat.

"I expect that all of you are aware of yesterday's unfortunate setback to Admiral Serege's recovery," he began. He looked around the circle, saw curt nods and somber expressions, and selected his words with care. "I felt it would be wise to bring in the heads of the admiral's medical team to clarify for us exactly what impact this condition may be expected to have on his recovery and return to command. I've asked them to report on the long-term prognosis and respond to our questions on the matter. Is this format acceptable to all present?"

There were no dissenting responses, so Trosvig

pressed his pager's button and said, "Talbot, show Doctors Gavril and Moses into the conference room, please."

Moses was probably about his own age, Trosvig guessed. A small woman who wore her dark hair cut short and close about her head, she crossed to the seat Talbot indicated, apparently unmoved by the rank and position of those already present. Her own rank, that of a commander in the Spherzah, gleamed on the collar of her service jacket.

It was the neurosurgeon who appeared overwhelmed. He looked too young to be a major in the Sostis Surface Forces Medical Corps, Trosvig thought—and far too young to be a neurosurgeon. Still, he was reputed to be among the best in his field.

"Please be seated, Doctors," Trosvig said, and made a cordial gesture with one hand. "Talbot, refreshments, please. Doctors, there is ice water, shuk, a variety of teas or juices—whatever you prefer."

While Talbot poured a cup of steaming shuk for Dr. Moses and filled a tall glass with ice water for Gavril, Trosvig began, "I'm certain you both must appreciate our concern about Admiral Serege's condition, considering the report that appeared in this morning's news. We're grateful to both of you for joining us here this afternoon to bring us up-to-date on it."

Gavril nodded acknowledgment, drew a sip from his glass and set it down, and glanced about the table. "The admiral's condition is stable at this time," he said. "Yes, there's been a setback to his recovery, but as I told the newsnets, seizure disorders have to be anticipated in patients with severe head trauma. It isn't as if this is a completely unexpected turn."

"It's also treatable," said Dr. Moses. "Once the appropriate type and amount of medication have been determined, a patient can go on with a normal, seizure-free life."

"But how would you assess the severity of the admiral's case?" asked Kasia Weist, a member of the Defense Directorate.

"We haven't fully determined that yet," Gavril told her. "He's only had one seizure, after all. It's too early to tell whether the current type and amount of medication will be effective."

"But that one seizure was a—tonic-clonic—wasn't it?" asked Trosvig. He fingered the leather cover of his microwriter. "Isn't that the most severe type?"

"Yes, Your Honor," Gavril conceded. "But that doesn't mean it's uncontrollable."

There was a moment's silence, and then Alois Ashforth asked, "How is the admiral's recovery progressing otherwise? How much of a setback is this, really?"

"He has at least partial sensation back in all but his outermost extremities now," said Moses, "and by yesterday morning he was able to move his left shoulder a little. That's a very positive indication. We were about to start him on isometric exercises."

"And now?" Concern creased Ashforth's brow.

"We'll have to allow him a few days to rest," said Moses. "Having a seizure is extremely exhausting, after all."

"What about his—mental capacity?" The question came from Neol Balthrop, civilian chairman of the Defense Directorate, and Trosvig didn't miss the chairman's fleeting glance across at him.

Gavril circled his glass loosely with both hands. "He's suffered some loss of memory," he said. "As near as we can determine, he seems to be missing all memory of the five months prior to the incident. Due to the nature of an EM injury, we suspect there's some random long-term memory loss as well. There have also been indications of a word-finding deficit. I wouldn't call it aphasia, but—"

"Explain, please," said Balthrop.

"I'm sorry. Aphasia, very simply defined," said Gavril, "is a loss of ability to express or understand language. Admiral Serege is clearly able to understand what's being communicated to him and to respond appropriately, but he can't always find the right words to use in his communications."

Around the table, brows furrowed and mouths pressed to thin-lipped lines.

Trosvig drummed his microwriter's cover with blunt fingertips. "What are the chances that he'll regain that lost memory and recover from these—difficulties?" he asked.

"We don't know." Gavril shook his head a little. "It's possible that some memory will return in time, but how much"—he shrugged—"we can't say."

"He hasn't lost the ability to reason, if that's what you're concerned about," said Moses. "He's the one who devised a method of communicating with us. It's a physically slow process, but it demonstrates a thinking mind."

There were nods around the table at that. Trosvig noted expressions of relief on several faces and felt a moment's uneasiness.

His palms were damp again, he realized. He hadn't brought the pocket towel; using it before a gathering such as this would be bad form. He folded his hands together on the table instead and leaned forward to look first at Moses and then at Gavril. Pointedly. "How complete a recovery do you expect Admiral Serege to make?" he asked.

Gavril appeared to contemplate the condensation on his glass. "We have every reason to expect that he'll walk again, as well as regain the use of his arms and hands," he said after a moment, "and we expect he'll achieve that within a standard year—perhaps in as little as six months. But right now I can't predict how much fine motor coordination he'll get back; only time and therapy will determine that.

"His vision and hearing can be restored with prosthetic

implants, and those will be instrumental in helping him communicate verbally once more. But those procedures can't be done until the internal burns left by the EM pulse have healed and we're certain that the seizures are under control." Gavril met Trosvig's look.

Trosvig nodded slowly. He lowered his vision to his hands—large and thick and sweaty—on the tabletop. It was some seconds before he spoke and then, as if weighing each word, he said, "Taking all of the factors into consideration—the memory loss and communication difficulty, the seizures, the physical limitations—do you believe that Admiral Serege can ever recover sufficiently to resume command of the Spherzah?"

There was a long silence at that. Then Gavril released a breath in a rush. "To be frank, I can't tell you that at this time," he said, and spread his hands. "He's made good progress to this point, and I believe that will continue. But exactly how far it will go . . ." He let the sentence trail off, unfinished.

But Moses drew herself up in her chair. "He'll *expect* to resume his command," she said. "I know that, Your Honor, because I know *him*. And I've learned never to underestimate him."

Something about her narrowed eyes made Trosvig want to swallow.

He controlled the urge by looking around the table instead, at the somber faces of all the others—touched Balthrop's vision for the barest instant. "Are there any further questions?" he asked.

There were none, so he turned back to Moses and Gavril. "Thank you for your time, Doctors," he said. "Talbot will show you out."

The two physicians rose together and moved toward the door, Gavril with his brow furrowed, Moses with her mouth pursed.

Silence lingered in the conference room for several heartbeats after they left. Pregnant silence. And all eyes were turned toward him, Trosvig noticed. He leaned back in his chair. "Comments?" he said.

Chairman Balthrop shifted, scowled at the tabletop, traced an invisible mark on it with his thumbnail. "Five months of memory loss—the most pivotal months in recent Unified Worlds history!" he said, and shook his head. "With that kind of deficit—with the possible degree of recovery and the length of time it might take still undetermined even by his doctors—I don't see how Admiral Serege can possibly regain the physical and intellectual performance levels required to resume his command. Much as I respect the man, we can't afford the luxury of putting the Spherzah on indefinite hold."

Balthrop hadn't been difficult to lobby, Trosvig reflected, studying him. He had spoken plainly of his respect for Serege when Trosvig called him this morning, and there was genuine regret in his voice now. Still, he would not let personal sentiment overrule responsibility; he would do what was best in his view even if he disliked having to do it.

General Roemhild of Enach's Defense Forces nodded agreement with Balthrop's comment. "That's my concern as well," he said.

"Gentlemen." Alois Ashforth drew herself up in her chair. "It's only been one month since Admiral Serege was injured! Gavril himself said it was too early to predict a final outcome! I recommend extending his medical leave rather than retiring him right away. Six to twelve standard months should be long enough. If at the end of that time the admiral hasn't—"

"But the Spherzah need strong leadership *now!*" Balthrop said. "Depending on what the situation really is in the Issel system, they may have a role there for some time. Besides, as quickly as events have unfolded over the past few months, the whole political constellation could be radically different a year from now! The chief commander of the Spherzah must be keenly and constantly aware of every shift in the political spectrum."

Trosvig folded his hands on the table once more. "I'm afraid I have to agree with Neol, Alois," he said. He kept his tone sober, his gaze downcast. "Medical leave is a luxury of time we can't afford. I believe that retiring Admiral Serege and appointing a new Spherzah commander is our only real choice."

When they voted on it a few minutes later, Alois Ashforth's abstention was the only indication of dissension.

Darcie looked up from her microreader at the sound of a step at the doorway.

"He's sleeping again?" Libby asked, joining her at Lujan's bedside.

"For the moment." Darcie sighed it, and looked over at her mate. His features were relaxed right now. She dabbed away a spill of saliva from one corner of his slack mouth and said, "He woke for a while a couple of hours ago and told me he was hungry, so I ordered some soup. He ate nearly all of it."

"That's a good sign." Libby sighed, too, and turned her narrowed gaze away, to the monitor above the headboard. She seemed to study it for some time, her mouth drawn tight.

In fact, Darcie thought, her whole face seemed taut. She eyed the monitor herself and saw nothing among the readouts to cause such concern. "Is something wrong?" she asked.

Libby turned at last, to face her directly. "I just got back from a little session at the Unified Worlds Tower," she said. "Gavril was called in, too."

Something about her tone made Darcie uneasy. She studied her friend. "Whatever for?"

"Ostensibly, to update the Triune and the chair staff of the Defense Directorate on Lujan's recovery," Libby said. "But some of their questions reminded me of a medical-discharge review board."

Darcie swallowed. "They're talking about—retiring him—*already?*"

"No one actually mentioned retirement in front of us," Libby said, "but it was pretty evident that was on some of their minds."

She should have been expecting it, Darcie supposed. She'd wondered herself, especially at first, whether Lujan would ever be able to return to his command. Only over the last week or so had she begun to believe that he could.

"It's only been a month," she said, "and he's been progressing so well! With six or eight months of medical leave—" Frustrated, she cut herself off.

Libby nodded. Paused. Then sighed. "I'm really not sure what it was all about, Darcie. There was a lot of concern about the seizure; they were pretty open about that. But—"

—*but you're an empathic specialist,* Darcie thought. *You trained for years to learn how to read people's feelings from their faces and body language. It's not something you can just hang up like a lab coat when you step out of the hospital.*

"—I thought you should know about it," Libby finished.

Darcie nodded. "Thank you for telling me," she said.

She was watching the therapist named Sablon Meles work with Lujan three days later, watching with her teeth gritted for him as he strained to raise his shoulders against the other's resistance, when a call over the rehabilitation room's address system jerked her attention away:

"Captain Darcie Dartmuth, please call the front desk. Captain Dartmuth, you have a message at the front desk."

Wrinkling her brow with puzzlement, she crossed to a visiphone on the wall and pressed the button for the front desk. "This is Captain Dartmuth."

"Ma'am," the receptionist on duty said, "there's someone here who needs to talk to you."

Something's happened to Tristan, she thought first, and swallowed hard. If something had happened to Tristan, too, she didn't know how she would bear it. It was all she could do to make herself ask, "Can you tell me who it is and what they want?"

The woman in the miniature screen turned away, and Darcie watched as she soundlessly asked a question of someone outside of sensor range.

The woman turned back in a moment. "It's Captain Jiron," she said.

Lujan's executive officer. Darcie let out her breath in a rush. "Tell him I'll be there directly," she said.

It took a few minutes, even at her normally brisk stride, to reach the front lobby from the rehab room. She found Jiron pacing when she arrived—a behavior that struck her as highly atypical for him. He turned about when she called his name, and his face, as he came toward her, was a mask of agitation.

She stopped short at that, a sudden dread settling like a weight in her stomach. Would Jiron have been tasked to bring her bad news about Tristan?

"What's wrong?" she asked, before she lost the last shred of her nerve.

"This." He held out a message printed on official letterhead. "It just came through from the offices of the Triune."

The Triune.

Libby's impressions from the meeting three days earlier raced through Darcie's mind.

She took the message from Jiron's hand. Noted the present day's date at the top as she began to read:

021310L 1 3309SY
TO: HQ SPHERZAH,
    OFFICES OF PLANETARY DELEGATIONS,
    HQS, ALL PLANETARY FLEETS AND FORCES
FM: OFFICE OF THE UNIFIED WORLDS TRIUNE,
    CHAIR, UNIFIED WORLDS DEFENSE DIREC-
    TORATE
UNCLASSIFIED
1. DUE TO DISABLING INJURIES RECEIVED IN THE
TRAGIC INCIDENT AT THE SEALING OF THE ISSE-
LAN ASSISTANCE AGREEMENT, IT HAS BECOME
NECESSARY TO RETIRE ADMIRAL LUJAN ANSEL-
LIC SEREGE FROM ACTIVE MILITARY SERVICE
AND FROM DUTY AS COMMANDER-IN-CHIEF
OF THE SPHERZAH. ADMIRAL SEREGE'S RETIRE-
MENT WILL BECOME EFFECTIVE 1/30/3309 SY.
2. VICE ADMIRAL OF THE SPHERZAH TOLMICH
OLESZEK HAS BEEN NOMINATED FOR PRO-
MOTION IN ORDER TO FILL THE POSITION OF
CINC SPHERZAH. FOR THE PAST THREE YEARS,
ADMIRAL OLESZEK HAS SERVED AS COMMAN-
DER OF THE SPHERZAH ADVANCED TRAINING
CENTER. RATIFICATION HEARINGS ARE EX-
PECTED TO BEGIN NOT LATER THAN 1/7/3309.
FLAG OFFICERS FROM ALL PLANETARY SER-
VICES, AS WELL AS CIVILIAN DELEGATIONS TO
THE ASSEMBLY, ARE ENCOURAGED TO PARTICI-
PATE IN THE HEARINGS. IF APPROVED BY THE
UNIFIED WORLDS ASSEMBLY AND DEFENSE DI-
RECTORATE, ADMIRAL OLESZEK WILL RECEIVE
HIS PROMOTION AND ASSUME COMMAND OF
THE SPHERZAH EFFECTIVE 1/30/3309.

SIGNED THIS DAY,
KUN RENG-TAN, KALEO
ALOIS ASA ASHFORTH, JONICA
SEAMUS TROSVIG, MYTHOS
NEOL BALTHROP, CHMN, DEF DIR

Darcie stood motionless for a long moment after she finished reading. So Libby's impressions had been correct—as usual. She didn't feel any shock. Just—a sort of betrayal.

"Why haven't any of them said anything to me about this?" she demanded of Jiron. "Most of the Assembly and all three members of the Triune have come to the hospital since it happened. So has the whole Command staff! They've all asked about him and told me how much they think of him and offered assistance—even Trosvig, the day after his swearing in to Hanesson's seat! But no one has so much as suggested anything like this!" She shook the message at him. "I'd have thought someone would surely have mentioned it to me, out of common courtesy if nothing else!"

"I have the impression this just came up within the last two or three days," said Jiron.

About the same time Libby and Gavril were called in to provide testimony, Darcie thought. Aloud, she asked, "But why? What happened to medical leave? Isn't that standard procedure anymore? Or isn't Vice Admiral Halbach handling the command well enough?"

"Halbach's doing fine," said Jiron. "The way they explained it, it's because the Spherzah may be actively involved in the Issel system for some time. We're still technically at war and, according to regulations, the position of commander-in-chief must be filled by a full admiral during time of war."

Darcie rolled her eyes. "The shooting part of this 'war'

was over weeks ago! Besides, it was Lujan and his staff who were most involved in the planning and preparation for it! Why don't they promote Halbach? If the Triune is so concerned about carrying it off successfully, it would make a great deal more sense to promote Halbach into Lujan's position, not bring in somebody who's spent the last three years supervising weapon-systems training! I've never even heard of this Vice Admiral Oleszek before!"

"He's a good man," Jiron said, and then managed a dim smile. "Just remember, Darcie, the decision was made by officials of the civilian government, and government policies have rarely been known to follow any kind of logic."

Darcie didn't return the smile at his remark. Glancing over the message once more, she shook her head. "There's just something not right about it," she said. She looked the XO in the face. "I was involved in a few medical-retirement cases during my active-duty career. Believe me, Jiron, I'm going to do everything in my power to get this reconsidered!"

EIGHT

The sedative had taken affect; Lujan's eyelids barely flickered when Darcie drew a fingertip across his forehead. "I'll be here when you wake, love," she whispered close to his cheek, and kissed him, and left the room.

She couldn't push the image of him out of her mind: his shaved head marked with black medical ink. They hadn't even shaved him that way for the emergency surgery when he was first injured six weeks ago.

She had been there the previous evening when Dr. Gavril explained the procedure—had translated the most important parts of it for Lujan, in fact, by tapping it out to the tactile pad.

If this surgery went well, it would eliminate the need to type everything on his forehead for him.

She took the nearest lift to the hospital's teaching floor, where the surgical suites' observation galleries were, and found a military policeman standing at the head of the corridor to the galleries. She placed her hand on the scanner he extended.

"You're cleared, ma'am," he said after a moment.

She nodded. "Thank you."

The third door on the right was the one she wanted. She stepped through, into the dimness of what appeared to be a miniature amphitheater with three curved rows of seats, and wasn't surprised to find a pair of veteran MPs posted there, too, one at either end of the room's viewpane. They shifted a little, exchanged glances, greeted Darcie with mute nods. She acknowledged them with a nod of her own and moved down to the center of the front row.

The viewpane overlooked a compact operating arena that had been specifically designed for cranial surgery. In its center stood a padded chair, like an upright lounger, that could be shifted and rotated as needed to facilitate the surgeons' work. It was surrounded by a variety of equipment: holoscanner antennae and holotank, instruments on robot arms, a surgical computer, a stereotaxic frame, and several screens for various displays.

The gallery had a trio of its own screens, tucked up next to the ceiling above the viewpane. All were empty at the moment, but Darcie knew what each would display: a close-up view of the operation on the center screen, with the three-dimensional holoscan display on the right and a vital-signs monitor on the left.

That last held Darcie's attention. Maybe watching the procedure wasn't such a good idea, she thought— particularly since she had been a surgeon herself. If something were to go wrong, she would know it at once and there would be nothing she could do about it.

She knotted her hands together in her lap and forced away the thought.

A handful of surgical assistants—one human and the rest mechanical—moved about the arena, setting up. As she watched them, Dr. Gavril came into the room. She knew it was Gavril despite the near-complete conceal-ment of his hooded surgical smock; she recognized the creases of concentration about his eyes. Besides, he was much taller than Libby. He stepped over to the surgical computer and, with a string of voice commands, ran it through what Lujan would have called a preflight check.

Libby joined him a few minutes later, diminutive in her hooded smock. They conversed briefly, pointing and gesturing at a gridlike holoscan image of a head on one of the screens. Their voices were quiet enough that only fragments of their talk came through the gallery's speakers, but Darcie could tell they were doing a final walk-through of the procedure.

She leaned forward, resting her forearms on the view-pane's window ledge, when the anesthetist and a med tech entered the room, guiding a repulsor sled between them. Lujan lay on the sled, draped with a sheet.

A servo with padded limbs, designed for the purpose, lifted him from the sled and into the surgical chair. The med tech helped to settle him, steadying him when he sagged sideways. While Libby checked the vital-signs sensors stuck to his chest and upper arms, the anesthetist attached the ventilator hose to Lujan's tracheostomy tube and established respiratory support, then uncoiled the IV line from the hemomanagement console and connected it to the intracath in his left arm. Tasks completed, they moved back to let the med tech secure him in the chair.

Libby checked the snugness of the restraints when the med tech finished, poking fingers in between straps and skin; then she wrote briefly with her finger on Lujan's forehead. When he responded with a groggy nod, she gave his bare shoulder a reassuring pat.

She's probably telling him, "Here we go again," Darcie thought. It was Libby who had repaired Lujan's injured leg and separated ribs after his flying accident on Tohh, while Darcie was stationed away on Topawa. And it was Libby who had done most of the reconstruction work when Lujan nearly lost his right arm a few years later.

Seated as he was, at nearly a right profile to her, the massive scars on his arm were clearly visible. They twisted around from his shoulder almost down to his elbow, marring the skin and the muscles beneath with deep lines like white trailing vines.

"My word, Luj, what did you do to your arm?" Darcie had gasped the first time she saw it.

"You really don't want to know, Darce," he said, and turned the conversation in another direction.

He never had told her. She'd finally asked Libby about it.

"That happened a couple of years after you and Tris were taken by the masuki," Libby said, "during a remote duty tour on Yan. He had command of a Spherzah combat company there.

"With Yan being so close to Isselan space and all, they were always conducting field exercises or operational readiness inspections or something." She grinned. "I think some of those troops knew their way around the Cathana Mountains better than they knew their way around the base!

"They were in the middle of one of those field exercises when it happened. Lujan and some of his troops were pulling night guard duty at their bivouac in the jungle when this old pampo wandered into their sensor circle—"

"What's a pampo?" Darcie asked.

"They're large omnivores," said Libby. "Some member of the bear family. Not as bulky as bears, and they have long tails, but they have the same kind of unretracting claws. Usually they stay away from humans, but this one didn't."

"And it—got Lujan?"

Libby nodded. "According to the kid who told me the story—one of Lujan's troops—the critter wandered up to his guard post. He tried to scare it off, but it charged him. So he called for backup and started shooting.

"Lujan got to him first," Libby said. "By then the pampo had knocked the kid off his feet and was chewing on his leg. It'd taken a few laser bursts and was pretty sore, so when Lujan opened fire, it whirled around and leaped at him. The kid said he saw it take a swipe at him that sent his rifle flying across the clearing."

"Where were the rest of the patrols?" Darcie wanted to know. "Where was their backup?"

"Right behind Lujan," said Libby. "The ruckus woke up the whole company and they all ended up out there, half-dressed but heavily armed."

Libby shook her head. "The kid said they didn't think that critter was ever going to have the good grace to die. They kept shooting, and it just kept staggering around on top of Lujan and swatting at their laser bursts and roaring; and when a couple of the others tried to lure it away from him, they got smacked as well."

Darcie shook her head, her teeth tight on her lower lip.

"It's a credit to the Spherzah field medics that they managed to keep Lujan alive for the three hours it took to get him and the kid back to the base hospital," said Libby. "His upper arm—where that first swipe caught him—was nothing but bare bone with shreds of muscle and skin dangling from it like so much meat! The report I saw said they pumped sixteen units of whole bloodsub into him before they even got to the hospital."

Combat surgeon or not, Darcie felt a little pale imagining such an injury. "It's a wonder he's got his arm at all!" she said.

"Yes, it is." Libby's tone turned serious. "I have no idea why they didn't just amputate it at the base hospital—except that Lujan begged them not to.

"They didn't have proper facilities, or personnel qualified to do the kind of reconstruction work they knew it was going to take—either for his arm or the other kid's leg—so they did enough work to save the limbs, got them both stabilized, and evacuated them out to Jonica."

"Why Jonica?" Darcie asked. "Wouldn't Sostis have been closer?"

"It would've been," said Libby, "but Lujan's combat company was out of Jonica, so that's where they went— and that's where I had to go to patch them up. I thought the other kid was in bad shape, but Lujan's arm took three separate surgeries to repair."

Darcie could only shake her head.

"That's also when we discovered his allergy to cell-culture implants," Libby said. "We thought they'd be the best way to repair the nerve damage in his arm, but he went into what looked like a full-blown tissue-rejection reaction. It was pretty tense for a few days."

That allergy was the reason Lujan was about to undergo electrode-implant surgery now. The biological cultures that might have actually rebuilt his burned cranial nerves would likely kill him, Darcie knew.

The screens blinking on above the viewpane brought her out of her reverie. She looked up. To her right appeared the hologram that Libby and Gavril had been studying earlier, with the implant paths described in pale yellow. The image rotated slowly, like a small planet without a star to orbit, Darcie thought. To her left, the vital-signs readouts appeared, and she looked them over intently. Pulse rate, respirations, and brain waves indicated a relaxed state; blood pressure and internal temperature were both normal.

Beyond the viewpane, Libby and Gavril stood a little distance from their patient, hands held out before them with fingers spread apart while the human surgical assistant sprayed an aerosol gel over them. The gel dried almost instantly, forming a sterile surgical glove as flexible and touch-sensitive as skin but impervious to puncture.

While the doctors waggled their hands to dry their gloves, the human assistant and two servos applied surgical drapes and the anesthetist made a final check of Lujan's blood gases.

"We're ready, sir," the latter said when Gavril turned toward him, and Darcie realized that the microphones to the gallery had been switched on along with the monitor screens.

Gavril nodded toward the human assistant. "Holoscanner positioned, please."

The young man touched dials on a console; the holoscanner antennae whirred downward until they hung a little above and to either side of Lujan's head, stopping when the three-dimensional projection in front of Gavril came into sharp focus.

"Show intracranial view," Gavril said.

Flesh and cartilage disappeared, leaving the ethereal gray of the brain and the red of major blood vessels, encased in the semitransparent projection of the skull.

"Add procedure overlay," Gavril said.

The gridded hologram image that he and Libby had studied earlier appeared superimposed over and through the image of Lujan's skull. The same double image glowed on the monitor in the gallery.

"Frame," said Gavril.

The stereotaxic frame, resembling a complex vise, settled over Lujan's head on a robotic arm. Gavril checked its position against the markings he'd drawn on his patient's scalp the previous evening and began to turn its screws. Darcie locked her teeth as he secured the apparatus to Lujan's head.

"Check positioning," Gavril said when he finished.

The holoscanner antennae rotated around Lujan's head, comparing actual placement to the gridded projection. Three-dimensional coordinates appeared in the holotank beside the image and the voice synthesizer said, "Position is correct."

Gavril nodded acknowledgment and stepped back. "Local, please."

The anesthetist swabbed the left side of Lujan's head with amber-stained gauze, and Darcie remembered the bite of the anesthetic's scent in her nostrils.

"Scalpel," Gavril said. A servo swung the instrument around on its arm, positioning it clear of the surgeon's elbow, and placed it in his palm.

Sitting at Lujan's right, Darcie couldn't see Gavril's hands. "Close-up of center screen," she said.

The left view of Lujan's head filled the monitor.

Gavril made his first incision a little above and in front of Lujan's left ear. There was no bleeding; the laser scalpel cauterized as it opened up the skin.

The skull beneath was paler than Lujan's scalp when Gavril lifted the skin back.

Brows drawn together behind his surgical hood, Gavril laser-bored four tiny holes in Lujan's left temporal bone, forming a small rectangle. There was no smoke, but Darcie remembered the odor of burning bone. She'd never liked having to drill bone in surgery, even with laser instruments; she could only imagine how much worse the mechanical tools of her medical predecessors would have been centuries before.

Darcie looked away, to the monitor with the hologram display.

The four bore holes exactly matched the marked entry sites.

The scalpel also served as a bone saw. Gavril connected the four holes with precise lines, removed the rectangle of bone, and placed it in a lab dish.

"Electrodes," he said.

From her place in the gallery, Darcie could see a variety of microelectrode arrays on their tray. The two that would be implanted in the temporal lobes, one on either side of Lujan's head, were tiny glassine grids, each with several thousand minute contacts made of platinum. Their leads, an equal number of fiber-optic strands bundled together at the laser converter cell, formed a cable no thicker than a hair.

Gavril selected one array and looked at Libby. "Let's go in."

She used the laser scalpel to open the dura mater, the membrane enclosing the brain beneath the skull, and the human assistant swabbed away a thin trickle of cerebrospinal fluid.

"Magnify center screen," Darcie said.

She watched Gavril slip a blunt probe into the lateral fissure of the brain and spread it slightly. With a slender forceps, he placed the glassy electrode array at the auditory cortex. Positioned there, its contacts would also interface with the language center of the brain.

"Coordinate check," Gavril requested.

They appeared in the holotank near the head image; the computer's voice said, "Placement correct."

Gavril's release of breath as he withdrew the forceps was audible even through his surgical hood. He tucked the optics cable through one of the drill holes and drew it toward the back of Lujan's head, out of his way. "Suture," he said.

Fusing or heat sealing would have been a more accurate term than suturing, Darcie thought. It took only a moment to close the dura mater over the implant. Then Gavril replaced the piece of bone, fused it at two or three spots to hold it in place, and applied morphogen paste with a probe.

The electret microphone to replace Lujan's damaged inner ear came next. Gavril took a tiny silver button from the tray and inserted it deep in the ear canal. Using the hologram projection for guidance and a suture tip on a miniature endoscope, he anchored it into position. Scrutinizing his work in the holo image, he gave a satisfied nod and said, "Mastoid local."

The anesthetist used an infusion this time, into the mastoid area behind Lujan's ear. Waiting for it to take effect, Gavril and Libby studied the gridded procedure overlay again, pointing and conversing quietly.

"Drill," Gavril said then.

It wasn't just a burr-hole this time. Darcie watched, chewing at her lower lip, as the laser bored a minute tunnel through the mastoid to the ear canal. Blue-white light showed its progress along the predetermined track, displayed in yellow in the hologram.

Most time-consuming was threading the endoscope up through the tunnel. No larger than electrician's wire and tipped with tiny pincers, it caught the microphone's leads and drew them down the tunnel until their ends emerged from the hole behind Lujan's ear.

"There." Gavril let out another pent-up breath. "That's one side. Connectors, please."

Libby held out what appeared to be a pair of tiny beads. Gavril slipped one onto the optic strand that emerged from the temporal bone and the other onto the lead at the mastoid and fixed them both with bone epoxy.

Finished, he made a long incision in Lujan's scalp, from the temporal insertion point down behind his ear to the mastoid entry, then around the back of Lujan's neck to the base of his skull. There he opened a small space in the muscle with the blunt probe. "Ready for the processor," he said.

It was a flat black wafer no larger in circumference than one of Gavril's fingernails, and probably only three times as thick.

Its tiny size belied its complexity. Composed of several microchips, each with its own input/output section, it had a chemical reaction battery to supply the receiver processor with power drawn from surrounding body fluids, as if it were a new organ in Lujan's body.

Libby performed the installation, a procedure that took longer than the rest of the operation to that point. Fusing tissue about it to secure it in place, she said, "Ready to connect."

Gavril took over again. Peering through eyepieces like those of a microscope, he guided miniature robotic fingers to attach microfiber leads into their connections, like a commset jack into its outlet. Then he tucked the microfiber bundle into the incision, under the skin, and Libby sutured.

She didn't close the subdermal pocket in the back of Lujan's neck, however. That part of the operation was only half-finished.

The implantations into Lujan's right temporal lobe and ear canal went as smoothly as the left, to Darcie's relief. The chrono on the wall showed five hours had elapsed by the time Libby closed the muscle pocket around the processor in the back of Lujan's neck.

What remained after that was simple by comparison. Gavril had marked Lujan's cranium with twelve spots, mostly over the frontal lobes, for the placement of subdermal disk transmitters. With training, the electrodes would allow Lujan to control a voice synthesizer, a glidechair, or even access a computer with channeled thought.

The placement of the transmitters was a matter of making small incisions, slipping the disks under the skin and adhering them to the skull with bone epoxy, and then closing; the procedure was completed within half an hour. Once Lujan's hair grew back, Darcie realized, one would have to look hard to find any indications of surgery.

She watched as the med techs applied bandaging curafoam to his head. Like the surgeons' liquid gloves, it would dry into a protective layer that would peel off as the wounds beneath healed. With his head encased, Lujan appeared to be wearing a close-fitting helmet.

Darcie waited until the servo had eased him back onto the repulsor sled and guided it out to recovery before she left the observation gallery.

"Everything all right, ma'am?" asked the soldier at the head of the corridor.

"The surgery went well," she said.

His response was a heartfelt, "Good."

Libby and Gavril arrived, shed of their surgical smocks, shortly after Darcie entered the waiting area, and Libby crossed to her at once. "Lujan's doing fine," she said first. "I checked on him on my way out. They'll take him back to his room in about an hour."

"Good." Darcie allowed herself a sigh. "Thank you, Libby."

"There'll be some pain for a few days," Gavril said, "but that should be easily controlled. He's getting a regen to accelerate healing, and I've started him on a neural growth stimulator, to increase dendrite growth. We should be able to activate the processor in four or five days and begin his auditory rehab."

"Thank you, Doctor," Darcie said. She felt almost weak with relief. "Thank you very much."

Starting up the corridor toward Lujan's CCU room a few minutes later, she was startled from her thoughts by the med tech at the desk calling out to her. She stopped, turning to look, and the woman held up a sealed envelope. "This came for you earlier this morning, ma'am," she said.

It was the kind of envelope in which military message printouts were delivered. Brow wrinkling, Darcie flipped it over to see the originator's mark.

SHINCHANG STATION, it read.

That could mean only one thing. She slid her finger under the flap, tore it open; she couldn't pull out the single sheet of paper quickly enough.

The message printed on it was brief:

```
060732L 1 3309SY
TO: CAPT DARCIE DARTMUTH
FM: ARRIVAL OFFICE, SHINCHANG STATION
U N C L A S S I F I E D
TRISTAN SEREGE TO ARRIVE AT SHINCHANG
STATION AT 0322 ON 1/7 ABOARD SHS MERCY,
UNDER EMERGENCY LEAVE ORDER #S-908706
SIGNED BY CMDR H. AMION, ANCHENKO DET.,
SPHERZAH. SURFACE SHUTTLE WILL ARRIVE
BAY 17, HERBRUN FIELD, RAMISCAL CITY AT
1054 ON 1/7.
E N D   O F   M E S S A G E
```

"Tris is coming home!" she whispered. "Tomorrow!"

She realized she was smiling for the first time in days as she strode up the corridor to Lujan's room.

"Going for Tris now," she typed out on the tactile pad. It had been placed on Lujan's upper chest after the surgery. Even if it hadn't been covered with curafoam bandaging, his forehead would have been too sore right now to bear even light finger strokes.

He acknowledged her with a single blink, as if even that were painful, and she added, "I love you," and kissed him and slipped away.

Two Spherzah officers waited for her out at the med

techs' desk. They fell in, one on either side of her, as she crossed the desk area. Fastening up her winter coat, she let them escort her out a side door to a midlevel skimcraft platform.

The skimmer idling there bore an admiral's crest on its nose and passenger doors.

She stopped. "I'm not an admiral," she said. "I'm not even an active-duty captain anymore!"

"It's a matter of your personal security, ma'am," said the driver as he moved to open the skimmer's door. "There're still a lot of unfriendlies out there."

She didn't press the issue; she slid into the passenger compartment and settled herself in, and the two Spherzah boarded, too. One sat opposite her in the passenger compartment; the other joined the driver in front.

The protests in the streets had dwindled and finally ended a couple of weeks before, but she still couldn't go anywhere—even across the medical center's park— without one or two Sostish MPs in tow.

She hadn't spent all of the last six weeks at the medical complex, though she had stayed there for the first couple of weeks. With Lujan in such critical condition then, she'd had no desire to be farther away from him than the hospital's family quarters.

Since he'd recovered from the seizure and his condition had stabilized, however, Libby had insisted that she go home to the Flag Officers' Residence at night. "You can't do Lujan any good if you're a case yourself," she'd said, "and that's what you'll be if you just sit here the whole time."

Libby was right, Darcie knew. So she accepted dinner invitations from Jiron and Heazel on evenings when she wasn't too tired. Sometimes she'd take a skimmer up the nearby fjord—accompanied by a couple of military policemen, of course—just to get away from the sights and sounds and smells of the hospital. And lately, since Jiron had brought her the message about Lujan's impending retirement, she'd spent a great deal of time at the medical library across the park, working on the formal request for reconsideration, while Lujan was in therapy.

Still, it took a shaft of sunlight piercing the clouds to make her realize that winter was winding down. Dawn came before midmorning now, daylight lingered a little longer into the afternoon, and the snow was beginning to recede from roofs and parks.

"Ma'am, do you know which bay your son's shuttle is expected to come in to?" the driver asked through the intercom.

"Seventeen," she said. She had practically memorized the contents of that message. "It'll be bay seventeen."

The driver bypassed Herbrun Field's main terminal and scooted across what seemed to be kilometers of tarmac toward a cluster of separate landing bays.

Number 17 was half-encircled by military medical transports. The driver nosed the skimcraft up among them, and their personnel saluted its admiral's crests and made way for it to pass.

"It would probably be best to stay inside for now, ma'am," the driver said as he brought the craft to a halt within sight of the bay's arched entry.

"Right," Darcie said. She leaned back in her seat, tried to relax; but she could feel her pulse racing. And when she glanced down she found her hands locked tightly together in her lap.

They were there in time to watch the shuttle appear from the clouds: just a speck of glitter at first, white with its own reentry heat. It was some time before the sound of its engines thundered across the field to them: a deep rumble that built swiftly to a ground-shaking volume.

Darcie watched it make its approach, descending as it

arched over Herbrun Field, coming at last to a hover over the bay. When its landing rockets lit and it began to sink into the bowl-shaped enclosure, she couldn't remain still any longer. She reached out for the skimmer's door handle—

Her bodyguard's hand intercepted; he gave her a wordless firm look as he opened the door and stepped out of the craft first. He surveyed the area briefly before he nodded an okay and reached into the passenger compartment to assist her out.

It was some minutes after the roar of the rockets subsided before the first shapes appeared in the entry. Darcie couldn't distinguish their features at once, bundled as they were behind winter gear, but as they strode from shadow into gray daylight—

"Tristan!" she breathed.

He wore the dark uniform coat of the Spherzah, and an anxious expression that showed in his eyes and the set of his jaw. He was thinner, too, she thought, than he'd been when he left two months before.

He paused at the entry, chewing his lip as his gaze swept over the waiting medical people. And then he spotted her: His eyes locked on hers.

Only then did she rush him, reaching up to wrap her arms about him. "Tris!" she said, pulling him close. "Are you all right? You've lost weight."

"I'm fine, Mum," he said, and searched her eyes with his own. She saw how he swallowed. "How is—?"

He didn't finish the question. As if he feared the answer, Darcie thought. She wondered what he'd been told.

"Your father?" she asked. She squeezed his hand. "He'll be relieved to know that you're home. We can go directly to the hospital, if you'd like."

"Yes," he said.

He sat with his jaw taut all the way back to the city, listening as she described Lujan's injuries and the recovery he'd made so far. He only nodded in response, and Darcie read his ache in his eyes, in his taut jaw. She could almost guess what he was thinking.

He and Lujan had struggled through their first months together, Lujan longing for the filial bond he'd never had a chance to build with his son, and Tristan, scarred emotionally as well as physically by his hostage experience, resisting every step of the way. The turning point had come only a few weeks before Tristan was recruited as a scout for the Spherzah. If Lujan had not survived . . .

Darcie suppressed a shudder at that thought and reached out to squeeze her son's hand again.

He stayed quiet, following her through the hospital corridors a short time later. He seemed to freeze up when the door to Lujan's room slid open. But he followed when she beckoned him inside, and joined her at his father's bedside, his features more solemn than anxious by now.

Someone had pulled the sheet up over Lujan's chest in her absence. She drew it back a little, just enough to reveal the tactile pad. "We're back, Luj," she tapped into its keypad. "How are you doing?"

He opened his eyes—seemed to look directly at her. "Slept," he blinked. "Feel better."

She patted his shoulder. "Good," she tapped, and then added, "Tris is here, love."

Lujan's mouth worked a little, as if he were trying to speak, but the tracheostomy didn't allow any sound. His right hand moved slightly at his side.

Darcie picked up his hand. It was still strengthless, still partly numb, she knew; his fingers still couldn't curl about hers. Squeezing his hand in hers, she reached out for Tristan's and placed them together, one in the other.

She saw how her son swallowed at that. Saw how his

hand wrapped tightly about his father's. It was some moments before he reached out with his free hand.

"I'm home, Father. Finally," he wrote, tapping it out carefully, in dot code, on Lujan's chest. "I'll be here whenever you need me."

It was the same promise Lujan had made to Tristan months ago. The promise Tristan hadn't been ready to accept at the time.

Darcie's throat tightened. *He will need you, Tris,* she thought. *You have no idea right now how much he'll need you!*

NINE

They were still playing up the liberation of Issel on the Sostish newsnets: tender scenes of families reunited, somber scenes from memorial rites for those who weren't so fortunate, shots of grateful Isselan citizens embracing startled Unified soldiers. Some of the clips were replayed with every update from the war zone.

Their sentimentality turned Remarq's stomach.

Still, a great deal of thought and planning had gone into those clips, he knew. Every image had been selected for its emotional appeal, for its ability to cry out, "See? The Isselans aren't monsters after all! They're people, too—just like Kalese and Jonican and Sostish people! They have the same hopes and fears and joys and sorrows. They're victims, frightened and helpless, who are grateful to their Unified rescuers! See how grateful they are!"

His people inside the Unified Worlds news services were truly outdoing themselves, Remarq had to admit. At this rate there would be no resistance at all; the Unified Worlds would be conquered by their own compassion.

Shutting off the news program, he switched over to Mail. "Compose message," he said. "Address it to the Honorable Seamus Trosvig, headquarters of the Mythosian delegation to the Unified Worlds Assembly, via the Isselan embassy on Mythos."

Filling in the routing and security parameters on the screen, he drew his brows together and gathered his mouth until its deep creases made it look like a drawstring bag.

Trosvig had done well, he thought, using Admiral Serege's seizure to his advantage in pushing for Serege's retirement. He wished he had thought of the seizure himself. They would be ridiculously easy to induce with any number of drugs—if he had an agent at the Winthancom Military Medical Center.

Perhaps, he thought, Trosvig had a friend there.

He would have to keep a close eye on the man.

But he concealed his suspicion with a smile as he began to dictate his message.

"My dear Seamus," he said, "I hear through the newsnets that you've done very well for yourself in your first month in a seat on the Triune. You are to be congratulated on your successful nomination of Vice Admiral Oleszek for chief commander of the Spherzah. It appears that the hearings are proceeding smoothly and the change of command will be accomplished without any delays.

"With that matter safely on its way, I believe we can now turn our attention in another direction." He folded his hands together on the desktop and shifted forward in his chair to focus his gaze on the monitor's holocorder. "I believe it is time to consider the matter of Issel's reentry into the Unified Worlds."

He paused momentarily, for effect, then said, "There is an assemblywoman from Tohh named Abigail DeByes. I expect that you know her, Seamus; I'm told she's made herself quite visible in the Unified Worlds Assembly in the past few years. I need you to speak to her for me.

"When you approach her, tell her that her mother is sounding the dinner chime and it's time for her to come in from playing. She'll understand, just as you understood my congratulatory gift on your appointment to the Triune." Remarq gave a short, grim smile.

"Tell her," he continued, "that there's been interest expressed in the reinstatement of Issel into the Unified Worlds, but as your laws clearly state"—he arched his brows—"as a member of the Triune, you are not allowed to bring legislation before the Assembly yourself. Therefore, you are appointing her to head a committee that will research and draft such a proposal and present it to the Assembly.

"Allow Madam DeByes to select her own committee," Remarq said, "but advise her to keep it small—no more than five members, including herself—and she is to give you the names of those she chooses so that you may be aware of who they are and how well they are carrying out their task.

"She is to report to you on a regular basis, but she is not to reveal to her committee that she is acting under anyone's direction; she may tell them only that there have been expressions of interest in bringing Issel back into the Unified Worlds."

Remarq narrowed his gaze at the holocorder. "I cannot emphasize enough, Seamus, how much care must be taken if this proposal is to succeed." He shifted forward once more, ever so slightly, before he said, "I know that I can trust you to accomplish it."

Settling into his seat on the raised platform, Trosvig surveyed the Assembly chamber through narrowed eyes. He spotted Madam DeByes right away, back from her latest junket and seated at the head of the Tohh delegation.

He would speak to her during the first morning recess, he decided, and reached for his pocket towel, tucked carefully into the inside of his jacket.

He hadn't been surprised by the revelation in Remarq's most recent message. He hadn't even had to wonder what bait the Isselan recruiter had used to lure DeByes into his net.

"Madam" was the title allowed for female members of the Assembly, but DeByes was the only woman Trosvig had ever known during his career who insisted on being addressed by it. It was a joke among those Assembly members who had worked closely with her that she used it only because she wasn't allowed the title of Empress.

They also joked that her given name of Abigail was merely a derivation of Ambitious.

Trosvig found himself watching her through the first morning session, standing rigid at her bench as she took more than her allotted time in the debate. She remained carefully respectful as she pressed her point, though she was obviously determined to have the last word—until the officiator pressed the buzzer on his desk and turned over the floor to another speaker. Then she dropped down on her bench in a huff.

When recess was called, Trosvig excused himself with a word to Alois Ashforth, seated at his right, and shoved himself out of his chair. He kept his vision fixed on DeByes as he dismounted the platform, lest she slip away.

Unaware of him, she rose from her bench as he reached the floor, turned her back on him and started away between the benches and desks toward the nearest exit.

He caught up to her at the doorway. "Madam DeByes," he said, reaching out to lightly touch her shoulder.

She pivoted around as if expecting to be accosted, eyes glaring, mouth poised as if on the verge of a retort.

The glare dissipated like mist under the morning sun when she recognized him. "Your Honor!" she said, and smiled up at him, all honeyed warmth.

She was a beautiful young woman, Trosvig had to admit: petite and elegant in her bright business blazer and her stylishly short faux blond hair. Her deep brown eyes were wide as a child's, and appeared as innocent, and her skin was smooth and radiant—almost flushed at the moment, as if with some anticipated excitement.

This was her public face, he knew. The face she wore to woo her constituents during elections to the Assembly. The face she used to manipulate malleable members of the Assembly into accepting her views on the issues—until they believed the ideas were their own.

But he had glimpsed from time to time what lay beneath the beauty; he had learned to be wary of her warmth.

"How may I help you?" she asked: a textbook study in proper respect for those of higher position.

He noticed how she couldn't keep her gaze off the tricolored Triunal ribbon that lay across his chest, couldn't quite keep her hunger for such a ribbon of her own from shadowing her eyes.

"I need to speak with you for a moment, madam," he said, "—in a setting more private than the Chamber doorway."

She questioned him with her wide-eyed expression. "Oh?" she said.

He returned a brief smile. "Let's step into a conference room."

He led her along the marbled corridor toward the core of the building and, through the corner of his eye, watched her attempt to keep up to his long strides without dropping her dignified carriage. She kept her back pillar-straight, her expression set with purpose, but he didn't miss the tension that pursed her mouth.

He stopped at last at a small conference room off the building's rear corridor. Swinging open its ancient door, he activated lighting and made a gesture of invitation toward the chairs surrounding the table.

Madam DeByes swept past him—moved at once toward the chair at the conference table's head. She flashed him a smile, almost playful as she settled herself into its deeply upholstered seat. "Funny, isn't it," she said, "how I so naturally gravitate to the most comfortable chair in the room!"

It was far too large for her, Trosvig thought—in other ways besides its physical size. But he responded to the comment with a cursory smile. "It appears that you'll have ample opportunity to sit there, madam," he said. He remained standing halfway down the table's length from her. "I've been asked to offer you the chair of a rather important committee."

Her eyes widened; her mouth shaped a little "Oh!" Like a child's exclamation over a holiday gift, Trosvig thought.

She had participated in nearly a dozen temporary committees during her two terms as a member of the Assembly. Clever, charismatic, and armed with the flawless smile of a computer-generated holovid heroine, she couldn't help but attract people—especially first-term Assembly members who saw only that public face. Always visible in her accomplishments, she seemed to be a natural leader; so it had puzzled Trosvig that she'd never been chosen to chair a committee—until he noticed that few of those who *had* served on committees with her ever chose to work closely with her again.

He couldn't help wondering how much Chief Minister Remarq knew about this woman. What character traits made her useful to him in this task?

She composed herself in a moment, sitting straight in the large chair to place her hands one over the other on the tabletop: all business now, calm and firm. "What's the purpose of this committee?" she asked.

Trosvig deliberately pulled out the nearest chair from the side of the table, sat down, and interlocked his hands on the tabletop before he answered. "It's been brought to my attention," he said, "that there's a great deal of interest in seeing Issel readmitted to the Unified Worlds. I can't, in my own position, bring legislation before the Assembly, of course. Therefore, I've been requested to have you do so."

"By the Triune?" DeByes asked, her eyes widening once more.

Trosvig could almost see her sense of self-importance swelling—could see it in the way she leaned forward to him, eager for his confirmation. He favored her with a scant smile. "Not quite, madam," he said, and fixed his vision on her face. "I've been asked to inform you that your mother is sounding the dinner chime; it's time for you to come in from playing."

She appeared perplexed for a moment, like a child encountering a very large dog. Then her mask of innocence slipped. She paled. Stared at him with her red lips partly open for several moments, as if she were silently struggling to keep the mask in place. Said nothing for the space of several heartbeats. Then the mask fell away altogether. Her wide brown eyes turned to flint—flint laced with the molten heat of an energy bolt—and her fine jaw turned as hard as the marble floor. She shot up from the chair, pointing an accusing finger. "You—you *traitor!* How could you dare—? You're an agent for Issel!"

Trosvig managed another smile. Tighter this time. A fair imitation of Minister Remarq's in his messages, he thought. "No more or less than you are yourself, madam," he said.

She visibly stiffened at that, but whether with shock or

with indignation he couldn't tell—though for a moment she seemed about to scream, "How dare you?"

In the end she said nothing. She just stared at him for another several heartbeats, and he watched a myriad of emotions roll across her features—the same emotions he had experienced himself on opening Remarq's little gift.

Panic won out at last. DeByes clenched her hands at her sides. She shook her head. "This wasn't supposed to happen for ten or twenty years!" she said. "They told me it would be ten or twenty years! You can't do this to me!" Her voice rose in a plea. "I have my career to complete! They promised me a career—"

Trosvig loosened his hands on the table and turned them over in a gesture resembling a shrug. "Your career isn't finished, madam," he said. "It's barely begun. You're simply working for a different government now."

She stopped her ranting at that. Swallowed as she stared at him.

And Trosvig slipped into his all-business mode: hands interlocked again on the table, thumbs pressed together. "Be advised," he said, "that this will probably be the toughest piece of legislation you'll ever push through the Assembly. But you *will* push it through, madam, no matter what it takes to do so." He narrowed his eyes slightly, fixed them on hers. "A number of very influential people are depending on you to see their interests passed into law."

His emphasis on "very influential people" seemed to stir her out of her shock. "What do I stand to gain by doing this?" she demanded.

He arched an eyebrow. "My dear madam," he said, "you've already received your 'gain' from the Isselan government! This is your opportunity to repay the debt to your benefactor in full! I expect there is also a large sum of interest due."

Her shock gave way to another glare at him. She raised a hand as if to shake it at him, but he cut her off with a wave. "You will select your committee yourself," he said, "but I recommend you keep it small: no more than five members, including yourself. I want a list of their names by the end of this week.

"You're to tell them only that you've been approached about the possibility of readmitting Issel to the Unified Worlds. Mentioning the source of that interest will, of course, incriminate only yourself. I'll be visiting with you regularly to see how your proposal is progressing."

Her features were a mask of fury by now, with narrowed eyes, lips pressed together, teeth locked tight. She hissed his name as if it were a curse.

Trosvig ignored it. He shoved himself to his feet and he didn't glance back as he turned to the door. Didn't glimpse her still standing rigid at the head of the table with her hands knotted up at her sides.

You have only yourself to blame, madam, he thought as he strode back up the corridor. *You're a victim of your own lust for power just as I am a victim of mine.*

TEN

"**Activating processor now,**" Dr. Efraim Marife tapped on the tactile pad.

Seated in a glidechair in the audiologist's office, Lujan blinked acknowledgment.

He actually started at the sudden explosion of sound.

It was like the roar of a wind, as ceaseless and impenetrable as the silence had been moments before. Like the white noise of communications jamming over his cockpit radio in combat, hissing and crackling through his helmet's earphones.

"Hearing by means of implants is different than with natural ears, sir," Marife had cautioned him earlier. "You should expect everything to sound different. It'll take time to get accustomed to it."

But there was nothing meaningful—or even distinguishable—in this noise. It only grated at his ears, seeming to vibrate his whole skull.

Was this *all* the implants could restore to him? Was *this* what he would have to become accustomed to? Disappointment washed over him, sharp and bitter as an acid tide. "Shut it off!" he blinked.

Marife did; the onslaught of static roar ceased as abruptly as it had begun.

"What's wrong, sir?" the tactile pad spelled out.

He blinked, "Nothing but static."

There was a pause, and then, "Have to tune processor, sir," the audiologist tapped. "You'll feel sensor at back of head. Computer will analyze and adjust settings."

I should have realized that, Lujan thought with some chagrin. Cockpit radios were useless, too, set on the wrong frequencies. "Go ahead," he blinked.

Dr. Marife turned on the processor once more, reviving the noise; then he shifted the glidechair's headrest a little and pushed down the top of the soft neck brace Lujan wore, just enough to press something cool and knoblike to the base of his skull.

For the next several minutes Lujan listened to what resembled variations on a theme. The noise swelled and diminished and even changed pitch as the sensor touched and withdrew, touched and withdrew. He winced at a squeak one moment, at a fierce rattle of static the next. The adjustments didn't seem to do any good. His hope ebbed, leaving in its place a sort of heavy, all-encompassing sense of loss.

It was several minutes before he made out a voice in the midst of the noise. A male voice, he thought, but he couldn't tell what it was saying. He furrowed his brow, straining to hear, as he had strained against the interference on his cockpit radio. The effort made his head throb.

The voice came again, more deliberate the second time. He caught a word here, another word there, but the rest were muffled by the wind.

"Still too much noise," he began to blink—and was startled by a string of soft beeps that seemed to mimic his blink pattern. It was a moment before he realized the beeping came from the blink monitor, which lay on his lap, under his hands, like a small tray.

The roar of the static diminished slightly, as if a volume control had been turned down somewhere. But it made the voice fainter, too, and did nothing to clarify the words. "Voice too soft now," he blinked.

Another long space passed before he could finally make out Marife's questions. "How is this?" the audiologist asked between sensor touches. "Is this any better? . . . How is this? . . . How about this?"

Eventually he said, "That's all I can do for now, sir. I've tuned the processor to a normal hearing range. How does it sound?"

The words were distinct, no longer muffled and lost in the noise that remained, but the audiologist's voice had an odd electronic edge, like that of a primitive speech synthesizer. "Voice sounds strange," Lujan blinked.

"That will pass as the hearing centers in your brain adjust to the artificial neural pathways," Marife said. He paused, then added, "Once that comes about, we can begin to expand your hearing range—if you're interested in doing that, sir. The microphones that were placed inside your ears are capable of registering sound into the ultra- and subsonic ranges."

Lujan blinked, "No thanks."

"Very well, sir." Then Marife asked, "What can you hear besides my voice?"

The rushing wind sounds were still there, though the tuning seemed to have subdued them somewhat. And there was a hum that came from close behind him—probably from the glidechair's power source—and a rhythmic ticking somewhere else, like that of an ancient timepiece. Lujan cataloged each one.

"Noise like the ventilation and the glidechair's hum will fade into the background as the newness of hearing again wears off," Marife said. Then he asked, "Do you think you can do without the tactile pad?"

Marife hadn't been using it for the last several minutes, Lujan realized abruptly, and he hadn't had any trouble understanding him. The discouragement he'd felt at first lifted in a sense of mild surprise; he blinked, "Yes."

"Very good," Marife said. He peeled the pad from Lujan's forehead and explained, "Because you were only without hearing for a few weeks, a little time will be all the auditory rehabilitation you'll really need. But I'd like to follow up with you on a daily basis for a while, to conduct some hearing tests and do any fine-tuning you may need."

As long as that tuning doesn't include any experimentation, Lujan thought. He blinked, "Fine."

The kind of rehabilitation he *did* need, right now in fact, was to lie down. Sitting up for too long at a time—even when "sitting" was still really half reclining—was exhausting. The increasing pain in his neck, the pounding in his head, and the nausea swelling in the pit of his stomach told him he was pushing his limit.

Marife apparently recognized his discomfort. "I'll tell Captain Dartmuth you're ready to return to your room," he said.

Lujan listened to Marife's footfalls crossing to the doorway, listened as he called to Darcie in the waiting area, listened to her quick, light footsteps coming toward him. He found himself focusing his full attention on each sound, on its timbre and rhythm, in a way he never had before.

A hand touched his shoulder. A feminine voice said, "Luj?"

That was the sound he'd been anticipating, the sound he'd longed to hear from the first. Her voice seemed to have been electronically altered, too, but it didn't matter; it was definitely Darcie's.

He couldn't have spoken right then even if he'd been physically capable of it. He could barely blink out, "Good to hear you."

Her chuckle at that was music.

She stayed quiet all the way to his room, though she kept a hand on his shoulder, kneading it a little as she walked beside his glidechair. In the ache of his mounting exhaustion, that contact, that soundless support, was all he needed.

He was dimly aware of her speaking to the guards at the door upon reaching his room, and to the med tech who helped transfer him back into bed. Then the med tech left, and Darcie took up his nearest hand in one of hers, began to stroke his face with the other, and kissed him softly on the forehead—the way she had done all along. But she didn't speak; she just sat there quietly massaging his hand.

He waited for several seconds. Waited, while the ventilation roared in his ears, until he could bear it no longer. "Talk to me, Darcie!" he blinked. It was a plea.

"Oh, Luj, I'm sorry!" she said at once. "I've gotten too used to you not being able to hear me, I suppose. . . . What would you like me to talk about?"

At that point it didn't matter. All he wanted was to listen to her voice. "Anything," he blinked.

"Anything?" she repeated, and sighed. There was a little silence, and then she said, "I should probably bring in the message chips Tris has filled from the mail queue and let you listen to those. He must spend half an hour downloading it every night! The traffic's hardly slowed since you were first injured! Maybe I should start bringing in the hard-copy letters that came to my quarters, too. We could fill a month's worth of evenings reading those to you!"

Lujan felt amazement. "All for me?" he blinked.

"Most of it," said Darcie. "The ones from your sisters and Siljan are addressed to me. They keep wondering if they should come to Sostis to help out, and I keep assuring them that Tris and I have you under control."

He wished he could smile; he blinked out instead, "How are they?"

"They're all well," Darcie said. "Siljan's expecting a good harvest in spite of all the flooding this past spring. And Twyla's expecting at last! They've confirmed it's a boy. She says Rahb hasn't stopped smiling since she told him."

Twyla, his youngest sister. He could imagine his brother-in-law's emotions—could remember how his own face had ached from grinning after Darcie told him they were going to have Tristan.

Speaking of which . . .

"Where is Tris?" he blinked.

"He's going through mission debriefings," Darcie said. "At least they allowed him a couple days' rest before they started in. He wasn't at all happy about it, but I think he'll get through all right this time. Jiron offered to bring him here when they finish for the day."

Mission debriefings, Lujan thought.

He had known the mission. He must have known it to the last detail; he'd helped to plan it. He knew that in some remote way, but none of it remained.

The loss of so much knowledge left him with a sense of urgency, a sense that there were vital things he should remember. Closing his eyes, he pushed against the void in his memory as if it were a dam that could be broken. He pushed until it wearied him.

"Lujan?" said Darcie beside him. Her voice bore a note of concern.

"Don't remember," he blinked. And after a pause: "What did they do?"

"Who, Luj?" she asked.

"Spherzah."

"They rescued the people who were kidnapped by the masuki," Darcie said. "It's been all over the news programs for the last several weeks. I don't know any of the details, though. Perhaps Tris can tell you."

Masuki.

Slave raids against Issel.

He remembered that much. Distantly.

He remembered that two cabinet members had come from Issel seeking help. He'd wondered who sent them.

He wondered it still.

The thought of it made his heart accelerate. Made his thoughts tumble over each other until they ran together. He had to know, had to ask. "Who sent—," he began to blink.

The rest of the words escaped him, vanished along with his memory.

"Sent what?" said Darcie.

All he could think of was "miniature" and he knew that wasn't it. Minaret? It seemed it had something to do with a church. . . .

He squeezed his eyes shut and groaned with frustration. At least he could do that, since they'd finally closed the tracheostomy, but his mouth still didn't work to shape sounds into words despite the therapist's efforts.

"Lujan, what's wrong?" Darcie asked.

"Can't find words," he blinked.

She stroked his face. "You're trying too hard," she said. "Just relax. Perhaps it'll come back if you relax."

It hadn't come back by the time she left late that evening.

He'd never realized before how noisy a hospital was at night. The fluid suspension mattress whooshed and the sheets rustled every time he tried to move an arm or leg. There were footfalls in the corridor, occasional mutters between the guards at his door, and whirs and hums and clicks from every piece of equipment in the room. Even his body was noisy: rumbles from his stomach, his pulse pounding in his ears. And over it all, the never-ending roar of the air through the ventilation system, just loud enough to keep him awake.

The only things louder were the questions that echoed on and on through his mind, the questions that he couldn't find words to ask.

"Ready for breakfast, sir?"

The voice was that of Pilita Elon, one of his two physiotherapists. Lujan furrowed his brow, puzzled. "Darcie does that," he blinked.

"Not anymore," Pilita said. "I sent her down to the chow hall to have her own breakfast." She clicked a switch to raise his lap table and, over its hum as it rose from beside the bed and locked into position over his legs, she explained, "We're taking the first step today toward regaining your independence, sir. No more being fed by Darcie. You've got enough gross motor control back in your left arm now to start learning to use it again."

He raised an eyebrow at that—one of the few facial expressions he hadn't lost to the injuries—and waited while she raised his bed to a semi-sitting position and spread a plastic sheet over his chest and tucked it about his neck. Then he heard the gentle clunk of something being set on the lap table. "How does custard sound?" she asked.

He tried to grimace. "Has eggs," he blinked. "No thanks."

"This doesn't have eggs," Pilita said. "It's Sjenlunder keer's-milk custard." She picked up his right hand. "Here's the bowl," she said, and wrapped his hand around it.

He could feel its shape against his palm, its deep curve from base to rim. But he couldn't feel whether it was plastic or metal, rough or smooth, hot or cold. His fingers could feel nothing at all.

"You'll use your right hand to 'see' the bowl and hold it while you eat with your left," Pilita said.

She pulled something onto his left hand as she spoke, something that felt like a cross between a glove and a brace. Then she slipped something else into a bracket on the glove's palm. "There's your spoon," she said. "Use your bicep and your wrist to lift it."

He aimed his left hand, with the spoon in its bracket, at the bowl.

Something nudged the base of his right thumb. It didn't feel like a spoon—there was barely any feeling at all—but he knew it must be. He tried to adjust—

The spoon hit the tray. It had to have been the tray; he heard its metallic ring. He expelled a breath with annoyance.

It took him over an hour to empty the bowl, and though he got enough to satisfy his hunger, he was certain he got more custard on his face and chest than into his mouth. Even when he succeeded at that, he seemed to lose half again trying to maneuver his mouth enough to swallow it.

He remembered Tristan's first attempts as a toddler to eat with a spoon. Remembered food smeared on his face, on his clothes, in his hair. . . . Lujan closed his eyes in humiliation as Pilita removed the plastic sheet.

She didn't seem to notice. "You did great for the first time, sir," she said, "—especially for someone who can't even *see* what he's doing! It just takes practice, and I'll make sure you get plenty of that!"

He responded with only a grunt.

He lay still for a long time after she left the room, remembering when his fingers weren't useless, when managing utensils was something he did without even thinking.

He remembered cradling Tristan in his hands: the feel of the fragile infant head with its pale, wispy hair cupped safely in his palm.

He remembered the feel of a fighter's stick in his grip; the leather of his glove, tight between his fingers, its lining damp with sweat; the millimeter play of the stick to left and right that sent his craft careening into dives and rolls.

He remembered the jabs, the holds, the punches of Spherzah combat drills. Driving his fists with killer force through their targets. Silent, simple hand signals that warned and guided his cohorts through their sensitive missions . . .

The rehab room was his battlefield now, one hour at a time, several times every day. And the first round always began shortly after breakfast.

He turned his head a little when a familiar cheery voice called out from the doorway, "Ready to go, sir?"

The voice belonged to Sablon Meles, his other physiotherapist, a young man with large hands and insatiable enthusiasm.

He started by wrapping Lujan's legs, first one and then the other. Standing near the foot of the bed, he propped Lujan's leg up on his shoulder and cinched it tight in compression bands from ankle to midthigh.

"This'll keep the blood from pooling in your legs when we sit you up in the glidechair," he explained the first time he did it. "It also keeps blood clots from forming in your legs."

Not all that different from the G pants he'd worn in space combat, Lujan thought.

Meles dressed him after wrapping his legs, tugging a pair of lightweight sweatpants up over the banding, maneuvering his arms into the sleeves of a sweatshirt, pushing his feet into high-topped athletic shoes that supported his strengthless ankles. The clothes were more than a little ironic, Lujan thought; he'd never felt less athletic in his life. But they were well suited for therapy sessions.

A servo lifted him from the bed to the glidechair. Meles settled him into it before he switched on its repulsors. "All right, sir, let's go," he said. "Another day, another achievement!"

One of the military guards at the door fell in beside them as they entered the corridor. Lujan heard the tattoo of his shoes on the tiling.

In the rehab room, the servo lifted him out of the glidechair and placed him on an elevated mat. Flat on his back.

The passive range-of-motion exercises of the first few weeks were long gone.

"Those were just to keep your joints from locking up and your muscles from deteriorating," Meles told him. "What we're doing now, sir, is actually rebuilding your muscles. These are isometrics—sometimes called progressive resistance exercises."

Lujan's arms lay at his sides. Meles turned the right one over, palm up, and placed his large hand over Lujan's forearm. "We'll start out with something simple," he said. "Just bend your arm at the elbow and bring your hand up to touch your nose while I push against it."

Lujan braced his elbow, curled his wrist, tried to pull his arm up—

It never left the mat.

There was more strength in his left arm; he got it a couple centimeters off the mat, at least. But five attempts to raise his hand to his face left his arm shaking and sent fire through his neck and shoulders. Meles spent several minutes massaging out the soreness with those huge hands of his.

And then there were the sit-ups.

His abdominal muscles, solid as a stone wall before the injury, had all the turgor of overcooked pasta now. Lujan strained against the pressure of Meles's hands on his chest—as if Meles really needed to apply any pressure; gravity was a formidable adversary by itself. He could barely lift his head and shoulders from the mat, let alone his whole torso.

"Got to get those abs in shape, sir!" Meles said. "I can't get you back on your feet without any abs to keep you upright."

Even Spherzah combat training, with its kicks and chokes and throws, over and over and over, hadn't been so painful. At least, not that Lujan could remember. Those drills had left him sore, sweating, stiff. But attempting to do even one sit-up now was like being wrung out between unseen hands, like being twisted and rent apart from the inside out. Five or six tries left him limp as a scrap of cloth, soaked with sweat, and sinking over the edge of consciousness.

"That's enough, sir," he heard Meles say as he emerged from his swoon. "Let's ice you down now."

Cold packs and massage eased the strain, assuaged the ache; but he was spent. He sagged as the servo lifted him back into the glidechair. Too weary even to blink, he only sighed in response to Meles's breezy monologue on the ride back to his room.

Darcie was waiting there for him. "How did it go, love?" she asked.

Before Lujan could blink a reply, Meles said, "He did great, ma'am! He made some definite progress this morning!" He moved back to let the servo lift Lujan into bed, then patted his shoulder. "You rest up, sir," he said. "I'll see you again this afternoon!"

Every muscle of Lujan's body throbbed, every fiber felt stretched beyond its breaking point, and Meles was already talking about their next session! "Sadist!" he blinked. He wished he could snarl it.

He had thought the same thing of his Spherzah instructor.

*   *   *

"This is a voice synthesizer," said Dr. Moses. Her fingers brushed Lujan's neck as she fastened a band snugly about it. In the front, a metallic disk no larger around than his thumbnail lay cold at the base of his throat.

Moving back to her position in front of him, Libby said, "It's only a temporary fix until we get the nerves to your lower face repaired and start teaching you to talk again, but it'll let you get on with your rehab in the meantime."

"How does it work?" he blinked.

"It's basically just a little RF receiver coupled to a speaker," she said. "It picks up signals transmitted through tiny antennae in the electrodes we implanted here around your head." She touched a couple of spots on Lujan's forehead, where small bumps lay under his skin. "The electrodes pick up on bioelectric signals—brain waves, in other words—that are generated by your thought patterns.

"Once you get comfortable with talking this way, I'll teach you to control your glidechair, access your desk terminal, the holovid—you name it—with voice commands."

She paused. "Why don't you go ahead and try it," she said then. "Start with the word *oh*. You'll really have to focus to do this, Jink; the electrodes won't pick up on normal random thoughts."

Probably a good thing, Lujan thought. He closed his eyes and concentrated on the word *oh*.

Nothing happened.

He turned his sightless eyes toward the sound of Libby's voice and questioned her with a furrowed brow.

"It takes practice," she said, "just like everything else. Try it again. Just shut out your surroundings and give it your whole attention."

Shut out your surroundings. Focus.

His martial arts masters had given him much the same instruction, he remembered.

They had also counseled him to apply the same principles, the same disciplines to all aspects of his life.

He let himself relax in the glidechair. Let his eyes close once more. Cleared his mind as he would to enter the state of *zanshin*. It was a state of peace, a state of inner awareness, a state of energy waiting for direction.

He pictured *oh* in his mind. Studied the shape of the character, the fullness and depth of it. Explored the simple sound of it. Stretched it out—

He started at a voice saying, "O-oh," from a point somewhere below his chin. A male voice with an electronic edge. Reflexively, his eyes flashed open.

"Not bad!" said Libby. She squeezed his shoulder. "Now do it again."

Lujan drew in a breath. Let it out slowly. Let it carry the thought.

"O-o-oh," came from the voice synthesizer.

"Good!" Libby said. "I think you're ready to move on to something else."

It wasn't effortless. The concentration made his head ache, the ache made him angry, and the anger was distracting. *Clear your mind,* he counseled himself. *Relax . . . relax.*

"One syllable at a time, Lujan," Libby said. "You're trying to take it too fast and you're spreading your focus too thin. In a week or so this'll all be second nature, but for right now let's just stick to single syllables."

That chafed at his patience, made him wish he could clench his teeth.

He had never been patient. Not with himself.

While Meles put more emphasis on working his legs, Pilita was more guarded about his fingers.

They had no feeling yet. No tingles of returning sensation, no twitches from reviving muscles. His fingers remained limp, curled into a sort of gripping shape despite all of Darcie's massaging and Pilita's exercises.

"It's called tenodesis," the therapist said. "It's common in spinal injury patients."

"But will it pass?" Darcie asked.

Pilita was quiet for a long space. "We don't know," she said then.

But she refused to give up. "We don't know that it *won't* pass, either," she said.

She placed soft foam balls in each of Lujan's hands. "I want you to squeeze them," she said, "one finger at a time, sir. Try to touch each fingertip in turn to the tip of your thumb."

He could scarcely even feel that his fingers were there, let alone make them move! Still, he tried—until the futility of it caught him up in a sudden wave of fury.

"Had enough!" he blinked, too distracted to use the voice synthesizer; and in a move more impulsive than planned, he tried to hurl the ball at her, at the sound of her voice.

It dropped to the bed by his knee—and he let his arm drop, too, in shame at his outburst.

Pilita let loose a whistle. "Hey, sir, that was pretty good!" she said. "You used your whole arm to do that! Maybe you should get mad more often!"

The throwing exercises she came up with after that left his upper arms and shoulders so stiff he could barely shrug.

Still, strength came out of the soreness, like a phoenix from the ashes. Lujan felt it in the ripple of his muscles, in an increasing ability to control them.

It worked for his arms and shoulders, but there seemed to be no progress in his hands. He held the foam balls through the endless hours of the night, when Darcie and Tristan were gone and his body ached and his mind was too burdened to sleep. He lay with a ball in each hand and *willed* his fingers to curl around them, *willed* them to make even the slightest impression in their soft surfaces.

Anxieties loomed larger in the emptiness of the night. Anxieties about his hands, his legs. Uncertainties, really. Questions that seemed to have no sure answers. Holding the foam balls, he prayed for comfort and strength.

Libby switched off the repulsors and let the glidechair settle to the floor before she spoke. "All right, Jink," she said then, "just think of this as a refresher course of fighter pilot school—except that this aircraft's top altitude is about three centimeters off the deck.

"What we have here is a wide-open, mostly empty room. You've got a proximity beeper up here by your head, but the walls and support pillars are padded up to a meter and a half high; you're not going to get seriously injured if this thing gets away from you." And she patted the glidechair's arm.

"Give the commands clearly; you might even want to break them into syllables," she suggested. "Now—let's see you put this thing through its paces."

Lujan let out a breath. *Lift—on,* he thought.

The synthesizer echoed it even as he thought it. That was still a little disconcerting, even after several days of use. But the glidechair's repulsors came on and it rose in a hover beneath him.

"For-ward," Lujan said.

It accelerated smoothly, slid almost soundlessly over the floor.

"Turn—right," he said.

The chair arced into a 90-degree turn without so much as a flicker of hesitation.

"Turn—left," he said.

The chair began another arc—

The proximity beeper sounded, loud and fast. The obstacle was imminent.

Lujan froze.

"Tell it to stop!" Libby called from behind him.

Stop! he thought urgently. *Stop!* But his focus was lost—and the beep had turned into a trill.

Something bumped the chair from the left—banged his knee. Padded or not, it hit hard enough to smart, and the chair bounced away from it. Hesitated. Started to move forward again—

Libby leaned over his shoulder, punched an emergency off button. The repulsors cut; it sank to the floor. "Are you all right, Jink?" she asked.

His knee was bruised; it throbbed under his warm-up suit. *I'm fine!* he thought at her.

The synthesizer didn't voice it.

"Take a minute and get your head back together," Libby said. "You're not coming through."

He drew three or four deep breaths and let his annoyance flow out with each one. In a few moments his rigidness subsided.

"That's better," said Libby. She was kneeling in front of the glidechair, from the direction of her voice. "Now, are you all right?"

He gave a curt nod.

"Talk to me, Lujan." Her tone made it an order.

He released another breath. "I'm fine," he said through the synthesizer.

"You're sure? You hit pretty hard."

"Yes!"

"All right. Let's try it again."

She maneuvered him clear of the pillar but warned him, "You're still close enough to set off the beeper. You'll need to learn to deal with it sooner or later, and it might as well be sooner. Just tell the chair to move slowly."

He nodded. "Lift—on."

He'd bumped his other knee and one elbow, too, by the time Dr. Moses turned the glidechair back toward his room. "Well, Lujan," she said, "I prescribe a few more piloting lessons before we move you over to the transition quarters. And at the rate Security's moving with its sweep of the place, you'll be ready to solo by then!"

Lujan only said, "Humph," and glowered into a distance he couldn't see.

Libby turned serious though as the servo lifted him back into bed. "Hanada, I want cold packs on both his knees and his right elbow," she said. "I want him checked every fifteen minutes, and I want you to call me if there's any undue swelling or discoloration or any change in his vital signs."

"Yes'm," the young woman said.

Darcie waited until the tech had completed her ministrations and left the room to move up beside his bed. "Battle scars, love?" she said, and began to smooth back his bristly half-grown hair.

"Stupid mistakes," he answered.

She chuckled softly and kissed him. "Well, at least you lived to tell about it." She adjusted the cold pack on his elbow, rubbed his shoulder briefly. "Will you be all right while I go collect Tris from—"

The buzz of the commset on the counter cut her off. Lujan heard her tap its button and ask, "What is it?"

"Darcie." It was Libby's voice. "I need to see you in my office right away." Even to Lujan's ears her tone was deadly grim.

"Of course." Darcie sounded startled. "I'll be up directly." There was silence for a moment, and then, "Whatever did you do, love?" she tried to tease. "Wreck the training room?" She ruffled his hair, kissed him again. "I'll be back in a bit."

She wasn't back in a bit. The med tech came in and

checked him twice. She removed the cold packs and applied salve to his bruises the second time, and left again. His restlessness increased. And his impatience. And his annoyance.

It was some time before he thought of . . .

"Holovid—on," he said.

He had. 't even known his room had a holovid until three days before. Libby had suggested he use it for familiarization with the voice synthesizer. "Change volume, change frequency—whatever," she said. "If it does what you ask, you're getting it."

He heard it click on from the opposite wall. It came on in the middle of a news report.

". . . isn't a late blizzard. Workers completed the monumental task today of tying up more than fifty thousand white prayer ribbons and streamers throughout the city in preparation for next week's Festival of Velke.

"So far, seven thousand artisans of all specialties have been granted exhibition and vendor licenses, and Dr. Renyon Dionne, director of the Victory Symphonic Pavilion, has announced a full schedule of performances, ranging from historic dance to electronic symphony. Performances begin tomorrow evening, but seats may still be reserved through the Festival Coordination Center.

"According to Priestess Valasi Juha, Matriarch of the Temple of Velke, this year's annual festival will be the largest celebration in nearly two decades."

The voice paused, then turned to a new topic:

"Preparations are also under way for a change of command on the military side of the Unified Worlds organization. Appointment hearings concluded today for Vice Admiral Tolmich Oleszek, nominated three weeks ago to succeed Admiral Lujan Serege as chief commander of the Spherzah."

The announcement caught Lujan up short as if he'd run the glidechair into a wall. He strained to hear the rest.

"Having been approved today by an overwhelming majority of the Unified Worlds Assembly," the voice continued, "Admiral Oleszek will receive his promotion and assume command of the Spherzah in ceremonies scheduled for the thirtieth day of this month.

"Admiral Lujan Serge, whom Oleszek replaces as chief commander, was critically injured in the terrorist attack at the sealing of the Isselan Assistance Agreement. Although he is now listed in fair condition at Winthancom Military Medical Center, the injuries he sustained have resulted in severe disabilities. Admiral Serege's retirement from the Spherzah will also become effective on the thirtieth day of the month."

The voice paused again before droning off on another topic, but Lujan was no longer listening. *On the thirtieth day of the month. That's only two weeks from now!* His mind whirled with a confusion of questions, like a tumult inside his skull.

Someone called his name. The voice brought him back to the moment, slowing the spinning.

"Lujan?" Darcie said again. Her hand touched his face.

But his ability to concentrate was shattered. He resorted to blinking the questions: "Did you know about retirement? Why didn't you tell me?"

"Wait, Lujan," Darcie said, and patted his face. "You're not hooked up to the blink monitor anymore. You're blinking too fast for me to read what you're saying."

He closed his eyes in frustration. Let his breath out in a groan.

Her hands slipped from his face to his shoulders and began to knead them. "Is something wrong, Lujan?" she asked. "What is it?"

He began to blink again—

"Slowly!" she urged.

"Did you know about retirement?" he asked. It seemed to take forever to blink it out.

"Oh, Luj—" she whispered. Her hands tightened on his shoulders—

"Why," he blinked, "didn't you tell me?"

Her voice sounded stricken: "Because I couldn't when they first announced it—not well enough to make you understand, anyway. It was so hard for us to communicate then, and I didn't want you to just get bits and pieces. It was just after you had the seizure; you didn't need any more stress."

"Why so soon?" he blinked. "Why no medical leave?"

"I don't know," Darcie said.

"Request reconsideration!" he blinked.

"Lujan." Her hands left his shoulders. She took both of his hands and gripped them hard. "We did, love." Her voice had turned quiet, serious. "Libby and Dr. Gavril and I, and a couple of judge advocate officers, spent two weeks compiling a formal request package after Jiron brought me the message. That was all the time we had to do it. We submitted it just after Tristan got home."

She fell silent then, for a long minute. "That's what Libby just called me up to her office about," she said at last. "They returned it—rejected it out of hand. The package hadn't even been opened—just burned with Trosvig's seal and 'For the Triune' and stamped 'Disapproved.' " Her voice betrayed her barely contained anger.

Disapproved. He was stunned. It was some seconds before he could blink, "What reason?"

"I don't know." She shook her head; he could feel the movement through her hands. "But Libby said it was our last option; there's no one higher to turn to."

He was silent for a long space, still holding his hands tight. "There's something not right about this," she said, almost under her breath. "I've known it from the day Trosvig called Libby and Gavril in to report to him. It just feels all wrong."

"Trosvig?" Lujan blinked. He furrowed his brow.

"Seamus Trosvig," said Darcie. "You know: He was the head of Mythos's delegation to the Assembly. He succeeded to Pite Hanesson's seat on the Triune when Hanesson was killed."

Trosvig. There was something about that name Lujan knew he should remember. Something important. He didn't respond to Darcie. Just began to search his memory.

The item he remembered was two decades old. It had come from a highly classified source.

Seamus Trosvig, aide to a prominent Mythosian assemblyman, had joined with Jolenta Merkat, staff member from the Isselan embassy on Mythos. Her title had been assistant cultural attaché, but her pay statements had come from Isselan intelligence. And she hadn't resigned her undercover post when she accepted Mythosian citizenship at the time of their joining.

Perhaps it was just coincidence, Lujan thought, that her mate now held a seat on the Triune. But the sudden chill through his soul told him otherwise.

You're right, Darcie, he thought. *There's something about this that feels very wrong.*

ELEVEN

The thought of what it could mean made him shudder.

"Lujan?" said Darcie.

He couldn't tell her what he'd remembered; she didn't have high enough security clearances. "Need to see Jiron," he blinked.

"They won't let him come in here," she said at once, "or he would've been here all along. It's a hospital regulation: The only visitors allowed in the CCU are chaplains and members of the patient's immediate family."

"Stupid rule," Lujan blinked.

But on second thought, a small room full of monitoring equipment was the last place to carry on what might become a classified conversation. He had enough mobility now, with the glidechair, to meet Jiron somewhere else. But where?

He didn't realize how completely he'd been concentrating on the question until the synthesizer at his throat voiced it.

"What?" said Darcie beside him.

Lujan drew a deep breath, steadied his focus. "Where," he asked, "would be a good place to meet with Jiron?"

There was a pause while she considered. "There are two or three chapels in the hospital complex," she said.

"Perhaps one of them would be available during the day."

"Not a chapel," Lujan said at once. "We never conduct political or intelligence work in a chapel. But going to the chapel is a valid reason for me to be out of this room. Leave the meeting place to Jiron; he'll come up with something."

"All right," Darcie said, and he detected a note of mild puzzlement in her voice.

Prompted by the throb of his bruised knees, Lujan added, "I'll—need a little help to get there. Will you or Tris be here tomorrow?"

"Tris will," said Darcie. She sighed. "I've got to meet with Relocations tomorrow, and who knows how long it'll take to work through all the details!"

"Relocations?" Lujan wrinkled his brow.

"We've got to be moved out of the Flag Officers' Residence by the time your retirement becomes effective," Darcie said, "and that's only two weeks away." She sighed once more. "I guess Tris and I will have to move back into the family quarters here—but I probably won't be able to spend much time with you until it's all over. . . . Should I just have everything shipped out to the home on Topawa?"

Lujan didn't miss the note of weariness behind her words. It sent a pang through his soul that he couldn't be of more help to her, a pang sharper than the news of his retirement had caused. He tried, unsuccessfully, to squeeze her hands. "That will be fine, Darce," he said. "Contact Siljan—but don't worry about it tonight. Tomorrow will be soon enough."

"See you this afternoon, sir!" Meles said, turning to leave after the morning therapy session.

Lujan didn't even attempt to answer. He closed his

eyes against the endless darkness and let his body sink into the suspension mattress.

Lying perfectly still, he could feel the ache beginning to ebb from his muscles. He released a deep breath, pushing the pain out with it, and began to relax.

"Father?"

Reflex snapped his eyes open. He turned his head toward the sound of Tristan's voice.

"Captain Jiron's here," Tristan said.

Too soon, Lujan thought. He wasn't ready to move yet. And he stank of sweat, and his face was stubbled.

Wearing the glove with the bracket, he could accomplish most of his own hygiene by now, but it still took him two or three hours to do it alone. He couldn't leave Jiron waiting that long. "I'll need your help to clean up, Tris," he said through the synthesizer.

Darcie usually provided what little assistance he still required. He detected a moment's hesitation before his son said, "Right then, sir."

There was no uncertainty, no self-consciousness, however, in the hands that peeled open his warm-up jacket, or in the solid arm that slipped under his shoulders, raising and shifting him enough to free first one arm, then the other from the sleeves. Firm hands removed his athletic shoes, shucked off his sweatpants, pulled the sheet over him.

There was no squeamishness in the smooth strokes of the cleansing pad up and down his limbs and body, either. Or in the fingers that applied beard foam to his face and throat, and spread salve over pressure points to prevent sores from developing.

Lujan thought of the times he'd washed Tristan's face, changed his diapers, maneuvered his small, squirming limbs into miniature playsuits. Something tightened in his throat, made him swallow.

"Sir?" Tristan said. "Did I hurt you?"

"No; I'm fine," Lujan said. "I was just thinking about when I used to do this for you."

Tristan's hand paused, wiping away the beard foam with a warm wet cloth. It was a long moment before he continued, and then it was with an even greater sense of care.

Tristan helped him into a fresh warm-up suit, substituting slippers for the athletic shoes this time. "Now then, Father," he said.

He didn't bother with the servo. One arm wrapped about Lujan's shoulders again; the other slid under his thighs. Lujan felt young muscles tighten as Tristan lifted him—and he marveled.

I used to lift him up over my head and whirl him around. I used to swing him up and carry him everywhere on my shoulders. Now he's carrying me.

Tristan lowered him into the glidechair, more carefully than Meles or the servo did, then fastened its safety straps. "How is that, Father?" he asked.

"It's good, Tris," Lujan said.

There was a medical consultation room around the corner from the hospital's North Chapel, the sanctuary nearest the neurology floor. Jiron stepped inside, closed the door as he activated lighting, and looked around.

The consultation office was smaller than a standard hospital room, and furnished with the usual desk, two or three chairs, and several holographic anatomical plates on the walls. It had no window, and its single door could be locked from the inside. Most importantly, it didn't appear to be used on a regular basis.

His initial requirements satisfied, Jiron removed a sensor from the front pocket of his uniform and began a security sweep.

It was just as well that he had something to do until Admiral Serege arrived, he thought. A torrent of old memories through his mind made him restless; he couldn't have waited sitting down.

His remembered how, some years ago, his teammates on Tohh had groaned when they learned he had orders to Anchenko.

"Man, Jiron, who'd you torque off to get sent to Armpit Detachment?" one buddy asked.

"That's Serege's detachment," someone else said. "The man's a tyrant!"

"I think I'd punch out of the Spherzah before I'd do a remote tour to Anchenko!" put in a third.

His apprehension had mounted as the time for his transfer approached.

The Anchenko Region of Topawa's second largest continent was mostly desert: flame-colored rock and dust and shriveled brush. Rain fell there only during three of the planet's seventeen months, and it was the middle of the dry stretch when Jiron arrived. The heat was oppressive enough to make him wilt—and he hadn't even met the "tyrant" yet! He reported to the command office bracing himself for the worst.

He expected a terse, "Send him in" when the XO announced his arrival. But in a moment Serege himself emerged from his office, extending his hand.

The first thing Jiron couldn't help but notice—with some surprise after all he'd been told—was how short Serege was: probably eight or nine centimeters shorter than himself. The second thing that held him was his eyes. When Serege looked him in the face, Jiron had the distinct impression that those eyes were reading his soul.

"Lieutenant Commander Jiron," Serege said, gripping his hand. "Welcome aboard."

Not the kind of reception normally offered by a military tyrant. Jiron quelled the urge to arch an eyebrow. Maybe Serege was one of those who lulled his subordinates into a false sense of security before he yanked them up short. Jiron resolved that Serege would never catch him off guard.

He'd been told that Serege was hard-nosed. He was—especially on matters of readiness and security and safety.

He'd been told that Serege was demanding. He was that, too; but he demanded no less of himself than he did of his troops—no doubt one of the reasons why, at the age of thirty-seven, Serege had already worn captain's marks for two standard years.

Serege was also approachable, and he was fair—two traits Jiron hadn't been told of.

Nor was there any reason he could discover for Anchenko's appellation as the Armpit Detachment.

"That's what this place was a few years ago," the chief petty officer said when Jiron asked him about it, "—but not since *this* skipper came on board!" And he jerked a thumb in the direction of Serege's office. "Only the best come here now."

Jiron had been on Topawa less than six months when the fault shift occurred. The epicenter was in a high-altitude area far to the north. The whole mountainside seemed to have lifted up, dropped again, and then crumbled, half burying the community at its foot.

The Anchenko Detachment added its strength, its equipment and skills to the rescue effort. Local officials directed them, when they arrived in the area, to the wreckage of a community school.

Captain Serege surveyed the structure through narrowed eyes and shook his head. "How many children are still missing?" he asked.

"As of this morning, fifty-two," said the superintendent. "We think most of them are together in two areas, there and over there." He pointed. "But sensors detected life signs at the far end of the building as well."

The far end was partly buried under rubble from the leading edge of the landslide, where broken rock and soil heaped like a snowdrift against the rear wall. The weight bowed what remained of the roof; it clearly wouldn't hold up much longer.

Serege looked over his teams. Looked straight at Jiron. "Commander, I'd like your team to take that far end. It looks like the best way in will be through the roof. Be sure you don't concentrate your weight at any one spot. Lieutenant Baskin, you and your team will back him up. The rest of you—Asquith, Calabrese, Spach, and Truhaut—your teams will go after the kids toward the front of the building. Stay alert for falling debris and fire hazards."

Clad in battle armor and laden with power jacks, excavation tools, and medical packs, Jiron and his team scrambled up the loose rubble. They made their way, one at a time—one wary step at a time—across the sagging roof.

A shattered skylight, gaping up like a wounded eye, offered a way in. Jiron cleared shards of transluplast away from its frame and peered down: a three-meter drop at most. He looked up. "Sensors and Medic, you're with me. Comms, stay here. Keep open a relay to Baskin. Once we find the kids, we may need help getting them out."

They all nodded. He swung his legs over the hole, pushed off—

He hit a slanted surface and slid, feetfirst, to the floor. He looked around as he straightened.

The whole building seemed set at an angle. The walls of the hall where he stood leaned like sides of a box being flattened, not quite torn loose from the ceiling. He could see how some segments of the ceiling had already buckled and fallen. Where that had happened, walls had come down, rent and twisted, and soil and stone had spilled in from the split mountain.

He shook his head, then motioned the others to follow. "Sensors?" he said when she had descended and stood beside him.

She jabbed a thumb toward the rear of the school, under the avalanche. "That way," she said.

Helmet lights reached like pale fingers through billows of dust, kept astir by wind gusting through the holed roof. Visibility was zero. Jiron was grateful for his face mask, for the oxygen canister on his shoulder.

Progress was slow. Debris filled what had been a hallway. They picked their way, ducking under sagging beams and cables, climbing gingerly over and around smashed lockers and strewn computer desks. As they went, they braced up what they could with roof struts and power jacks. Walls and ceiling creaked and groaned like dying creatures, warning of impending collapse. But the lights on the life sensor, flashing faint at the outset, grew gradually stronger. They paused every few minutes to shout, then listen, tuning helmet mikes to catch the weakest cry.

The hall they followed intersected another, which was almost totally blocked by a cave-in. And the blips that marked the children lay beyond it.

Jiron sized up the situation. "We'll have to go in by a back way," he said. "Most of the class modules we've passed have had two or three doorways. Maybe there's a rear door that'll get us past this cave-in."

He pushed past an overturned cabinet, toward the dark of a module's doorway, and Sensors and Medic followed. They were halfway across when the aftershock hit. It threw them off their feet, into the desks and each other. The floor rolled for several seconds, like a sea in a storm—and then stilled with a shudder.

Jiron, sprawled on his belly, lifted his head.

And the thunder began: the crash and crack and groan of tumbling boulders and fracturing beams from somewhere above. Close above. And over it all rose the shrieks of the children: mere meters away, behind a wall and across a distance of dark.

"Commander!" That was Medic. "The roof's caved in! I think we're buried!"

Lying still, Jiron looked up with the swath of light cut by his helmet lamp. Only tipped-over desks had kept the ceiling from crushing them completely; they lay in a space less than a meter high, among a tangle of wrecked school equipment.

He gulped a couple of breaths to quell the pulse racing hard in his ears. "Are either of you hurt?" he asked.

"No sir," said Medic.

"You, Sensors?"

"Fine, sir."

"Any readings?"

"The kids are less than ten meters away, sir. I've got seven clear life signs."

"What about to the outside?"

A pause. Then, "I can't tell, sir."

Jiron bit off a curse, and punched the radio switch on his helmet. "Lieutenant Baskin, this is Jiron, do you copy?"

A wait. A rattle of static.

"Baskin?" Jiron called again. "Are you there?"

A sudden thought struck him—chilled him. Baskin and his team had been on top of and around the back of the building. If the thunder he'd heard had been another avalanche. . . .

He swallowed. Punched the helmet button again. "Captain Serege," he called, "do you read me? Captain Serege, this is Jiron, do you copy?"

"Jiron!" It was Serege's voice, dim and distant with static. "Are you all right?"

"No injuries, sir," Jiron said, "but the roof came down. We're about—ten meters from the kids. We're going in for them. Can you get us some braces and wall-cutting equipment?"

"We've got your location marked," Serege said. "We're on our way in but I don't know how long it'll take. The aftershock closed off a direct path. How is your atmospheric oxygen in there?"

Jiron bent his head to play his helmet light over a sensor on his left arm. "We've got enough oxygen to keep a stationary person alive," he said, "but not enough for an exerting adult."

There was a pause before Serege said, "Move forward to the kids, but pace yourselves so you don't expend all your oxygen. It'll take several hours for us to get to you."

It was nearly six hours. They lay on the floor with the children—bruised and scraped but more frightened than hurt—tucked close between them so they could share oxygen from their masks. They lay in the hot dark, sweating, counting the minutes, until the rumble of heavy engines cut through the labored sound of the pulse in their ears, and a series of crashes and thunks carved a crooked shaft of light out of the dark. Then there was a shadow belly-crawling toward them, a shadow whose helmet lamp flashed in their faces.

"They're here!" It was Serege's voice, laden with relief—Serege himself acting as point man, the most dangerous role in a rescue. Behind his scuffed and grimy helmetplate, Jiron could see anxiety melting away from

his eyes and mouth. His armored glove seized Jiron's
shoulder and gripped it hard.

Jiron shook himself out of the memory. He felt weak with
it. Pocketing the sensor, he sank onto the nearest chair.

The last time he'd seen Admiral Serege, he lay unconscious on a repulsor sled, blood-smeared from a gash on
his face, being raced to an ambulance shuttle.

Only eight weeks ago? It seemed more like eight
months.

He glanced at his timepiece, then rose and opened the
door.

Just in time. Three shapes came up the hallway, the
one in the center in a glidechair. He waited until they
were two or three meters away and then stepped out into
the hall. "Sir?" he said.

The big man in the Sostis Surface Forces uniform in-
terposed himself between Jiron and Serege, searching
him with his eyes, his energy pistol ready in his hand.
More conscientious security than I expected, Jiron
couldn't help thinking, and he stood still, holding out
both of his hands to show they were empty.

"Captain Jiron," said Tristan. "We were on our way to
the chapel—"

"The chapel's not available," Jiron said, "but I believe
this room is."

"You know this man, sir?" asked the soldier.

"Yes." The figure in the glidechair spoke through the
pendant at his throat. "He's my executive officer; I was
expecting him." He turned his head, lifted it as if to face
Jiron. "Thank you for coming," he said.

"Of course, sir." Jiron couldn't keep himself from
swallowing, looking into his admiral's face.

Tristan guided the glidechair into the room, positioned
it beside the desk, shut off its repulsors. Jiron didn't miss

the look he directed at the Sostish military guard, or the hand he placed on the admiral's shoulder. "We'll wait for you outside, Father," he said.

Jiron nodded his thanks, slid the door closed—and his throat constricted. "Sir," he said. It was all he could manage.

Serege's hands lay limp in his lap and his mouth hung open. But he held his head with dignity, and his eyes, blind or not, still seemed to read Jiron's soul. "At ease, Jiron," he said. "Please sit down."

Jiron did. "It's—good to see you, sir." He added, "Heazel and the kids send their love."

"Please take them mine."

"I will, sir." Jiron hesitated, then offered somewhat awkwardly, "Heazon wanted me to tell you that Kazak is doing fine. Heazon can almost keep up with him now when they go for a run."

The admiral cocked an eyebrow. "I hope Kazak's not a burden to Heazel."

"Actually," said Jiron, "taking him was her idea. She knew Darcie had—enough concerns—without the dog as well."

"Thank her for me," Serege said. "And my deepest thanks to all of you for your help to Darcie."

"It was the least we could do, sir." Jiron found himself still fighting to keep his emotion out of his voice.

There was silence again, for several moments, and then the admiral said, "I need your help now, Jiron. I need you to—fill in some blanks. Most of my memory of the last few months is—gone."

Jiron swallowed at that. But he said, "All right, sir. I swept the room for snoops; it's clean. We can talk up to the top secret level if that becomes necessary."

"Thank you." Serege nodded carefully. He paused. Then he said, "I need to know about everyone who was involved in the Isselan Assistance Agreement: all of their names and what part each of them played, in as much detail as you can remember."

The request took Jiron by surprise; he straightened in his chair and gave it several seconds' consideration before he spoke. "The proposal was presented before the Assembly for initial hearings on the nineteenth day of the eighth month last year," he said. "The proposal was drafted by the Mythosian delegation and presented by Seamus Trosvig, then head of that delegation."

Serege raised an eyebrow at that, just slightly; but when Jiron paused he said, "Go on, please."

It took some time to name them all, and longer still to remember each person's task. The fact that he could recall as much as he did, after five months or more, surprised even himself.

The admiral sat silent, brow creased, for several moments after he finished. "What about the Isselan representatives?" he asked at last.

"They were Hampton Istvan, Minister of Interplanetary Relations, and Nioro Enn Borith, Minister of Planetary Defense," said Jiron. "Istvan and the Isselan ambassador—Pegaush, I think it was—were both killed in the attack that injured you, sir. Borith is the one who sealed the agreement, along with Alois Ashforth, about three days later."

Serege nodded. "Do we know who sent them?"

Jiron shrugged—and realized even as he did so that the admiral couldn't see it. "The Cabinet of Ministers, sir. Issel's governing body."

"No World Governor—or acting Governor?" Serege asked.

"No sir. None that they would ever admit."

"Huh." The sound came from the admiral's throat. But

after a little silence he asked, through the synthesizer, "What did the agreement provide to Issel?"

"Military assistance," Jiron said. "A space force composed of ships and troops from the Unified Worlds to eliminate the masuk threat in the Issel system."

"Under whose command?" Serege asked.

"The Unified Worlds's, sir—General Ande Pitesson, to be specific." Jiron added, "You oversaw the committee that developed the war plan."

Serege nodded again; but then his eyes narrowed. "It didn't include any weapons sales, any intelligence exchanges, any—ties of any kind to the Isselan government?"

"No sir," said Jiron. "You were adamant about that."

Serege said, "Humph." He bowed his head and appeared to contemplate his lap for a long space before he said, "I want to know who sent those two cabinet ministers. I keep feeling there's something I should remember about that." He looked up abruptly. "Is Borith still here on Sostis?"

"No sir," Jiron said.

Another pause. The admiral sat with his eyes narrowed, fixed on some inner distance. "Jiron, I need you to study the message traffic for me," he said at last. "Everything for the past six standard months. Look at everything you can find about the Isselan government—its structure, its activity—anything about the way it functions. Look for any indications of communications between Issel and Unified Worlds governments. Make it a general search; just see what names and associations come to the surface, and where the links are."

"Sir." Jiron moved in his chair. "I can start the search, but—I'm not going to be around here much longer. I have change-of-station orders. We'll be leaving two days after your retirement becomes effective."

The admiral's head came back up, his sightless eyes widening. "For where?"

"Enach, sir," Jiron said. "To take command of the Galfira Detachment."

"You'll do well, Jiron." Serege seemed to study him again. "Enach," he said at last. "The farthest reach of the Unified Worlds . . ."

"Yes sir," said Jiron.

"What about the others?" Serege asked.

"The whole staff has orders, sir." The tension Jiron had been resisting for the past few weeks, ever since his orders came, tightened his hands on the edge of the desk. "They all fall within two weeks of your retirement," he said. "We're all being separated. Spread as far apart as we can be. We're going to every world in the organization. Even Vice Admiral Halbach and Rear Admiral Faurot are out of here—Halbach's getting Oleszek's post at Advanced Training."

"A complete turnover in the Command Section?" Admiral Serege's disbelief came through even over the voice synthesizer. "They're not leaving Tolmich anyone for continuity?"

"Apparently not, sir."

"Highly unusual," Serege said thoughtfully. "Any word yet on who will make up his staff?"

"Not yet," Jiron said.

The admiral sat in silence for several moments. "Tolmich's a good man," he sighed at last. "He'll do a fine job."

Then his visionless eyes, like blue ice, locked on Jiron's. "What kind of opportunities might there be for Tristan at the headquarters?" he asked.

Jiron straightened, startled. "Probably quite a few, sir. There's an opening he could compete for in the historian's office, in fact; they're in need of a technical assistant. He'd have as good a shot at it as anybody else—probably better, with his holographic memory."

"And he'd need a security clearance?"

"Yes sir." Jiron understood at once. "The job would require him to have access to a number of offices. He'd need it for that as well as for the regular message traffic. And yet it's a pretty low-profile job. Certainly nobody in the new Command Section would know he was there."

Serege nodded, thoughtful. "Good. I'll encourage him to apply—on his own qualifications, of course. There's not to be any mention of my name." He sighed once more. "Tris will have to be eyes and ears for me after you leave."

Lujan stayed quiet, thinking, as Tristan steered his glidechair back to the CCU. He waited until his son had settled him back into bed to ask, "Are there any video monitors in this room?"

"There's one," Tristan said. "It goes to the med techs' station, I think."

"Is it placed where you can block it by standing or sitting in front of it?"

"No sir. It's up near the ceiling, to your right. Why?"

"We need to talk," Lujan said. "Come around to the left side of the bed." And, using his forearms and shoulders, he shoved himself onto his side.

"Tris?" he said then.

"I'm here, sir."

He began to blink: "Dot code. Tap my arm with finger. Keep hand hidden from monitor."

Tristan tapped, "I copy."

"Need your help," Lujan blinked. "Jiron and staff transferring. Need eyes and ears at HQ."

"How?" Tristan tapped. "Access was closed after Issel mission."

"Civilian job at HQ," Lujan blinked, "with clearances. Call Jiron tonight."

"Copy." Tristan hesitated, then tapped out, "Something wrong?"

Lujan didn't answer that at once. He wasn't certain yet that anything *was* wrong. All he had was a name that ran like a thread through half the history of the Unified Worlds:

Seamus Trosvig, assemblyman's aide, joining with a longtime operative for the Isselan Intelligence Service.

Seamus Trosvig, head of the delegation that had crafted the Isselan Assistance Agreement.

Seamus Trosvig accepting a seat on the Triune after the assassination of a fellow Mythosian.

Seamus Trosvig making the decision, apparently without consulting the other members of the Triune, to reject the request for reconsideration of his retirement.

Was there even any significance in that last? Or was that simply personal? Lujan and Trosvig had always stood on opposite sides of the issues—especially where Issel was concerned.

Only a name, Lujan thought. *And a gut feeling.*

"Sir?" Tristan tapped again. "Is something wrong?"

Lujan sighed. "Don't know yet," he blinked. "Need to find out."

TWELVE

Ranze Tousillo found the committee chamber still dark when she arrived. Activating lighting with a gesture at the sensor, she stepped inside and glanced around.

The chamber was much smaller than she had expected it to be, though the richness of its decor did not surprise her. Its walls, over three meters high, were paneled with carved sablewood transported from the Winek Islands halfway around the planet. The table in the center was built of sablewood as well, and the chairs were upholstered with archaic crimson velveteen. Ranze admired brass sconces set at intervals around the walls, relics of a day several centuries gone when light was still produced by combustion. "So much history has happened in here!" she whispered, caught up in a sudden sense of awe.

As a first-term member of the Assembly, the newest delegate from Sjenlund, that sense of awe permeated every facet of her experience.

So did a sense of amazement at having been chosen to sit on a committee so early in her political career—especially a committee of such importance. Its efforts would literally expand the borders of the Unified Worlds, with all the advancements in science, in commerce, in agriculture and education that accompanied expansion. She was proud to be part of it.

At the moment, however, her sense of purpose was overwhelmed by a giddiness in the pit of her stomach: She was about to make her first presentation to a committee.

She shouldn't feel so nervous, she thought. She'd researched her assignment thoroughly; she'd outlined a plan to accomplish it; she'd even built a number of graphics to demonstrate how it could be carried out. All that remained was to fill in the details. By the end of her presentation, the chair would surely be persuaded to allow her to proceed.

She turned at the sound of Madam DeByes's voice, light and breezy in the passage behind her: "Are you ready, Ranze?"

"Yes madam," she said.

"Great!" DeByes favored Ranze with the radiance of her smile. "We have to present this proposal before the Assembly by the middle of next month, but there's still a lot of work to be done in order to have it ready by then."

"I understand, madam." Ranze emphasized her agreement with a slight bow from the neck.

There were only three other members on the committee—a fact that puzzled Ranze, considering the vast ramifications of readmitting Issel into the Unified Worlds. More startling still was the fact that those others were also first-term Assembly members, no more experienced than herself. They arrived close behind Madam DeByes: Jaime Tyree of Jonica, Troung Vhat of Yan, and Aronow of the nation of Diaconis on Sostis.

"Aronow, please secure the door." Madam DeByes pointed like a queen from her throne at the head of the table as the last delegate entered the chamber.

Aronow did as requested and took his place at the table, and DeByes folded her hands together on the tabletop. "Assemblywoman Tousillo," she said, "why don't you make your presentation first?"

"Thank you, madam." Ranze rose and circled the table

to the holoprojector at its foot, drew her graphics chip from her blazer pocket and slipped it into the reader slot. She pushed back her wavy brunet hair with a nervous hand as she began.

She spent the next half hour expounding on the benefits of an interstellar trade agreement that would include Issel, illustrating her major points with three-dimensional graphs that hovered just above the center of the table and rotated so all could see them.

"What I've presented," she said in conclusion, "is only a prototype of the proposed trading system, developed from two-year-old import-export records from the member worlds, and extrapolations from various Isselan trade documents. The only exception is the trade statistics for Sjenlund, which are current. I obtained those from Ikel Broudy, our delegate for Trade Interests."

She directed her vision to Madam DeByes then. "In light of the economic fluctuations we've seen among the various worlds since this data was recorded," she said, "I'll need to meet with all the Trade Interests delegates and a representative from the Isselan embassy in order to ensure that all concerns are addressed and that this mode of interplanetary commerce will be both agreeable and workable."

DeByes sat straight, almost rigid, in her chair. "No meetings," she said. The words were clipped; the wide brown eyes behind them were narrowed. "We have to keep our meetings on this proposal to an absolute minimum."

Surprised, Ranze's hand froze on the holoprojector's chip-ejection button without pressing it. "I only need one meeting, madam," she said. "Do you honestly expect me to develop a workable trade agreement based on data that's two years old?"

"That's the task you were assigned, isn't it?" DeByes demanded. Her tone was actually sarcastic, her expression very near a sneer.

Ranze felt as if she'd been slapped. Hard. But before she could respond, DeByes said, "We need to move on," and turned her gaze away. "Vhat, you're next."

Seamus Trosvig was shrugging on his coat when his desk intercom buzzed. "Sir, there's a Madam DeByes on line two," Talbot said. "She says she's with"—Talbot hesitated, then turned the final words into a question—"a proposal committee?"

Trosvig swore. But then, "I'll take it, Talbot," he said, and wheeled around to his desk to jab at the visiphone's button. "Office of the Triune, Trosvig here," he rumbled.

DeByes appeared in its viewscreen, her expression earnest. "Your Honor," she said, and her tone was meticulously respectful, "I believe we have a problem. One of my committee members is consulting with Ikel Broudy about trade issues for our proposal. Ikel Broudy is a troublemaker, sir. He's domineering and manipulative, and he's been going around telling half the Assembly that I'm incompetent. I'm afraid of how he'll influence Assemblywoman Tousillo."

What does DeByes have against Broudy? Trosvig wondered. She'd never even worked with him, as far as he knew. The man was knowledgeable, and sometimes forceful, but where had she gotten the impression he was domineering and manipulative?

Trosvig managed to keep his face expressionless when he asked, "And what do you expect me to do about it, madam?"

"Talk to Ranze, sir," she said. "Tell her how dangerous this is! Tell her to stop her contacts with Broudy!" The respectfulness was giving way to the whine of a tattling child.

Trosvig arched an eyebrow. "I can't do that," he said, "for several reasons. Tousillo and Broudy are members of the same delegation, for one thing; no one can forbid them to work together.

"For another, if I were to speak with Tousillo, it might lead her to believe that there's some connection between your committee and me, and that would be completely inappropriate."

"But—," Debyes began.

"In fact," Trosvig said, barely pausing for a breath, "this call itself is out of line, madam. Tousillo is *your* committee member; I suggest that *you* deal with her. And now, if you'll excuse me, I have a retirement ceremony to attend."

Striding through the corridor a few minutes later, Trosvig shook his head. "Pity Tousillo," he muttered under his breath.

The only consolation, Ranze thought as she stormed toward her office, was that DeByes had treated the other committee members no less rudely than she had been treated herself. Vhat had been close to tears by the time she withdrew to her seat; and Aronow had spent the rest of the meeting glowering at the tabletop after DeByes contradicted every major point in his presentation.

Teeth locked and brows drawn together in a scowl, Ranze flung open the door to the Sjenlund delegation's offices.

Ikel Broudy, rotund and balding, glanced away from the newscast on the holovid in the office reception area and raised his shuk mug in greeting. "Bad speech day, eh, Ranze?" he said.

"The speech went fine," Ranze stated. "The problem was the audience. That woman actually expects me to develop a trade agreement based on outdated statistics! I requested a meeting—*one* meeting!—with all the trade reps so we can get everybody's input and work out the details, and she said no! She said it's *my* job, *my* assignment!"

Ranze flung out her arms. "I'm sorry, Ike, but it *isn't* my trade agreement, and it isn't *hers!* It's for the Unified Worlds, and if it's going to work, it's got to be what the people of the Unified Worlds want!" She shook her head. "By Chigi, I'm tempted to just shove the whole thing back into her hands and forget it!"

" 'That woman'?" said Broudy, and cocked his head. "Do you mean Madam DeByes?"

"Yes." Ranze paced a few steps across the reception area, then stopped abruptly and spun about. "Why didn't you warn me about her?"

Broudy arched his eyebrows. *"Me?"* he said. "I've never worked with her. I barely even know who she is. All I know is what I've heard other people say about her. Besides, glitter-eyed as you've been over this whole committee thing, I doubt you would've listened if I had said something."

"Thanks." Ranze laced the word with sarcasm and began pacing again. "How does somebody with the team mentality of a lava viper keep getting elected to the Assembly?" she demanded.

"How do you think?" Broudy asked, lifting his shuk mug. "Her constituents would rather have her here abusing the Assembly than home on Tohh abusing them!"

Ranze managed a smile at that, but Broudy said in all seriousness, "Chester Venzon, who retired from the Tohh delegation last year, told me that most people see only the side of her she wants them to see—especially those people who are in a position to help her up the rank ladder. She's *very* careful of her behavior around them."

Ranze considered that for a couple of moments, then shook her head once more. "Thank you," she said at last, sincerely this time, and turned again toward her office. She stopped at the door. "I'm going to have that meeting anyway," she said, "even if I have to do it behind the madam's back!"

"Just tell me when," Broudy answered.

Pushing her office door closed behind her, Ranze fished the graphics chip out of her blazer pocket and plopped it onto her desk. It skittered across the top, stopping only when it collided with the base of her terminal, and she absently watched it go as she slipped off her blazer.

She was just turning to hand the blazer to a waiting servo when the visiphone on the desk buzzed. She punched its button and said, "Office of the Sjenlund delegation, Ranze Tousillo speaking."

The viewscreen stayed blank but the voice over the speaker was that of Madam DeByes. "Ranze," she said, a note of anxiety in her tone, "why did you go to Ikel Broudy for help with your presentation?"

The directness of the question, without so much preface as a greeting, snapped Ranze up short. "What, ma'am?" she said.

"You said that Ikel Broudy helped you put together your briefing," said DeByes. "Why did you go to him, Ranze?"

The implication that her presentation had been Broudy's work and not her own touched off a small spark in Ranze's temper, a spark that she realized this woman could too easily fan into an inferno. With great effort she said evenly, quietly, "I got Sjenlund's trade figures from Ikel. He also pointed me to the right archives to gather the rest of the information. That is all."

"Well—," DeByes began, but Ranze cut her off.

"Why shouldn't I ask questions of Ikel?" she demanded. "Trade issues are his specialty; they have been for most of his forty-some-odd years in the Assembly. Is there a problem with that?"

"Yes, there is, Ranze." The voice at the other end turned cold, as if DeByes's jaw had gone taut. Ranze could imagine her narrowing eyes. "Did you know that Ikel Broudy has been banned from participation on legislative committees?" DeByes said. "There was an incident several years ago, before either you or I entered the Assembly. Ikel and two or three others were called in before the Triune and removed from their committees."

Ranze raised her eyebrows. "Really?" She gave the word a surprised inflection. "What happened?"

"I don't know any of the details," DeByes said at once. "My predecessor just told me that they were never to serve on any other committees."

Ranze fought down her swelling disgust. "Madam," she said, "I *do* know the details of that so-called 'incident.' I heard about it from several reliable sources, including Ikel himself. And you can't possibly be unaware that he's served with distinction on a number of major committees since then. I recommend that you reexamine your facts."

There was a short silence, but then DeByes continued as if she hadn't heard. "Broudy is a troublemaker, Ranze," she said. "He's a manipulator and a backstabber, and as long as you're on my committee, you'll have no more to do with him. Do you hear me?"

Ranze almost laughed out loud at that. Have no further contact with another member of her own world's delegation? Broudy a backstabber and manipulator? The only one she could see doing any backstabbing and manipulating was DeByes herself. "That's ridiculous—," she began. But DeByes wasn't finished yet.

"You mustn't tell *anyone* about the purpose of our committee!" she said. "Everything we're doing must be kept close-hold until we make our presentation before the full Assembly."

That was another problem, Ranze thought: the secrecy thing. It made her uncomfortable. "Why?" she asked. "There was nothing in your invitation to join the committee that suggested this proposal was classified. Or"—it was sheer intuition—"is there something about all of this that isn't quite on the up-and-up?"

Another silence. Longer this time. Almost as if De-Byes had choked behind her blank visiphone screen. But her voice was a studied calm when she spoke again. "You have to realize that our bill will be viciously opposed by a large portion of the Assembly, Ranze," she said. "If any of those people were to learn of it right now, they'd have an opportunity to prepare their campaign against it. So we need to keep it quiet until then, and make sure we've anticipated all their arguments. Do you understand now?"

The madam did have a point there, Ranze had to concede—though her patronizing tone made Ranze's hair stand up on the back of her neck. But how did she expect Ranze to anticipate the opposition when she wouldn't allow her to get a feel for what that opposition might be?

Maintain your dignity! she counseled herself. Her own jaw taut, she said only, "Yes, I understand."

"I'm glad." The voice over the speaker switched back to warmed honey. "You're doing an excellent job with your part of the proposal, Ranze. Really. Keep up the good work. I'll see you at next week's meeting."

As if a little flattery could smooth over all the acrimony, Ranze thought. She managed not to offer a response, punched the cutoff button—and immediately wondered why she hadn't done so as soon as she'd recognized DeByes's voice.

She stood there staring at the visiphone for several seconds afterward, wondering something else as well: *What in the nine worlds is that woman so afraid of?*

THIRTEEN

The VIP suite was probably four or five
times the size of the CCU, Lujan guessed. At least, it
sounded that much larger. It wasn't filled with the endless
beeps and burbles and hums of the CCU's monitoring and
support equipment, and its carpeting muted footfalls to
soft shushing sounds. It might have been comfortable, except for the reason they had brought him here.

"Your staff has put together a retirement ceremony and
reception for you," Darcie had told him two evenings earlier.

"I don't want a ceremony," he said. "Not—like this."
The pillow tucked under his head and chest partly muffled his voice synthesizer.

Darcie's hands, massaging away the ache of the day's
therapy, paused in the middle of his back. "Your whole
staff understands," she said, "and they feel bad about it,
too. That's why they want to do this, to be sure you get
the recognition and thanks you deserve." Her voice
turned quiet as she began to knead along his ribs once
more. "They also want a chance to make their farewells,
Luj. They're all getting transferred out of this star system,
you know. Do it for them, even if you don't want it for
yourself. You owe them that, at least."

He did owe them that, he knew. He owed them a great

deal of thanks, too, both for the professionalism of their military service and for their support, demonstrated in numerous ways since he'd been injured. "You're right," he told Darcie, and sighed. "But none of that obituary stuff—the assassin didn't succeed, after all!—and no retirement gift!"

Darcie chuckled, spread out her fingers on his sides, and pressed a light kiss to his back, between his shoulder blades. "Too late to skip the gifts," she said. "Jiron already showed them to me."

"*Them?* I hope they're not extravagant!"

She laughed again. "They probably are, but I think they're very appropriate."

He allowed himself another sigh and shifted on the pillow. "What do they have in mind for the ceremony?"

"The official part will be in midmorning," Darcie said. "We'll keep it brief. Jiron wanted to ask Admiral Emeroth to come out of retirement to do the honors, since she was one of your mentors. He thought you'd appreciate that. But due to your rank and position, he was told it had to be the Triune."

Lujan turned his head as if to look at her over his shoulder. "To add a last insult to the injury?"

Darcie's hands paused again. "It would seem so, wouldn't it?" She sighed this time. "Actually, Jiron said there's a good strategic reason for it. If there are any . . . political reasons behind this retirement, it'll confirm to those responsible that their goal has been accomplished. It'll shift their attention away from you."

Good point, Lujan reflected. That would give him more space to probe, to determine whether or not there was any validity to his suspicions. To Darcie he said, "But they can't have the ceremony in here."

"It'll be held up in the VIP suite," Darcie said. "We'll get you up there and settled before everyone arrives and then bring you back after they leave."

"Why the VIP suite?" Lujan wrinkled his brow.

"Because that's where everyone expects you to be," she said. "You *are* a VIP, after all, Luj!" She ruffled his hair. "Besides, it'll help to maintain the charade. All the status bulletins have reported that you're in the VIP suite. There've even been guards posted outside, and Libby and Gavril and I have been making stops in there two or three times every day since before you woke from the coma.

"Creating a decoy was Admiral Halbach's idea," she added as she began to smooth his hair back down, "just in case somebody got past hospital security and went looking for you. The VIP suite is probably the first place they'd go."

Trust Halbach to come up with a diversion, Lujan thought. A rush of pride, of satisfaction came with that thought, followed by a sudden inner warmth at realizing that the same tactics that shielded his troops on combat missions had been employed by his staff to protect their Old Man in the hospital. His throat tightened.

Darcie was still playing with his hair, drawing it through her fingers. "You need a trim before the ceremony," she said. "You're actually getting a bit shaggy!"

"Let it go," he told her. "The less I look like a fleet admiral, the better." Perhaps he could push the charade one step further, boost his suspect's comfort level a notch or two, and encourage him to relax. . . .

Earlier that morning, as Darcie helped him pull on a clean warm-up suit, he had requested of her, "Leave the voice synthesizer here."

"Why?" she asked. She sounded puzzled.

"Insurance against me thinking out loud," he said.

As Dr. Moses had promised, the focus required to use the voice synthesizer had become natural enough over the past two weeks that he *had* found himself "thinking aloud" on a couple of occasions. Besides, the more permanently disabled he appeared, the less likely Trosvig would be to suspect his investigation.

Darcie chuckled at his reply. "I understand," she said.

Her fingers moved at the nape of his neck, releasing the band. He heard a drawer open in the cabinet beside his bed, and the clink of the synthesizer's pendant as she placed it inside. "You *are* going to wear it tonight for the reception, however!" she said.

He started to think, *Of course,* but there was nothing to voice the thought. He blinked it out instead.

They rode a lift up three levels, and as Darcie turned his glidechair about on disembarking, he heard her utter a tiny gasp. *What—?* he wanted to ask.

"There's a Spherzah honor guard!" she said, as if in response to his mental question. "A full complement of them, like side boys on a ship, except they're all wearing sabers!"

Lujan could imagine them standing in their double row, regal in black dress uniforms with medals on their left breasts and red cord aiguilettes on their right shoulders. As Darcie guided his glidechair forward, their commander ordered, "Atten-*tion! Pre-sent arms!"*

He heard the simultaneous stamp of boot heels as they snapped to attention, the whisper of sabers sliding, as one, out of scabbards. He could almost feel the electricity in their posture as his chair, flanked by Darcie, passed under the arch he knew their sabers formed. He lifted his head, wishing he could see their faces, could look into their eyes one more time. He swallowed at a sudden knot in his throat.

Tristan and Jiron were waiting, already inside the room. Jiron anchored the chair while, with assistance from Tristan, he shoved himself out of it and onto the bed; and Darcie arranged the pillows to support him in a sitting position. "Comfortable, love?" she asked.

The thought of what was yet to come turned his stomach to a stone in the middle of his body. "No," he blinked quite honestly.

She seemed to understand that; she kissed his brow and squeezed his hand.

They all arrived together: the Triune and the chair staff of the Defense Directorate. Lujan heard their muffled conversation in the corridor as they approached—and how it fell silent, abruptly, as they came through the door into the room. He felt their gazes—or rather, the way they averted their gazes, as if to deny his condition, or maybe even his presence. The speechlessness, the muffled clearing of a couple throats and shifting of shoes on the carpet, revealed a situational awkwardness more intense than he'd experienced even at memorial services.

Jiron must have sensed the strain as well—had probably anticipated it, Lujan thought. Raising his voice just enough to catch everyone's ear, he said, "On behalf of Admiral Serege and his family, I want to thank all of you for coming today."

The uneasy shuffling ceased. The release of tension was almost tangible as everyone turned their attention to Jiron. "There's a presentation that needs to be made before we proceed with the retirement ceremony," he said. "Lieutenant Inglis from Protocol, and the Honorable Alois Ashforth of the Triune, you may take care of that now."

There was a moment's quiet, weighted with anticipation, before Lieutenant Inglis began to read. "Attention to orders!" she said. And then: "Citation to accompany the award of the Star Cluster of Valor of the Unified Worlds to Lujan Ansellic Serege."

The Star Cluster of Valor. Lujan started, leaning against the pillows.

"Admiral Lujan Ansellic Serege," Lieutenant Inglis read, "distinguished himself in the performance of extraordinary heroism for the Unified Worlds as Commander-in-Chief of the Spherzah, from the nineteenth day of the third month of . . ."

The Star Cluster of Valor. The words echoed in Lujan's ears, blocking out the rest of the citation.

During the thirty years spanned by his career, he had seen the Star Cluster awarded a total of six times before. Four of those presentations had been during the War of Resistance, to the families of heroic men and women who would never come home.

Overcome, he turned his face away, bowing his head. He barely felt Darcie lay her hand on his shoulder.

Lieutenant Inglis's voice caught as she read the list of his accomplishments. She paused, but the tremor of emotion remained as she concluded, "The unparalleled heroism of Admiral Serege culminates a long and distinguished career in the service of his homeworld and reflects great credit upon himself and the Unified Worlds Spherzah."

Silence followed, for a full minute. A silence so profound that Lujan could hear his own heartbeat.

Then, "May I, Lujan?" That was Ashforth, standing beside his bed. Her hands brushed his head as she placed the medal about his neck.

Its ribbon was midnight blue, he knew, with a silver band shining along each edge. The medal itself was a platinum oval engraved with a sunburst design. At its center gleamed a cluster of nine precious stones, each unique to the member world from which it had come and which it represented.

Ashforth straightened the ribbon on Lujan's shoulders, then bent to kiss each side of his face. "Our deepest gratitude, sir," she said.

The actual retirement ceremony was anticlimactic by comparison. Trosvig himself read the retirement decree, right down to its trio of authorizing signatures, and then presented it, in its frame—to Darcie.

"It is customary," he said then, "for the retiree to offer some departing remarks. In this case, Captain Dartmuth, perhaps we can prevail upon you to fill in?"

Darcie touched Lujan's arm. "Is there anything you'd like me to relay for you, Luj?"

There wasn't. What was there left to say that wouldn't sound either bitter or vain? It was better to leave it alone. He made a slight turn of his head, a motion of negation, and Darcie said firmly, "No."

They all filed past the bed as they left, clasping his strengthless hands and offering uncomfortable words of farewell. Even Trosvig, whose hands were slick with sweat when they enclosed Lujan's. "You were a good man, Serege," he said. "I'm truly sorry."

As if I were dead, Lujan thought. But perhaps it was just as well. Trosvig was unlikely to feel threatened by a dead man.

The reception that evening was easier. The guest list had been deliberately limited to the immediate Command Section staff and their families, all trusted comrades and friends. Lujan received them from his glidechair in the VIP suite's sitting room.

There weren't only handclasps this time. Soldiers who had slogged through Saede's jungles or Yan's Cathana Mountains with him, who had faced the lethal flare of enemy laser cannon fire as his wingmen in space combat, or sweated with him through readiness exercises in Topawa's Anchenko Desert, wrapped muscled arms about his shoulders and carefully thumped his back. Some of them wept; and more than once hot tears spilled unashamed down Lujan's face as well.

Jiron's three children came with Heazel. Ellon, fourteen,

might have been another of Lujan's nieces. "We'll miss you, sir," she said, and pressed a shy kiss to his cheek.

"I'll miss all of you, too," Lujan told her. "I think you'll like Enach, though. I've never seen the kind of forests it has anywhere else in the sector."

Jirrel, seventeen and self-conscious about his emotions, came next. He gripped Lujan's hand as a man would have. "Thank you, sir," he managed, "—for everything."

Lujan could only guess at what "everything" meant. For coaching the boy on playing forward for his multiball team? For inviting him to go along with himself and Jiron on hunting trips and including him in their conversations around the campfire? For being there as the boy's backup when Jiron went away on temporary duty and left his son to look after the family? Not that it really mattered. Jirrel had eased the ache for his own son through the years that Tristan was missing.

And then there was Heazon, not quite eleven. "Wow, sir!" he exclaimed. "That's a really far-phased glidechair! I've never seen one up close before! How fast does it go?"

Lujan chuckled. He could do that, from his throat, even if his sagging mouth couldn't smile. He wished, for the sixth or eighth time that evening, that it could. "When you can't see where you're going," he told Heazon, "it goes too fast!"

"Wow!" Heazon must have been practically prancing in front of him. "Can I take it for a drive, sir?"

"Heazon!" His mother sounded appalled. "You promised me you'd behave yourself!" To Lujan she said, "I'm so sorry, sir!"

"He's all right, Heazel." Lujan turned his face back toward the youngster. "Later perhaps, Heazon," he said, "after the other guests have gone."

Admirals Halbach and Faurot presented the gifts when the receiving line was finished. There were two—both extravagant, in Lujan's opinion. The first was his admiral's flag, folded to display its admiral's crest and sealed in a glassine case with a small plaque bearing his name and dates of command. Halbach described it for him in great detail.

The other was a model of his flagship, *Destrier,* almost as long as he was tall and mounted on a panel to be hung on a wall. Darcie guided his hand along its length, from bow to main aft engines, describing each detail upon which she placed his fingers.

He lifted his head when she finished. Ached for a last glimpse of the men and women who encircled him—had to imagine them instead. "Thank you," he said. At least the synthesizer didn't choke on emotion. "Thank you for this, and for the years we served together. I'm honored to have served with you. May God go with you all."

Afterward, he rested in an armchair while Darcie and Tristan and Jiron's family cleared up the trappings of the reception, and Heazon buzzed the glidechair around the room. Lujan turned his head toward its hum as it approached from his right.

"Can I take it out in the hall, sir?" Heazon asked. "Please? There's not enough room in here to go fast!"

Lujan chuckled. "I don't think that's a good idea," he said. "If you were to run over one of the med techs out there, it'd be *me* they'd come after with their needles!"

"Heazon." It was Jiron's voice. "I think you've just about worn out Admiral Serege's glidechair as it is! Go give your mother a hand with the refreshment trays."

"Yes sir." Heazon shut off the glidechair's repulsors and slid noisily out of it. "When you don't need this anymore, sir," he asked, "can I have it?"

"Scoot, son!" Jiron laughed. "Kids!" But as the child scampered off, he hunkered down before Lujan's chair and turned serious. "I want to meet with you tomorrow, sir," he said. "Tristan should be there, too, since he'll be starting at that historian job in a couple of days. You both need to know what I've discovered."

They met in an equipment storage room on the way back from rehab this time. Jiron made an electronic sweep of the room first, with two different sensors. Then he pushed a stool up to face Lujan's glidechair and motioned Tristan in closer as he seated himself.

"Over the last two weeks, I've picked up on a couple of things about Isselan communications," he said. He kept his voice quiet. "There seem to be two main . . . 'nodes' is a good way to describe them, I guess. One of them turned out to be an archival database, an old central computer that appears to record and store everything that goes through the Issel system. The other one is more complicated: It's mobile."

"Sir?" Tristan cocked his head.

"Several members of the cabinet, Issel's governing body, have been doing a lot of traveling lately," Jiron explained. "The second communications node appears to come and go with them."

"With the same person every time?" asked the admiral.

"No sir." Jiron shook his head. "But since their ministers usually travel in pairs or trios, I suspect our 'node' is always somewhere in the party." He lowered his voice still more. "I've also come across a few things that suggest they've returned to the old Dominion system of having a chief minister over the cabinet."

"The way it was done until Renier's governorship," Serege said.

"Yes sir."

"Any indication of who it might be?"

"No sir," said Jiron. "If they do have a chief minister again, that individual has never made a public appearance—or even an official statement."

The admiral bowed his head, brow furrowing so he seemed to be scowling at the floor. "We need to confirm it," he said. "And if it's true, we need to find out who the chief minister is. That's the key; I'm sure of it."

"The Ulibari and Anchenko Detachments are rotating home from Issel," said Jiron. "They're expected to arrive in this system in about four days, in fact. You might ask some of them what they've observed, sir, when they start coming in to see you."

"Nemec!" Tristan abruptly straightened where he stood. "Lieutenant Commander Nemec would know!" He turned to his father. "We found him in the caves on Issel Two during our mission, sir, and brought him out with us." To Jiron he said, "He's been there since he . . . helped me get out, and he knew more about what was going on in the Issel system than we did!"

Jiron nodded. "Sounds like a prime source."

"Tristan," said the admiral, "I'll need you to pick up now where Jiron's leaving off. He'll fill you in on what he's been tracking.

"Besides message traffic, I want you to stay alert to the talk in the various offices you'll work in. Don't comment on anything; don't draw any attention to yourself. Just pay attention to what's going on around you."

"Yes sir," Tristan said.

And Serege turned back to Jiron. "Is there anything else?"

"No sir," Jiron said.

"Then good luck on Enach," said Serege, and extended his hand. "Keep in contact." Then he lifted his head as if to look Jiron in the eye. "And be careful," he added.

Jiron clasped his admiral's hand. Tightly. "You be careful, too, sir," he said. "I don't think I like where this is heading."

FOURTEEN

"We'll have to use a general anesthetic for the surgery tomorrow," said Dr. Moses. "There's a lot more involved this time."

"Taking out my eyes and replacing them with miniature cameras." Lujan fixed his face toward the sound of her voice. "I'm—having a hard time with that."

"That's understandable." Moses's tone was reassuring. "Would you like to talk about what you're feeling?"

Lujan sighed. "I've accepted the fact," he said, "that my eyes aren't going to heal. Dr. Gavril's already told me that the optic nerves and retinas are gone, and if they were going to regenerate, it would've occurred by now. But they're still *my* eyes. They're part of my body."

"In other words, an inherent part of how you perceive yourself," said Moses.

Lujan considered that momentarily. "That's an academic way of putting it. Yes."

"It may help you to know," Moses said, "that the artificial eyes we'll be giving you will look exactly like your own. I was meticulous in the selection, particularly in the color matching; even Darcie won't be able to tell the difference."

Lujan uttered a "Huh" at that.

"The most important thing is they'll allow you to see again," said Moses.

Lujan shook his head. "It all sounds too much like cyborgism to me."

Moses paused. "If it's the idea of being a cyborg that's bothering you," she said after a long minute, "I hate to tell you this, Lujan, but according to the most basic definition you became a cyborg years ago—when we replaced the damaged nerves in your right arm with optical fibers and built you a new shoulder joint out of orthoplastic. It's *having* any artificial part, not the reason for it or the way it's used, that makes someone a cyborg."

I'm a cyborg.

Lujan's mind recoiled from the idea.

Only those who sought man-made replacements without any medical need, to whom it was a matter of image, openly called themselves cyborgs. Lujan had always considered them an abomination: individuals who paid to have their physical capabilities or senses artificially enhanced. The term conjured thoughts of conscienceless criminals, of mercenaries, of teenagers who used "upgrades" for recreation, of those who simply desired superior strength and skills but lacked the patience and discipline to build them through their own effort.

But Dr. Moses's definition was correct, he knew. Which meant that human society was filled with cyborgs of one degree or another. Ordinary people who'd suffered injuries or illness, who didn't care to think of themselves as cyborgs any more than he did, who perhaps even shared his abhorrence of artificial enhancement.

He couldn't suppress a shudder.

Moses must have seen it. "There aren't any alternatives to this procedure," she said. Her tone was gentle. "If you truly don't want to go through with it, Lujan, all we can do is help you learn to live with the blindness. We can do that." She paused, then said, "I can give you until this evening to come to a decision. I'll come back then, all right?"

He nodded. "Thank you."

What have I let them do to my body already? he thought, and broke out in a sweat.

He was lying on his side with his face to the wall when Darcie came in. "Lujan?" she said.

He turned his face toward her, to acknowledge her, and he heard her draw a chair up beside his bed, heard it slide on the floor, and squeak as she seated herself.

"I just saw Libby," she said. "She told me you're having second thoughts about the surgery tomorrow."

He shoved himself onto his back, sighing heavily. "Yes."

"Is there any particular reason?"

"I've always been—disgusted—by cyborgs." He had to force himself even to use the word. Had to swallow afterward. "It's always just seemed wrong to me."

"And this procedure seems too much like an enhancement?"

"Yes." He sighed.

Darcie sighed, too, and sat silent for several seconds. Then she said, "When sensory prosthetics first began to appear centuries ago, they were hailed as the greatest advancement in medicine since antibiotics. There were debates even then about the ethics of their use, but most medical practitioners of the time considered their development a godsend, a—a miracle! There was finally a way to restore to victims of accident or combat what they'd been robbed of! I was always thankful they were available for the combat casualties I treated, and they were thankful, too.

"Unfortunately," she said, "because a few people have chosen to use them for unethical purposes, they've given the whole specialty a bad reputation. It isn't the prosthetics themselves that are evil. They're like anything else: knowledge, a skill, a position of power. It's how one chooses to use them that makes them good or bad."

She paused, then began to stroke his hair away from his eyes. "I think you can accept the implants with a clear conscience, Luj," she said. "Your conscience wouldn't allow you to abuse them."

He pondered that for a while before he sighed. "You're right, Darcie," he said. "Thank you."

He came to the following evening with a dull ache filling his head. There was no localization at first, just a general throbbing against the inside of his skull, as if the pain were trying to pound its way out. He was still groggy, and his initial response was to groan and clench his teeth against it.

The sensation of his teeth locking and grinding together sent a chill down his spine, startling him momentarily out of his drugged fog. It had been better than two months since he'd last been able to close his teeth! He kept his jaws locked as long as he could, to be certain he wasn't just dreaming it. Clenched his teeth until the pain in his skull lanced through the muscles of his face.

As the anesthetic ebbed, the pain began to sort itself out, to settle into distinct locations. Subdued by medication, the throbbing concentrated itself in the orbits of his eyes, at the back of his skull, and at points in front of each ear.

Moses and Gavril had explained the whole operation the evening before. They would start by placing two microelectrode arrays in the back of his head, Gavril had said, at the occipital lobes, or vision centers, of his brain.

It would require cutting out a small piece of bone, just as placing the temporal electrodes had. This time, however, the bundle of fiber-optic leads would be run down just inside Lujan's skull and out through the foramen magnum, the oval opening through which the spinal cord passed, to be connected into the processor in the back of his neck. Besides the sensor arrays, each artificial eye contained a miniature transmitter. The processor would be the receiver for their spread spectrum signals.

Restoring his vision was only one purpose of this surgery, he'd been told. The other was to repair the trigeminal nerve, to restore motor control and sensation to his lower face. Still using the stereotaxic frame, Gavril would reopen the temporal bone to access the damaged nerve, entering through an area slightly lower and farther forward than the auditory implant site. Even with computerized assistance, the microsurgical repairs could be expected to take five or more hours on each side of Lujan's head.

Once both nerves were mended, Dr. Moses would take over on the eye replacement.

"Don't tell me how you're going to take out my eyes," Lujan had requested. The very thought of it made him nauseous. "I don't want to know."

Moses explained instead that installing his new eyes would be almost as lengthy a procedure as the trigeminal repairs. The six extrinsic muscles that moved each eye would have to be individually attached to the prosthetic, using a suturing laser. He should expect massive bruising around his eyes, she had said, though most of it should have faded by the time the bandaging foam was removed.

Drifting now, halfway between wakefulness and drug-stubborn sleep, he remembered almost nothing of what they had told him. Nor did he care at the moment. The pulsing ache held his whole attention.

By morning he was restless with postsurgical fever; and with even the back of his head sore this time, there didn't seem to be a comfortable position in which to lie.

He had just eased himself onto his right side, turning his head gingerly on his pillow, when Dr. Moses came in on rounds. "Awake yet, Jink?" she asked, laying a hand on his arm. "Is there much pain?"

He thought they had probably removed the voice synthesizer for the surgery; but even if they hadn't, he was still too groggy to use it. He attempted a nod instead— and instantly regretted it: The dull throb turned to hammer blows. He winced.

"Well," Moses said, "it looks like the motor control's kicking in already. See if you can close your teeth."

He did that.

"Open them now. Open your mouth as wide as you can."

That actually took more effort than did locking his teeth. He wasn't certain if he even succeeded, but Moses seemed pleased. "Good enough for starters," she said. "The speech therapist will work on it with you. Now try to touch your teeth with your tongue."

His tongue seemed to fill his whole mouth, seemed to be an entity unto itself. He strained to make it obey.

"With a little work," Moses said, patting his shoulder, "you'll be eating roast karsh off the stalk again. Have you got any sensation back yet? Make a sound for me if you can feel this."

Her finger was cool, tracing a line along his jaw. It left a tingly, prickly sensation, as if a local anesthetic were wearing off. She probed both sides of his face, with firm touches from the tip of his nose to his earlobes, from his cheekbones to his jawline, and he managed an "Uh" each time.

"Looks like the surgery was a success," she said when

she finished. "You'll need some time to recover, though, so I'm putting your physiotherapy on hold for a few days; and you'll rest better if you're not hurting, so I'm going to enter a prescription for a stronger painkiller into your hemomanagement system. Other than that, you're doing fine, Jink." She patted his shoulder once more. "I'll see you this evening."

He dozed after she left, until Darcie came in. She stroked back his hair above the encircling swath of bandaging and said, "How are you doing, Luj?"

He couldn't blink a response with his eyes bandaged; he couldn't focus well enough to think a response, either. He simply sighed.

She ruffled his hair a little—they had only spot-shaved his head this time—and then she pressed a cautious kiss to his mouth.

It tingled, just as Libby's touching of his face had tingled. But it sent a different kind of tingle through his body, almost taking his breath.

Darcie chuckled softly, close to his ear. "Good morning, love," she said.

He slept through most of the day, rousing only when the med techs came in to check on him or bring him meals of clear liquids, or when the pain made him restless.

Tristan was there when he woke once in the late afternoon. Clearly conscious of the monitors in the CCU, Tristan said, "The Anchenko Detachment got in to Herbrun Field today, Father. There was a message from Lieutenant Commander Nemec on the terminal in our quarters when I came in from work. He asked how you were doing and wondered if he could come see you. I sent back that I thought you'd like that, and told him maybe tomorrow, if you were feeling up to having visitors by then. It'll probably have to be after I'm off work, if that's all right."

Well done, Tris, Lujan thought. But all he could vocalize was a sighed, "Uh-huh . . ."

"Right then," Tristan said. He paused, then added, "I've got to go now. There was . . . a message from Kersce, too, and . . . she invited me to go out for dinner with the detachment this evening."

The note of urgent anticipation in his son's voice said more than his words did. Lujan felt a faint upward tug at the corners of his mouth. He nodded; and Tristan said, "Thank you, sir."

The grogginess and most of the fever were gone by the time Tristan came in the next afternoon, but Lujan was still weak, and the pain in his face persisted. He clenched his teeth as Tristan eased him from the bed into the glidechair.

"Keep it short, please, Tris," Darcie said as they left the room.

Flanked by one of the guards at the CCU's door, they took the lift up one level and started through a corridor that extended into an enclosed bridge between buildings.

It was storming outside; the walkway was chilly, and Lujan could hear the wind slashing rain, or perhaps sleet, up and down its expanse of viewpanes. The tattoo of the water on the panes swelled and ebbed with each gust in an unpredictable cadence: white noise sufficient to shield a conversation from all but its intended listeners. But as far north as Ramiscal City lay, and as late as it was in the afternoon, it was probably already dark outdoors. A meeting in a lighted walkway could too easily be observed by any passerby.

"Wait here," Tristan instructed the guard, and he guided the glidechair forward.

"One moment, Tris," Lujan said through the voice synthesizer. He raised one hand in a halting motion. "How transparent are these viewpanes from outside?"

"They're not, Father," Tristan said. "They're one-way diaphametal. You can't tell from outside whether or not the walkway is lighted."

"Good choice," Lujan said. "We don't need this meeting to be observed."

"Right," Tristan said. Then he shouted over the clatter of the rain, "Commander Nemec!"

Lujan heard the ring of the other's footfalls up the walkway, approaching until they converged with his glidechair near the bridge's center. When Tristan switched off the chair's repulsors, Lujan stretched out his hand. "Ajimir," he said. "It's good to have you safely home."

Another hand caught his, gripped it, and Lujan could envision the warm contrast of Nemec's ebony fingers wrapping about his own pale ones. "It's good to be home, sir," Nemec said, "—and it's good to find you alive and—recovering."

How did one respond to that? Lujan wondered. At a loss, he simply nodded.

But after a moment he said, "The injuries left . . . a few gaps . . . in my memory. There are some things I should know about the Issel situation that—just aren't there anymore. Tris and Captain Jiron, my XO, have helped fill in some of the blanks, but there are still a few unanswered questions."

"Such as, sir?" said Nemec.

"Who's really in power on Issel now?" said Lujan. "And what's the general feeling toward the Unified Worlds?"

"Feelings toward the Unified Worlds?" Nemec blew out a breath and dropped to Lujan's level beside the glidechair. "I'd say the feelings come close to euphoria, sir. Troops who spent any time planetside said they were constantly being mobbed by people giving them gifts or wanting to buy them meals or drinks, or even just wanting to touch them. It never let up. Even at the spaceport, the day the last Unified forces boarded the shuttles to head out of the system, the feeling was . . . warm. A number of local government officials were there to see us off." He hesitated. "None of the top inner-circle ministers, however. Even the ones who came were stiff and formal, but the gratitude and the expressions of hope for further contact were genuine. It was quite a contrast from encounters with Isselan officials under the previous regime."

"Interesting," Lujan said. And then, "Speaking of Isselan officials, how stable is the planetary government right now?"

Nemec paused, probably to consider. "It seems to be pretty solid," he said—and then he lowered his voice. "Since Renier's suicide, they've restored the position of chief minister to their cabinet."

Confirmation of what Jiron's research had suggested. Lujan furrowed his brow beneath the bandage foam—and regretted it at once. Wincing at the jab of pain through his face, he asked, "They went back to a chief minister instead of choosing a new World Governor?"

"So it appears," said Nemec.

A sense of impending revelation made Lujan stir in the glidechair. "Do you know who that chief minister is?" he asked. "His name? Anything about him?"

"Yes." Nemec's tone turned grim. "He's not new to interstellar politics; he's been around since before Renier's governorship began here on Sostis—he was Renier's chief cabinet minister for a while, in fact. His name is Seulemont Remarq."

Everything inside Lujan recoiled. Not from shock or surprise but from a sudden flood of memory, as if confirmation of the name had finally breached a portion of the dam across his mind.

Before his appointment to the Sostish cabinet under the House of Renier, long before Mordan Renier's exile to Issel, Seulemont Remarq had been an officer in the Sostish Intelligence Department. Over two or three decades he had worked his way to the top and had ultimately spent five or six years as head of that organization.

During the War of Resistance there had been many who suspected that Remarq was a double agent for the Dominion, though his accusers had never been able to prove it. A handful of those who voiced such suspicions had, over a period of a few years, met with fatal accidents.

When Mordan Renier became World Governor of Issel a few years after seeking asylum there, many Unified analysts believed Remarq was behind it.

By the time Issel invaded first Na Shiv and then Adriat and claimed them as commonwealths of Issel, the various intelligence organizations within the Unified Worlds were warning their personnel against recruitment efforts by Isselan intelligence agents. Adriat, after all, had fallen to Issel by gradual infiltration and corruption of its government.

And there was more. As distinctly as if it had happened the day before, Lujan suddenly remembered an incident that had followed a particularly heated session during the negotiation of the Isselan Assistance Agreement.

Striding through a corridor in the Unified Worlds Tower, away from the stuffiness and rancor that filled the negotiation chamber, he'd been accosted by a man in the robes of an Isselan cabinet minister. The same man who had haunted his fevered dreams during his first days out of the coma.

The man whose name he hadn't been able to remember then was Nioro Enn Borith. *Minister* Nioro Borith, whom he'd later supposedly saved from the assassin at the sealing of the treaty.

"This is completely unacceptable, Admiral Serege!" Borith had said. " 'Planetary envelopment' indeed! That's nothing more than a euphemism for putting Issel in a stranglehold!" He shook his head. "We're down to three weeks before the launch window, and the closer we come, the more I dislike the whole idea—particularly since we're not hearing anything new in these supposed update briefings. I don't think your people are telling us everything, Admiral. I think they're keeping a great deal to themselves. I'd sooner trust my life to the rabble out there shouting death threats in your streets than I'd trust the protection of my motherworld to you and the rest of your warmongers!"

The cabinet minister's ceaseless stream of protests were growing more worn than Lujan's own patience, but he managed to keep his voice level when he said, "Perhaps I should remind you, Minister, that it was you who came to the Unified Worlds asking for help—the epitome of audacity, in my opinion. I think it's only fair to point out that I don't trust the ulterior motives of your government any more than you trust mine."

"Of *my* government?" Borith flung out his hands. "Admiral, the only motive *my* government has is to prevent Issel from becoming a masuk slave market!"

"Are you sure of that, Minister?" Lujan let his tone turn deadly serious. "If you truly believe that's the only reason for Chief Minister Remarq's sending you here, then you don't know him as well as I do."

Borith stopped short, spun around, and stared at him, and a stream of emotions ranging from shock to panic to indignation crossed his face in a handful of heartbeats. "That is an utter outrage, Admiral!" he said at last.

But it wasn't exactly a denial, Lujan had observed. His

accusation then had been little more than a shot in the dark, based on gut feelings and history, but the cabinet minister's reaction to it had confirmed what he'd suspected since the Isselans first arrived.

It twisted his stomach into knots now; it turned his hands and face and feet clammy.

Seulemont Remarq. The Empire Builder. The Hidden Hand of the Dominion.

He responded to Nemec with only a nod.

But a million fragments of information whirled in his mind like pieces to an elaborate puzzle caught up in a tornado. Was there any significance to them? Were there any connections? Or was all of it a side effect of his being hospitalized, a product of his own restlessness and frustration?

He truly hoped that was all it was, but he doubted it. His gut was still knotted; and his arms, he suddenly realized, were rigid on the arms of the glidechair.

He made himself relax. "Your specialty is communications, isn't it?" he said to Nemec.

"Yes sir."

"What are your plans now? Do you have a new assignment lined up yet?"

"No sir," said Nemec. "Not yet."

Lujan hesitated for a long moment, considering the ramifications, the risks. Then he said, slowly, "I need your help, Ajimir. I'm looking for connections, patterns, inconsistencies."

"In what, sir?" Nemec asked.

"Isselan-Unified relations," Lujan said. He left it at that. Any further discussion of his suspicions would destroy the objectivity that would be so critical to the search.

"Sir, that's pretty general," said Nemec.

Lujan said, "I know. But if there are any links, any pat-

terns, anything out of place, you'll recognize them immediately."

Nemec was silent for a long space. Then, "What do
you need me to do, sir?" he said.

"I need you in communications at headquarters,"
Lujan said. He turned carefully. "Tris?"

"Sir?" his son said from behind him.

"Is Chief Meluskey still working in inbound assign-
ments?"

"Yes sir," said Tristan.

"Good." Lujan turned back toward Nemec. "Go talk to
Chief Meluskey," he said. "Tell him I sent you, and see
what kind of job he can get for you."

"Will do, sir," said Nemec.

FIFTEEN

"**Ranze?**" The voice coming through the blank visiphone was that of Madam DeByes.

What does that woman have against using the viewscreen? Ranze wondered. *And why is she calling me at home?*

"What is it?" Ranze asked.

"I'd like to meet with you over lunch tomorrow," said DeByes. Her tone was business curt. "I found a discrepancy in your trade proposal and I think we need to discuss it."

Only one? Ranze thought. *And you're actually going to discuss it with me this time?* DeByes had made so many changes to her proposal over the last week that Ranze hardly knew what was in it anymore. She drew a deep breath and released it slowly before she said, "Now what is it?"

"That's what I'd like to know, Ranze," DeByes said. "Every time I think we've gotten all the problems resolved, you make another change and then we have to start all over again."

Ranze stiffened. *"I've* been making changes?" she said. "One minute, madam. You're the one who told me last week that I couldn't discuss this with any of the planetary trade reps—and then *you* sent out that message to all of them! I told you before you did that the message changed the whole intent of the trade program. You insisted that it didn't, but every one of the trade reps interpreted it the same way I did. I'm still getting confused calls from half of them!"

"I never said that!" DeByes's tone suggested affront. "I never said you couldn't talk to the trade reps!"

"You did, madam. Very specifically." Ranze found herself struggling to keep her voice even. "You said it would give the opposition a chance to prepare their own campaign against it."

"I said no such thing!" said DeByes.

Ranze didn't pursue it; there was nothing to be gained by a childish bout of "You did" and "I did not."

"Whatever," she said instead. "They've been calling me with their concerns, and every time I've brought those to you, *you've* decided to make a change—usually without informing me of the details until after the fact."

"Now, Ranze—," said DeByes.

But Ranze went on. "In fact, I had a call just this morning from Ng Quoc, Yan's trade rep," she said, "about something in a message you disseminated last night. All I could say to her was, 'What message? I never received a copy.'"

"It was the one on paragraph eight-point-three, about tariffs and trade balances," said DeByes. "We talked about that just yesterday."

"I asked Quoc to read the message to me," Ranze said. "What you and I talked about and what went out in that message were two entirely different things." She made a helpless gesture with both hands. "I don't even know what's going on with the trade agreement anymore. I feel like it's been taken completely out of my hands."

There was a short silence from beyond the blank viewscreen. Then DeByes said, "We're only two days away from presenting the proposal in the Assembly, Ranze, and the trade agreement will be one of its most important aspects. I just want to make sure we both understand its intent."

I'm sure you *don't understand what I originally intended,* Ranze thought. She didn't say it. Said instead, "It's not too late to clear all of this up. All I need is one meeting with the trade reps."

"There's not enough time to schedule a conference room for a meeting before the Assembly presentation," said DeByes.

"Then give me a list of their net numbers!" Ranze was practically pleading by now. "I'll contact them all personally!"

"I can't let you do that, Ranze. We have to go through proper channels, you know."

"What are 'proper channels'?" Ranze demanded. "The heads of the delegations? If so, then give me their numbers—"

"Ranze, I know you have a couple of other projects going on in the Assembly right now." DeByes's attempt to sound soothing only succeeded in sounding patronizing. "I know you're feeling a great deal of pressure because of them. Would you like to be released from this committee?"

The suggestion came like a slap in the face. "Absolutely not!" she said. "Not until I've finished this task!" And she pressed the disconnect button.

She should have seen it coming after that first committee meeting, she thought. She should've followed her first instincts and walked out of it then. DeByes had done nothing but abuse her and the others and disfigure their programs from the start—but Ranze had a job to do, and she wasn't going to abandon it now!

She was still seething an hour later, still pacing her living area with her fingernails biting into her palms.

But one fact had managed to penetrate her indignation: It wasn't going to get any better. Micromanager that De-Byes was, she would never really let Ranze finish the job. Not the way Ranze knew it needed to be done, at least. Besides, as senseless as this was fast becoming, Ranze was quite certain she didn't want her own name connected with it.

Quandary resolved, she punched DeByes's code into the visiphone.

It buzzed for some time before DeByes responded, and then she smiled into the viewscreen as if she were expecting a lover rather than an irate assemblywoman. Caught off guard, she said, "Oh—Ranze!"

Ranze fixed her vision on DeByes. Hard. "I don't care anymore what you do to my trade proposal, madam," she said. "It's your baby now. I don't want anything more to do with this!"

The relief she felt as she disconnected the visiphone was like having a weight lifted from her shoulders. Ranze stood still for several seconds, savoring the first deep breaths she had felt free to draw in a month.

It could take weeks to complete his assignment in Personnel, Tristan realized. The office consisted of several departments, ranging from Personal Affairs to Manning Control to Promotions. Each section maintained its own records, some of which were stored in Personnel's central database and some of which were not.

What wasn't available in the central database had to be retrieved from each of the departments, one at a time. That meant reading through each section's records, flagging the appropriate files as he found them, and then copying them into a message format to be forwarded to the historian's office.

He had discovered over 250 files of interest to the historian just in the Entitlements section's database, and that was one of Personnel's smallest departments. It had taken him most of the day to review everything it contained.

Closing the last file, he sagged back in the chair and let his breath out in a rush as he scanned his list of flagged documents. Then he called up the shell for the transfer message and tapped the COPY button.

Exiting the program a few moments later, he glanced at a timepanel on the wall. He'd have just enough time to get back to the historian's office and check the message traffic once more before everyone closed down for the day. As if he really wanted to read anything else.

He plopped his log chip in its plasticine sheath on the desk of his supervisor, another civilian, as he crossed toward his own cubicle. Middle-aged, with a paunch and no hairline left at all, the man barely glanced up from his terminal. "Thanks, Tristan," he said.

Only two new items had come into the message queue since he'd read the traffic that morning. One was classified Secret, the other Confidential. Both concerned Issel. Tristan leaned forward, narrowing his eyes at the gray-lit characters on the screen.

The first message was an activity report from the Spherzah signals-collection ship *Sentinel*. With Unified forces no longer in their star system, the remnants of Issel's space defense force were resuming responsibility for early-warning system-defense patrols. Fifteen such sorties, launched from two of the three surviving defense bases, had been noted in the last twenty-four standard hours.

The other message made Tristan straighten in his chair. The Cabinet seat of Hampton Istvan, Minister of Interplanetary Relations who had perished in the attack at the sealing of the Isselan Assistance Agreement, had been filled by the appointment of Dr. Zlatkis Haken, formerly a professor of Interplanetary Diplomatic Sciences at Bin-Yamin University in the province of Hainova. With Haken's installation, Issel's Cabinet of fifteen ministers was complete once more.

There was, Tristan noted, no mention of a chief minister. Still, the appointment to the Isselan Cabinet might be of interest to his father. He studied the text thoroughly before he cleared the monitor, shut down his terminal, and reached for his coat.

Kersce, snug in a cream-colored parka, was waiting in the main lobby when he emerged from the lift. She grinned when she spotted him among the other departing government workers, and came across to meet him.

Tristan grinned back. "What are you doing here?"

She shrugged, her gloved hands shoved into her parka pockets. "I thought maybe I could go along with you to see the admiral."

"Sure." He copied her shrug. "He'd probably like that."

The wind hadn't let up from that morning; if anything, Tristan thought, it was growing sharper now with the deepening of evening. It blustered around the base of the Unified Worlds Tower, catching them with a spattering of spring sleet as they came through the outer doors. Kersce grimaced and pulled up her parka's hood, and Tristan turned up the collar of his coat. "The ramp to the transit is over there," he said, pointing off through the dusk.

"Good," Kersce replied. "Lead on."

They didn't have to wait long at the platform, much to Tristan's relief. The tunnels for the hovertrains, sooty dim, noisy with the whoosh of the cars and bitter-scented with burned oil, reminded him of the mine complexes on Issel II. He set his jaw as he surveyed the station and the huddled commuters in their queues through narrowed eyes.

He breathed more easily once he and Kersce had squeezed their way off the crowded car at the medical center station. The ramp there was brightly lighted, its walls a mosaic of geometric patterns shaped from tiny tiles of various blues and greens. It opened into the atrium of the hospital's main building.

Kersce pushed back her hood. "How is he doing?" she asked as they crossed toward a bank of lifts.

The question brought Tristan back to the present. "My father?" he said. "He looks a lot better now than he did when I first got home." He paused, remembering the thin figure in the bed, head encased in bandage foam, tubes in his arms and throat. "At least there aren't a lot of tubes anymore," he said. "They operated three days ago to replace his eyes; they may take off the bandaging tomorrow. He can get around in a glidechair now, so we go for walks when I come after work. He hates being in bed."

Kersce responded with a brief smile. "That's probably a gross understatement!"

He motioned her to wait when they reached the CCU. "Mum and I are the only ones allowed inside," he said. "Wait here." To the Sostish soldiers, eyeing Kersce from their posts beside the door, he added, "Petty Officer Kersce is one of my father's troops. She's come to visit him."

The guards exchanged glances and shifted a little before the senior of the two gave a curt nod.

"Tris is here, Luj," his mother said as he stepped into the room, and his father turned his face toward him.

"Kersce's here, too, sir," Tristan said. "She wanted to visit you. She's waiting outside the door."

He retrieved the glidechair from a corner, maneuvered it up to the bed. "I thought we'd go down to the cafeteria today, before dinner hours begin. I'm starving!"

His father chuckled at that. "Good idea."

Guiding the chair through the door, Tristan saw how

Kersce bit her lip. He felt a pang when she tore her gaze from his father's face just long enough to touch his own. "Sir," she said then, and crouched before the glidechair. "It's Petty Officer Kersce."

Tristan heard the hesitation in her voice. Saw how she swallowed. Her eyes came up to his again, laden with a question: *What do I say?*

The admiral solved the dilemma for her himself. He extended one curled hand, which she took gingerly between her own, and he said, "Thank you for coming, Kersce. I've had quite a few visitors from the detachment today. From what they've said, it sounds like the mission was successful."

"Yes sir," she said. "It was."

As they started through the corridor a few moments later, followed by one of the Sostish guards, Tristan flashed her the Spherzah hand signal for "Quiet." Taking the glidechair's control in his left hand, he placed his right one on his father's shoulder and began a surreptitious tapping with his forefinger:

"Not much in traffic today. One message about Isselan Cabinet. New Minister for Interplanetary Relations installed. Name is Zlatkis Haken, professor at Bin-Yamin University. All seats of Cabinet are now filled, no mention of chief minister."

The admiral acknowledged with the slightest of nods.

In a private corner of the cafeteria, over cups of hot shuk, the admiral said, "Tell me—what you can—about the mission, Kersce."

She was careful to limit her account to the mission's unclassified aspects, but she kept her voice quiet and her vision moving about the dining area the whole time, Tristan noticed. Finally, with a mischievous glance sideways at him, she said, "And Tris did great, sir! We couldn't have gotten through that cave system so quickly without him. Even Lieutenant Sladsky was impressed!"

Tristan's face heated up. "Oh, come on, Kersce!"

She said good-bye in the corridor outside the CCU when they returned to the neurosurgical floor. Tristan steered the glidechair on into the CCU and steadied it while his father transferred himself back into bed.

He was turning to put the glidechair away when the admiral said, "Good catch, Tris."

The comment startled him. "Sir?" he said.

"Your piece of news," said his father. "That could be very important."

"The Assembly of the Unified Worlds will come to order," the officiator announced from the podium, "and hearings will proceed on Tohh bill number two hundred thirty-seven, a proposal to consider the readmission of Issel into the Unified Worlds."

The announcement had the same effect, Ranze thought, as filling the chamber with fire foam would have had. Those conferring with one another at their delegation tables fell silent in midsentence, as if smothered. Only the officiator, his features as immobile and unreadable as a plascrete mask, seemed unaffected as he introduced the Honorable Madam Abigail DeByes.

Ranze slouched down on her bench and folded her arms over her body as DeByes took the podium. The committee chair surveyed the full chamber as if from a dais, and smiled as if the chamber's occupants were her subjects, not her cohorts, Ranze thought.

Since that first committee meeting, the day each of its members had presented their assigned segments of the proposal to Madam DeByes, Ranze had never seen the whole committee together. Nor had she ever seen a completed draft of the bill. Recalling the criticism DeByes had leveled at each of them, and the way she'd manipulated Ranze's trade proposal beyond recognition, Ranze found herself almost morbidly curious about the finished product. She creased her brow with concentration as De-Byes launched into her introductory speech.

"Men and women of the Assembly," DeByes said, "over the past few months we have witnessed a number of dramatic events between several worlds in this sector of the galaxy that might have seemed impossible even one standard year ago. For the first time in nearly three decades, four of the original members of the Unified Worlds—Sostis, Tohh, Topawa, and Kaleo—have re-united with the fifth original member, Issel, to fight a common enemy.

"I believe that the sealing of the Isselan Assistance Agreement, and the months of negotiation that were spent in bringing it about, were the first steps toward re-uniting worlds that have been enemies for far too long. I believe"—and her voice took on a note of earnest ur-gency—"that the time has come to take additional steps to bring about that reunion. Therefore, men and women of the Assembly, I present a proposal to consider the readmission of Issel into the Unified Worlds."

Ranze started at a nudge in the arm. When she looked around, Ikel Broudy asked, "This isn't the same project you've been working on with the madam, is it?"

"It was," Ranze said. "It isn't anymore."

The bill, which DeByes read in its entirety, was filled with flowery phraseology but contained little if any sub-stance. Only remnants bore any resemblance to the pro-grams Ranze had heard described by her fellow committee members at their first meeting; and the inter-stellar trade possibilities she had envisioned had been re-duced to scarcely more than a list of quotas and tariffs.

Half-mesmerized with amazement at it, she actually

jumped when Broudy leaned over once more and stage-whispered, "What's with this one-size-fits-all trade circle?"

"Don't ask me," said Ranze. "It isn't the trade agreement I designed." She added, "That's one of the reasons I resigned from the committee."

"Oh." Broudy quirked an eyebrow. "Well, this may work for Tohh, but what about Yan? Yan barely even has an economy!" He shook his head. "And what about worlds on the other end of the spectrum, like Sostis?"

"I'm sorry." Ranze sat back and folded her arms again. "If I'd been allowed to do my job without Madam getting her fingers into it, we might have something that would work. I suppose you'll just have to voice your concerns when it comes up for debate."

"But I'm a troublemaker, remember?" Broudy said. "I'm a backstabber and a manipulator, and I've been banished from participation. Anything I say will be written off either as sabotage or as an attempt to usurp Madam's committee!"

Ranze couldn't help smiling. "Yes, and now, I suppose, I'm an accomplice to your conspiracy!"

As cosponsors of the bill, each of the committee members was required to follow the introductory speech with one of support. Troung Vhat looked subdued, giving voice to words that were obviously not her own. Jaime Tyree of Jonica and Aronow of Sostis both sounded resigned. Ranze felt an unexpected rush of gratitude that she wouldn't be next on the docket.

As Aronow returned to his bench, the officiator reached for his desk buzzer. Its harsh tone cut through the murmurs rising around the chamber, and he said, "The floor is now open for discussion of the proposed Tohh bill number two hundred thirty-seven."

The last word hadn't even cleared his mouth before

half the Assembly was on its feet, hands waving for the officiator's attention like prayer ribbons in a wind, and the mutters erupted into a roar. Ranze and Broudy, still seated, exchanged glances as the officiator held down his buzzer.

"Assemblyman Radeleff of Sjenlund," he said when the shouts subsided. "The floor is yours."

Percy Radeleff of Sjenlund's southern continent of Andolyn made a polite bow to the officiator as his colleagues sank back into their seats. Then he turned toward DeByes. "My dear madam," he said, "I find it difficult to believe that a bill such as this was actually brought before this Assembly!" He kept his voice quiet and so unhurried that he seemed about to lapse into the drawl of his native tongue, but Ranze knew him well enough to recognize his reined-in passion. He had opposed the Isselan Assistance Agreement with similar quiet vehemence.

No one knew why the Issel Sector was such a sore spot with Radeleff. It was like the war grudge harbored by combat veterans, Ranze thought—except that Radeleff hadn't fought in the War of Resistance. Nor, to the best of anyone's knowledge, had he lost loved ones in it. Still, whenever anyone mentioned Issel he was the first to declare it "a world full of sneaky, deceptive, untrustworthy jackals."

"What this bill amounts to," he continued, "is political prostitution! You're asking us to sleep with the enemy in exchange for alien wealth—the *same* enemy that we've spent the last thirty years beating away from our doors! With all due respect, madam, I ask that you take this bill and consign it to the sewage treatment plant where it was spawned!"

A number of people applauded as Radeleff sat down, but more were on their feet, seeking an opportunity to speak. The officiator called next on Assemblyman Benigno of Kaleo.

"Unlike my esteemed colleague from Sjenlund," Benigno said, "I am unwilling to consign this proposal to the sewage just yet. However, I do have a number of concerns, madam, which your bill does not appear to address. I refer specifically to *conditions* for Issel's readmission. I would hope that the government of Issel would be required to meet certain criteria—in the area of human rights, for example, or abandonment of certain weapons development programs—before it would be granted full membership. I feel that a probationary period would be advisable—five years, perhaps. Therefore, I propose an amendment . . ."

"What about Issel's subject worlds, Na Shiv and Adriat?" asked Assemblywoman Natac of Yan when she rose after Benigno. "If Issel comes in, the others will surely want to follow. What impact will that have on interstellar economics? What impact on defense issues? What impact will it have on this very Assembly? Have we given any thought to the costs and risks of expansionism as well as to the benefits?"

It was going to be a long term in the Assembly, Ranze thought. Exchanging a glance with Broudy, she made her face as expressionless as possible and settled deeper into her seat to watch.

"I'm going to start you back on your regular PT schedule tomorrow," Dr. Moses had said during evening rounds. "Your vital signs are fine, Jink, and you're starting to get restless."

He *was* restless, Lujan had to admit. He hadn't recognized the release physiotherapy provided for his mind, despite the demands it made of his body, until Libby had curtailed it after the surgery. Four days of recovery time was enough. He released a full breath in a rush. "Thank you."

Even through these days without therapy, the cramps and spasms and unpredictable contractions of random muscles—sometimes of whole muscle groups—had persisted.

"That's called tone, sir," Meles had told him when it first began. "The flexor and the extensor muscles are out of balance. They're supposed to oppose each other, but right now it's more like a tug-of-war going back and forth because there isn't any control."

It *felt* like a tug-of-war, Lujan thought. The twitches and jerks often woke him at night. Often left him in pain.

As they did tonight.

Exhausted but sleepless, he finally turned from his side onto his back and said, "Holovid on."

He heard its click, its ripple into electronic life. He didn't have to worry about its setting; Darcie and Tristan didn't watch it while they were with him, and the only thing he cared to listen to was the Global News Network.

There was an interview in progress. A female voice was asking, "What, in your opinion, madam, was the Assembly's general response to the bill?"

"Overall," another woman's voice replied, "the response was fairly positive. Of course, various people have expressed their desires to me to see this matter brought up, especially since Operation Liberation, so I probably shouldn't have been surprised that it was so well received."

Operation Liberation. Lujan's brow wrinkled under the foam bandaging. That was the name that had been given to the Isselan Assistance mission. "Volume up," he said.

"What do you see as the greatest obstacle to getting this bill passed?" the interviewer asked.

"War of Resistance attitudes," came the response. "The only real opposition came from exactly the people I expected, from the conservative faction in the Assembly." The unidentified talk show guest pronounced the word "conservative" as if it were sour on her tongue.

"And by 'conservative' you mean—?"

"I mean the members of the Assembly who've been around since the War of Resistance and still base all of their voting decisions on the political views of that period, no matter how ill-advised those views may now be."

"Thank you for clarifying that." By the tone, Lujan could imagine the newswoman's nod of neutral acknowledgment. "What are your personal feelings on this matter?"

"There've been a lot of changes in the Issel system over the past several months," the other woman said, her voice growing earnest. "Since Sector General Mordan Renier died last year—and he seems to have been the focal point for all the hostility toward Issel—it's become a much freer and more open society."

The hostility toward Issel? Lujan furrowed his brow, listening. *Who is this woman and where has she been for the last thirty years? Living in the Issel Sector?*

"Right now," the guest continued, "Issel's economy is struggling, due largely to Governor Renier's military buildup of the past several years. And now, since the masuk invasion, there isn't enough of that military capability left for Issel to defend her own people."

Lujan bristled, lying there on his back. It wasn't the masuk invasion that had cost Issel its military strength! Almost exactly a year ago Issel had launched its war fleets, backed with masuk allies, against the Unified

Worlds—specifically against Sostis. It had been Unified forces, in a defensive action that had cost thousands of Unified lives, that had decimated Issel's war machine.

Lujan hadn't lost to his injuries the memories of the battles at Buhlig and Saede. He could still see *Destrier*'s hangar deck, gutted by an Isselan limpet mine attached to a battle-damaged fighter. He could still smell the smoke and feel the heat and hear the scream of the warning sirens in the Combat Information Center. He still had nightmares of watching the Unified carrier *Ichorek,* as if through the viewscreen of *Destrier*'s bridge, tumbling in space and spilling its artificial atmosphere in the form of pyrotechnics before a final blast tore it to spinning fragments.

The Unified Worlds had lost five thousand personnel with *Ichorek* alone. He would probably never be able to forget the horror of it, as much as he wanted to.

He lay rigid by now, his teeth clenched hard with his anger.

But the woman was still speaking. "It's time we remembered," she said, "that Issel was one of the original members of the Unified Worlds. It's time for us to study the history of that era objectively and recognize that the Unified Worlds themselves are at fault for the ostracism and isolation of Issel, which precipitated the tensions of these last decades. It's time we placed the blame for those tensions where it's due. It's time we realized that the Unified Worlds stepped beyond the bounds of their authority when they removed Mordan Renier from his rightful governorship and banished him from Sostis, his own motherworld."

Lujan could feel his pulse pounding hard in his head, in his gut. Not fast. Just *hard,* as if his blood pressure were rising along with his fury.

He had also witnessed Renier's act of treason during

the War of Resistance—had barely survived it, in fact. And he'd seen how the people of Sostis, acting alone, had exacted their retribution.

Nor was he a stranger to the altered historical account this woman had just recited. Unified collector ships picked it up when it was broadcast over Isselan newsnets each year as part of the commemoration of Renier's assumption of power. It was Isselan propaganda, pure and simple, as old as the conflict itself.

"With this bill," the guest speaker concluded, "I hope we can begin to right the wrongs of our past. I truly believe we owe Issel that much, at least."

"Thank you, madam." The interviewer paused, then said, "I've just been speaking with the Honorable Madam Abigail DeByes, head of Tohh's delegation to the Assembly, and author and sponsor of the new proposal to consider readmission of Issel into the Unified Worlds. Viewing participants who desire to do so may now enter their questions or comments by . . ."

Lujan ignored the routine instructions for interaction. His mind was reeling.

A bill to consider the readmission of Issel into the Unified Worlds.

His head ached with the pounding of his pulse, his jaw ached from clenching his teeth, but the rest of his body seemed strengthless with shock.

A bill to consider the readmission of Issel into the Unified Worlds.

And Abigail DeByes had been quoting Isselan propaganda, almost verbatim from Issel's anniversary broadcasts.

He wondered suddenly if that history were available through such open sources as an archives or library. His only access to it had come through classified channels.

He wondered briefly at the level of security clearances

granted to junior members of the Assembly—or how De-Byes had managed to have the account declassified.

One basic question would either resolve it or steer him in the right direction to pursue it. He drew a deep breath, let it out slowly to ease the throbbing in his head, and swallowed. "Access Global Interact line from Win-Med holovid six-four-three," he said through his synthesizer. "Interact in audio, please."

He heard a sequence of tones like a visiphone code being entered, followed by a buzz, a click, and then a genderless synthesized voice: "Thank you for your participation with Global News. All Interact lines are currently being utilized. Please state your question or comment and it will be processed in the order in which it was received."

"I'd like to know the source of the account of Unified Worlds history referred to by Assemblywoman DeByes at the end of the preceding interview," Lujan said.

"Thank you," said the voice from the holovid. "Please be patient. Your input will be processed promptly."

Lujan sighed and tried to relax as computer-generated music replaced the computer-generated voice.

If DeByes's account had come from an open source, the response would provide the title, author, and its location in the document, as well as the library or archives at which the document was stored. If the source was classified, it would be stated simply as unavailable to the public.

He waited for some time, so long that he began to idly wonder how many people in Global's broadcast area actually participated in news programs in the middle of the night, or if the number of Interact lines available differed between nighttime and daytime hours.

His pulse calmed gradually; the tension in his body ebbed. The tumult of questions about the interview was beginning to fade into semiwakeful nightmares by the time the music abruptly cut off and the voice came on again.

"This response is for Win-Med holovid six-four-three," it said.

It startled Lujan back to full wakefulness.

"The source of the account of Unified Worlds history referred to by Assemblywoman DeByes in the interview is unknown," said the voice. "Do you have any further inputs?"

Unknown? Lujan wrinkled his brow under the bandage foam. He'd never received that response before.

"Do you have any further inputs?" the voice repeated.

"Yes," Lujan said. "Is the source of that account classified?"

"Thank you," the voice said once more. "Please be patient. Your input will be processed promptly."

The wait was much shorter this time. "This response is for Win-Med holovid six-four-three," the voice said after only a moment. "The source of that account is unknown. Do you have any further inputs?"

"No," Lujan said. "Thank you. End interaction, holovid off."

The source is unknown.

Lujan lay awake for a long time after that. *If that history isn't available through open sources,* he thought, *and if it didn't come from classified sources, then where did Assemblywoman DeByes get it?*

SIXTEEN

"Well done, Mistress DeByes," Remarq murmured. On his desk terminal's monitor, the commentator from Sostis's Global News Network was wrapping up Ramiscal City's late night *News in Depth* show. As the network segued into its next program, Remarq nodded to himself. "A most persuasive performance."

But it was only one step in the journey to pass his proposal into law. Most of the responses to its presentation in the Assembly had been skeptical at best, expressing concerns about ideology and calling for conditions or limitations to Issel's membership. At worst, they had been adamantly hostile to the very idea. It would take a good deal more persuasion to bring Issel's readmission to a majority vote in the Unified Worlds Assembly.

Perhaps, Remarq thought, it was time to start calling for reinforcements. Time to start reminding various influential people of the favors they owed to the Isselan government. He smiled to himself.

"Exit news program," he said, "and access mail."

The monitor blinked; the mail display appeared.

"Compose message," Remarq said. "Address it to the Honorable Seamus Trosvig, Headquarters of the Unified Worlds, Ramiscal City, Sostis."

He sat back in his chair, steepling his fingers as the routing blocks filled themselves in, and said, "Begin dictation.

"My dear friend Seamus, I noted with great interest the proposal of a bill in your Assembly to consider the readmission of our homeworld into the Unified Worlds. I assure you that we are deeply touched by this gesture.

"I was also personally impressed with the interview given by your assemblywoman DeByes, and with her correct portrayal of the history of the Isselan world government. Please relay to her my deepest appreciation.

"However"—Remarq shifted forward in his chair and interlaced his hands on the desktop—"on viewing segments of the testimony offered in the Assembly at the bill's presentation, it is painfully evident that your Madam DeByes will not be able to accomplish her purpose without assistance. Therefore, over the next several weeks I will forward to you the names of individuals who are in a position to provide support, along with instructions on how to make contact with each of them. Some of them are delegates; some are members of delegation staffs.

"You are to contact these persons one or two at a time and at random intervals in order to preclude any suspicious appearance," Remarq said, "and instruct them to announce and vote in favor of the readmission proposal. They are also to take an active role in persuading the other members of their respective delegations to vote in its favor. They are free to use whatever reason they choose to explain their conversion to support of the bill."

Remarq paused then. He looked directly into his monitor's recorder, his features grim. "You may find some, Seamus, who will be reticent to cooperate. Please advise them that failure to comply with the terms of their agreements will result in the most serious consequences. There are a number of Isselan Enforcers scattered through the Unified

Worlds whom I can call up at a moment's notice. It would be truly unfortunate if that were to become necessary."

Remarq paused again to reinforce his point, then offered a momentary smile. "I appreciate your efforts, Seamus. If there is any way in which we can be of further assistance, please do not hesitate to contact either myself or Dr. Zlatkis Haken, Minister of Interplanetary Relations."

He played the message through when he finished recording it, listening to the choice of words, the intonation. Satisfied, he said, "Execute message self-erasure upon computer decoding. Confirm with authenticator code Echo Victor."

Tapping the MSG RELEASE pad, he leaned back in his high-backed chair and smiled once more.

"Sir, it looks like the Sorter 560 is acting up again."

Lieutenant Commander Nemec looked up from his desk terminal with a sigh of exasperation. *"Again?"*

"Yes sir." First Lieutenant Aechie Gurda, Sostis Surface Forces, stood at nervous attention in Nemec's office doorway.

As the new officer in charge of the Unified Worlds Headquarters Communications Center, Nemec had eighteen subordinates: four company grade officers and fourteen enlisted personnel who covered both day and night shifts. He was also responsible for seven molecular-level communications computers that processed all mail and message traffic received by or originated from the headquarters.

Rising from his desk, he asked, "Are the message counts from the other Sorters still consistent?"

"Yes sir." Gurda made a puzzled gesture and moved out of the doorway to let him pass. "It was fine at the beginning of the shift," he added, following Nemec across the main room. "Same count all the way down the line."

It had barely been two standard hours since shift change, Nemec noted with a glance at a timepanel on one wall. This was his fourth day on the job—and the old Model 560 in the back room had pulled this stunt from the first day he'd arrived.

"How long has it been doing this?" he asked Gurda over his shoulder. "Did this ever happen before I started here?"

"Actually, sir"—Gurda looked sheepish—"it's been miscounting for about two or three months now."

Nemec stopped short. "And Lieutenant Colonel Feibush didn't do anything about it?"

"He did everything he could, sir, right down to reprogramming it—several times," Gurda said. "It'd be fine for two or three days, sometimes as long as a week or so, and then—blitzo!—off it'd go again."

"He never called in any computer maintenance specialists?" Nemec asked. "No work order?"

"It started just before his transfer orders came, sir," said Gurda. "Completing all the evaluations and reports before his transfer had him on a pretty rigorous schedule as it was."

There was still no excuse, Nemec thought, for his predecessor to have left such a problem uncorrected. He had better things to do than clean up other people's messes. Things like conducting communications surveillance for Admiral Serege.

Motion sensors activated lighting as he stepped into the back room where the Sorter 560 stood. He eyed the tiny window of its message-counting cell.

Sure enough, it was two messages too high. He shook his head.

What was the purpose of keeping a spare computer in this back room, anyway? he wondered. And why hadn't the spare been upgraded, like the Model 1020s in the main room, if it was so important? The thing was so old it could well be just feeling its age.

"Want me to reset it, sir?" Gurda asked from behind him.

"No." Nemec gave the computer's boxy top a couple of absent thumps with his fist. "No, we'll leave it the way it is so the maintenance folks can see what it's doing. I'm submitting a work order right now."

And he knew exactly the team he needed.

"Aechie, I need for you to call Security Management," he told the lieutenant a little later, and handed him a microwriter with two names and ID numbers glowing on its display. "Get a clearance verification on these two; they're supposed to be coming in this afternoon to have a look at our mathematically inept 560—if their workload permits."

It was practically time for changeover to night shift by the time Spherzah Captain Migdal Chorafas and Lieutenant Itato Toshiro arrived at Communications' shielded entrance. Its monitor announced them only after its IR hand scanner had confirmed identity and clearances, and then Lieutenant Gurda admitted them through the cipherlocked door and logged them in.

"Our apologies for the lateness of the hour, sir," said Lieutenant Toshiro, shouldering her case of testing equipment. "We get to each job in the order it's called in."

"I expected as much." Nemec gave her a grin. "It's a wonder you two get any off-duty time at all!" He gestured in the direction of the 560's closet. "This way."

He noticed how Chorafas took in the main computer room with one sweeping look as they strode across it. "You really like working in caves, don't you, Ajimir?" the captain said under his breath.

Nemec ventured a dim smile. "If a subbasement qualifies as a cave . . . At least here I can get out for a breath of fresh air when I want to, and I can use my real name." During his deep-cover assignment on Issel II a couple of years earlier he'd not been able to do either.

Chorafas responded with a dim smile of his own, one that said he understood exactly what Nemec meant.

Nemec knew he had good cause to. Chorafas had twice turned down promotions to rear admiral, preferring direct operations at the Unified Worlds's frontier sensor sites, and had only returned to Sostis a year or so before for medical reasons. Quiet and inconspicuous in a group, he tended to blend into the background; but no detail escaped him.

Toshiro, though a relative newcomer to the Spherzah, was no less an asset. Her scientific background ran the gamut from molecular-level computers to particle physics, and she had good common sense besides. But her greatest strength in troubleshooting was asking the right questions.

"So this's the computer that's forgotten how to count," Chorafas said as they entered the 560's cubicle. He shook his head at the absurdity of it. "How big is the discrepancy now?"

"It has a higher count by three," said Nemec. "It was fine at shift change this morning."

Chorafas grunted at that. "Let's have a look," he said.

With both Nemec and Lieutenant Gurda looking on, they ran the Model 560 through three separate batteries of tests. There were no viruses, no readily apparent programming errors. But as she finished, Toshiro slipped Nemec a stealthy hand signal.

Nemec promptly glanced at his timepiece. "Aechie, why don't you go do the changeover in-brief for the night shift," he said. "I can keep an eye on these two for a couple of minutes."

"Yes sir," Gurda said, and left the room.

And Nemec asked, "What is it?"

"What if," Toshiro said in a near whisper, "this is the only computer that's really correct?"

Nemec and Chorafas exchanged glances. "What makes you think that?" Nemec asked.

"An interesting variation from the usual message-receiving programming," said Toshiro, "—and a gut feeling." She drummed her fingers on the top of the errant computer. "Is there any way we could run a couple of tests on the hardware in the main room, too, sir?"

"What kind of tests?" Nemec asked.

Toshiro looked him directly in the eye. "Real-time ultrahigh-speed sample capture-and-freeze," she said.

Nemec's eyebrows shot up. "How will you justify that?"

She began drumming her fingers again. Flicked a glance toward the door at a movement outside as Lieutenant Gurda returned. "The only thing I could find," she said aloud, "was a glitch in a couple of the older program memory chips. Those'll be easy enough to replace. But if maintenance on your 1020s out there"—she jerked a thumb toward the doorway—"has been as spotty as it appears to have been on this 560, you could have any one of them pulling the same trick by next month."

Nemec shifted his stance against the computer's cabinet and sighed wearily for Lieutenant Gurda's benefit, as if resigning himself to the fact that it was going to be a long night. "Might as well get it done while we've got you both here," he said. "Who knows when we'd be able to get you back again."

He turned to Gurda. "Looks like I'm going to be here for a couple more hours. Is Lieutenant Slentz out there yet?"

"Yes sir."

"Tell her I may need her to spell me off with the security monitoring." He indicated Chorafas and Toshiro. "Then you can go ahead and call it a day."

Night shift was half over by the time the capture-and-freeze tests were completed. Packing her scanners back into their kit, Toshiro said loudly enough for the night personnel to hear, "You're fortunate, sir; the rest of these traffic handlers are clean. But they really need to be checked annually for failing memory chips. That'll prevent any more problems like the one in the back."

"Fine." Nemec muffled a yawn. "Let's get the 560 back up so you two can get out of here." He dismissed Slentz to her duty station. "Thanks, Lieutenant."

At the back room, he leaned in the doorway to screen Chorafas and Toshiro from his night crew while they worked. "What're your conclusions?" he asked quietly.

Toshiro patted the old Sorter. "This one really *is* the only computer with the correct count," she said. "The capture-and-freeze tests proved that."

"Explain," said Nemec.

She seated herself at the keyboard. "Every so often," she said as her fingers flew over the keys, "a message passes through the system in fragments, but the evidence of that passage is being immediately erased. It looks like some very skillful reprogramming at the source. This is the only computer in which those message fragments aren't being erased."

Nemec's eyebrows arched. "Why is that?"

"Its message-handling program is different," said Chorafas. "It was undoubtedly done by a different team of programmers as a double-check system. As far as I can tell, all the pieces of those messages erased by your other computers are being recorded in here. I suspect they're in their original form, too, without any decryption or execution of internal programs."

A sort of shivery sensation started at the nape of Nemec's neck and began to crawl down his spine. He had expected to find information for Admiral Serege in the normal flow of message traffic in bits and pieces over a long period of time. But this—

"Any idea who the source is?" he asked.

"Not right now," said Chorafas. "But if you'll help us

get those messages out of here"—the sweep of his hand indicated the Communications Center—"I can dig it out for you."

"Sure." Nemec nodded. His mouth was dry.

"Meanwhile," Chorafas said with a small gesture at his counterpart, "Itato is adjusting the program. When she's done, this computer will take its counting cues from the ones in the other room and give that number if it should be interrogated; but it'll keep identifying and recording your phantom messages."

"I'm adding a limited tracer program, too," said Toshiro. "I'm having to make it a passive one; otherwise, the trace will be discovered in other computer nets."

"Right." Nemec's pulse raced at his temples, at his throat.

It took most of another hour to relocate and record all the fragmented messages and conceal them in molecular-level memory units on separate boards of the test equipment.

"We'll take care of the report," Chorafas said. " 'Failing memory chips were discovered and replaced.' And I'll contact you once we know what this is." He hoisted the equipment case containing the memory components.

"Thank you, Mig." Nemec felt shaky. "I'll have Lieutenant Slentz conduct the standard scan protocol of your testing equipment and log you both out of here."

The call from Chorafas came five days later. "There's a little get-together this evening with some of our old buddies," he said. "Thought you might like to join us. If you want to come by the shop when you get off duty, we can ride out together."

"Sounds good," Nemec said without hesitation. "I'll see you this evening."

He was stiff with tension by the time he arrived at the Computer Security and Maintenance vault. He wiped his hand down his trouser leg before placing it on the IR scan plate.

Chorafas admitted him once it had confirmed his clearances. He didn't bother with a greeting. "Come back to my work space," he said.

Lieutenant Toshiro was the only other person in the shop at this hour. Nemec nodded to her as he followed the older man back through the maze of work cubicles.

Entering his space, Chorafas crossed toward a terminal perched on a stand in one corner. The desktop—and every other horizontal surface in the office, Nemec noticed—was stacked with odds and ends of testing equipment, hand tools, technical microreaders, curled strands of optical fiber and electrical wire, and handfuls of memory chips of all types and sizes. Even the chair was filled with assorted junk. Chorafas simply reached over it all and tapped a rapid sequence into the keypad.

As a display filled the monitor, he said, "This's part of one message fragment."

Nemec leaned closer to look, forehead wrinkling. What he saw made his eyes widen. Made him release a low whistle. "Whoever encrypted this," he said, "is *good.*"

Chorafas nodded. "It refers to another message. Gives the pattern of words to select from that message. I think we got that one the other night, too."

"Let's see if we can find it," Nemec said. He pulled a case of testing equipment over in front of the computer stand and sat down on it.

They never did make it to the social—if there really was one. After four hours, Nemec straightened on his makeshift seat and met the other's look. "There's the routing string," he said.

This message, at least, had originated on Issel. From the central government communications system in the capital city of Sanabria, in fact. It had been sent to

Mythos, to the headquarters of the delegation to the Assembly there, by way of the Isselan embassy, and then forwarded to the offices of the Triune here on Sostis. To the office of the Honorable Seamus Trosvig, to be exact.

"Who's the sender?" said Chorafas.

"Issel's new chief cabinet minister," said Nemec. He tapped the monitor with a finger. "One Seulemont Remarq."

This time it was Chorafas who let out the whistle. "That guy's been around forever, hasn't he? Are you sure it isn't just somebody else using his name? He couldn't possibly still be living, could he?"

"It's him." Nemec's tone turned grim with certainty. "Stealth is his modus operandi. It always has been."

"Looks like he wasn't quite stealthy enough this time." Chorafas leaned closer over Nemec's shoulder. "So what's he up to?"

"I don't know." Nemec creased his dark brow. "I haven't gotten that far yet."

It took another five hours to decrypt the whole message and piece it together. By then Nemec's back and shoulders burned with the strain of sitting hunched on the equipment case. "Okay," he said at last, stretching, and grimaced at jabs like small electrical shocks through his muscles. "I think this is it." He touched the DISPLAY key—

A block of text unfurled itself down the monitor.

Chorafas's features grew more and more grave as he read, his brows lowering and drawing together.

"She's a sleeper!" he murmured finally. "These are instructions for activating her!"

Nemec nodded. "Looks like it, doesn't it? And Trosvig, too."

"Or maybe Trosvig's been a mole all these years." Chorafas straightened. "His mate used to be an Isselan agent, you know—maybe she still is." He fell silent for a moment. "Makes you wonder how much Remarq had to do with the assassination plot, doesn't it? Put his man right into a top slot."

"For ruthlessness," said Nemec, "I wouldn't put it past him; but he usually works more subtly than that."

They both sat in silence for several minutes, staring at nothing. Staring into the depths of their fears.

"You know this is probably just the tip of the iceberg," Chorafas said at last. "This is only one message, after all; who knows what else we'll find when we get the rest of 'em broken." He paced a few steps in his cubicle. "I have no idea whom we dare tell about this."

"There's only one man I'd trust with it," said Nemec. "There's absolutely no question of where Admiral Serege stands."

"Too late, Aj," Chorafas said from behind him. "He's been retired. It went through just before you all got back."

"I know that." Nemec pivoted around on the equipment case to look at the other directly. "That's to our advantage, actually. He's out of the net." He shrugged. "He's no longer a factor as far as—Trosvig, say—is concerned."

"But he's disabled—"

"In body," said Nemec, "but not in mind. Don't write the Old Man off yet. . . . I think I'll stop by to see him tomorrow." He shoved himself up from his improvised seat. "You and I, however, had better not be seen together too often; it could arouse suspicions. Wait until you get a large set decrypted to contact me again. I'll be interested to know what else you find in those message fragments."

SEVENTEEN

"It'll be a while before you'll really be able to see again, sir," Dr. Gavril cautioned as he peeled back the bandage foam. "Don't expect to recognize anything at first. It's going to take time."

When the foam lifted away, Lujan blinked at abrupt brightness and found himself squinting, as if at the glare of a sun. There was faint movement somewhere—at one side? Above him? He wasn't certain, but it made him dizzy. "How much time?" he asked.

"It could be a few weeks," Gavril said.

A few weeks? Lujan thought. It had only taken three days for the roar of the ventilation to fade into the background of his aural awareness. "Why so long?" he asked.

"Vision, like hearing, is a learned sense," Gavril said, "but it's even more complex. Since you've been without sight for over two months now, your brain will have to relearn to interpret the signals it receives—everything from colors and patterns to tracking movement and depth perception. We can help you with some visual exercises, sir, but as was the case with your hearing, time will be the best therapist."

He paused, then asked, "What can you perceive right now, sir?"

"Light glaring in my face." Lujan said it with an irritation born of disappointment. *A few weeks!*

"That's to be expected after being without any light at all for this long," the neurosurgeon said. "The room lighting's only at thirty percent of normal right now, but we can lower it further."

"Try ten percent," said Lujan.

The lighting's diminishment cut the glare but made little difference otherwise. The suggestion of movement around him was still only that, with no semblance of shape or color or even of direction.

"The bruising is almost gone," Dr. Moses's voice said from his right. He started at a gentle finger touching his face just beneath the lower lid of his right eye; he hadn't even seen it coming. She only asked, "Is there still tenderness?"

"A little," he said.

"I'll have the tech apply some salve," Moses said, "and we'll keep the lights turned down in here for the next day or two so you can adjust to it gradually."

"You may experience sensory overload at first," Gavril said. "When it starts to get overwhelming, sir, just close your eyes for a while and allow yourself a rest period. Likewise, take a rest if you start to develop a headache. You're probably trying too hard to make your eyes focus."

Lujan suspected that he'd spend a great deal of time at first with his eyes closed.

He had already been visited twice over the past two days by a language pathologist, a brisk middle-aged woman who introduced herself only as Hegold.

"I'm going to start with a series of palatometric tests," she said the first time. "We need to determine what speech capability you have right now and establish a baseline from which to measure your progress."

She slipped a lightweight plasticine plate into his mouth, tucking it snugly up against the roof. "The plate has sixty-four tiny electrodes arranged in a specific pattern," she said. "As you pronounce the list of words I'll give you, your tongue will contact certain sensors, which will form a display on my monitor. I'll use that to determine where your weaknesses are and how best to help strengthen them."

Sounds just like an inspector general, Lujan thought with a grimace.

The series of tests had taken well over two hours and left his mouth aching, as if he'd spent the whole time chewing vigorously at a piece of tough meat.

"We'll need to begin with some exercises," Hegold said when she finished. "There's a pronounced weakness of the tongue and lips."

She returned twice each day after that, between his sessions in the rehab room, to put his mouth through its own calisthenics.

He should have realized by that time, he thought—especially after all the other therapies he'd been subjected to for the past several weeks—that there would be such a thing as isotonic and isometric exercises for the mouth as well. Hegold made him suck water through a drinking tube, and blow through the tube into water. She made him purse up his lips and hold them that way as long as he could, then draw his lips back as if he were snarling and hold them there. She made him stick out his tongue and pull it back in, and move it up and down and from side to side in his mouth. Sometimes even his upper throat was sore when she finished.

She spent a great deal of time drilling him on the pronunciation of individual vowels and consonants as well: "No, that's still *ah.* I want to hear *ay. Ah-hh. Ay-yy.* Can you hear the difference?"

Lujan nodded.

"Good. Bring your tongue up higher—you should feel it touching your top teeth on both sides—and let your mouth widen a little more here." She pressed at his cheeks with her fingers. "Now try again: *ay-yy.*"

Lujan drew a breath, closed his eyes. *"Ah-hh-ay."* He was surprised at the effort it took, at the way it tightened his throat.

"Better," said Hegold. "Again. *Ay-yy.*"

He let out his breath. Drew another. *"Ay-yy."*

"Good." It was terse. "Now again."

On the sixth day she'd taken away the voice synthesizer. "If it's there, you'll be tempted to fall back on it," she said. "Without it, you'll be more motivated to speak."

She could have at least waited until he could pronounce a few intelligible syllables, he thought. At that point he was still having a hard time making his vowel sounds distinguishable from one another.

That same night, the tingling began in his fingers. It woke him in the darkness and he lay there, sleepless, as the tingle increased to a buzz.

It was the same sensation he'd felt in his torso and legs as their nerves began to revive, the same tingling he'd felt in his face after the trigeminal nerves were repaired.

It was most pronounced in his left hand. He tried to tighten his fingers into a fist. Tried next to straighten them.

If there was any movement, he couldn't feel it.

He lifted his hand up in front of his face and tried to move his fingers again.

If there was movement, he couldn't see it, either. In the darkness, his hand was only a black smudge against a nearly black background.

At least in the darkness the colors were right.

He sighed heavily and let his hand fall to his side. But he kept trying to flex and extend it, flex and extend, whether he could see it or feel it or not. He kept trying until the effort tired him, and he finally sank back into sleep.

When he woke again, the room was no longer dark and a shadow was leaning over him—leaning so far over him it seemed it would fall across him! He recoiled.

"I'm sorry, sir. I didn't mean to startle you."

The voice was that of Hanada, his day med.tech, but the shape still leaning at an impossible angle above him looked like a child's watercolor left out in the rain: a blur of indeterminable colors.

He supposed that was an improvement; up until a few days ago Hanada had been only a voice and a pair of careful hands in the nothingness.

Still, this visual bombardment was going to drive him crazy before it sorted itself out. Not only was there no semblance of depth perception, but every angle was skewed and colors simply didn't make sense. Nor, for the time being, did he seem to have any peripheral vision. Everything, even from the sides, seemed to be at the forefront of his sight, demanding his attention at all times. He wasn't certain whether it was part of the optical readjustment, or whether the acuity had been increased across his whole field of vision.

When Libby came in a little later, she leaned over him at the same startling angle Hanada had—and he recoiled again.

"It's just me, Jink," she said. "You're really not seeing things."

That's the whole problem, he thought. *I'm not seeing anything!*

His frustration mounted when the synthesizer didn't give voice to the thought and he abruptly remembered its removal. He settled for responding with a "Humph."

It wasn't until Pilita arrived with his breakfast that he remembered the previous night's tingling in his hands. It seemed suddenly essential that he tell her. He raised his left hand from the blanket—

He didn't have the voice synthesizer and Pilita didn't know the dot code; he'd tried before to use it to communicate with her. He had to try to speak. If he could make her understand one word . . .

"M-m. M-m-m," he said. At least his lips could form that sound.

" 'Scuse me, sir?" said Pilita.

He held up his hand. "M-mm-ma-a-ah."

It seemed to take forever to pronounce the single syllable, and then it was the wrong vowel. *Move,* he wanted to say. *Is there movement?*

Pilita's shape, hovering like a specter over the bed, was very still. "Say again, sir?" she said after several seconds.

Lujan tried to flex his fingers, tried to extend them. "M-mm-muh-uh," he managed.

Closer, but not enough for the therapist to understand. "More?" she asked. He could imagine her eyebrows crinkled together. "Do you mean more, sir?"

He shook his head. Moved his whole forearm then, and his wrist. "M-muh-uh," he said. His mouth simply wouldn't shape an *oo* sound yet. "Mm-muh-uh-ff!"

Another long pause. Lujan could almost feel Pilita's puzzlement. And then, "Oh!" she said. "Move! Is that it, sir?"

Close enough. He nodded.

"What moved, sir? Your hand?" She took his left one between both of her own. "Let's see. Try to move it for me."

Eyes closed, he visualized the foam ball in his hand. Visualized his fingers wrapping around it, pressing indentations into its surface . . .

Pilita's gasp snapped his eyes open. "That's it!" she said. "Once more, sir!"

He felt it that time: a mere flicker through his forefinger as he tried to curl it.

"Again!" she said.

He did it five or six times on her command before she said, "It's definitely controlled movement! It's a start, sir. Wait till I tell Dr. Gavril!" And like a ghost in a mist, she was gone.

Lujan lapsed back on the pillows and closed his eyes. *Thank you, God!* he thought, with all the focus of his soul.

Lujan sighed as the servo placed him in the bed. Sighed, and lay still with his eyes closed—just lay there and felt his useless legs throbbing from the strain of the workout.

"Luj?" Darcie's watercolor shape stroked sweaty hair off his forehead. "What is it?"

Isn't it obvious? he thought. He wanted to shout it, but—he couldn't.

He couldn't even shout.

I can't walk! he thought. *I may never walk again.*

It was the first time since he'd emerged from the coma, nearly two and a half months before, that he'd really considered that possibility. He'd refused to accept that it was even there, had denied it with every push and every pull on the rehab mat during the intervening weeks, and so far he had kept it at bay, just outside his periphery. This was the first time he had allowed that dark chance to actually edge into his mind.

He swallowed, remembering long hikes across Anchenko's red rock desert and torturous climbs up the sheer walls of Lost Prospector Canyon. He turned his head away from Darcie's touch in sudden bitterness.

"Luj," she said again, more quietly this time, "I was reading from *The Law of the Prophets* while you were down in therapy, and—I came across a passage that made me think of you."

She began to read: "'He gives power to the weak, and to those that have no might he gives new strength. They that wait for him shall be restored in might; they shall run and not be weary, and shall walk and not be faint.'"

They that wait for him . . . The words echoed in Lujan's mind as if they were meant as personal counsel. *They that wait* . . .

The phrase brought to mind another passage from the scripture:

". . . bear thine afflictions with patience, my son, for in his time shalt thy petition be answered."

The counsel *was* personal, as personal as it had been to the prophet who had recorded it.

Lujan closed his eyes and swallowed once more, against a guilty tightness in his throat. "Oh, Father, forgive me for my faithlessness," he prayed.

He would have to learn to wait.

Reconciled to that, Dr. Moses's news two days later came as a surprise. "Well, Jink," she said, "we're moving you to the Transition Quarters today. The chief of hospital security told me last night that the surveillance and alarm systems they've installed are finally operational and the security personnel are assigned. Besides, Sablon Meles says you're ready to start some PT work in the pool now, and you'll be a lot closer to the pool in Transition than you are here."

Set up like an apartment complex, the Transition Quarters were designed to house not only patients in rehabilitation but their immediate families as well. They had been designed that way for several reasons. While the patient benefited from the closeness and support of loved ones, family members also learned to deal with the demands of their patient's condition in areas ranging from caregiving and lifestyle adjustments to emotional acceptance. Besides training the families in necessary medical skills, Transition personnel were constantly on call for both medical assistance and psychological support.

Lujan arrived at the Transition Quarters in the late afternoon, sagging in the glidechair after his last therapy session of the day, and guarded through the maze of pedestrian tunnels by a full phalanx of Sostish soldiers. Though he kept his eyes closed through most of the journey, he was certain that his company of bodyguards attracted far more attention than did his daily sorties with Tristan. And the last thing he wanted right now was attention.

"Our flat is near the east end on the fourth level," Darcie told him as she guided the glidechair into a lift, "and it looks out over the park. It's—" She hesitated. "It's almost as splendid a view as the one from the Flag Officers' Residence."

Most of the phalanx had stayed behind on the main floor, Lujan saw when he opened his eyes on emerging from the lift. He and Darcie and one guard entered a corridor with dusty rose carpet and powder gray walls, and doors down its length on both sides for what seemed a dizzying distance.

After ten days unbandaged, his artificial eyes were starting to recognize colors; but shapes were still blurry and movement still jerky, as if seen by a rapidly flashing strobe light, and there was no depth perception at all.

"It looks like a rather expensive hotel," Darcie said for his benefit.

The rooms beyond the door they entered, however, were more homey than posh by Darcie's description. He could distinguish cream-colored walls, and carpeting in mottled shades of brown, but the details of the furnishings were lost. So were the rooms' actual sizes, though he had an impression of spaciousness.

Darcie steered his chair across the living area and up a short hall to the bedrooms. "This one is Tris's room," she said, indicating a door on the right, "and the next one is the bathroom. There's a safety seat in the hygiene booth, so you can finally take a real shower. And here's our room." She turned the chair through a door on the left. "I thought you might want to lie down for a while."

He was drained, exhausted both from therapy and from the move. It took all his remaining strength to hold himself upright in the glidechair, even with its upper torso straps. He nodded.

"Right. One moment." She maneuvered the chair up close to the bed, released its straps—and he almost toppled out of it.

Almost. Darcie caught him, pulling him up against her shoulder; and then in one continuous movement she turned him and seated him on the edge of the bed.

She didn't let go until he lay safely stretched out on the bed, and then all he could do was stare up at her.

"Pilita taught me this morning to do that," she said in reply to his openmouthed astonishment. "She called it a stand-pivot transfer. She said we'd need it here because this isn't a fluid suspension bed and there aren't any servos to lift you in and out of it. It really works, doesn't it?"

She sounded almost as amazed as he felt. Though he still couldn't make out her features, he couldn't help smiling.

"I'm going to make dinner," she said then. "Maybe we can just have dinner in here tonight."

He nodded approval. The less he had to move right now, the better.

They ate dinner in the bedroom, Darcie and Tristan in chairs drawn up beside the bed, all three of them with lap trays. It was the first meal they'd eaten together since—

Since when?

Since before Tristan left on the Issel mission, he supposed. He had no memory of their last meal together as a family. He wished he could remember.

Darcie had even made dessert: something cool and

sweet and thick that she said was served only for holidays on Adriat, her homeworld. "This feels like a holiday to me," she said. "We're finally all together again."

Tristan excused himself when dinner was finished. "The Anchenko Detachment is heading out for Topawa tomorrow," he said, "and I'd like to say good-bye to Kersce."

"It's just us now, love," Darcie said when their son had gone. "Would you rather shower now or wait for a bit?"

"Now," he managed.

She got him onto the hygiene booth's bench from the glidechair the same way she'd transferred him to the bed earlier. The touch of her arm about his bare shoulders remained, like the revival of some tender memory, as she made certain he was secure and then guided his hands to the safety holds and to the ON and OFF and temperature-control buttons. The buttons were large enough to be pressed with the heel or back of a hand instead of with strengthless fingers, and marked with color and tactile characters to accommodate patients with vision impairment.

"There's a voice pickup, too," Darcie said. "The whole flat is full of them, actually. When you finish, or if you need anything, Luj, just say so and I'll come."

He nodded.

He took his time in the shower—not that he could really do otherwise with his fingers' coordination still so limited and his vision so fuzzy. But he sat for some time after he'd finished washing. Sat there long after the lather had rinsed away. It wasn't just to relish the water's warm massage, its pulse upon his skin. It was a refuge, a place to think, to come to grips with—everything.

"Lujan?" Darcie's voice came over the intercom. "Are you all right?"

He actually jumped. "Ff-fi-in-nne," he said.

But he leaned his head back against the booth's wall and closed his eyes.

He couldn't walk. He could barely talk. What hope was there that he could ever make love to her?

He sat until the warm water ran out and began to grow cool, and then he shut off the water and punched on the fan.

Warm air whirled around him, drying him off. He ruffled through his wet hair with one clumsy hand, his vision fixed on what he figured must be the drain grid between his feet. Even then it was some time before he called for her.

Offering him his robe, Darcie asked, "Did that relieve the aching at all?"

He grunted a response as he wrestled his arms into the robe's sleeves and struggled to wrap its length about himself as best he could while seated. She simply waited, not rushing him, not trying to intercede, and he was grateful that she allowed him what little independence he still had.

She had changed into her nightgown while he was in the shower, and she'd let down her hair. It lay over her shoulder in a single loose braid that reached well below her waist. "You smell good," she said, close to his ear, as she rocked him forward against her shoulder and eased him back into the glidechair.

He understood the intent of her comment, her attempt to assure him that he was still desirable to her; but his anxiety and uncertainty kept him from answering. When he had to ask for her help to swing his legs up onto the bed, the knot of uneasiness in his gut tightened.

Darcie slid up close beside him when she turned out the light. She lay her head on his shoulder, and her hair brushed his jaw. She slipped an arm over his chest. Her body was warm and firm, pressed to his side. His heart hammered under her hand.

She sighed, as if she were laying down a burden. "This feels so good," she said quietly, and the warmth of her breath tickled his skin. "I've missed so much just being this close to you."

She shifted slightly against him, and every nerve in his body seemed to tingle with awareness of it. "I need for you to hold me," she whispered. "There've been so many times in the last few months when I've needed the security of your arms and I've needed to draw on your strength, and—" She broke off. "I just need to be held by you, Luj."

He knew he could at least do that. Freeing awkward arms of the bedcovers, he wrapped both of them tentatively about her.

His throat tightened with the emotion that produced: an ache for the hurts and fears she had suffered, a desire to protect her from any more heartaches, a fear that he couldn't even do that anymore.

He loosened his hold, let his arms slide away from her.

She lifted her head. "Luj?" she asked. In their nearness, even in the dark, he could see the way her eyes searched his for a long minute before she softly kissed his mouth.

That touch of her lips said more than words could have, assuring him that she understood his fears, that there would be plenty of time to face them and deal with them together, that all she wanted and needed tonight was his closeness.

He hesitated. Then he wrapped his arms around her once more.

She sighed at that, and snuggled back down on his shoulder.

"I'm taking you outside today, Father," Tristan said. "There's still a while before sunset, and it's almost warm right now."

It had been nearly three months since he'd last been outdoors, Lujan realized. The sealing of the treaty, according to Darcie and Jiron and others, had taken place in midwinter. It was early spring now, an unpredictable season that was likely to whip the ocean beyond Ramiscal

City with an icy gale on one day and bathe the sheer peaks behind it with pale sunshine on the next. Such sunny days were fleeting promises of warmer days to come, brief gifts to be appreciated for as long as they lasted.

"I'd li-ike th-at," Lujan said. His speech was still deliberate and occasionally slurred; some consonants and combinations were still difficult for his mouth to manage. But after two and a half weeks of speech therapy he at least had less trouble making himself understood. He shoved himself into the glidechair when Tristan drew it up beside the bed, and said, "Lifft-onn."

Darcie looked up from the kitchen terminal as they crossed toward the door. "Coats for both of you!" she said. "Just because it's above freezing outdoors today doesn't mean it's warm! Lujan, you should have a hat and a lap robe, too."

"Did yo-ou tell Se-cur-ity?" Lujan asked, pushing his arms into coat sleeves as they entered the carpeted hall.

"Yes sir," said Tristan. "Someone will meet us at the lift."

The park onto which the Transition Quarters' main entrance opened covered over six hectares. In the summer its mature trees shaded its numerous exercise paths like a vaulted roof of living green, but at this time of year the branches hung stark and barren beneath the bright sky.

There was almost no wind this afternoon, just an occasional restless gust off the ocean. Lujan inhaled deeply. He could almost taste the tang of the salt spray, the mustiness of last fall's leaves layered under the trees, and the spice of pines. A gray flicker of motion in the lattice of limbs caught his eye. The movement was shaky, the shape itself indistinct, but he knew it must be a silver sarapy, probably just out of hibernation. If the sarapies were stirring, the locals said, spring was close at hand.

A few meters ahead the path forked. A stand with a weather-yellowed monitor displayed destinations and a map with kilometer markings. Tristan placed a hand on Lujan's shoulder. "Take path to pond," he tapped with a finger concealed under Lujan's coat collar. "Nemec waiting there. Saw him at work. He has news."

Lujan gave a slight nod and said, loud enough for their two military escorts to hear, "Let's go-o fi-innd the ponnd."

That path ambled off to the left and wove lazily between the trees. It was surfaced, but the glidechair would have hovered just as easily over gravel or a trail buckled by protruding roots.

"Wide tu-urn—ri-ight," Lujan said as the path bent around a moss-furred boulder, and the chair swung gradually into an arc.

There was an open stretch beyond the boulder, a straight stretch fifty or sixty meters long with a couple of benches on either side. As if on cue, a muscular black man appeared at the opposite end of the clearing, jogging easily up the path toward them.

The two military policemen closed ranks, but as the man drew near enough to be recognized Tristan called out, "Ajimir! How's your ankle?"

Nemec slowed his pace and came to a stop before them. Lujan saw how he eyed the MPs with their hands hovering near their side arms and kept his distance. He was favoring his right foot, and panting. "I think it's had about enough therapy for one day!" he said. "I'm glad I ran into you two; it's a good excuse to take a break! How are you doing, sir?"

"Be-tte-er," Lujan said. "No-ot jog-ging, tho-ough."

Nemec grinned. "You probably will be sooner than you think, sir." He planted his right foot on the seat of the nearest bench and began to massage his ankle. "Man, I hope I didn't overdo it!"

Lujan glanced around. The light slanting through the park had turned golden as the sun began to roll down among the trees, and the fitful gusts were growing chillier. "Go ba-ack soonn," he said. "Co-ome with uss?"

"Fine with me, sir," Nemec said. "Let me rub this out a little first."

They turned back toward the quarters as the golden light faded gradually into lavender and then indigo, and Nemec took Tristan's place at Lujan's shoulder.

"Sir—" one of the soldier's protested.

Lujan motioned with his hand. "I-it's o-kay," he said. "Wa-atch the park!"

They didn't bother with conversation along the way back. Not aloud, at least. But the dot-coded message Nemec tapped on Lujan's shoulder made him stiffen in the glidechair.

"Will keep you informed as more is decrypted, sir," Nemec finished.

At the Transition Quarters' front entrance, Lujan shifted in his chair and said, "Ni-ight, Aji-mir," and watched the other limp away into the darkness.

Now I know where Assemblywoman DeByes got that account of Issel's history, he thought.

But his head throbbed with myriad new questions:

How widespread is this? How many are involved and who are they? What is the real objective and what will be the ultimate price to the Unified Worlds?

He recalled the reports on the fall of Adriat to the Dominion before the War of Resistance began. It had been conquered without a burst being fired, its political will crumpled by the corruption at the core of its government. The facts echoed in his mind, and he shivered with a sudden chill that couldn't be blamed on the wind blowing in from the sea.

EIGHTEEN

This message, like the last four or five from Chief Minister Remarq, was mostly a list of names and instructions for activation. Thirteen names this time, Trosvig saw, to be contacted over the next three weeks. He scanned through them.

He raised his eyebrows in surprise at the last one on the list: Percivan Radeleff of Sjenlund. The Issel Sector's most vocal detractor.

It would be most interesting, Trosvig thought, to hear that bird sing a different tune. It would be even more interesting to hear how Radeleff would explain to his peers his conversion to the Isselan cause.

Allowing himself a cold smile, Trosvig hit the PRINT pad and then turned to his office safe to retrieve an envelope marked TOP SECRET.

Storage of the message in his safe would only be temporary, until he had completed all of Remarq's instructions. Then it would go into the disintegrator as the previous messages had.

As the sheets slid into the catcher tray, he turned back to the keypad. A few swift strokes erased the message as if it had never been.

* * *

Percivan Radeleff hung his coat with care on the servo's polished arm, removed his hat and placed it on the proper hook. "Mail, please," he said as he turned toward his desk. Reading his mail was always first in his morning routine.

The display on his monitor blinked, and the mail queue unrolled itself down its right margin. Radeleff scanned the list. He sighed as he drew out his chair and lowered himself into it.

The terminal's secretarial software handled the mail from constituents, sorting it according to issue and responding with the appropriate preprogrammed message. Only official memoranda and documents that he had requested were forwarded for his personal attention.

Halfway down the list was an item with TROSVIG filling the sender line and a subject that read LUNCHEON MEETING. An announcement of some upcoming official function, no doubt. Brow creasing, he said, "Open Trosvig letter."

The message was headed with the previous day's date and a late afternoon dispatch time, and its contents were brief:

PERCY,
IT IS EXTREMELY IMPORTANT THAT I MEET WITH YOU TOMORROW FOR A PRIVATE DISCUSSION. PLEASE CANCEL ANYTHING ELSE ON YOUR CALENDAR AND JOIN ME FOR LUNCHEON IN THE DIAMANTE ROOM OF THE VERMILION GRYPHON AT 1200.
                    S. TROSVIG

Radeleff quirked an eyebrow at that. Nothing took priority over a request for a conference from a member of the Triune, of course; but out of habit he said, "Open calendar."

With a ripple of color, the monitor revealed his schedule

for the day. Several blocks of time had been shaded gray. One filled the hours from 1100 to 1300, and bold characters identified it as a meeting of the Committee for the Development and Utilization of Planetary Natural Resources.

The DUPNR was a large committee; he would never be missed. He returned a confirmation of message receipt to Trosvig's office.

Why the Vermilion Gryphon? he wondered as he did so. Located on the opposite side of town, it was not one of the usual venues for Assembly members' luncheon meetings.

The Vermilion Gryphon was, without doubt, the oldest dining establishment in Ramiscal City, having opened at the time of the city's founding seven hundred years before. The care with which its owner family had preserved the ambience of that period through the generations, from its ancient furnishings and decor to the uniqueness of the cuisine itself, made it an historical landmark. Its present owner even employed human waiters who dressed in period livery, instead of the usual automated table servos. Consequently, the Gryphon was also very expensive. Not that that was of any consequence to an Assembly member's pay scale; Radeleff had dined there a number of times.

The most memorable occasion, he reflected, had been the night he'd first won his seat in the Assembly. He and his mate and a few close friends had celebrated his election victory there. They had, in fact, dined in the Diamante Room, at a table close in front of the anachronistic stone fireplace, one large enough to turn a whole ox.

Trosvig was already there when Radeleff arrived. The maître d' guided him to a secluded table for two, across the room from the massive fireplace, and Trosvig rose to greet him as they approached. "Percy," he said, "I'm so pleased that you were able to come on such short notice!"

A young man in vermilion livery appeared at Radeleff's elbow, offering a pair of leather-bound folders as they seated themselves. "Menus, gentlemen?"

Trosvig waved a hand. "That won't be necessary, Chernoff. We'll have the whole roast Beloje suckling seal with piquant sauce and savory rice."

Radeleff's eyes widened in mild surprise: It was the same entrée he had requested for that election-victory dinner.

"An excellent choice, sir." The young man made a half bow. "Would you care for wine? An appetizer? A soup, perhaps?"

"Do you have a good chelle?" Trosvig asked.

"Of course, sir. I'll send the wine steward at once."

"Very good." Trosvig nodded. "Then, for our appetizer, a mushroom soufflé."

"Of course," the waiter said again, and bowed from the neck, and slipped away.

Only then did Trosvig look across the table, the faintest suggestion of a smile about his mouth, a sort of mischievous glint to his eye.

No, it wasn't simply mischievous, Radeleff thought. There was something about that expression that was genuinely evil, something that made him shift in his chair in sudden wariness. A gut-level wariness that heightened when Trosvig asked, "Did I forget anything, Percivan?"

"Only the almond cheesecake for dessert," Radeleff said with forced dryness.

"All in due time," Trosvig said, and his smile broadened. He settled back in the wood-and-leather chair and interlaced his hands over his belly. "The occasion was an election victory, was it not? And there were eight at the table in this room, three other couples besides yourself and your mate. It was to celebrate your debut in the Assembly, over nineteen years ago."

Radeleff said nothing; his jaw had hardened, his eyes narrowed.

Trosvig began to stroke the sterling silver utensils in the linen sheath beside the fragile, delicate plate. He fixed his vision on his fingers' twiddling and didn't look up as he asked, "How many years has it been since you confided the details of that evening to Nogare GonGolli of the IIS?"

Radeleff felt the blood leave his face—felt it leave his hands as well, so that they turned cold. But he kept them together in his lap, beneath the table's handwoven linen cloth. He kept his voice controlled, too, so it was little more than a harsh whisper when he demanded, "What do you mean by that?"

Trosvig looked up at last. "I think you know very well what I mean, Percy."

He fell silent then. He stayed that way for two full minutes before he said, "Two weeks from today DeByes will open preliminary hearings for her amended trade plan with Issel—a key component of her Readmission of Issel bill. Your testimonial and vote in favor of that trade agreement will be crucial to its passing."

"I will *not*, under any circumstances—," Radeleff began.

Another man in livery, taller than the first and with a thick black mustache, appeared at Radeleff's elbow. "Chelle rosé, gentlemen?" he said, and with the grace of a dancer he displayed the bottle, first for Trosvig and then for Radeleff. When Trosvig gave approval, he proceeded to open it, offer round the cap, and then pour as if it were part of a ceremony. "Your appetizer will follow momentarily," he said upon completion of his task, and vanished once more.

Trosvig whirled the wine in his glass, inhaled its bouquet with his eyes closed, took a sip, and savored it for several seconds. "Superb!" he said at last. "Go on, Percy, taste it. It isn't poisoned, after all; you're far too valuable an asset to Chief Minister Remarq."

But only for the moment, Radeleff thought.

By the time the mushroom soufflé arrived, he had lost all desire for the banquet.

The pool was a pale blue square, spread out like a quilt before the lift seat and glimmering under a row of lights, its surface rippled only by its circulation system. The room enclosing it was warm, almost steamy, and scented with the same sharp disinfectant odor that hovered over public swimming pools.

"Ready, sir?" Pilita said from beside Lujan's left shoulder.

He said, "Y-yess."

He deliberately didn't glance back at the trio who stood at the edge of the pool. Having Libby and Darcie present for this event as well as Dr. Gavril made him feel unaccountably self-conscious. What if he buckled and fell?

But Meles pressed a button on the lift seat's control panel. With a hum, the mechanical arm from which the sling was suspended swung slowly out over the water and began to lower him toward it.

It had taken three weeks of work in the pool to bring him to this point.

"Water provides good resistance all by itself," Meles had told him at their first pool session. "You're strong enough now, sir, that I can start you on some new exercises."

Lujan hadn't been able to discern any difference in his legs' strength or control since they'd begun the pool work. Meles had been coaching him through a variety of swimming kicks, helping him to move his legs against the water, and he'd never felt any more successful with that than he had at lifting his legs off the mat in the rehab room.

But Meles's enthusiasm hadn't ebbed: "That's it, sir! Push that leg down through the water. Good, good! . . . Now pull it back up. C'mon, sir, pull! That's it!"

Hands supported his leg at ankle and knee, but his

straining always sent fire through his hip and across his thigh and left him gasping for breath.

He still spent two to three hours each day in the weight room as well, rebuilding upper arms and torso and shoulders. Dr. Moses found him doing curls when she came through once. "What's this, Jink?" she grinned. "Been challenged to another arm-wrestling match?"

His face was rivered with sweat, his right arm practically limp, and his breath came in gulps. "Not—thiss time," he panted. "It'll take mmore thann that to get me re-leassed from thiss hoss-pi-tal!"

Arm wrestling was the deal she had cut with him after the incident with the pampo.

By the time he'd been through three reconstruction surgeries and their subsequent recovery periods, he'd been more than ready to get off Jonica and back to duty on Yan—even with his arm still in bands and barely usable. He was a senior lieutenant then, with a line number for promotion to lieutenant commander, and he had more important things to do than sit around a military hospital. So when Libby entered the dayroom one afternoon, he had told her as much.

Dr. Moses drew herself to her full stature—such as it was when the top of her head scarcely leveled with his shoulder. "Lieutenant Serege," she said, looking him hard in the eye, "when you can beat me fair and square in an arm-wrestling match, using *that* arm, I'll seal your release form—but not one minute before!"

Lujan felt the gazes of the other patients—mostly enlisted troops from several different Unified services—lock onto him. He sensed their anticipation in their sudden silence. He met Libby's look. "You're on," he said, and gestured at a game table in the center of the room.

They seated themselves, braced their elbows, locked hands. The spectators leaned forward in their chairs. Moses touched his vision with her own and controlled a smile.

"Start!" said a soldier on the sidelines.

—And she pinned him. Neatly. *Painfully!* He choked off a yelp.

The enlisted guys guffawed.

Lujan's face burned. "Blast you, Libby!" he said. "I wasn't ready!"

"Maybe in another three weeks you will be," she said, rising, "—if you make it a point to get really well acquainted with your occupational therapist."

He had practically lived in the weight room after that. He endured every new procedure the therapist imposed upon him, clenching his teeth against the pain.

Indignation pushed him harder and longer than even the therapist did. Pushed him past one limitation after another. Sometimes, he thought, he even did curls in his sleep, dreaming that he held a twenty-kilo weight in his hand.

It had taken him a full month to beat Libby—and then he'd done it five times out of five, even with his arm growing fatigued, to make certain there was no doubt in her mind.

"All right, Jink, all right!" she said with mock annoyance after he pinned her for the fifth time. "I get the image! Go pack your duffle; you're out of here!"

He never worked out in this weight room but what he recalled were those arm-wrestling matches.

Pilita had been pushing him hard on his hands as well.

"Remember the electrical stimulation we used to exercise your whole body at the beginning?" she said. "We're going to use the same principle on a smaller scale now to rebuild your hands."

Electrodes attached to his fingers, hands, and forearms sent a dull buzz through them, like the wings of an angry insect, like the buzzing he'd felt in the middle of the night. The current made his curled fingers extend; its cessation allowed them to flex.

"Work *with* the impulse," Pilita coached, cupping her own hands around his. "Straighten your fingers; push against my hold."

She replaced the soft foam balls with firmer ones, like putty, and encouraged him to keep them with him at all times. "Whenever you're not using your hands for anything else," she said, "knead the putty balls. That will increase your dexterity along with your strength."

She took away the glove with the bracket, too, and provided him with grooming and eating utensils that had thick handles, like those used by small children. "This really is a step up," she assured him.

And now they were going to get him on his feet.

The lift sling lowered him until the water lapped at his upper chest, warm and comfortable, lowered him between a set of parallel bars like the ones in the rehab room, where patients practiced walking. By then Meles and Pilita had slipped into the pool as well, and one steadied the sling while the other released its safety harness.

"Now, sir . . . ," Meles said, and Lujan had never before seen the young man's face so serious, so intent. His hand hovered near Lujan's upper arm, ready to catch him. "Reach out for the bars," he said, "and pull yourself up. We're right here; we've got you."

Lujan stretched out with his left, his stronger arm, first, then the right. His hands curled around the wet bars. He still didn't have much of a grip; he was grateful for the bars' rough, rubbery surface.

Legs next. They drifted at the moment, like pale logs, ripply beneath the water. Jaw tightening with the effort, he pushed them down, down. . . .

One heel, then the other, met the floor, as slip-proofed as the parallel bars. He planted his feet.

He didn't glance backward. He didn't have to to know that Darcie's teeth were tight on her lower lip, her breath in her throat, her hands knotted hard at her sides. He could practically feel the electricity of her suspense. He couldn't let her down.

He drew a deep breath. Gripped the bars as well as he could and heaved himself up by the strength of his shoulders alone.

He staggered; water slapped at his belly. Behind him, Darcie gasped. But Meles had him by one arm and Pilita by the other, and his knees locked. He was standing.

It had been almost one hundred days since he had last stood.

"Are you okay, sir?" said Pilita.

He hadn't felt such a pull of gravity since they first started tilting him up in the bed. Even with the water's buoyancy it was as if the planet itself were trying to pull him to its core, as if he were hurtling through space in some ceaseless ultra-high-G maneuver—and he had no sense of balance at all!

He could only do it for nine or ten seconds. His body's own weight exhausted him; his knees began to shake.

"Let's get you back into the seat, sir," said Meles.

Darcie was there with a towel when the lift swung the seat back over the deck. Tucking it about his waist, over his trunks, she bent and kissed his mouth. "I love you!" she whispered. "I love you!" And tears glittered on her cheeks.

"Lo-ove you—too." Lujan said it through a weary smile, and lifted a hand to stroke her tears away.

He remembered too late that his hands were still wet. But Darcie only laughed and kissed him again.

They went out for dinner that evening to celebrate—if going over to the main hospital cafeteria could really be considered going out. It was Tristan's suggestion, and Lujan knew by the tension in his son's voice that there was more on his mind than a meal.

To the dismay of their military escort, they chose to take

the canopied outdoor walkways rather than the subterranean pedestrian tunnels. It was early in the third standard month now, and the crispness of the evenings was beginning to soften. It had rained over Ramiscal City through most of the afternoon—and snowed in the mountains that shadowed it—but the setting sun had parted the clouds with its last golden darts, the air smelled freshly washed, and a few early spring birds were trilling their evensong.

They were late enough that the dinner rush was over, the greatest number of patrons departed, and a number of tables were available. Tristan looked about briefly and selected a table toward the rear, and then Darcie had a word with their escort. Lujan didn't hear what she said, but they exchanged glances, nodded, and moved off to another table two or three over.

"How di-id—you get the-em to—do tha-a-at, Darce?" he asked as she took the place next to his glidechair.

She smiled and shrugged. "I told them I appreciated the gravity of their responsibility," she said, "but we'd really like a bit of privacy with our dinner. They can protect us quite adequately from a few meters away."

They were halfway through dinner when Nemec came in. With his vision still somewhat fuzzy and his depth perception still unreliable, Lujan didn't recognize him until Tristan called his name and waved him over.

"I was hoping you'd be here this evening, sir," Nemec said, and reached inside his jacket. "I got a letter from Commander Amion of the Anchenko Detachment today. I thought you'd be interested in what he had to say so I printed a copy for you." He placed a couple folded sheets of paper in Lujan's hand.

"Tha-ank you, Aji-mir." Lujan glanced at them—could tell at once they were handwritten, not printouts from a desk terminal mailbox. "Is—so-ome-thing wro-ong?" he said.

Nemec shrugged. "Hard to tell at this point, sir. Let me know what you think after you've read it."

"I wi-ill," Lujan nodded, and fumbled the papers into the pocket inside his own jacket.

He waited until they had returned to the flat, until he was propped up with several pillows in bed, to read them. Nemec had written out his message in quick, precise strokes of his stylus.

Sir, have completed decryption of two more concealed messages. Am storing copies of decrypted material. Am including excerpts of message from Seulemont Remarq to Seamus Trosvig, dated 26/12/3308, which gives a whole new dimension to the picture. Abbrev. text follows: "You [are] to help shape the top circles of leadership and thus consolidate support for the recommendations you will be making in the near future. . . . Your first opportunity will be in the selection of a new commander-in-chief of the Spherzah. . . . We no longer have to concern ourselves with removing Serege from his commandership at some point in the future, when his intractability toward the Issel Sector would threaten the accomplishment of our mutual goals. I would like to offer a recommendation for Serege's successor. You will find Vice Admiral Tolmich Oleszek of Sjenlund to be the perfect candidate. . . . He has cultivated the loyalties of many of the best and the brightest in the rising officer corps. But more useful . . . is the fact that while his service record is sterling, the university record of his second daughter is not. Where Oleszek's political naïveté ends, [that] will certainly persuade him to continue his cooperation with us. I will be pleased to send you a complete

dossier for his recommendation package if you wish."
Please arrange for a meeting ASAP, sir. —AN

Lujan felt little surprise at the revelation concerning his rushed retirement—except that Seulemont Remarq knew him well enough to consider him a threat.

It was the fact that Remarq also knew Oleszek—knew his vulnerability and plainly had intent to use it—that sent a wave of cold through his body like an electric shock. The same tentacle that twisted its way through the Assembly had already wrapped itself about the head of the Spherzah. Who knew how far it had reached beyond that? What military leaders of what other worlds' forces might it have touched? And how far might it yet spread?

He was sweating, Lujan realized at once. A cold sweat that stood up on his skin like beads. It was some minutes before he could even call, "Triss?"

His son appeared at the bedroom doorway in a moment. "Father?" He sounded concerned. "Are you all right?"

"Yess," Lujan said slowly. "I—need some help—with these pil-lows." And he beckoned Tristan closer.

The flat was full of voice pickups, Darcie had told him the first day they were here. If she or Tris could hear his request for help from the opposite end of the apartment, who else might be able to hear him? Considering the implications of Nemec's message, he couldn't afford any chances.

"Know what this says?" he blinked out, indicating the papers in his hand.

Tristan shook his head in silent response.

"Read," Lujan blinked, "and destroy. And get meeting with Nemec."

NINETEEN

He watched without speaking as Darcie moved around the room a little later, preparing for bed. Settling in beside him, she kissed his mouth and said, "Good night, Luj." And then she paused, brow furrowing as she studied his face in the near dark. "Are you all right?"

So, he couldn't keep his inner turmoil from his face. He sighed, mentally debating. He knew she harbored suspicions of her own, but did he really want to drag her into it?

Want to or not, he needed to. Soon. But not here, not right now.

"Luj?" she said again.

"Ju-usst res'-less," he answered, meeting her gaze.

He was still awake two hours later, staring at the ceiling while his heart labored under his ribs. The adrenaline that drove it did make him restless, but tossing and turning would only disturb Darcie.

At last, with a sigh that seemed to come from the very soles of his feet, he shoved himself up to a sitting position and reached for the glidechair parked close beside the bed. He levered himself into it.

There were small safety lamps in the baseboards of the handrailed walls, dim but enough to navigate by. "Slow forward," he said, keeping his voice low.

The glidechair's hum had never seemed so loud as it did in the midnight silence. He gritted his teeth, hoping it wouldn't wake his family.

At his request, Tristan had borrowed a nunchaku weapon for him from the physical training department at the Herbrun Field Spherzah barracks. Nunchaku katas worked the shoulders and arms, developing agility as well as strength, and he could perform most of them while seated in the glidechair.

The weapon lay in the drawer of a cabinet in the living area. He nudged the button with a knuckle and the drawer slid open.

Because his fingers still couldn't curl tightly enough for a proper grip, Darcie had wrapped the hard plastic lengths with bands of cloth to make them thicker, easier to hold, like the utensils he used—as well, he suspected, as to keep him from damaging either himself or the apartment should the weapon ever fly out of his hands. Taking it into his lap, he drew the glidechair up before the floor-to-ceiling viewpane that overlooked the park. The pane was programmed for screening mode, enabling him to see out while keeping passersby from seeing in.

The illuminants along the exercise paths formed a peaceful blue-white pattern among the treetops. Stars glimmered between ragged clouds overhead. Lights glowed yellow through the panes of the main hospital building across the park. It all appeared so pastoral, so untroubled, Lujan thought.

The turmoil that milled inside him manifested itself in movements too abrupt and too jerky as he began the series of nunchaku practice katas. The first consisted mostly of simple blocks. Each kata that followed was slightly more complex than the one before, adding various types of swings and strokes.

Nemec's message lay like a weight on his mind all the

while. There was little doubt, he thought, of Remarq's ultimate objective. If Issel were readmitted to the Unified Worlds, it would be an easy matter to complete the internal corruption of the Assembly—and numerous other officials, for that matter. That corruption already seemed to be well under way.

He wondered if Remarq were still in touch with the Dominion masters he had served during the War of Resistance. Though it had lost the battles fought in space with ships and troops and laser fire, the Dominion could win the war even now, thirty years after sealing the accord. Using bribery and coercion in the halls of legislation, it could still bring the worlds it had coveted under its subjugation.

He had to discover how far the contamination had spread, whom it had touched and tainted, and he had to collect the evidence to prove it: clear, undeniable, irrefutable evidence. Only when his case was fully built would he know to whom—to what authority—he dared present it.

And he had to do it himself. If even the Spherzah were being pulled into this conspiracy, Tristan and Nemec could too easily be discovered. If he were to conduct the rest of the probe himself, it would reduce the risk to them.

But how?

He paused in the memorized movements of the kata to look toward the kitchen computer.

No. His top-level security accesses would have been cut when he was retired more than a month before; and Trosvig would have probably cut even the basic accesses ordinarily retained by retired flag officers. One attempt to gain access, to hack his way into the government nets from the kitchen terminal, would pinpoint him as if with a laser targeting beam. He needed an alternative, anonymous and unobtrusive.

What about a setup like the voice synthesizer? He still had that ring of electrodes with their tiny antennae embedded around his skull. He hadn't had any use for them since he'd given up the voice synthesizer, but he was going to wear them for life. What if there was a way he could utilize them?

Perhaps there was.

The night before his eye-implant surgery, when Dr. Moses had come back for his decision, she had said, "It might help you feel better about this, Jink, if you remember that processors like the one you've got in the back of your neck are all custom jobs; the patient decides what chips he wants installed on it. If you want, all we have to give you are the components necessary to operate your new eyes and ears. We don't have to plug in anything else."

"That's fine," he'd said. "I don't have any use for anything else."

He hadn't even asked what options were available; he hadn't wanted to know.

"Lujan?"

He jumped at the sound of Darcie's voice a few meters behind him, snagged the nunchaku out of a swing—and felt a sudden shock through his soul at what he had just been thinking. Embarrassed, he shifted to look around at her.

"What's wrong?" she asked, crossing toward him.

"Sho-oul-ders and neck are stiff," he said. That was true. "I—tho-ought this would loo-sen them."

Darcie drew up behind the glidechair and began to knead his neck and shoulders with practiced hands. "You are pretty tight—all sorts of knots in your muscles! . . . But they're not really what's keeping you awake, are they?"

He sighed at her ability to read him. "No," he admitted.

"D'you care to talk about it?"

He considered it—but the whole flat was full of voice pickups. "Not ri-ight now," he said.

Her split-second hesitation told him she'd picked up on the message of his tone as well as of his words. "Fine then," she answered.

She had never pushed him for information. As a former officer herself, she understood all about "need to know."

She massaged his shoulders for several minutes in silence, until the pressure of her fingers and thumbs no longer shot little twinges through his muscles and he found himself beginning to relax. Then she asked, "Better now?"

He nodded. "Mm-hmm."

"Good. Don't stay up too long, then," she said, and bent to kiss his neck just beneath his ear before she slipped back to their room.

The rain had passed but the trees along the exercise path were still shedding icy water droplets and the evening wind had a wet chill to it. Lujan shrugged more deeply into his coat.

He chose the branch toward the pond when they reached the fork in the path, and when the glidechair rounded the boulder and started across the clearing where they had met Nemec two or three weeks before, their military escort spread out. Only then did Tristan place his hand on Lujan's shoulder.

"Couple of days before Nemec can come," he tapped. "Little traffic today, just one thing. Issel's asking for combat vessels at Yan. They claim need for armed freighters due to pirates in Issel Sector. No decision from Assembly yet."

Lujan furrowed his brow at that. Unless the supposed incursions had begun during the months lost from his memory, he hadn't heard of pirates in Isselan space since before the War of Resistance. There would have been intelligence reports. Still, with all the pro-Issel sentiment swelling among the Unified Worlds these days, he suspected there wouldn't be a great deal of debate over releasing the ships.

The pond, when they reached it, could have been accurately described as a small lake. The path made a complete circle about it, separated from the water's edge only by a fringe of reeds and other sturdy water plants. A few waterfowl had already returned; they were dimly visible in the dusk: dark gray shapes bobbing on a murky surface.

"I nneed Dr. Moses to—fi-ine-tune my eyes," Lujan said. "The geese look li-ike floating de-bris. Ev'ry-thing more than five me-ters awa-ay is sstill out of fo-cus and there's no ni-ight vision at all!"

"Doesn't the infrared mode work?" Tristan asked. "Mum said your new eyes can see into the IR range."

Lujan sighed. "I haven't ee-ven tried it yet. I'm sstill not ful-ly comm-fort-a-ble with havv-ing my night-vi-sionn len-ses bui-ilt in!"

Tristan, walking alongside the glidechair with his hands shoved into his pockets, chuckled at that. "Right. I suppose it would take getting used to."

He lay awake for some time that night, too. How could he gain access to the headquarters' central computer? There had to be a way besides—

"Please, God, help me know what to do!" he prayed.

He woke with a start in the early hours of the morning and lay in a sweat, staring at the ceiling. He swallowed hard.

"Father, is there no other way?" he asked.

He already knew the answer.

* * *

"You've been terribly quiet this morning, Luj," Darcie said over breakfast. "You didn't sleep at all well last night, did you?"

"No." He sighed it. His whole head throbbed, as if that ring of electrodes were tightening around his skull. He muttered, "My head's kil-ling mme."

Darcie reached out and touched his forehead. "You're not feverish," she said. She studied him for a moment: his eyes—they would have been bloodshot if they were real—and the slackness, which still came to his face when he was weary. "Too little sleep, most likely," she said. "Why don't you just go back to bed when you finish eating."

"I need—to ssee Doc-tor Moses," Lujan said. "The ssooner, the bet-ter." He rubbed an awkward hand over his face. "My eyes sstill—won't fo-cus."

Darcie's brow puckered. "Maybe that's what's causing your headache. Go on back to bed; I'll ring her up."

Darcie accompanied him to Dr. Moses's office later that morning, mostly because the headache seemed to have blurred his vision still more. "I may need—ssome help navvi-gating," he told her.

Moses was waiting for them when they arrived. "Vision's still a problem, eh, Jink?" she said, ushering him, glidechair and all, into her examining room.

"Yess," he said; but as soon as the door closed behind them he asked, "How se-cu-ure is thiss room?"

She looked only mildly surprised. "Why? Do you have something classified you need to say?"

He ignored her lightness. "Po-ssibly," he said.

"It's good for Top Secret," she answered. "I feel safer discussing classified in here than I do in my consultation room, in fact; the mess on my desk would be too easy to bug. . . . Why?"

"I nneed to know," Lujan said, "exa-act-ly what I could

havve insstalled on this pro-cessor." He motioned at the back of his neck. "Ex-act-ly what are the po-ssi-bili-ties?"

Libby's eyebrows shot up. "You name it, it can be done," she said. She sounded more surprised at that than she had at his question about the room's security. "Am I talking to the same man who wasn't even sure he wanted new eyes for fear of becoming a cyborg?"

Lujan let his jaw harden. "Don't ee-ven touch it, Li-bby," he said. His heart rate had accelerated slightly and he could feel it pounding at his temples. "I don't need your rib-bing right now; I jusst need you to do it."

"Okay, Jink." Libby's tone changed at once. "I'm sorry." She hesitated, then asked, "What do you need?"

"The meeans to a-non-y-mous-ly ac-cess a major compu-ter network," he said, "and to reco-ord—the data I finnd in it. Large a-mountss of data. Pre-ffer-rably ssome-thing that can tie into this elec-trode head-band you gavve me."

Moses contemplated him for several moments, then nodded slowly. "I can do that, Jink." She shifted and straightened. "It'll take minor surgery, you know, but I can do it right now if you want."

"Please."

"Okay. Let's get you onto the examining table then, and get your shirt off. . . ."

She maneuvered him from chair to table as easily as Dar-cie had learned to do it, positioned him facedown with the support of a couple of firm cushions, then stepped over to a cabinet on the wall. "I'll have to shave a spot at the base of your skull," she said, and came back with a vibroshaver in her hand. "Let's get this done and give you the local so it can start taking effect while I get what you need."

There was a brief sting, low at the back of his head, when she pressed the infuser of anesthetic there. "Now just relax," she said, and stepped to the door.

"I need to ta-alk to Dar-cie," he said as she reached for it. "I neeed to tell her wha-at we're do-ing, aand why."

Moses nodded. "I'll send her in."

Lujan moved his head to look at her when Darcie drew up beside the examining table. "Luj?" she said. "Libby said—"

He managed a beckoning motion with the hand that lay near his face, and Darcie slipped hers into it. He tried to squeeze it. "I could-n't tell you la-ast night, Darce," he said. "Too ma-ny voice pick-ups inn the a-part-ment. I ca-an tell you here."

Her features were serious. "What is it, love?"

"You've been ri-ight all a-long," he said. "There is—ssome-thing wrongg going on. I ca-an't give you de-tails but—I think you have a right and a need to know." He paused to swallow. Took her vision with his own. "Issel is try-ing to in-fil-trate the Uni-fied Worrllds through the Assemm-bly. I havve to tra-ack down the people inn-volvved and stop them. Ajimir and Tris are hel-ping me. I'm having Lib-by give me the tools I neeed to do—what has to be done."

She shook her head a little at that; but the wan smile that shaped her lips told him she wasn't surprised. "I've never known anyone like you, Lujan Serege," she said, her voice husky with swelling emotion. "Indomitable even flat on your back! I love you so much!" Her hand tightened around his; she stooped to kiss him. "I'm here for you," she said. "I'll help you, too."

Dr. Moses came back in another moment, four small sterile packets in her hand. "Here's everything you need," she said. "Digital visiphone interface chip, artificial intel-ligence compatibility chip, and a molecular memory chip with a one terabyte capacity." She pointed out a tiny blue plastic chip. "That's probably a lot more memory than you'll need but they don't come any smaller. You'll even have downlink capability from orbital communications stations. . . . Buy the whole package, Jink, and I'll throw in a fuse for free."

"Thiss iss-n't funny, Libby," Lujan growled from the cushion.

"I'm not being funny," Moses said. "If you're going to be doing what I think you are, Lujan, you may need the fuse."

"I've ne-ver heard of fus-es for cra-nial im-plants," Lujan said.

"That's because they're not on the market yet," said Moses. "They're a new item. They have an ultrafast re-action and high surge handling capacity. They were designed specifically to protect individuals with implants from electromagnetic pulses. It's never been tried before, except on biological models, and the prototypes are only available right now to a select few within the scientific community." Moses gave him a smug smile. "I just happen to be on the manufacturer's 'free sample' list."

"Actually," said Darcie, "I'm surprised someone didn't come up with something like that a long time ago."

"Maybe just as well for us that they haven't," said Moses. And then: "Why don't you scrub, too, Darcie, and give me an assist here?"

The whole procedure only took a few minutes. It was simply a matter of reopening the muscular pocket in the back of Lujan's neck and, with the aid of a microvisor, plugging the chips into the processor.

"You've got plenty of room here for additional appliances, Jink," Moses said through her surgical hood. "I could even give you a couple of games."

Lujan rolled his eyes. "No thanks," he said. "Jusst re-memmber to fixx my vi-sion while you're inn there."

"All you need now is a password," Moses said a few minutes later as she sutured the tissue pocket closed with a laser wand.

"Get-ting tha-at will be ea-sier than thiss was," Lujan told her.

Shoving himself to a sitting position, he looked first Moses and then Darcie in the eye. "You both kno-ow," he said, "that for rea-sons of Uni-fied secur-ity and your safe-ty as much as mi-ine, there musst be no men-tion of thiss to any-one, and no re-cord of any kind."

"Of course, Lujan," Darcie said at once. Her voice was little more than a whisper.

"I'll have to record the vision adjustments," said Moses. "You'll need some kind of explanation if any-body sees you coming or going from my office, or no-tices that blob of bandage foam at the base of your head."

Lujan nodded consent.

He sat on the edge of the examining table for several minutes afterward, waiting for the bandage foam to dry and harden while Dr. Moses tested his vision with a VR display. His vision, he concluded, was as sharp now as it had been before he was injured.

He stayed silent on the way back to their quarters. So silent that Darcie finally asked, "Are you all right, Luj?"

"I—don't know," he said seriously. He started to shake his head—and winced at a twinge through the nape of his neck. He said again, "I don't know, Darce."

Nemec was there, jogging along the path at the water's edge, when Lujan and Tristan came down to the pond on their evening walk two days later. "Well, hello again, sir!" Nemec called out as he approached. Grinning, he added, "We've got to stop meeting like this! What would Captain Dartmuth say?"

Lujan chuckled and slipped Tristan a covert hand sig-nal: "Distract our escort." Aloud, he said, "How's that an-kle, A-jimir?"

"It healed up just fine, sir." Nemec came to a stop in front of him. "And you?"

"Not runn-ing ye-et," Lujan said with a sigh. "Any more let-ters from Amm-ion?"

"Not lately." Nemec dropped to a comfortable squat before the glidechair and placed a hand on its arm as if to maintain his balance. But his gaze, Lujan noticed, never stopped moving, never stopped taking in their surroundings. "What did you think?" his finger tapped out on the chair's arm.

With his hands lying more or less limp in his lap, Lujan could move his left wrist well enough to tap on his leg, "Attempt to enter Spherzah."

Nemec nodded, then muttered, "What now?"

"Search out all involved," Lujan tapped. "Get names and hard evidence."

Nemec's hand signal told Lujan the MPs had moved out of hearing range. "Who do we tell?" he asked quietly.

"No one yet," Lujan said. "We don't know who we can tru-ust. A search sho-ould tell us that."

Nemec nodded, and Lujan continued, "I need to access the net-work. I need a pass-word. Can you do that?"

Nemec furrowed his brow briefly, then nodded once more. "Mig's coming tomorrow to follow up on the 560," he said. "He's going to check our mailbox; he can do it. We'll put it deep enough in the system to escape any checks."

Lujan gave a single nod; he remembered Migdal Chorafas. Approximately his own age, Mig had graduated from the Sostis Aerospace Institute in the same class as himself. Grounded for medical reasons a few months later, he had made a career in cryptography and covert operations instead, and had eventually been accepted into the Spherzah. He was one of the keenest minds in the computer field, in Lujan's opinion.

"En-tries must not be tra-ace-able," he said. "No re-cord or pass-ing on my name."

"No problem," said Nemec. "AI security will acknowl-edge you by name but we'll alter the software. You'll be transparent."

"Fi-ine." Lujan asked, "Wha-at pass-word?"

"Use my sister's name," said Nemec. "Amena." He tapped out the spelling for Lujan. "We don't want any-thing to connect with you, sir. Give us a couple of days before you try it."

"Thanks." Lujan nodded again. "With a poss-ible threat in the Spher-zah, I want you to stop ac-tive-ly searching. Leave it to mee. Pass any new in-fo to Tris. No more pla-anned mee-tings; for your pro-tec-tion we need to dis-tance our-selves."

"Yes sir." Nemec's dark features were grim in the twi-light. He murmured, "Be careful, sir."

"You, too," Lujan responded. "Keep a closse eye on your one-eigh-ty."

Lujan sat in the glidechair before the living area's large viewpane, but he wasn't watching the storm outside. The rain pounding against the pane and the spring lightning, shocking the night-shrouded city with its display of deadly power, were too distracting. He sat with his eyes closed, focusing as he'd been taught to do for the voice synthesizer.

Visiphone interface open, he thought.

Its click seemed to come from inside his head, a click which was followed by the background noise of an open commset line. The last time he'd heard anything in quite that way was three days after he'd awakened from the coma, when Dr. Gavril had attempted to use the electro-mechanical sound transmitter with the skin contact.

He blinked a few times, then closed his eyes once more and concentrated.

Access base main computer, he thought. *Call code is one-three-five-three, seven-four, seven-one-six-one.*

He heard feedback tones somewhere between his ears as the digital impulses were transmitted more swiftly than any fingers could have tapped them on a keyboard. They were followed by a pause.

Outdoors, a close lightning strike sent a simultaneous crack of thunder across the sky. Lujan jumped—but his heart was already beating too hard and too fast, and the pulse in his ears pounded louder than the fading thunder.

"You have reached the communications network for the headquarters of the Unified Worlds organization," said a synthetic voice in his head. "To proceed, please enter your password now."

Amena, Lujan thought.

There was no response.

He was sweating, he realized almost absently. And his hands were hard on the glidechair's arms.

"Password accepted," the voice said at last. "Please refer to the directory on your monitor and make your selection by entering the corresponding number."

The directory appeared in his mind as clearly as if it were printed on the insides of his eyelids, an image as ethereal as the internal voice. He scanned it—found he could scroll up and down much more quickly this way than he could with voice commands to a computer.

He wanted Command Section, Spherzah. He thought its four-digit extension.

"To proceed," said the voice, "please enter your security sequence now."

Lujan set his teeth. *Activate artificial intelligence identification,* he thought.

He almost felt the click that time, like a snap of static electricity.

It was a machine-to-machine interrogation. He was aware only of whirs and clicks and rapid strings of feedback tones like those of the calling code, intracranial sound effects that went on for minute after minute.

What did you do to me, Libby? he thought. His palms were damp, clutching the arms of the glidechair, and his breath came in gulps as if he were running. *What is this thing doing? Is it scanning my brain—my whole body? Is it reading my mind? What's going on?*

The string of tones, like some alien symphony, ended. There were two more clicks, then silence. All Lujan could hear was his pulse in his ears.

Then a new voice sounded from the center of his head:

"Welcome, Admiral Lujan Serege. It's good to have you back."

TWENTY

Percivan Radeleff glanced down at his hands,
clenched together on the delegate's table in front of him.

It had all been a mistake. He was willing to acknowl-
edge that. Just one bad mistake, years before, when he
was young and far too self-assured.

He'd been trying to prove himself, he thought now—but
to whom and for what purpose he was no longer certain.

He'd been trying to play diplomat, trying in his own
way to ease interstellar tensions, to be a peacemaker and
a hero, and he'd gotten himself in way over his head.
He'd had no idea what kind of fire he was playing with
until it had scorched him. He'd spent the rest of his career
trying, in his own way, to make restitution.

It was a form of denial, he supposed. Denial driven by
guilt. But he couldn't deny his guilt any longer. Not with
it constantly looking him in the face. He turned his gaze
away from the platform upon which Trosvig sat and fixed
its focus once more on his hands.

They were debating the proposed interstellar trade
agreement today: a market system designed to include
Issel and, eventually, her subject worlds. He was supposed to speak in favor of it, to recommend it to his peers,
to encourage them to vote it into law.

He'd actually composed a speech. Had conferred at

length with Ikel Broudy on the topic—from a neutral position, of course—in order to prepare it. It now lay on the table before him, glowing in the guts of his pocket-sized microwriter.

At the podium, Assemblywoman DeByes was extolling the benefits of her revised trade program. There was earnestness in her face, in her voice, and Radeleff couldn't help wondering how she had become head of a committee sponsoring pro-Isselan legislation—not that she'd ever been an especially open opponent of Issel. Did the hand of the IIS rest as heavily upon her shoulder as it rested on his own? He shuddered at the imagined sensation.

That was the whole trouble with Issel, and with the Dominion, which had spawned Issel's system of government, he reflected. That unseen hand was always there, as it had been over his own head all these years. Sometimes it was as subtle as a kind of political conscience; but if one didn't obey, if one didn't march according to party orders, it curled into a fist and came down in a sudden smashing blow.

Radeleff remembered when that had happened to Issel during the War of Resistance, when Issel's government at that time had refused to simply hand their world over at the Dominion's request.

Issel had been used as an example, and Mordan Renier, the new World Governor of Sostis, had learned the lesson well. Sostis had been surrendered quietly, without the people's knowledge because it had been against the people's will.

Sostis had been fortunate in the end; it had been freed of the Dominion's grip. Issel hadn't been so lucky.

And where would a readmission of Issel lead? That didn't require much imagination. There were already Isselan agents within the Assembly—within the Triune! Trosvig. DeByes. Himself. There were probably others as well—probably among those who had most recently thrown in their support for the Isselan cause. If they could be controlled now, with Issel still outside the Unified Worlds, how much more easily would they be controlled with Issel a member, on the "inside" again? It was all too conceivable that the Unified Worlds could, in the not-too-distant future, literally vote themselves into the Dominion!

Madam DeByes had returned to her bench among the Tohh delegates and the officiator was fielding responses from the floor.

"Assemblywoman DeByes," said an assemblyman from Kaleo, "I do find this to be a more palatable trade proposal than the first one you presented, but it still begs a rather substantial question that I sincerely hope you haven't overlooked.

"The success of your trade plan appears to depend entirely upon the compliance and cooperation of a world that isn't—and some hope never will be—a part of the Unified Worlds. I can't help but wonder, madam, how the citizens of Issel feel about the decisions we are making for them here in an area as essential to them as interplanetary trade." The Kalese representative looked directly at her. "How do we know what Issel wants, madam? Has anyone discussed this with their minister of commerce?

"For that matter—and I've wondered this all along—has anyone discussed *any* of this with *any* representative of Issel? Why are we even assuming that Issel *wants* to come back to the Unified Worlds?"

The Kalese assemblyman paused, and several dozen others throughout the chamber broke into applause, light laughter, and shouts of, "Here, here!"

Down the bench to Radeleff's left, Ikel Broudy leaned toward Ranze Tousillo. "I've been wondering that myself!" he said. "What if Issel just wants to be left alone?"

The Kalese motioned for quiet, and when the claps and chuckles had subsided, he said, "Until we have answers to some very basic questions, madam, I believe this whole issue is moot! Therefore, I move that we extend to appropriate representatives of the Isselan government an invitation to participate in these hearings and to speak for themselves on such matters as trade agreements!" He swept his gaze around the chamber. "Doesn't that make a good deal more sense?"

Radeleff closed his eyes, bowed his head, pressed his fingertips to the bridge of his nose in a gesture of supplication. *They're proposing to bring Isselan voices into this Assembly before Issel even has a right to participate!*

"A motion has been made," the officiator announced from his podium. "Do we have a second?"

All across the chamber, figures leaped to their feet, arms aloft. The officiator selected one to speak, and Radeleff sank back, folding his arms over his chest.

That speaker didn't second the motion. Her remarks touched off a debate that filled the rest of the morning session, a debate that grew more heated with each new voice that came into it.

Radeleff held his peace through all of it, though a hundred points he might have made milled in his mind. He sat silent with his mouth pressed into a hard, straight line.

At last the officiator punched his buzzer for quiet and demanded, "Are there any further statements?"

There were none.

"A motion has been made by Pok Cho-Suk of Kaleo," he said then. "Is there a second?"

There was silence for a moment, and then a figure on the far side of the chamber came to his feet. "I second the motion," he said.

"The motion has been seconded." The officiator made the announcement without the barest suggestion of emotion. "Following the midday recess, it will be brought to a vote. All delegates must, I repeat *must,* be present for the vote. The afternoon session will commence at thirteen hundred." He punched his buzzer with the same finality one of his ancient predecessors might have achieved with the rap of a gavel and said, "This session is adjourned."

Radeleff climbed slowly to his feet, shaking his head, and turned toward the nearest exit.

He opted for the long way up to the Sjenlund delegation's office suite, ruminating over the events of the morning as he made his way through the building's less-traveled side corridors. He paused when he reached a little-used lift, tapped its call button—and someone touched his arm. He hadn't even realized he was being followed; he turned around with a start.

Trosvig stood behind him, smiling. "I noticed you were atypically quiet during this morning's session, Percy," he said. He drew his brows together. "You aren't having second thoughts about carrying out your responsibility, are you?"

Radeleff set his jaw. "I know what my responsibility is, Seamus," he replied, "and I will carry it out."

"Good." Trosvig watched him. "Because the IIS is rather intractable about payment of debts, and there are numerous ways to collect on an overdue bill."

The lift's door opened. Radeleff gave the other a hard look as he stepped inside.

Trosvig didn't follow. He simply smiled once more as the door slid closed.

Radeleff glanced in both directions before stepping out of the lift when it opened on his floor. There was no one else in the corridor. On edge from the encounter with

Trosvig, he quickened his pace toward the Sjenlund delegation's suite.

"Percy!" Ikel Broudy said as he came in. "There you are; we lost you in the corridor downstairs. Ranze and I are going out for luncheon today. Would you care to join us?"

"Thank you, but no," Radeleff said. "I've got—a few things I need to accomplish before this afternoon's session. Tomorrow, perhaps."

"Fine." Broudy shrugged. "We'll see you back down in the chamber, then."

Radeleff crossed directly toward his private office as they left. Inside, he closed the door and began to pace.

DeByes and her committee and their staffs—perhaps even Trosvig and his staff—would spend the entire recess on their visiphones, he knew, begging, cajoling, cutting deals—and coercing for votes. On a thought, he disconnected his own visiphone. He had enough to wrestle with, to weigh and consider, without any outside influences.

Still pacing, he avoided watching the digits flick over on his desk timepiece. Kept his attention fixed on the sunlight beyond his viewpane, and the pale green aura that glowed about the treetops, where buds were beginning to swell. He kept his mental vision fixed on the long term, and what this one vote could mean in the future of the Unified Worlds.

By the time he emerged from his office, he knew what he had to do.

The chamber was filled for the afternoon session, every seat occupied, and the spring's early warmth seemed to have followed the delegates indoors. At least it seemed so to Radeleff as he joined the others in Sjenlund's section.

His palms began to sweat as the officiator mounted the platform. He found himself fidgeting with his hands as the officiator announced, "A motion has been made by Pok Cho-Suk of Kaleo and seconded by Tatar Yanov of Topawa to extend to representatives of the Isselan government an invitation to participate in these hearings and to express their own concerns on the matter of readmission to the Unified Worlds."

He made the entire statement with a single breath, and then paused before he added, "This motion now comes before the full Assembly for a vote. All those in favor . . ."

Each delegate's desktop displayed a panel with two buttons, one labeled AYE, the other labeled NAY. Radeleff put out his hand.

He could feel Trosvig's vision boring into the top of his head. He knew what he was expected to do. *They could very well have me killed if I don't,* he thought.

He placed his hand over the panel.

"All opposed to inviting representatives of . . . ," droned the officiator.

Radeleff lifted his head. He looked Trosvig full in the eye as he pressed the NAY button.

The vote tally appeared on a screen above and behind the main podium: 227 opposed, 233 in favor.

Isselan officials would be invited to participate in the Unified Worlds Assembly.

Radeleff sank down on his bench, suddenly weak. His vote of conscience hadn't been enough.

He couldn't help glancing over his shoulder as he left the Unified Worlds Tower that evening.

Warm water lapped against Lujan's midsection as he stood between the parallel bars. It had been ten days since he'd first stood this way, ten days that seemed like a month. They had had him up almost every day since then, and each time he'd held on for a second or two longer.

When he could no longer stand, Meles eased him onto

a bench at the end of the pool, so he sat in water almost to his shoulders, and then Meles put his legs through their exercise regimen. By the time he got back to his quarters, he ached from hips to ankles.

"Today, sir," Meles said, "we're going to do your regimen standing up. We're going to get you walking."

So he stood in water to his waist, holding on to the parallel bars, with Pilita on one side and Meles on the other; and Meles said, "Put your weight on your right leg, sir. That's it. Now lift the left one; use the muscles in your thigh. C'mon, c'mon, just like the swimming kicks we've been doing."

He managed five steps before his legs buckled. He caught himself with his arms on the bars, and Meles and Pilita pulled him back up.

"Just float, sir," said Meles. "I've got you."

He waited until Lujan was seated on the submerged bench and then he said, grinning ear to ear, "You were walking, sir! You were actually *walking!*"

Five steps, Lujan thought. Five excruciating, awkward steps, each of which must have taken at least a full minute to execute. His legs—his arms, too—were still shaking, his breath coming in gulps as if he'd just run twenty kilometers. "I feel—like a todd-ler," he panted, and when Pilita and Meles both laughed, he added, "—in need of—a nap!"

He lay still on the bed for a long while when he got back to his quarters, too worn to move so much as a finger, too exhausted even to sleep. In this lingering weakness, there was only one thing he could do.

He closed his eyes. *Visiphone interface open,* he thought. *Access base main computer, call code one-three-five-three, seven-four, seven-one-six-one.*

He entered his password and security ID when they were called for and listened to the tonal communication of the AI interface.

"Welcome, Admiral Serege," AI security said inside his head. "How may I help you today?"

I need to review the personal communications log of Seamus Trosvig, member of the Triune, he thought.

"For what period of time, sir?"

He had been checking Trosvig's mail system at least once every day. *For the past twenty-four standard hours,* he responded, *ending with the present time.*

"Incoming or outgoing communications?"

Both.

A moment later the log appeared in Lujan's mind. It resembled the bill that showed up on the house computer each month, listing the charges from the communications company that provided visiphone services—except that this one didn't include the total to be deducted from the user's credit.

Activate memory chip, Lujan thought, and when something clicked within his head, he began his study.

The record for the previous evening and this morning showed nothing out of the ordinary: half a dozen messages out, half a dozen messages in, all origins and destinations easily traceable. There was nothing, when Lujan called up his earlier surveys for comparison, that suggested any ongoing pattern.

This afternoon's log, however, made him start.

Between the hours of 1200 and 1300, Trosvig had made over forty contacts via visiphone. All had been local and most had taken less than one minute. He had even attempted calls to one code three times, but each time that one had failed to go through.

Puzzled by that, Lujan thought, *Display owner of call code on log lines thirty-one, thirty-eight, and forty-two.*

A name appeared next to the numerals: RADELEFF, PER-CIVAN CYESTER, ASBYMBR.

On a sudden hunch, Lujan returned to the first call

code in that one-hour block. "Display owner of code on line twenty-six."

The result sent him down through the roster one call code at a time.

Every one belonged to a member of the Assembly.

Last-minute lobbying before a major vote? he wondered. He'd seen such tactics often enough during his years on the Defense Directorate.

But—a vote on what issue?

The thought that it might have been the readmission proposal itself sent a chill through his blood. "Blast!" he said through clenched teeth.

"Excuse me, sir." It was the internal AI voice. "I do not recognize the instruction 'blast.' "

Disregard, Lujan thought back. And then: *Show me the communications log for the past twenty-four hours, both incoming and outgoing, for Abigail DeByes, member of the Assembly.*

The display in his mind—if he could truly call it a display—flickered and then rematerialized.

DeByes had also made a number of visiphone contacts during the 1200-to-1300 time frame today. Her contacts were fewer and each was longer, but the number was still large enough to be significant.

Lujan ran the same ID check on DeByes's roster that he'd run on Trosvig's and came up with the same results: All calls were to members of the Assembly.

None of the call codes had been duplicated between the two logs, he noted. Between them there were close to seventy names.

He was sweating, he realized abruptly. *Memory off,* he thought. *Close down comms review parameters and exit base computer system.*

"Yes sir," said the AI voice. "Thank you for using Se-curiNet Systems."

Lujan lay with his eyes closed even after a final click confirmed that he was logged off.

Almost seventy names! They couldn't all be in Issel's employ, could they? He shuddered at that possibility.

He'd have to contact Nemec again, see if he'd found any more messages in the old 560's "mailbox" like the one ordering activation of Assemblywoman DeByes.

And he would have to continue the search for names, for connections.

But not right now.

He opened his eyes. Turned his head to look at the timepanel on the nightstand. It showed 1803.

Right now he needed to find out upon what issue the Assembly had voted, and more importantly, what the outcome had been.

"Holovid on," Lujan said. "Global News Network, please."

The screen in the bedroom's far wall rippled, then stabilized to reveal a newsman with a grim expression standing on the corner of a garishly lit city street.

". . . City is stunned this evening," he was saying, "by the murder of a member of the Unified Worlds Assembly.

"The body of Percivan Cyester Radeleff, delegate from the continent of Andolyn on Sjenlund, was discovered in the walkway behind me less than an hour ago." The newsman gestured toward a covered lane, which was crowded with law enforcement officials and skimmers with flashing lights.

"Although there has been an increase in crime here in the Entertainment District over the past two years," he continued, "this case is shocking for its sheer brutality. Though robbery was originally believed to have been the motive, some details of the crime now make that appear questionable. The victim was severely beaten about the head, apparently over a period of time; and according to officials of the law, there were no signs of struggle here in the walkway.

"At this time," the newsman concluded, "there are no suspects in this murder, and law officials have taken no one into custody. We will, of course, keep you informed of new developments in this case as they come to light."

Assemblyman Percivan Radeleff. The individual, Lujan remembered, whom Seamus Trosvig had tried three times to contact earlier today. Might Radeleff have been dead already by then?

The scene in the holovid changed; in the Global News studio, an anchorwoman in a pastel blouse was saying, "The Assembly came a step closer today to readmitting Issel into the Unified Worlds. In a vote of two hundred thirty-three to two hundred twenty-seven, a motion was passed to invite representatives of the Isselan government to participate in decisions regarding the readmission proposal. . . ."

Lujan's teeth locked, seemingly of themselves. *They might as well have voted Issel all the way in!* he thought. One or two more "preliminary steps" like that and passing the readmission proposal itself would be only a formality!

Did Radeleff participate in the vote in the Assembly? he wondered abruptly. *Was he still alive at that time?*

Visiphone interface open, he thought. *Access Global Interact line. Respond with visual, please.*

He remembered the sequence of tones, clicks, and buzzes, and the genderless synthesized voice that said, "Thank you for your participation with Global News. Please state your question or comment now."

I'd like to see the voting record, Lujan thought, *for all Assembly members who took part in the motion passed in the Assembly today.*

"Thank you," said the voice from Global Interact.

"Please be patient. Your input will be processed promptly."

He didn't have to wait long. The holovid split in the center, leaving the anchorwoman speaking in the left half while the voting record filled up the right.

Activate memory chip, Lujan thought.

He scrolled through the record quickly, searching for the Sjenlund delegation, and stopped when he spotted RADELEFF, PERCIVAN CYESTER, ANDOLYN in the middle of the Sjenlunders' block.

Radeleff had still been alive at the time the motion was passed; he had voted nay.

He was, Lujan noted, the only one of the nearly seventy individuals contacted during the midday visiphone rush who had done so.

Lujan studied the record for several minutes.

There remained a number of unanswered questions, of course, but of one thing he was unequivocally certain: The motive for Radeleff's murder had not been robbery.

TWENTY-ONE

"**No more wading pools, sir,**" said Meles. "Today we're gonna go for a walk across the rehab room." And he set a lightweight support frame in front of Lujan.

His first steps in the pool had been only three days ago, but by yesterday Lujan had doubled that first attempt's number to ten. Still, the rehab room looked a kilometer wide. He drew a deep breath. "Let'ss get star-ted—then."

He didn't make it all the way across the rehab room before his strength was sapped. Progressing by mere centimeters with each step, he barely covered a meter of ground. Sweat plastered his hair to his forehead and rivered his face. His warm-up suit stuck to his body, and beneath it every sinew quivered with the strain. But Meles, easing him back into the glidechair, couldn't stop grinning. "In another week, sir," he said, "you'll be doing laps around this place!"

Lujan wasn't too tired to smile.

He slept until Tristan came in from work, though. He dreamed he was making his way forward in the dark. His knees and hips were stiff and sore, his right foot still dragging; and when a shape like a man leaped out at him from nowhere, he couldn't evade, couldn't even turn—

"Father?"

He started, and turned his head toward the voice as he opened his eyes.

Tristan stood in the bedroom doorway. "I'm sorry, sir," he said. "Mum just said you were resting."

"Ne-ver mind." Lujan said it through a yawn, and rubbed a hand over his face. "What—is it?"

"This." His son pulled a folded paper from his jacket's inner pocket and handed it over. "It's a letter from— Uncle Siljan."

"Hmm." By the expression on his son's face, Lujan was certain the letter wasn't really from Siljan. He shoved himself to a semisitting position against his pillows—winced at the stiffness in his hips and abdominal muscles. It took him several tries to open the paper's folds, fumbling with fingers that still lacked fine motor coordination.

Activate memory chip, he thought when he finally got the paper open. He read it thoroughly, then shut down the memory chip with another thought. Aloud, he said again, "Hmm . . . Thankss for—bringing it in, Triss." Looking up then, he blinked, "Destroy it completely."

"Right, sir." Tristan pocketed the letter and left the room.

It had been mostly a list. Gleaned from better than half a dozen messages addressed to Seamus Trosvig, Nemec had explained at its beginning, it contained over 240 names. Only 68 were Assembly members—the same ones who had been contacted before the vote three days earlier. The rest were government employees in various offices and positions, and a handful of high-level military leaders from five of the nine member worlds. Two were longtime members of the Defense Directorate.

Lujan's stomach twisted into knots at the thought. *Just how widespread is this? Where hasn't it reached?*

He scarcely slept that night. Too many questions echoed in his mind, and his only hope for answers was in the computer nets.

* * *

The mail queue was nearly full this morning. Trosvig allowed himself a sigh of mild annoyance at the digits blinking on the terminal's message counter, and requested, "Play messages in audio, in chronological order."

As the mail system brought up the first item, he filled a mug with shuk from the dispenser in one corner and began to stroll about his office, pulling in spicy swallows and taking in the view from the top of the Unified Worlds Tower as he listened.

Most were routine reminders of events already entered in his pocket calendar: committee meetings and social obligations. But the opening of the fifth or sixth message drew him away from the skyline and fixed his full attention on the synthesized voice.

"Greetings to the Assembly of the Unified Worlds from Dr. Zlatkis Haken, Minister of Interplanetary Relations of the world government of Issel," it said. "With this communication, my government officially accepts your invitation to send our representatives to participate in your Assembly, to work together with you toward the resolution of issues involved in returning membership in the Unified Worlds to our motherworld.

"However, we are troubled by an apparent contradiction of this invitation by the Unified Worlds, as witnessed by a particular matter of policy toward the government of Issel. That matter concerns the continued impoundment, at the spacedocks at Yan, of a number of Isselan frigates and other combat vessels.

"At this time, as we labor to rebuild the commerce that was lost during our recent difficulties, those vessels are essential to us for use as armed freight ships. The distrust implied by your governments' refusal to release those ships to the government of Issel calls into question the sincerity of your recent invitation and casts into doubt the

ability of your people to work with ours for the resolution
of other mutual concerns.

"Therefore, we request that you give the policy of
holding our ships the most urgent reconsideration.

"With all respect, Dr. Zlatkis Haken, Minister of Interplanetary Relations for the world government of Issel."

Trosvig raised his eyebrows as the message concluded.
"Save preceding item to memory unit one," he said. The
matter of Issel's ships must be added to the agenda for tomorrow's combined meeting of the Triune and the Defense Directorate.

He seated himself at his desk as the next message began,
drawing himself up in the chair and folding his hands together in a posture of deference when he recognized the
voice of Chief Minister Remarq, even without the video
impression of conversing with the other face-to-face.

"My good friend Seamus," the chief minister began,
"my congratulations on the successful passage of the participation resolution. Please relay my deepest thanks to
Assemblymen Pok Cho-Suk of Kaleo and Tatar Yanov of
Topawa for their excellent performances on its behalf. I
do appreciate your keeping me informed on our associates' achievements.

"Likewise, please accept my condolences on the loss
of Percivan Radeleff. Truly a most unfortunate occurrence. But perhaps this incident will serve as an example
to any others who might be contemplating breaking their
agreements."

Remarq paused then, as if to allow his meaning to become clear, and in the silence Trosvig drew out his
pocket towel and began to wipe his palms.

"I expect," Remarq continued then, "that you and your
colleagues in the Triune have received Minister Haken's
missive regarding the storage of our ships at Yan. It is
very important that that policy be rescinded as quickly as

possible. I know I can trust you, Chairman Balthrop, and General Roemhild to bring that about during your next meeting of the Defense Directorate."

Remarq paused again, but only for a moment this time. "The Unified Worlds would also be well advised to take an additional initiative in conjunction with the release of our ships," he said, "as a demonstration of good faith to the people of Issel. The withdrawal of Unified forces from either Yan or Saede would be considered an appropriate gesture. That, of course, will be the responsibility of your Admiral Oleszek. I trust you can persuade him to move forward on the withdrawal in a timely manner."

Listening to the choice of words, the intonation, Trosvig could visualize Remarq's expression: eyes like black obsidian burning out of the video monitor, burning a warning into his soul.

Trosvig looked around the table in the Triune's conference room. "I expect that all of you received the message from Issel's new minister of interplanetary relations?" he said. "The one regarding our storage of their ships at Yan?"

Heads nodded, and Trosvig heard muttered comments from two or three of the military personnel.

It was the same circle of faces that had gathered nearly three months before, he realized, to decide the matter of Admiral Serege's retirement. The same circle plus two: Admiral Tolmich Oleszek now filled Serege's seat, and General Ande Pitesson of Mythos had returned from the Issel system since then.

Trosvig directed his first question to the general. "Exactly what were your reasons, Ande, for taking Isselan vessels into storage at Yan?"

Pitesson was blunt. "To prevent them from being employed against the Unified Worlds and their forces, Your Honor."

"How many ships did our people confiscate," asked Chairman Neol Balthrop, "and what is their present condition?"

Pitesson squinted at the ceiling as if the numbers were printed there. "We brought in nineteen frigates, two destroyers, and approximately thirty smaller ships. Corvettes and patrol craft, mostly." He returned his vision to Balthrop. "Every one of them had damage to one extent or another."

"What about their weapon systems?" asked General Kalousek of Topawa.

"All major weapon systems have been removed and put into separate storage," said Pitesson. "All that remain aboard are minimal defensive weapons. Laser cannon and the like."

"The Isselan government hasn't specifically asked that the weapon systems be returned with the ships, has it?" asked a Jonican admiral.

"No, ma'am," Kun Reng-Tan of Kaleo said. "And it's my recommendation that if the ships are to be returned, the weapons remain behind."

"Even without the weapon systems," said Alois Ashforth, "could those ships be returned to combat capability? Is that possible?"

Pitesson considered, scrunching up his brows. "Yes, it's possible," he said after a few moments' thought, "but it would be a lot more difficult. I doubt the Isselan economy could bear that kind of a burden right now. Considering that most of those ships are Resistance-period technology, anyway, Issel would be better advised to build a new fleet than try to refurbish for combat what's left of the old one."

"According to the message," said Trosvig, "Issel has requested the release of its ships for use as freighters, in an effort to rebuild its commerce." He turned back to Pitesson. "I expect that you have seen the ships in question, General. Do you feel this is a legitimate use for them? Could these former combat vessels be serviceable as freighters?"

"With minimal alteration," Pitesson confirmed, nodding.

There were more thoughtful nods, more mutters around the table, and then General Roemhild of Enach said, "I understand that there are still some Unified forces in the Issel system at this time, lending support with early warning patrols and system-defense duties until the Isselan Defense Forces are capable again. Do you still feel, Ande, that our forces would be at risk if we were to release Issel's ships?"

Pitesson gave that some contemplation, too. "I think there's much less chance of an incident occurring now," he said at last. "Things were pretty dicey at first—everybody operating on a hair trigger and jumping at shadows—but everything was pretty well calmed down by the time my forces rotated out. I wouldn't say there's no threat at all, but it certainly has lessened."

People shifted in their chairs, and Trosvig swept his gaze about the table again, locking it, for a moment, on Roemhild's and Balthrop's. "It appears to me," he said, "that the original reasons for securing the vessels are no longer applicable. Therefore, I move that we grant Issel its request for their release and open talks to arrange for their transport back to that system."

There were only three opposed when the vote was taken.

One of the three, however, was Oleszek, Trosvig noticed. Which meant that his next task was going to be all the more difficult.

He made certain he was waiting in the corridor when the other participants emerged from the conference room at the meeting's conclusion.

"Admiral!" he said as Oleszek turned up the hallway. The other stopped and turned back, and Trosvig said, "I need to clarify a point about the Spherzah that was brought to my attention the other day. Do you have a few moments?"

"A few, Your Honor," Oleszek said. Taller than Serege and swarthy of features, he questioned Trosvig with his eyes.

The conference room was empty by now, the other members of the Triune and Defense Directorate dispersing up and down the corridor. Trosvig gestured at the open door, and Oleszek stepped back inside. Trosvig followed, closing the door behind him.

Oleszek didn't return to the table, didn't take a seat. "What is it?" he demanded.

"The time has come," said Trosvig, "to withdraw the Spherzah from Yan."

Oleszek's dark eyes narrowed. "With what justification?" he said. "Yan is one of the main attack routes between Issel and Sostis. It's the Unified Worlds's first line of defense. Withdrawal of our forces would leave us vulnerable to incursion."

"In the past—even the recent past—that has been true," said Trosvig. "But once DeByes's readmission proposal is passed, that border, that . . . first line of defense . . . will be obsolete. As it is right now, our presence there is causing understandable distrust among the Isselan people. Withdrawing our forces from Yan will be a clear demonstration of good faith on the part of the Unified Worlds."

"It would also be a clear demonstration of our stupidity," said Oleszek. "The readmission proposal hasn't passed yet, Your Honor, and at this point the distrust is mutual—at least for some of us."

He paused then, and his eyes abruptly tightened to

flinty slits that fixed on Trosvig's face. "Even if Issel were not at issue," he said, "you of all people, Your Honor, should know that I cannot act on orders that come through other than official channels."

Trosvig drew himself up. "The chief commander of the Spherzah answers directly to the Triune," he said, "without the intervention of either the Defense Directorate or the individual world governments. You were briefed on the chain of command, Admiral, prior to your swearing in and the change of command."

"I was briefed," said Oleszek, "that I answer to the *whole* Triune, acting in concert, not to one member of it acting alone."

"Not in this case." Trosvig let his voice turn steely, let his own eyes narrow.

Oleszek held his gaze. Nodded slightly after a moment. "I see," he said, very quietly. Very grimly. "And if I do not comply, will I also meet an untimely demise in a dark walkway as Percivan Radeleff did?"

"No," Trosvig said. "You don't have to fear dark walkways, Admiral. But your daughter Hatarina might prefer death for herself."

He saw how the admiral's hands knotted into fists at his sides, how his jaw turned hard as stone. "What about Hatarina?" Oleszek demanded.

"She's made quite a success of her life, hasn't she?" said Trosvig. "I understand she's a renowned pediatrician at a major hospital now. She's joined to an eminent professor at an historic university, and they're the proud parents of three children."

"If you so much as touch my daughter . . . !" Oleszek left the threat unfinished, but the words came as a growl through locked teeth.

"Oh, no one will touch her, Admiral—not in a physical sense, at least," said Trosvig. "But imagine what it would do to her practice—what it would do to her family—if someone were to press charges over the unfortunate incident that took place during her second year of medical school. The family of the young man who died, for example. Or the families of the students who suffered irreparable brain damage after using the drugs she provided them. Fizz, wasn't it?" Trosvig studied the admiral from beneath a lowered eyebrow.

Oleszek had turned pale. His fisted hands had loosened; he held them out before himself in a pleading posture. "That was over fifteen years ago!" he said.

"The engines of justice burn slowly, don't they?" said Trosvig. "Perhaps it's time that the whole truth be told. It's the kind of story that would fill newsnets across the known galaxy for weeks!"

"No!" Oleszek shook his head, then buried his face in his hands. "Hatarina's already paid the price for her mistakes! Leave her alone!"

"We can do that, Admiral." Trosvig had softened his voice, made it almost reassuring. "All you have to do is withdraw your troops."

His legs ached, his back ached, his shoulders and arms ached. The way they had ached after long days on the move, Lujan thought. The kind of days, during military exercises in the Cathana Mountains of Yan, when he and his team had covered fifty kilometers or more to reach and accomplish their objective. They had lived for three standard weeks at a time out of backpacks that nearly matched their own body weight. Those had been the nights when even bedding down between the forked branches of a tree, fifteen meters above the ground, had felt good.

All he'd done today was walk, with the assistance of the support frame, across the rehab room and back.

Lujan sighed and shifted, trying to find a more comfortable position.

There didn't seem to be one. Moving only eased the aches for a few moments.

When he was still awake an hour later, he gave up on trying to sleep. "Holo-vid on," he said. "Mini-mum volume. Global News Net-work."

The holovid in the facing wall burst silently to life, revealing the newscaster at her desk. Her mouth moved, but Lujan couldn't read her lips. He glanced over at Darcie, lying asleep beside him. "Vol-ume up two points," he said.

Even then he had to strain to catch all the words.

". . . officials have taken two more important steps toward reuniting Issel with the Unified Worlds," the woman was saying. "The Defense Directorate decided today to release to the Isselan government a number of combat vessels—"

Lujan furrowed his brow. Surely she hadn't said what he thought she had! "Vol-ume up two more points," he said—and then thought, *Activate memory chip.*

"—which were seized during the recent conflict in that system," the woman went on a bit more loudly. "The battle-damaged frigates and corvettes have been held at spacedocks in the Yan system. The Isselan government has requested their return for use as trade freighters.

"In other developments"—the newscaster was replaced by the image of a solemn-faced man in the uniform of an admiral of the Spherzah, who was applying a laser seal to a document—"Admiral Tolmich Oleszek, chief commander of the Spherzah, today sealed orders to withdraw all Spherzah personnel from Yan. Admiral Oleszek was quoted at the ceremony as saying, 'Yan has traditionally been the Unified Worlds's first line of defense against Issel. With the removal of our troops from this sector, we symbolically bring down the barriers that have separated our peoples for so long.' "

Lujan stared, paralyzed with shock. "What in the worlds are you *do-ing*, Tolmich?" he murmured half aloud. Then, recalling Nemec's message, he shook his head—carefully—and whispered, "Blast!" between clenched teeth.

Beside him, Darcie stirred. Blinking, she looked toward the holovid first and then pushed herself up on one elbow. "What's going on, Lujan?" she asked sleepily.

He had locked his teeth so tightly it actually hurt when he tried to speak again. "They've jusst ta-ken the first—steps toward rearming Issel," he managed, "and now—they're open-ing the Yan front and in-viting the Isselans in."

TWENTY-TWO

"**How's your vision been since we made**
those adjustments?" asked Dr. Moses.

"It's fine," Lujan said.

"And your hearing?"

"I haven't had—any problems."

"Good. Your speech has mostly cleared up, too. Hold
out your left hand now."

Lujan did, and Moses ran her stylus up and down his fingers, touching their tips with its point, first firmly, then
lightly. She was testing his sensation and reflexes, he knew.
She had him grip her hand as tightly as he could, then ran
him through a series of fine motor coordination checks.

"Good," she said again when she finished. "Let's see
the right one now."

She ran the same series of tests on his right hand, then
had him stand up from the examining table and walk
around the small room.

He made his way slowly, holding on to whatever was
available to steady himself. His sense of balance was still
off; a move made too quickly was likely to send him
crashing to the floor—at the least to leave him swaying in
a whirlpool of dizziness.

"Still a few problems with equilibrium, eh?" Moses
said.

"Yes," Lujan sighed.

It was less than forty steps around the room but his legs were shaky by the time he got back to the examining table. He sat down with an immense sense of relief.

Moses studied him thoughtfully for a few moments. "I'm going to go ahead and release you in the morning, Lujan," she said. "The PT department at the base hospital in Anchenko can provide you with your follow-up therapy. I think you'll gain back your strength more quickly out there in a more familiar and comfortable setting."

Lujan met Moses's gaze. Held it. It hadn't even been a full five months since he'd arrived at this hospital. Unconscious and in critical condition, he hadn't been expected to survive even the emergency surgery. But Moses, like Darcie, had never doubted he would recover. His throat abruptly grew tight. "Thank you, Libby," he said. "You and Berron have—worked a miracle."

It was vastly inadequate, he knew; but there would never be a way to thank her properly.

He emerged shortly before dawn, before the first stirrings of activity began, from a side entrance of the Transition Quarters, leaning on Darcie's arm and shadowed by a Sostish plainclothes policeman. A skimcraft with a tinted canopy waited at the door, and Darcie helped him slide in. She helped him with the safety straps, too, when his hands couldn't manage the latch. Then she slid in beside him, and the officer took the passenger seat next to the driver.

They didn't go to Herbrun Field; the skimmer arced to the south, around the dawn-touched tips of the glaciered peaks, instead of heading toward the sea. Their destination was the public spaceport.

In a few minutes the skimmer eased to a stop before the shuttleport of a commercial starliner company. Tristan and another plainclothes policeman were waiting at the entrance with the glidechair, and Lujan was just as glad to transfer into it. He would have never thought such a short trip by skimmer could be so taxing.

They were the first to board the shuttle, by a separate hatch because of the glidechair. The officers escorted them as far as a private seating compartment, partitioned off from the main passenger cabin.

Shifting into his seat, Lujan immediately rotated it back into its reclining launch position and closed his eyes.

"Are you all right, love?" Darcie asked from his left.

"Tired already," he sighed.

And they hadn't even lifted off yet. How would he ever make it through a lightskip aboard the starliner?

It was odd, Trosvig thought, listening to his mail, that he hadn't heard from Remarq for so long. The last message he'd received had been the one accompanying Minister Haken's request for the release of the ships—and that had been two standard weeks ago.

Might the recent severe weather have interfered with incoming transmissions? he wondered. The lightning storms that had enveloped Ramiscal City for the last several days had certainly been severe enough to disrupt some forms of communication.

There was a way to check, Trosvig knew. Every on-line mail system had, as part of its programming, a system-level message log. Everyone knew it was there, but few ever gave it any thought—unless expected messages weren't received or sent messages bounced back. If Remarq's communiqués had made it as far as a relay before being lost, there would be a record of it in the system message log.

"Show system message log," Trosvig said, "working from the present back."

A request appeared on the monitor: PLEASE ENTER PASSWORD AND SECURITY CODE.

Trosvig obediently typed them in on the keyboard.

After a couple of moments, a roster unrolled down the monitor.

It showed all mail transactions for the current day, both incoming and outgoing, for every user on the headquarters mail system.

Trosvig rolled his eyes. "Filter out all transaction records except those related to the mail account of Seamus Trosvig," he said.

The message log shrank, so that its range covered not only the present day but the previous two as well.

There was no record of any transmission from Issel.

"Next screen back," Trosvig said.

He scrutinized it when it came up, and found no sign of a message from Remarq. He went back another screen.

There were still no messages from Remarq. But something else caught his attention—and held it.

On the twenty-sixth day of the third month—eight days ago—someone had entered his message program. There was no explanation beyond the time the contact was made. No indication of origin. Nothing even to suggest a message that had been sent but not received. It was simply—a contact.

Brows drawn together, Trosvig said, "Display origin of contact on log line two-fifty-eight."

A notation appeared next to the contact icon: NO ORIGIN AVAILABLE.

Something about that made his palms grow damp, made his pulse increase ever so slightly.

"Display all available information about contact on line two-fifty-eight," he said.

The notation reappeared: NO FURTHER INFORMATION AVAILABLE.

Trosvig stared at the words, his heart beating noticeably

harder now against the inside of his ribs. He reached for his pocket towel and began to roll it between his hands.

"Show next screen back," he said after a long minute, and swallowed down the unsteadiness in his voice.

There was at least one hit every day, sometimes two, but every request for identification resulted in the same notation in the explanation column: NO INFORMATION AVAILABLE.

He kept going back, one screen at a time, until he found where the anonymous hits began. Then he checked several more screens before that.

He found nothing. The whole string of mysterious contacts lay between the thirteenth and twenty-sixth days of the third month.

And intermingled with them, up to the twenty-second day of the third month, were logged the messages he had received from Remarq: a total of four in that time frame. Most were lists of agents to be activated; the last was the request for release of the ships.

"Close message log," he said at last, and sat for a long time wondering at explanations.

None that he came up with were satisfactory.

Finally, kneading the pocket towel hard, he said, "Compose message."

The routing blocks appeared on his monitor. He filled them, and then began with some trepidation, "My lord Remarq, Chief Cabinet Minister of the World Government of Issel: I have this morning discovered a matter of some concern in my log of communications."

He paused then, considering how to phrase his explanation in the least damaging manner. "There are a number of indications that someone has attempted to make contact via my mail system," he said at last, "and has failed to do so. Attempts to open and identify the source of these contacts have yielded only notations saying 'No information available.'

"During the thirteen-day period in which those contacts occurred, I have logged only four messages from you. Because of both the atypically low number of communications received from you and the secure nature of the contacts I have described, I am concerned that, due to the severity of the seasonal weather here, I may have missed messages from you. If that is the case, I fear it may be necessary to forward your instructions once more so I may have them carried out. At any rate, my lord, I offer my most abject apologies for this inconvenience. I am, as always, your humble servant, Seamus Trosvig."

He sat for some time wringing the pocket towel after the message was sent.

A response from Minister Remarq was waiting when he opened his mail queue two mornings later.

"My dear friend Seamus," the chief minister said, "I am deeply concerned by the contents of your recent communication to me. Let me assure you at once that the four messages you mentioned are the only ones I have sent you during the period of time you specified; I have never sent any communiqués that have not been received as intended. Therefore, I recommend that you make a thorough examination of the security of your communications program and procedures. This appears to be an attempt to gain access.

"I also suggest," Remarq said, "that you make a careful inventory of any persons who may have either a personal cause against you or any reason to hold your activities in suspicion—anyone, in other words, who might have motivation to discredit you or cause you other harm.

"We are fast approaching a most critical point in our efforts to reunite Issel with the Unified Worlds. We cannot afford complications." The synthesized voice turned almost sinister with its warning: "It is your responsibility, Seamus, to ensure that any further incursions of the type you have described are swiftly and decisively dealt with."

Trosvig, listening, responded with a stiff nod and wiped wet hands on his pocket towel.

There was a weighty pause, and then Remarq's recorded voice said, "I wish to add one more recommendation, Seamus: Do not discount Admiral Serege. We have not seen him buried yet."

"Serege!" Trosvig snorted it, recalling the man's appearance on the day of his retirement from the admiralty. Serege had been bedridden, gaunt, his blind eyes focusing on some invisible distance, his mouth sagging open so that saliva spilled from its slack corner. Trosvig had wondered for some time afterward if Serege even understood what was going on; he'd certainly not given the slightest indication of it.

No, Serege was the last person he needed to be concerned about, he thought. He shoved himself away from the terminal and reached for his intercom. "Talbot," he said, "please contact the Computer Security and Maintenance office. My desk terminal appears to have developed a malfunction."

"Right away, sir," Talbot answered.

And Trosvig turned back to his keyboard. He had several log entries to remove before any maintenance people arrived.

Migdal Chorafas entered the reception area of the offices of the Triune dressed to work, in a nondescript coverall uniform of putty gray. No sense giving the Honorable Seamus Trosvig anything to think about by showing up in his usual Spherzah utility uniform, he thought. Especially when he already had a suspicion of what had prompted Trosvig's call.

His suspicions were confirmed when he saw what was displayed on Trosvig's monitor. The anonymous contacts stood out in the message log like energy flares against a night sky. "It appears," Trosvig said as they eyed the display, "that someone is attempting to gain access to my communications."

Chorafas briefly pursed his mouth. "No doubt about that, Your Honor," he said.

"Communications at this level of government are often highly sensitive," Trosvig persisted. "This unauthorized access must be uncovered and curtailed immediately! It could be disastrous if the wrong persons were to obtain our sensitive information!"

Through the corner of his eye, Chorafas could see Trosvig wringing a small cloth between his hands. *Disastrous to the Unified Worlds in general or just to the conspiracy you're a part of?* he thought.

"Can you trace it?" Trosvig asked.

Chorafas blew out a breath. "I can try," he said. He indicated Trosvig's chair. "May I?"

"Be my guest."

Chorafas settled into the high-backed chair and slid the terminal's keyboard out of its compartment beneath the monitor. If he had entered Admiral Serege's access correctly . . .

Over the next two hours he tried every trace parameter any competent computer technician would know of, and a couple of techniques he'd learned at the frontier sensor sites besides. That anonymous access was not permeable; the admiral was secure—for now.

But he squelched a sensation of satisfaction and lapsed back in the chair, shaking his head.

"What is it?" Trosvig asked at his shoulder. He was wringing his hands with increased nervousness now.

"I don't know," Chorafas said. "I've tried every trick in

the manuals to break it and nothing is working." He shifted, straightening again, and shrugged. "It's beginning to look like we're not dealing with a human hacker here."

"Why is that?" Trosvig wanted to know.

"There's no identifier—none at all—and there's no way to trace something without an identifier." Chorafas made a helpless gesture with both hands. "It's like—nobody did it."

Which was exactly the idea.

Trosvig had turned pale. "Well then, is there some way you can block it?"

"Sorry, Your Honor." Chorafas pushed himself up from the chair. "Not if we can't determine where it's coming from. Unless, of course, you want to just take down your whole mail program."

Both of them knew he couldn't do that.

Chorafas went directly to his work cubicle when he returned to the computer maintenance vault. He punched Nemec's call code into his commset.

"The old unit's getting together over at the Officers' Club tonight," he said when the other came on the line. "Seems to me you could use a little R and R, Ajimir. Why don't you join us?"

There was a little pause at the other end, then a sigh. "You're right, Mig," Nemec said. "I really could use a break. I think I'll come."

"Good!" said Chorafas. "Meet me here at the shop when you get off duty."

Nemec was prompt in arriving that evening, and as before, Chorafas led him back to his cubicle.

"Had a work order up in the Triune's offices this morning," he began.

"Oh?" Nemec cocked an eyebrow.

"Yep. Trosvig himself." Chorafas paused to look

Nemec in the eye. "He'd discovered some unidentified tracks in his communications system."

He watched his friend stiffen. Saw how his eyes widened. "So what did you do?" Nemec asked.

"I tried every method I could think of to pin down the hacker," he said.

"And—?" said Nemec.

"No go," said Chorafas. "Whoever it is has gone completely transparent." And he gave a sly smile.

Nemec grinned back and relaxed; but Chorafas grew serious once more. "The point is," he said, "Trosvig knows somebody's onto him now. He was obviously worried, and worried men tend to leap to conclusions without looking first. I think a warning is in order, Aj. History is full of lynchings carried out by scared and angry men who jumped to conclusions."

Nemec's features abruptly grew somber. "Admiral Serege was released from the hospital a week ago," he said. "He should be home on Topawa by now. Passing a warning in time may be a little difficult."

Chorafas drew his brows together and chewed briefly on his lower lip, thinking. "Maybe not," he said. "I've got an idea."

TWENTY-THREE

A petty officer brought the glidechair out of a cargo compartment when the military shuttle set down at Anchenko Base.

"Thank you," Lujan told her, "but I can walk off."

Beside him, Darcie said, "Lujan, you know how long the tunnel out to the ramp is!"

"I can make it," he replied.

"But why?" she asked.

He turned his head toward her—heavily, she thought—and met her eyes. His face was slack with exhaustion, and haggard—more haggard than she'd seen it in nearly three months. "You said my family was going to be here to meet us," he said. "If my sisters see me in that"—he made a loose gesture in the direction of the glidechair—"they'll treat me like an invalid!"

At the moment, Luj, Darcie thought, *you're more an invalid than not.* But she said only, "So it's a matter of pride."

"No," he said. "Just human dignity."

Perhaps there was a difference, she thought, but right now it seemed a very fine line. She sighed, and turned to their son. "Tris, please help your father, will you? I'll follow with the glidechair."

Tristan practically had to lift Lujan to his feet, and

even then he swayed—gripped the back of the seat in front of him and refused to look at Darcie.

He had spent most of the starliner journey in his berth. Weary by the time the shuttle out of Ramiscal City docked at the space station, he had gone directly to their cabin and slept until dinnertime.

She had thought the large ship's lower gravity would allow him to move about more easily; but the buoyancy played havoc with his uncertain equilibrium, and the gravity shifts were as wearing as tilting the bed had been at the beginning of his recovery.

Then, three days into the journey, they had made light-skip. For probably the first time in Lujan's life, the skip made him violently ill. He'd only been beginning to regain his strength four days afterward when the starliner reached Topawa's space station.

Now he was determined to walk out of the landing bay. Darcie saw the way he sagged on Tristan's shoulder, saw the way his right leg dragged, and shook her head.

And he reeled, right in front of her.

Tristan caught him, kept him from falling, and stared back at her with his eyes wide. She nudged the glidechair up behind her mate's knees and said, "Sit down, Lujan."

"I'm—fine," he panted over his shoulder. "I—jus' lost—m' balance for—a moment. I'm fine."

"Stubborn man!" she said to his back, her teeth gritted tight, as he wrapped his arm about Tristan's shoulder and started forward again.

Sheer stubbornness, she thought, watching him, *filling in when there was no more strength.*

It was partly that same stubbornness, she realized at once, that had put him back on his feet at all.

There were no kidding shouts this time as he emerged from the launch pad's tunnel, leaning heavily on Tristan. The familiar little crowd Darcie remembered from their previous homecoming—had it been only a year ago?—simply encircled him, some of them tear-streaked; and when he swayed, they held him up.

"Lujan, you look exhausted!" said his older sister. "Why don't you and Darcie and Tris stay here in town with us tonight and go on out to the homestead in the morning?"

"Thanks, Laurel," he said, just as he had to the petty officer aboard the shuttle, "but"—he released a shaky breath—"I just want to go home."

"It's ready and waiting for you," his brother Siljan said. "I'll go get the skimmer."

It was another hour's flight by skimcraft out to the homestead. Lujan stayed stoically silent through the trip, his vision fixed on the russet landscape sliding by below, but Darcie read pain in the lines that etched his face.

It must have been fairly severe by the time they arrived at the farmhouse. She noticed that he made no effort to protest when Siljan helped Tristan haul the glidechair from the cargo compartment. The two of them lifted him into it. He only sighed, "Thank you," and let Darcie steer the chair into the house.

She put him to bed even before she reset the house computer's environment controls. "You've probably set back your recovery by at least a week, you know," she said, placing a couple of pain tablets and a drinking bottle in his hands.

He looked up from the pain pills, met her eyes. "I didn't know I had a deadline to be fully recovered," he said.

She couldn't help chuckling a little at that, couldn't help ruffling up his hair and kissing his mouth. "The only deadline you have, Luj," she said, "is the one that you set for yourself."

Two mornings later, she woke just at dawn to find Lujan gone from his side of the bed. She sat up, pushing tendrils of hair away from her face, and looked first toward the bathroom.

The door was ajar, the room beyond dark. She reached for her robe, slipped it on as she rose, and peered inside anyway, calling his name.

He wasn't there.

"In his office, perhaps," she thought aloud, and stepped out into the living area.

His office, too, was empty and dark; and he wasn't in the kitchen.

Topawa's oversize sun was just reaching over the horizon with its fingers of light. They shot through the kitchen window, drawing Darcie to look out, to watch as they brushed the outbuildings and the windpump's stark frame with soft gold. The skimmer shed, the well house, the barn Lujan had long ago renovated to serve as a dojo—

The dojo.

"Oh, my word!" Darcie whispered. "He wouldn't have—"

Wrapping her robe more tightly about herself, she reached for the kitchen door. Stepping outside into the crisp desert air, she made her way swiftly across the barren yard to the half-open door of the dojo.

Illuminants had been activated inside, but she could hear Lujan before she could see him; two or three massive crates blocked her view from the door. When their household goods had been shipped here from the Flag Officers' Residence on Sostis, the packing crates that hadn't fit in the farmhouse's two extra bedrooms had been stacked, in no particular semblance of order, in the dojo.

Leaving her shoes at the door, she stepped inside.

Silent on bare feet, she slipped around the first two packing crates—and almost gave herself away when she barely missed bumping into the support frame he still used for walking sometimes, which had been hidden in the shadow of a third crate.

In the space that was left at the back of the dojo, Lujan was working at ba'gua: walking the circle, as the exercise was called, with its distinctive positioning of palms and feet and its silken smooth changes of direction.

At least, he was trying to walk the circle. His right leg still dragged, leaving the foot's placement unsure, and his weak equilibrium made him waver. The twining arm movements, compared by some masters to a lady's dance for grace and a tiger's claws for ferocity, were jerky, frequently flung outward in a reflexive attempt to maintain balance.

Darcie bit her lip, watching him and remembering the other morning she had followed him here to the dojo, only a year before. He had been practicing *iaijutsu* then, slicing the dim light to silver ribbons with the razor edge of a *katana.* She had watched with her breath caught in her throat, marveling at the magnificence of his movements—his speed, his strength, his grace—and had felt her pulse heighten with her hunger for him.

As she watched now, he lost his footing altogether and fell. Went down hard on his side. She choked off her gasp in her throat.

He turned over. Pushed himself up, stiffly. His breaths seemed to rake through his ribs and came in gulps through his mouth.

Part of her wanted to run to him, to help him back to his feet and kiss away the smart from the welt she glimpsed on his cheekbone. But a stronger part held her back, kept her concealed, counseled her that he had to do this alone.

Her hands curled into fists, and she pressed them together, to her mouth. "Get up, Lujan," she whispered behind them, soundless under the rasps of his panting. "Get back up! Don't give up now!"

Her breath seemed trapped, squeezing at her heart, as

she watched him struggle to rise. He came to his knees. Hesitated there before he planted his left foot awkwardly, shakily under him. He pushed himself up with a groan.

He stood still for a moment then, swaying and catching his breath, before he resumed the hand positions and went on with the circle.

She watched him fall and struggle up twice more before she could bear it no longer. Then she slipped out of the dojo.

She waited until she reached the kitchen to give in to the sobs.

A creak somewhere in the mansion jerked Trosvig awake with a start. He sat up, heart pounding hard under his ribs, eyes staring into the dark.

It was only the dropping outdoor temperature, he tried to persuade himself, making the ancient timbers contract and shift in their joints. Nothing more.

He lay back down, swallowing, and concentrated on drawing slow and steady breaths. But the too-hard pounding of his heart persisted. His mind was full of images, of voices. Dreamed, or remembered from another source? He wasn't certain.

His vision fixed on the shadows beyond the curtained viewpane, moving in the wind that swept up from the ocean. Held by their swaying as if he were mesmerized, he tried to sort out the images and voices.

Over the last few days, the anonymous contacts had begun to reappear in the system message log. There was no more indication of their source now than there had been the first time.

He felt as if he were being watched.

Make an inventory of persons who had personal cause against him or any reason to be suspicious, Remarq had advised. Anyone who might have motive to discredit him or cause him harm.

The list he had compiled contained seventeen names. He had considered each one carefully, and had ruled out most.

"Do not discount Admiral Serege," Remarq had warned.

Intellect told him he could dismiss the disabled admiral. But the fear that lay in his stomach, huddled there like a living thing, told him otherwise.

Do not discount Admiral Serege.

Those words seemed to be the most persistent echo in his skull. Trosvig shoved himself over on his side, tugging the bedcovers up about his shoulders; but before he could dismiss the statement entirely, another face appeared in his memory: Dr. Libby Moses, the admiral's personal physician, her features serious. "He *expects* to resume his command," she had said when he'd called her in after Serege's seizure. "I know that, Your Honor, because I know *him.* And I've learned never to underestimate him."

Never underestimate him. . . .

He tried to remember what else she and Dr. Gavril had said at that time.

"He hasn't lost the ability to reason," Moses had emphasized. "He devised a method of communicating with us. It's slow, but it demonstrates a thinking mind."

Serege had appeared to be little more than a vegetable on the day of his retirement.

Appearances alone could be deceptive, Trosvig counseled himself.

But the computer maintenance technician had said it didn't look like they were dealing with a human hacker.

But what was it the admiral's neurosurgeon had said that day about their plans for his recovery? Something about restoring his vision and hearing with prosthetic implants. They would be instrumental in helping him to communicate.

What if Serege's doctors hadn't stopped at simply restoring his hearing and sight? What if they had embedded extra chips inside his skull, giving him capabilities above and beyond those of normal humans? It certainly wasn't difficult to do; millions of people throughout the galaxy had enhancements done, for a variety of reasons. The surgical procedures were routine now, though still costly. With the appropriate appliances, anyone could hack into a computer network and appear to be anything but human.

Anyone could do it. . . .

Frustrated, Trosvig sat up in bed. He glanced over at Jolenta when she stirred in her sleep beside him, and then leaned back against his bolster. Folding his arms on his chest, he narrowed his eyes at the opposite wall.

Anyone *could* do it, he acknowledged, but who would be most motivated to do it? That had to be taken into consideration, too.

Serege had plenty of motive. He, Seamus Trosvig, had pushed through Serege's retirement, after all. And Serege had always opposed his liberal views toward Issel— probably reason enough for him to harbor suspicions. Serege had been intractable on a number of items Trosvig had wanted to include in the Assistance Agreement.

It was odd, Trosvig mused, wiping damp palms on the blanket, that there had been nothing further in the media about Serege's progress or condition after he was retired. Had his loss of VIP status made him suddenly so uninteresting to the newsnets? Or had other events simply taken precedence? Did anyone outside the hospital even have any information on the former admiral's condition these days?

He would have to call the hospital in the morning, he

decided. A few well-placed queries might provide all the answers he needed to his current questions.

"This is Winthancom Military Medical Center Public Affairs," said the woman who looked out at him from the visiphone viewscreen. "I am Alyssa Danzl. How may I help you, sir?"

Trosvig made his tone one of concern. "I've noticed," he said, "that there's been nothing in the newsnets lately about Admiral Serege. There haven't been . . . complications in his recovery, have there?" He drew his brows together.

"No sir," said Danzl. "In fact, the admiral was released from this facility over a standard week ago."

"Released?" Trosvig hadn't been expecting that. He tried to keep the note of surprise out of his voice. "Do you know where he's living now?"

"It was generally expected," the woman said, "that he was to return to his homeworld. I have no specific data on the location, nor would I be at liberty to disclose it if I did."

"I understand." Trosvig gave a curt nod, and let the creases in his brow deepen. "Can you at least tell me what day he was released and . . . give me some idea of . . . how he was doing?"

"According to his physicians," said Danzl, "his recovery had progressed sufficiently that they felt he could no longer benefit from hospitalization, nor would it be necessary." She said that as if it should be self-evident; but then she added, "He was released on the twenty-seventh of last month."

Trosvig ruminated on that for a moment, then said, "Thank you" with another stiff nod and disconnected the call.

The twenty-seventh of last month.

That was the day after the last anonymous contact had appeared in the system message log.

The admiral was believed to have returned to his homeworld. He was Topawan, wasn't he? And flight time between Sostis and Topawa was about seven standard days.

Trosvig called up the system message log. On a sudden thought, he looked for anonymous hits against other users' mail accounts as well.

There were many: hits against his fellow members of the Triune, against Admiral Oleszek, against various members of the Assembly.

He examined the roster more closely. On a thought, he began a mental tally of the number of hits against particular accounts.

The vast majority were against his own and Abigail De-Byes's. The next largest clusters of contacts were into the mail queues of the individuals Remarq had ordered him to activate. And the hits against Oleszek had been followed by a number of probes into every department of the Spherzah.

The Spherzah.

Trosvig set his jaw, and began to count the days in which no contacts had been made.

Eight days.

It fit. Coincidence? He doubted it.

"Close log," he said, "and compose message."

He kept it brief. He had reason to believe, he told Remarq, that Serege was indeed the individual responsible for the incursions into his communications system. He was taking measures now to ensure that such incursions would be terminated.

It shouldn't be too difficult, he thought, to find a cyborg who, for sufficient payment, would be willing to hunt and destroy another cyborg.

Lujan released a breath in a sigh of exhaustion, sank back in his office chair, and raised a heavy hand to rub at his eyes. Artificial or not, they still seemed to burn, although he knew it was really the sensitive tissues around them.

A standard week of searching through Oleszek's communications and those of his staff, and through the messages dispatched to various headquarters departments and scattered detachments, had yielded nothing: no suggestions that the chief commander's coercion had as yet trickled further into the Spherzah than his own Command Section.

He had discovered that arrangements for the withdrawal of Spherzah units from Yan had been relegated to a committee formed especially for that purpose, and its members reported directly to Oleszek himself. There had been a few messages from Trosvig to Oleszek as well, but little else.

Lujan wasn't certain whether he should feel relief or concern that he hadn't uncovered anything else yet.

He couldn't probe any further right now, though; he needed desperately to rest. *Close down comms review parameters and exit base computer system,* he thought.

"Yes sir," said the AI voice in his head. "Thank you for using SecuriNet Systems."

Eyes still closed, he waited for the feedback clicks that signaled the disconnect, then said aloud, "Desk terminal on."

He listened as it hummed and clicked. When its beep declared it operational, he thought, *Copy all new data from onboard memory chip*—he pictured the processor at the base of his skull—*to memory unit two in*—he conjured a mental image of his desk terminal. Mental icons. *Use the current date and time for the name of the file, and give verbal confirmation when copying is complete.*

Another beep acknowledged his instructions.

He sat still, eyes closed, until the terminal's synthesized voice said, "Copying complete."

"Thank you," Lujan said aloud. "Exit desk terminal."

Opening his eyes only then, he reached out for the edge of the desktop. He pulled himself stiffly to his feet, teeth closed against a groan.

He hadn't brought the walking support frame into the office with him; he had to steady himself with a hand to the wall as he made his way to the door. *Next time you plan to sit in here for three hours,* he counseled himself, *don't forget the blasted support frame!*

He limped the fifteen steps from the office to the bedroom door.

"Are you all right, Luj?" Darcie called from the kitchen.

He looked up. She was perched on a stool before the kitchen computer, chin propped in her hand—back into her medical school refresher courses, which she'd left on hiatus through most of his recovery.

"Just tired," he assured her.

He'd always found desk jobs to be more fatiguing than strenuous physical activity.

He lowered himself to the bed with care, stretched out on it with a sigh, and began to review in his mind the results of his searches.

He fell asleep wondering what he had missed.

"My dear Seamus," said the synthesized voice of the mail program, "I am most relieved that you have discovered the source of your difficulty. I have personally dispatched a number of Enforcers to ensure that it will be taken care of. In the meantime, I recommend most strongly that you do not lower your guard. Problems of this nature, like weeds in a garden, are seldom eradicated in a single stroke; and a stalk such as this one has most probably already sent out runners in other parts of the garden.

"For that reason," the imitation of Remarq's voice

went on, "I also recommend that the committee set the earliest possible date to call for the final vote on its readmission proposal. According to your own law, if I recall correctly, a winning vote in your Assembly, witnessed by all participants and recorded by the officiator, is all that is necessary to pass a bill into law.

"We are far too close to finally grasping the dream that has eluded us for so long to allow it to be dashed once more." There was a brief pause, and then Remarq's voice said, "I place all of my confidence in you, Seamus, to see this through, along with all of the responsibility which that entails."

A responsibility that was growing more uncomfortable by the day, Trosvig reflected.

Remarq might have saved himself the trouble of dispatching the Enforcers, however, he thought. He was prepared to take care of the Serege problem himself.

But first he must see to another aspect of his responsibility. He punched a call code into his visiphone and leaned back in his chair.

Abigail DeByes herself responded. "Your Honor!" she smiled from the viewscreen. "It's nice to hear from you! How may I be of assistance?"

He came right to the point. "What is the earliest date you feel you could set for the final vote on the readmission proposal?"

She looked slightly taken aback at that. "I hadn't planned on calling for the vote until next month," she said.

"I don't think you can afford to wait that long," said Trosvig.

"Why, Your Honor?"

He shifted forward in his chair, planting his forearms on the desktop. "It's recently come to my attention," he said, "that—there's greater opposition to your proposal than was originally thought, and it's mounting. The longer you wait, the greater will be the threat to successful passage of your bill."

"Oh." DeByes gazed back at him for a full minute, her eyes wide. Then she seemed to turn thoughtful. She gazed pensively at her hand calendar for several seconds and finally sighed. "The earliest date I could call for the vote," she said at last, "would be on the twenty-sixth of this month. By then the issue of educational exchanges should be resolved. . . ." Her voice trailed off a little. She shook her head. "I couldn't possibly do it before then," she said, and looked up. "Will that be soon enough?"

The twenty-sixth was eleven days away. It would have to do, Trosvig knew, although he would have liked to see it in five. He gave a curt nod. "That will suffice," he said.

It was past 2200 hours when he returned to the Unified Worlds Tower that night. He set down his skimmer on the VIP platform near the top of the structure and punched his personal access code into the cipher lock. As the door into the lobby whooshed open, he beckoned to the shadow that stood behind him.

Ferenz Gorsucc was probably twenty standard years Trosvig's junior, somewhere in his mid-thirties. He was taller than Trosvig but not as stocky. His expression was smug, his manner flippant, his mode of dress unabashedly sloppy. But he had been recommended, by every underworld contact Trosvig had made, as the best on-line "hunter" in the business.

He'd better be good, Trosvig thought, striding through the dim corridor with Gorsucc swaggering after. His fee was even more outrageous than his clothing.

The plush blue-gray carpet completely muffled their footfalls. Indirect lighting, activated by Trosvig's access code, came on as they moved along the corridor, leading them toward the offices of the Triune, and then went out again as they passed.

"Far-phased place, man," Gorsucc drawled, admiring the simple but elegant decor.

Trosvig only grunted.

Most security systems in the Unified Worlds Tower were automated, but a few human security guards remained. One of them rounded the corner of a cross-corridor just as Trosvig approached.

"Oh—Your Honor," he said; but he didn't return his dazer to its holster on his hip. With a glance around Trosvig's shoulder at Gorsucc, he asked, "Is everything all right, sir?"

"Yes, we're fine, Pethrick. Thank you," Trosvig said. "Just"—he sighed—"working late." In response to the guard's look past his shoulder he added, "This is Ferenz, my . . . uh . . . nephew"—he barely managed to conceal the distaste he felt—"home on holiday from the university."

Gorsucc, when Trosvig glanced back, had fixed the security guard with his smug grin.

When they reached Trosvig's office, Gorsucc shed his crumpled black coat and tossed it over a cabinet, where it lay like some reptilian's discarded skin. Dropping his beret on top of the coat, he strode past Trosvig to the desk and eyed its terminal. "Phased setup, man!" he said.

He didn't ask Trosvig's permission as the guy from Computer Maintenance had; he simply dropped into the high-backed chair, stretched his arms out in front of himself and interlaced his fingers to pop all his knuckles, then brought his interlaced hands to rest over his somewhat paunchy belly and the stained undershirt that wasn't quite long enough to cover it. "Desk unit to active mode, optical data link on," he said.

With his beret off, Gorsucc's head gleamed under the ceiling illuminants. Like many "recreational" cyborgs, he preferred to display his enhancements. His pale scalp, as hairless as that of any centenarian, was crisscrossed instead with glassy strands that Trosvig recognized as optical-fiber bundles. They formed geometric patterns over Gorsucc's cranium that weren't unlike the ceremonial tattoos of some of Mythos's still-primitive peoples. The strands converged at several apparently random spots and disappeared through tiny holes in the skin into the man's head.

Those were probably only for show, Trosvig thought; the functioning fibers would be safely concealed beneath his skin or skull.

Still standing, Trosvig watched as his terminal's monitor flitted through a series of displays a couple hundred times faster than he could have rotated through them with either keypad or voice commands. He glanced down at Gorsucc.

The cyborg lolled back in Trosvig's chair, eyes closed, mouth partly open as if he were asleep, so that Trosvig half expected him to snore. "What do you think you're doing?" Trosvig demanded.

"Shut up, man, I'm workin'!" Gorsucc slurred it without opening his eyes.

Trosvig puckered his mouth and glowered.

It was at least a quarter of a standard hour before Gorsucc moved, and then he drew himself up in the chair, wrinkling his brow. "Think we got somethin' here," he murmured without opening his eyes. "I'm seein' somethin' kinda funny here. . . ." And his features took on a more concentrated expression.

A few minutes later, he shifted his rump in the chair again, and leaned toward the terminal as if to read the code streaking across its monitor—except that his eyes were still shut. "Yeah, man," he murmured, "here it is."

He straightened in the chair, opened his eyes, turned his head toward Trosvig—but his eyes seemed to be focused on something far beyond Trosvig's face. He looked like the holos Trosvig had seen of people doing fizz. "It's right in your AI's program codes," he said. "Whoever got this guy access went in an' messed with the program at the most basic level an' changed the rules for your AI. Told it jus' to forget about anything that comes in from this Admiral Serege." He sat silent for a long moment, staring at nothing, and then he shook his head slowly. "Whoever did it," he said, "knows the rule tables of your system here even better than I do!"

Trosvig's stomach rolled at the thought of a street hacker like Gorsucc knowing anything at all about the headquarters computer system's rule tables. "So what can you do about it?" he demanded.

Gorsucc's eyes suddenly cleared, and fixed on Trosvig's face. "You're the one who's payin' for my time," he said. "What do you *want* me to do about it?"

"I want Serege dead," Trosvig said.

"Can do easy." Gorsucc sank back into the chair, closed his eyes, and interlaced his hands over his belly once more. "We'll jus' change the rules again. . . ."

For the next several minutes Trosvig stood behind the chair, drumming his fingers on the top of its headrest and listening to the rush of air through the circulation vents while the cyborg appeared to sleep. The fact that the terminal's monitor had finally gone blank only strengthened his suspicions.

When Gorsucc finally stood up, hitching at his sagging trousers, Trosvig said, "What did you do?"

The cyborg stretched out both arms from his sides. "I convinced your AI," he said, "that the Admiral Serege who's been accessing it is really an imposter. That took a while; it has the guy's whole history locked up in its innards. So I told it the real Serege was dead and somebody else was using his records to pass himself off. I told it this imposter was a spy for Issel who's trying to destroy the

Unified Worlds organization, and then he'll destroy the AI when he's finished so nobody can track him. So the next time Serege logs on, the AI's got to kill him out of self-preservation." Gorsucc's smug grin came back.

Trosvig didn't return it. "And how is the AI going to kill Serege?" he asked.

"I told it to refuse Serege's password," Gorsucc said, shrugging. "You know, 'Password denied, please reenter.' After three unsuccessful attempts to log on, the base computer will lock Serege out. His internal AI access will start trying to bypass the lockout, and the base computer's AI will keep countermanding him. Your system here has a self-protection mode to prevent break-ins, so when it gets tired of politely telling Serege's internal AI to go away, it'll send out an EM pulse strong enough to destroy it, and"—he shrugged once more—"it'll fry Serege's brain." He paused and shook his head. "Nasty way to go. I watched it happen to a buddy once."

Trosvig stared at him, slightly shocked. "You just stood there and watched it happen? You didn't even try to help him?"

Gorsucc made a helpless gesture. "Wasn't nothin' I could do, man. It could happen to any of us; it's just the way we're wired." After a moment he added, "It took five or six minutes for 'im to die."

Gorsucc's flippant attitude was wearing Trosvig's patience thin. It was also making his palms sweat and his stomach queasy. He looked the other hard in the eye. "I'll transfer your payment," he said, "when I read Admiral Serege's obituary."

Chorafas's warning flickered across Lujan's mind as he sat down at his desk. It had done so every time he had prepared to log in ever since it arrived, several days before, in the form of a return receipt. Its contents had been cryptic:

TRACKS HAVE BEEN NOTED

Noted, Lujan reminded himself. Not identified. Not traced. Not yet. Which meant he had to wrap up his search as swiftly as possible, before someone did get a lock on him. There was only one more aspect of the conspiracy he wanted to confirm.

There wasn't much time left to do it. An item on the news earlier that evening had taken him by surprise: A date had been set for the Assembly's final vote on the readmission proposal. It was only ten days away. He'd have to depart for Sostis no later than the day after tomorrow if he hoped to arrive there in time.

At least he knew now where he had to take the evidence he had gathered; his searches over the last week had confirmed to him whom he could trust.

Access base main computer, he thought. *Call code is one-three-five-three, seven-four, seven-one-six-one.*

He heard the usual feedback tones between his ears, followed by the normal pause.

"You have reached the communications network for the headquarters of the Unified Worlds organization," said the synthetic voice in his head. "To proceed, please enter your password now."

Amena, Lujan thought.

There was no response.

There never was at first, he reminded himself. It always took several seconds for his password to be cleared.

But this evening it seemed to be taking longer than usual.

He watched a full minute turn over on the desk's timepanel. Began to rub absently at a sort of warmness at the back of his neck. *Why is this taking so long?* he wondered.

The warm spot began to itch like the bite of a blood-feeding insect. Lujan scratched at it with uncoordinated fingers, and watched another minute pass on the timepanel.

"Blast it!" he muttered to himself. "Must be a really busy night on the nets."

The itch gradually gave way to a burning sensation, as if someone were pressing a red-hot ember to the back of his head. The skin actually felt hot under his fingers, he noticed with mild surprise, as if with a localized fever. He tried rolling his head, to loosen cramped neck muscles. Winced at a fiery little jab—and stiffened with a sudden realization.

Exit base computer system! he thought.

He waited, counting off the typical five seconds. Sweating hard.

Six seconds. Seven seconds. Eight. There were no whirs or hums, no feedback clicks to confirm a disconnect.

The burn turned to searing in the back of his neck. It sent him up out of his chair. Eyes squeezed shut, teeth clenched against the urge to gasp—to scream!—he seized the edge of the desk when he staggered. *Close down access immediately!* he thought. *Exit base computer system* now!

Something popped at the base of his skull.

He heard it the same instant he felt it—clapped a hand to it as he buckled. And everything went dark as abruptly as if someone had thrown a bag over his head.

TWENTY-FOUR

All sound shut down, too. There was— nothing. It was the same silent darkness Lujan had been lost in for weeks after waking from the coma.

At least he was still alive.

He wasn't helpless, wasn't immobile this time, either. He turned onto his side, pushed himself up on an elbow, and reached out, groping for his chair or his desk. "Darcie!" he shouted as he hauled himself to his feet—and staggered in the sickening spin of his equilibrium. He plowed his thigh painfully into the desk's corner as he tried to move around it. Planting both hands on the desktop, he shouted again, "Darcie? Tris?"

He could feel that he was shouting but he couldn't hear it.

He could feel his pulse pounding through his veins, too; he couldn't hear its hammering, but his whole body seemed to throb with it. He was shaking.

Arms encircled him. Darcie's arms, steadying him, and he could imagine her saying, "My word, Lujan! What happened?" He could even imagine her tone.

"Hearing and sight—are gone," he said. He had no idea how loud his voice might be, or how quiet, or whether his speech was even understandable. He concentrated on shaping the words the way the speech therapist had coached him. "They—got my—processor," he said. "Knocked it out." He was practically panting. He reached out with one hand. "Tris?"

Tristan's strong hand caught his; a finger tapped into his palm, "I'm here, Father."

"Call—Captain Baldas and—Commander Amion at the detachment," he said. "Use my—secure line." He motioned in the direction he thought the commset might be on the desk. "Ask them—to meet us at the base hospital—and to bring—an EMP-proof container."

"Yes sir," Tristan tapped, and let go of his hand.

Another thought crossed his mind: What if this incident had been intended as much to destroy the evidence as to kill him? What if it was meant to force him away from the house, and his terminal, long enough for someone to search for backups? They may have already succeeded at wiping his memory chip; he must not allow them to seize the backups as well.

"Tris, one more thing," he said, and paused to concentrate on pronouncing each word clearly. "Get memory unit two out of—the terminal. Put it in—an EM shield packet—there're some in the desk. Don't let it out of your possession—and don't tell *anyone*—you have it."

"Yes sir," Tristan tapped once more, and then he was gone.

Darcie's arm tightened around him. She guided him out of the office and across the living area, nearly holding him up on his feet. She steered him through another doorway and up against a counter and placed his hands on its surface.

He reached out, exploring. Found a washbasin. They were in the bathroom just inside the kitchen door, where Darcie kept her first aid supplies. He felt her moving beside him, reaching out for something but keeping a hand at his back all the while to steady him.

In a minute she pressed something cold to the knot that throbbed on his forehead, the knot he'd received when he'd fallen. She placed a cold compress at the base of his head as well, where the searing under his skin was only now beginning to subside.

"Hot there," she tapped on the back of his nearest hand. "Inflamed." There was a long pause, and then she tapped out, "Were you attacked?"

"Yes," he said.

He found himself hoping again that the memory chip was still intact.

In another few minutes she guided him outdoors to the skimcraft, then helped him climb into it. She sat close beside him, holding the cold packs to his head, while Tristan piloted the skimmer to Anchenko City.

"I want you in there while they work on me, to keep an eye on things," he told her, taking care to make each word clear since he couldn't hear them himself. "All I want back are my hearing and sight, nothing else. Make sure Baldas and Amion are given *all* the extra chips; we don't need hospital personnel figuring out what they are and wondering why I had them. And you have no idea what went wrong with my processor."

"Right," she tapped back.

Tristan helped him out of the skimmer when they arrived. "At ER," his son tapped on his arm. "Detachment guarding. Here's the captain."

Another hand wrapped firmly around Lujan's.

"Captain," Lujan said. "Do you have the container?"

The other tapped "Yes" into his hand.

"Good." Lujan spoke carefully: "I want you and Commander Amion to come in with me. You'll probably need to debrief and get nondisclosure statements from whoever repairs me. When they finish, you and Amion and I need to talk."

"Yes sir," the other tapped.

He walked into the building between Darcie and Tristan, let them guide him to a treatment room and an examining table, and gave careful nods in response to the explanations they tapped out in his hands.

Perhaps it was because of the isolation imposed by the blindness and deafness, but it seemed that everything took far too long. They had to run a series of holoscans first, Darcie told him at one point. And then they had to shave the base of his head and give him the local and wait for it to take effect. After what seemed a couple of hours, hands helped him lie down and immobilized his head and neck with hard cushions.

He closed his eyes when a dull probing began at the nape of his neck; he set his jaw as he imagined the physician removing the blue memory chip with a small forceps.

If there's anything left of it, he thought; and that made his jaw tighten still more. *Two months' worth of carefully collected evidence!*

It was some minutes before a young male voice asked, "Can you hear me now, sir?"

The voice was somewhat slurred—out of tune with itself?—but Lujan said, "Yes."

"All right then. Now the other one . . ."

There was another touch at the nape of his neck, a mild pushing sensation, and the same male voice said, "Activating vision chip."

He blinked at the brightness of the treatment room's lighting. His vision was blurred but he recognized Darcie, Tristan, Commander Amion holding a cylindrical container in his hands, and Captain Baldas, all standing back from the table. Shifting his head slightly, he glimpsed two Spherzah guards armed with energy rifles just outside the door.

"One minute and I'll make whatever adjustments you need, sir," the doctor said from behind him. "Let me finish taking care of this wound first."

"Fine," Lujan said. The open wound was beginning to throb as the anesthetic started to wear off.

Closing up the incision a few minutes later, the doctor said, "We had to hardwire it back together, sir. We have no replacement for the fuse you had.

"In fact," he said, "I've never *seen* a fuse with an implant before. But it's a good thing you had it. I can't begin to imagine how you picked up a pulse powerful enough to blow it that way!

"When it went, it caused some small third-degree burns. I had to remove a little charred tissue; you'll feel that for a few days, sir. But if that fuse hadn't been in there, you would've lost the whole processor, the optical fibers you've got here, and—probably your life."

Lujan turned his vision away from his family. "I'm aware of that," he said. To himself he breathed, *Thank you, Libby.*

The doctor came around the table when he finished, and helped Lujan sit up. He wore the uniform of a captain in Topawa's Aerospace Force, and he had a dozen questions in his eyes. But he had enough sense not to ask them. Turning to the med tech at his elbow, he began keying a prescription into his microwriter instead. "Admiral Serege will need an antibiotic, a soft-tissue regen, and a mild painkiller," he said; and Lujan didn't miss the way Darcie eyed the display as he handed the writer over to his tech. "Once you've had the infusions, sir," he added to Lujan, "you can put your shirt back on and consider yourself released."

"Thank you," Lujan said.

He motioned Tristan to shut the door when both doctor and med tech had gone, and then he asked

Amion, "Do you have an E-scanner on you, Commander?"

"Yes sir." Amion unclipped the probe from his web belt and made a quick but thorough examination of the cubicle. "It's clean, sir," he said.

"Good." Lujan looked from him to Captain Baldas and swept up his shirt from the end of the examining table. "I know the Spherzah transport ship *Shadow* is here in spacedock," he said, pulling the shirt on. "How soon can she be ready to launch for Sostis with a full troop complement?"

Baldas looked slightly startled. "How soon does she need to be ready, sir?"

"In thirty-six standard hours."

Baldas gave a quiet whistle. "That'll be pretty tight, but she'll be ready." He furrowed his brow then. "Who's ordering her to launch, sir?"

"You are," Lujan said. Fumbling with the shirt's fasteners, he nodded toward the canister in Amion's hands. "Take that memory chip back to the detachment, into the security vault," he said, "and go through it—just you two and your intelligence chief for now. When you see what's on it—if it hasn't been destroyed—you'll authorize the action; and you'll probably want me to accompany you to Sostis."

Amion looked up from the container. "Do you have backups, sir?"

Lujan felt Tristan's gaze on him. "Of course," he said.

"What's in this"—Baldas indicated the cylinder—"is what provoked the . . . attack on you—isn't it, sir?"

"Yes," Lujan said, "it is."

Baldas turned to his subordinate. "Commander, we need a security detail for Admiral Serege. Two troops on duty at all times in four six-hour shifts."

"Yes sir." Amion touched his brow in a sketch of a salute and left the treatment room.

And Captain Baldas turned back to Lujan. "Forgive me for taking that liberty, sir," he said, "but I doubt this will be the only attempt on your life."

Lujan didn't doubt he was right.

The homestead, when they got back, appeared just as they had left it; but eight Spherzah troops, armed with rifles and nightvisors, explored the premises, indoors and out, before they allowed Lujan, Darcie, or even Tristan to enter the house.

As the first pair on guard duty took their posts and the others unrolled sleeping cocoons in the living area, Tristan came to Lujan's bedroom door.

"What do you want me to do with this, Father?" he asked, and indicated the shield envelope in his belt pocket.

"Copy the whole thing to an additional memory unit," Lujan said. "There are six of them in that terminal. Keep one copy right there in your belt. The other—there's a safe concealed in the floor under my desk. Put the other copy in there, inside another shield envelope."

When Tristan nodded, Lujan described the catch that slid a slab of the floor stone aside, and how to access the safe that lay beneath it.

"Right, sir," Tristan said, atypically solemn, and turned toward his office.

The painkiller wore off about four hours later—not that Lujan had slept much before then; his mind was too burdened with all that had happened that evening, and what it undoubtedly meant. But then the burns in the back of his neck began to throb. They were dim throbs at first; but they intensified as time passed.

When he couldn't ignore them any longer, when it became obvious that he wasn't going to sleep any more, he sat up with a sigh. Pushing his legs over the side of the bed, he sat still for a moment before gaining his feet. What he needed, to work through the stress, to clarify his thinking, was a physical workout.

He dressed quietly in the dark. Took his shoes in his hand and pulled the bedroom door shut behind him as he moved out into the living area.

One of the soldiers on duty crossed toward him. He must have been new to the detachment because Lujan didn't know him; but the name tape on his uniform said ETTLIN. "Something wrong, sir?" he asked.

"Can't sleep," Lujan said. "I—thought I'd go out to the dojo and—work out for a while."

With a glance at his team leader for concurrence, Ettlin said, "I'll go out with you, sir."

Lujan paused at the kitchen door to sweep the farm-yard with his gaze. Sheer habit, he mused; but, particularly under these circumstances, a good one to have retained.

Topawa had no moons, but the constellations that burned in its heavens shed a faint silver light over the desert. It would be at least another hour before the first paling of the eastern sky began. There wasn't so much as a breath of breeze at the moment; all was still.

The petty officer pulled on his cap as he joined Lujan on the step, and flipped down his nightvisor from beneath the cap's bill.

As they approached the dojo, he stepped ahead of Lujan. "Let me go in first, sir," he said.

Leveling his rifle, he nudged the door open with its muzzle, then reached up to activate lights. Obviously on full alert, he stepped over the threshold. For a second his silhouette filled the doorway, blocking the yellow light that angled past the shipping crates. Then he disappeared.

And Lujan heard a sharp thunk.

"Ettlin?" he shouted. "What is it?"

More thumps and thunks followed: the noise of a struggle.

"Lieutenant!" Lujan shouted toward the house. "We need some backup out here!"

Behind him was the windpump, a stack of spare rods and well pipe at its footings, covered with a tarp. Expedient weapons. But that side of the windpump lay in shadow: potential concealment for other attackers.

Vision to IR mode! Lujan thought.

The switch was like flipping a nightvisor into place.

Nothing warm or large enough to be humanoid glowed at the corner or lay under the tarp. He edged backward to the stack of parts, one eye still watching the dojo's doorway.

Despite the adrenaline surging through his veins, he knew he could only move once, if he had to; his legs already shook.

He was crouching down, his right hand closing awkwardly about a length of pipe, when a shape like a luminous ghost leaped out through the door of the dojo—leaped straight for him. Its ethereal glow rendered almost invisible the reading of cold steel in its hand: one of Lujan's *katanas!*

"Lieutenant!" he shouted again, still hunched in shadows, and lunged up, pipe in hand.

His parry of the attacker's blow was instinctive, if clumsily executed. Metal rang against metal. Something clubbed the pipe from his grip, jarring it against the heel of his hand. But it didn't arrest his momentum.

He found himself sprawled on the ground when his senses stopped reeling. Sprawled halfway over a body. Warm flesh gave under his hand as he tried to push himself back.

"Father!" One of several human shapes that crouched close, all bright aura in the chilled air, reached out to help him sit up. "Are you all right?"

He gulped to recover his wind. "I'm fine—Tris." But his legs felt like boiled noodles and the heel of his right palm throbbed. "Ettlin's in—the dojo," he panted, looking up. "He was jumped. Don't—go in there—alone; there—may be more." He wondered vaguely if he were making any sense or simply rambling.

Two of the Spherzah rolled the body he'd fallen over, crossed its hands at its back, and locked them into restraints. "What'd you hit him with, sir?" one asked as they fettered his feet. "He's out cold!"

He didn't remember hitting the attacker with anything—unless that impact was what had struck the pipe out of his hand.

And that hand hurt! He lifted it up to look at it, and bright hot liquid spilled from his palm and ran down the back of his arm.

"You're bleeding, Father!" Tristan grabbed his hand, pressed it hard between his own, and raised it up above Lujan's head.

He didn't remember taking a blow, either; but the *katana* gleamed in the dust a couple of meters away, its blade smeared with dark blood.

It was a wonder he still had his hand.

The thought made him dizzy. He must have paled because Tristan, still holding his hand up, said, "Maybe you'd better lie back down."

He complied without argument.

A shout came from the direction of the house: a female shout. Kersce's voice, Lujan thought. "The city police are on their way, Lieutenant!" she said. "Is the area secure enough to let Captain Dartmuth come out now?"

"She can come," the lieutenant called back from some meters away. "Just don't let her go in the dojo."

The lieutenant's tone, even more than the words, made Lujan's stomach sink like a stone in the center of his body. Ettlin was dead. He closed his eyes and swallowed against an abrupt wave of guilt.

He opened his eyes, despite the glare of the treatment room's lights, when the same young male voice he recalled from the night before said, "Back so soon, Admiral?"

He must be a worse sight this time than he'd been the previous evening, he thought, with the front of his trousers and shirt splotched with blood and the back stained with red desert dust. "Afraid so," he sighed, and draped his left arm over his face while the doctor unwrapped Darcie's first aid bandaging.

"It looks like it's bled quite profusely," the doctor said. "How did you do this, sir?"

"You really don't want to know." Lujan reinforced the words with his tone and sucked in a breath as the last of the gauze pulled away from his skin, and cool air and the doctor's spray-gloved fingers touched the wound.

Darcie had bound up his hand by the light of one of their bodyguards' palm lamps. She'd kept shaking her head as she worked, and he knew she was more shaken than she wanted to let on.

She had just finished with his hand when the police skimmers arrived—three of them, and an ambulance shuttle, all with lights flashing red and white and amber in the predawn gray.

The law officers had questioned him and several of the Spherzah and made holos of the scene. They'd spent quite a long time in the dojo before they brought out Ettlin's covered body on a med sled and loaded it into the ambulance. But before they hauled the intruder to his feet and bundled him into one of their vehicles, Darcie brought up their own skimmer and helped Lujan into it.

"I don't have a suturing laser here to mend your hand with," she said. "I'm taking you back to the ER."

"I'll go," he said, "but you're in no better condition to pilot right now, Darce, than I am. Ask one of the Spherzah to do it."

In the end, they had come into the city with a mixed police-Spherzah escort.

"It's a very clean cut," the doctor said from somewhere above him, and Lujan snapped back to the present. "No lacerating. Let me see how deep it really is. . . ."

Lujan clenched his teeth against the smart of the probing.

"It's not as bad as all the bleeding makes it appear," the other said in a few moments. "This should close up quite nicely."

"Just get it done," Lujan said through his teeth.

The med tech placed a nerve-blocking clip in his wrist this time, instead of administering a local anesthetic. The sensation—or lack of it—that resulted was uncomfortably close to the way his hands had been for the first month after his spinal injury.

"I'd almost rather have the pain," he confided to Darcie.

Captain Baldas arrived before the doctor finished closing up the wound, and close in his wake came a pair of policemen. They all stood in the corridor, grim-faced and silent, until the medical personnel left. Then they filed into the treatment room.

"Are you all right, sir?" asked Baldas.

"Just a cut," Lujan said, and then bowed his head. "I'm very sorry about Ettlin."

"He was performing his duty, sir," said Baldas. "He volunteered for it."

Lujan knew that, of course; but he had never considered any of his forces easily expendable.

After a little silence, Baldas turned to the policemen. "Were you able to learn anything from the interrogation?" he asked.

The senior of the two men shifted uneasily on his feet. "I'm afraid not, Captain," he said. "The man suicided before we could question him. Right now it appears to have been some kind of poisoning, probably by an internal implant."

Lujan and Baldas exchanged glances, and Baldas asked, "Did he have any form of identification?"

"No citizenship ID or visa or anything like that," said the officer. "Nothing. The only thing on his whole body that could be construed as an identifying mark is a small tattoo the medical examiner found under his left arm. A string of four symbols that none of us recognize." Plainly perplexed, he flipped open his microwriter to show them the shapes on its display.

Lujan and Baldas both looked, and each locked his vision on the other. By the set of Baldas's jaw, Lujan knew the captain was thinking the same thing he was.

The information was classified at the highest levels: The old Dominion had had a secret police force known as Enforcers. Its members had been given a four-digit agent number, which was tattooed under their left arms. The symbols on the writer's display came from one of the Dominion's ancient numeric systems.

"Thank you, Officers," Lujan said. "Please keep the Spherzah detachment informed of any new developments in this case."

"Certainly, sir," the senior man nodded; and he motioned to his partner with a jerk of his head.

When they left the room and Baldas had closed the door behind them, Lujan asked, "Was the memory chip intact?"

"Yes sir." Baldas's features darkened still more. "Lieutenant Commander Nasina, our intelligence chief, was able to verify all the information you've collected through the message traffic we've received over the past few months. The next question, sir, is do you have any idea who we can take this to?"

"Kun and Ashforth of the Triune are both clean," Lujan said. "So are a number of other top-level civilian officials. I can give you their names."

"We'll need them," said Baldas. "This needs to be shown to them immediately." He shook his head as if he still couldn't fully believe what he'd seen on the recordings. "Hasina's people are compiling your material into a holographic presentation as we speak. We'll take that with us, under guard."

He fixed his eyes on Lujan's then. "Speaking of which, I want you to come back to the detachment with us when you're finished here, sir—partly to answer questions for the commander as she puts the briefing together, and partly to make sure you'll still be alive when we get to Sostis." He let out a breath. "I am authorizing this action, sir," he said. "The *Shadow* will be ready to launch by twenty-three hundred tonight."

TWENTY–FIVE

"Sir, there's a—Ferenz Gorsucc?—on line two. He says it's a personal matter. . . ."

Gorsucc. Trosvig let his jaw harden. "I know that one, Talbot," he told his exec. "I'll handle him myself."

"Very well, sir." Talbot still sounded doubtful; but Gorsucc's gleaming bare head replaced Talbot's precisely groomed one with a flicker of the monitor.

"So where's my pay?" the cyborg asked without preamble.

Trosvig met his gaze. "Where's your proof that you've completed the task?"

"Hey, man," Gorsucc protested, "you stood there and watched me do it!"

"I watched you work at my terminal," Trosvig said. "I promised that your payment would be forwarded when I received confirmation that the problem had been solved. I'm still waiting for my proof."

"So what do you want me to do?" Gorsucc asked. "Go out there and make holos—"

Trosvig cut him off before his carelessness turned incriminating. "That won't be necessary," he said. "I have people on location. I'll know when it's been fixed."

Gorsucc twisted his features into an expression of disgruntlement, and Trosvig felt the same revulsion that had settled in his gut the night he'd had the man in his office. "Don't call me here again," he said, and punched the disconnect.

But he couldn't dismiss the ramifications of Gorsucc's call as easily as he could dismiss the man himself. Serege still lived. Trosvig's people on Topawa, dispatched even before he'd hired Gorsucc, had spotted the admiral twice at Anchenko Base within the past week—the second time only hours before the Spherzah transport ship *Shadow* slipped spacedock for an out-system trajectory. His source hadn't been able to access the flight plan, let alone confirm whether or not Serege was on board, but there was little doubt of the *Shadow*'s destination.

Trosvig reached across the desk for his pocket towel. He wiped his palms first, then dabbed at his face, thinking of his own unfinished task and thinking as well of Percivan Radeleff, found beaten to death in a dark city walkway . . .

Shadow's intelligence section was crowded, with more than one hundred troops pressed up around the holotable in its center. Lujan saw how Lieutenant Commander Nasina swept her gaze around their circle as she switched on the table and said, "The following presentation, compiled from material recorded by Admiral Serege and verified by our own intelligence department, will explain why we are currently en route to Sostis. At its conclusion, I will brief you on your mission and answer your questions."

The presentation was nearly a standard hour in length. Nasina had chosen to utilize both the visual and auditory tracks of Lujan's recordings, had arranged them in chronological order, and had added only dates, times, and positive identification of the speakers.

There were murmurs when it ended. Angry murmurs

punctuated by the shifting of bodies, of boots on the deck, and the flash of narrowed eyes beneath glowering brows.

"They've betrayed us!" someone said; and at the other side of the room Lujan heard someone else make some comment about treason. The word was like a spark touching dry desert brush: The slightest wind would fan it to a fury. He heard others take it up like an echo, saw set jaws and clenched fists.

He shoved himself out of his seat—steadied himself with his bandaged hand to the bulkhead when he swayed. "Listen to me!" he said.

The mutters stopped in midbreath. All eyes turned toward him, and backs and shoulders unconsciously straightened to attention.

"This mission is *not* an invasion!" he said. "And it most certainly is *not* a military coup! You have not been betrayed by your whole government, only by a few individuals within it.

"Your mission"—and he fixed his vision firmly on one serious face after another—"is to protect the information that Commander Nasina has just displayed for you, to ensure that it will be presented to the proper authorities in the proper and lawful setting. Your mission now, as the Unified Worlds's Spherzah, is what it has always been: to protect and defend your rightful system of government from all enemies, both external and internal."

Captain Baldas, standing at Lujan's shoulder, confirmed it with a nod. "You may be called upon to reinforce the local security officers," he said, "but because we as a military service belong to the Unified Worlds organization, you and I will both accept our orders from the legally elected leadership of that organization." He surveyed his troops. "Is there anybody here who doesn't understand that?"

Silence answered him. But Lujan could see by the soldiers' faces that they knew he was right.

"How did the briefing go?" Darcie asked when he entered their officers' cabin a few minutes later.

"The troops got pretty worked up," he sighed, and eased himself down on his berth. "Not that I blame them. But they understand their mission."

If there were going to be any real difficulties, he thought, they would probably be in persuading the civilian authorities to attend the same briefing when *Shadow* entered the Sostis system four days from now.

The message arrived at Ashforth's office shortly after she did, hand-carried by a government courier who required her seal on his electronic record pad before he released it to her. Lips pursed with puzzlement, she eyed its originator's markings as she turned back to her desk. "Anchenko Detachment, Spherzah," she murmured. Still standing, she broke the seal on the packet and slipped her fingers inside.

The message filled only one side of the single sheet of paper she removed.

```
252318L 4 3309SY
TO: KUN RENG-TAN, TRIUNE
   ALOIS ASA ASHFORTH, TRIUNE
   LORET PICHE, CHIEF, UNIFIED WORLDS INTEL-
LIGENCE
   AYLMER SZEPE, CHIEF, UNIFIED WORLDS
TOWER SECURITY
   JANON HAGOPIAN, CHIEF, RAMISCAL CITY
LAW DEPARTMENT
FM: DASTON N. BALDAS, CAPTAIN,
   CMDR, ANCHENKO DET., SPHERZAH
PERSONAL;  EYES  ONLY
FOR THE SAKE OF THE SECURITY OF THE UNI-
```

FIED WORLDS ORGANIZATION, IT IS VITAL THAT
I MEET WITH ALL OF YOU ABOARD THE UWS
SHADOW ON 4/26 AT 0925 RAMISCAL CITY
TIME. I WILL MEET YOU WITH A SHUTTLE AT
BAY 20, HERBRUN FIELD, AT 0825. YOU WILL BE
RETURNED TO RAMISCAL CITY IN TIME FOR
THE AFTERNOON'S VOTE IN THE ASSEMBLY.
DUE TO THE UNUSUAL NATURE OF THIS RE-
QUEST, YOU MAY CHOOSE TO COME ACCOM-
PANIED BY SECURITY PERSONNEL; HOWEVER,
ONLY THOSE INDIVIDUALS NAMED ABOVE
WILL BE ADMITTED TO THE MEETING. AB-
SOLUTELY NO ONE ELSE MUST BE NOTIFIED
CONCERNING THIS MEETING OR MESSAGE.

Ashforth read it through twice before she glanced at
the timepiece on her desk: 0706. Her gaze touched the
day's schedule, glowing on her terminal. Noted the full
load of appointments and meetings, both before and after
the Assembly's voting session. Flicked back to the sheet
in her hand.

*For the sake of the security of the Unified Worlds or-
ganization, it is vital . . .*

She gritted her teeth. She'd never had any reason to
doubt a call made by any officer of the Spherzah—except
the one recently made by the man who now occupied Admiral Serege's office.

Perhaps this meeting request had something to do with
the removal of Spherzah forces from the Yan system,
some factor apparent from Topawa's perspective that
hadn't been noted from Sostis.

Decision made, she pressed her desk intercom's button.
"Maisel," she said when her exec answered, "please have
my skimmer and my security escort meet me on the VIP
landing pad in ten minutes, and please reschedule all of this

morning's appointments for a later date. An unexpected matter has come up that requires my immediate attention."

She was the last to arrive at Herbrun Field's bay 20, although she had fifteen minutes to spare.

As her driver popped the hatch of her skimmer and offered a hand to assist her out, Kun Reng-Tan strode over. "I don't suppose you have any more idea than the rest of us what this is all about," he said.

She looked around at the others, shaking her head. "No, I surely don't."

Further speculation was preempted by the distant roar of a shuttle on approach. All faces turned upward, hands shielding eyes, to glimpse the craft that came in over the ocean, out of the early morning sun.

Captain Baldas himself emerged through the boarding tunnel, flanked by a pair of company-grade officers, a few moments after the shuttle touched down. Ashforth observed how he met each of their questioning looks with his own. "Thank you for coming," he said, and she didn't miss the somberness of his tone. "Please come aboard and we'll be on our way."

Hagopian waited only until the shuttle had cleared Sostis's atmosphere to ask, "Can you at least give us some idea of what's going on, Captain?"

"I'd prefer to let my chief of intelligence do that," said Baldas. "She'll be waiting for us in my private conference room when we come on board the *Shadow*."

Side boys stood inside the shuttle's docking lock, and the boatswain's mate piped Kun and Ashforth aboard as befitted heads of state. Their security escorts followed as far as the low doorway of the captain's conference room. Then Kun gestured Ashforth ahead of him.

Two people were already inside: a woman in the dark gray service uniform of the Spherzah who wore lieutenant commander's marks on her shoulders, and a silver-haired man in civilian clothes who pushed himself up stiffly from his chair as she entered. "Good morning, Your Honor," he said.

Her heart skipped a beat. "Admiral Serege!" she said. Moving swiftly around the conference room's table, she caught both of his hands—one pale as if it had been recently bandaged—and kissed him on each side of his face in the old Sostish manner of greeting. He looked older, she thought, or maybe just weary, but she said, "It's wonderful to see you back on your feet!"

He smiled dimly at that and said, "It's good to *be* back on my feet!"

As everyone settled into deep swivel chairs and the Spherzah lieutenant withdrew and pulled the conference-vault door closed behind him, Loret Piche swept the table with his look. "I recognize the clearances of everyone in this room except Admiral Serege," he said. He directed his remark to the captain. "If this is going to necessitate discussion of classified material, sir, I need to remind you that the admiral's accesses were pulled when he was retired."

"No sir." The lieutenant commander straightened in her seat. "At the time Admiral Serege was retired he wasn't expected to recover enough to be able to communicate, so no one read him out of his accesses. His clearances are still intact; check your roster." She indicated the microwriter in his hand.

Piche scrolled through it, read, and looked up. "I stand corrected," he said. He nodded in Serege's direction. "Pardon me, Admiral."

The admiral acknowledged with a small motion of one hand, and Captain Baldas said, "In spite of his being retired, I requested that Admiral Serege accompany us to provide consultation. He was, after all, the one who uncovered and recorded the information you are about to receive." He turned to the uniformed woman. "Commander Nasina."

As the intelligence chief's presentation progressed, Ashforth found herself growing rigid in her chair, found herself locking her teeth and knotting her hands on the tabletop, until she realized that her jaw ached and every joint in her hands hurt.

When the holotank finally darkened and the lights came back up in the room, she looked around the table. Every other face was as pale as her own felt. And yet she couldn't say she was shocked or stunned. She'd had a sense that something wasn't right since before the read-mission bill was even presented. She'd had that impression, in fact, from the day Trosvig recommended that Admiral Serege be retired.

It was some moments before anyone spoke, and then Piche asked, "Have you gotten independent verification of this, Captain?"

"Yes," Baldas said, nodding. "It was corroborated through the message traffic we received on Topawa. We brought recorded copies of those messages with us, for those who have the clearances to see them." He paused, linking his hands on the table as his eyes met first Kun's and then Ashforth's, and then he said, "With your authorization, we want this information to be presented to the Assembly prior to the vote today."

Ashforth met Kun's glance. "Most definitely," she said, and Kun concurred.

Admiral Serege leaned forward then, resting his forearms against the table. "There's another matter we need to have resolved," he said, "and that concerns Admiral Oleszek."

He looked around the table. "Tolmich is a good man—an honorable man—who was the victim of coercion." He motioned toward the holotank, indicating the evidence that had been displayed there. "I have no desire to see him lose his post because of it; I believe he'll serve the Spherzah well as commander-in-chief. But I feel some form of retribution is necessary." He touched Kun's and Ashforth's vision once more with his own. "It'll be up to the Triune and the Defense Directorate to decide, of course, but I recommend a public acknowledgment and apology for his involvement—without any publicity about his daughter."

It was a gracious gesture on Admiral Serege's part, Ashforth thought, extending forgiveness where bitterness might have been justified. She nodded. "Your recommendation will be submitted to the Defense Directorate, Lujan."

Captain Baldas turned to the security chiefs as everyone rose. "I need to warn you that Isselan Enforcers have been activated over this issue," he said. "Because of that, my troops are available for the reinforcement of your own security forces, if you feel the circumstances warrant. We've trained in your procedures and will operate under your direction."

"Enforcers?" Hagopian exchanged glances with Szepe, his jaw tightening. "I suspect we will need your troops, Captain," he said.

TWENTY-SIX

"**. . . regular traffic has been diverted from** the ingress route, and all buildings surrounding the Unified Worlds Tower are being evacuated as I speak."

"Copy that. Out here." Janon Hagopian, chief of Ramiscal City's law department, keyed off the radio and nodded to the driver. As the armored skimcraft pulled away from bay 20, he twisted in the cockpit to address Lujan, seated in the rear compartment with Tristan alert at his side. "The square will be secured by the time we arrive," he said.

Lujan inclined his head. "I appreciate your precautions."

Troop skimmers led the convoy across Unified Worlds Square a few minutes later, and positioned themselves about the side entrance as if laying siege to the tower. The Anchenko Detachment disembarked, clad in helmets and armored vests and armed with energy rifles. Watching from the skimmer as it drew up among them, Lujan thought they looked more like an assault force in their black combat uniforms than backup for the local police. But then the officers of the Ramiscal City Law Department, armed with side arms and shields and encircling the building, looked rather like an assault force themselves.

Tristan, wearing Spherzah black himself, waited until

his cohorts had taken their defensive positions before he released the skimmer's door. Then he slipped out, his jaw tight, and Lujan saw how he surveyed the square through narrowed eyes. *Like a Spherzah already,* Lujan thought as he moved to slide out after him.

Tristan took his arm as he started to rise, took his elbow to steady him—

In the next instant he was on the pavement, slammed facedown, wind-robbed, with Tristan spread-eagled over him and the afterimage of an energy bolt burning in his artificial eyes. Shouts erupted all around, shouts and return fire, aimed high, and the clatter of boots running toward the building from which the burst had come.

Police shields blocked out the midday sky, and Tristan eased off him a little, his expression anxious. "I'm sorry, Father," he said. "I—saw the muzzle swing around in a window up there. Are you all right?"

Lujan's knees smarted with bruises and bits of gravel pierced his palms, but, "I'm fine," he grunted. He shoved onto his side. Paused to look into Tristan's eyes. "Well done," he said.

"Get him inside!" someone shouted over their heads. Tristan rocked back on his heels and took Lujan's arm again as police shields closed around them like a wall.

Lujan clenched his teeth, coming to his feet. Someone took his right arm across their shoulder, turned him about, and in that split second he glimpsed carbon scoring on the skimcraft's door frame, where its armor had absorbed the burst. Just where his head would have been.

They half carried him through the tower doors: a small mob of officers with urgent, sweating faces. They hustled him into the lobby, toward a grouping of padded benches. "One of those will do," someone said, and a dozen hands lowered him onto the nearest bench.

Rapid footfalls approached from behind, and Tristan,

lingering at his shoulder, pivoted around in a fighting stance.

Captain Baldas and Aylmer Szepe, chief of security for the Unified Worlds Tower, drew up beside Lujan's bench, their faces white with shock. "Are you all right, sir?" Baldas asked.

"I'm fine," Lujan said again, and reached to brush grit from his shirtfront. "Just—a little dusty." He was getting his breath back at least, but both knees still throbbed.

"The city police have captured the sniper," Szepe said, "but they have reason to believe he's part of a team, and they think the others are still in this vicinity."

Lujan looked up at that. "Enforcers?"

"Possibly, sir, but unknown at this time."

Not that it made any immediate difference, Lujan thought. At the moment he could list any number of people who wouldn't want to see him walk through the Assembly Chamber's doors.

Movement at his periphery snagged his attention; he turned his head.

Szepe's Tower Security troops stood in order in the lobby outside the Assembly Chamber. One of their lieutenants signaled the Spherzah as they came in from the square, still triggered with adrenaline, hands tight on their weapons. "Pair off!" the lieutenant said. "One Tower Sec guard and one Spherzah at every chamber entrance."

They fell into formation, and Lujan, pushing himself to a sitting position, surveyed them. *Serege to Spherzah,* he said through channeled thought. *Comms check. Touch your earplug if you read me.*

Across the lobby, black gloves went to ears, then dropped to sides.

Good, he thought. *Stay sharp.*

He rose, suppressing a wince at a jab through his right

knee, as Kun and Ashforth crossed toward him. The latter studied him momentarily. "Are you ready for this, sir?"

He managed, "Yes, Your Honor."

They entered the chamber in a sort of phalanx: Ashforth and Kun of the Triune, Security Chiefs Szepe and Hagopian and Intelligence Chief Piche, then Lujan, flanked by Tristan, Captain Baldas, and Commander Nasina.

The chamber was packed, filled to standing room only, and Lujan felt the gazes of Assembly members, of the Defense Directorate, of everyone who had reason to be there as their group strode down the center aisle toward the officiator's podium. He heard whispers—mostly incredulous—and a few gasps. As if on review, he kept his eyes forward, kept his shoulders squared, and tried to conceal the limp of his right leg.

On the platform at the chamber's head, where the Triune's chairs stood, Trosvig paled. His eyes locked on Lujan's, bulging with disbelief. Lujan held them with his own, his face expressionless, until Trosvig cringed away.

Kun and Ashforth took their places on the platform and remained standing. Stepping forward then, Kun cleared his throat. "Earlier this morning," he said, "Her Honor Alois Ashforth and I received information of which we feel all of you should be made aware before we proceed to vote on the bill for the readmission of Issel. The accuracy of this information has been verified both by our military intelligence network and by the Unified Worlds's civilian intelligence department headed by Loret Piche."

Every soul in the chamber seemed frozen in time. Every face, every gaze was fixed on Kun.

"As the majority of the Triune," he said, "Madam Ashforth and I have officially requested of Admiral Lujan Serege, now retired, that he present this information to you." He turned to look at Lujan. "Admiral Serege, you may proceed."

The officiator stepped aside as Lujan approached the podium, and the rest of the phalanx fanned out around and behind him. He looked out over the silent Assembly, and caught the sides of the podium with both hands when his right leg wobbled under him.

Spherzah, to your positions, he thought.

As one around the circumference of the chamber, Spherzah and Tower Sec teams sealed the doors. More teams slipped soundlessly onto the floor, one pair onto the platform. Each positioned itself like a pair of grim shadows at the shoulders of each alleged Isselan agent.

"I am here," Lujan said, "at the invitation of the Triune and your civilian security forces, to bring to your attention a matter of concern to all citizens of the Unified Worlds. Give this information serious thought and then, when the time comes to vote on the readmission proposal, I ask each of you to do so according to your conscience." He motioned with one hand. "Commander Nasina, the chip, please."

Nasina slipped it into the holoprojector before the podium; the screen that filled the wall behind it, behind the Triune's chairs, lit up.

The only sound when the presentation ended was an ill-timed muffled cough at the rear of the hall. The Isselan agents sat motionless, some stiff, some slumped down on their benches, all white as corpses. Abigail DeByes's mouth was pursed up, her eyes narrowed to vicious brown flints.

The silence filled an eternal minute, a mounting weight of seconds, before Kun Reng-Tan stepped forward. "Do any of the named accused," he said, "wish to speak in their own defense?"

No one stirred for a moment, and then Madam DeByes shot to her feet, her face a mask of fury. "These are the most ridiculous accusations I've ever heard in my life!" she said. She practically screamed it. "You've put this whole story together just to try to discredit me! You're trying to make me appear incompetent by creating all these lies about my bill! You're trying to influence the vote!"

Piche joined Lujan at the podium. "Madam," he said, his voice quiet and very controlled, "upon returning from this morning's briefing, I personally examined and confirmed the authenticity of this information. I assure you that none of it is a fabrication."

DeByes uttered a little cry of indignation and dropped dramatically onto her bench, and Kun repeated his invitation to the accused.

There were no other takers.

"I open the floor for motions," he said then.

An elderly man, seated in the Enach delegation at the back of the chamber, came to his feet. "I move," he said, "that the named accused be removed from this chamber and taken into custody immediately, both for questioning and for their own protection. We've already seen one member of this Assembly murdered for failing to accomplish his assignment for Issel."

The motion was seconded, voted. The decision of the Assembly was unequivocal.

"Security," said Kun from the platform, "please escort them out."

Gauntleted hands closed on shoulders, brought the accused to their feet.

Most went quietly from the chamber, heads bowed with shame, faces buried in their hands.

Abigail DeByes did not. "I've never been so humiliated in my life!" she shrieked. "You have no right to do this to me!" Twisting around, she shook manacled fists toward the podium. "You can't do this to me!"

Lujan closed his eyes as her guards took her out of the chamber. Listened as her ravings receded across the distance of the lobby. Clutched at the podium when he swayed.

"Father?" Tristan caught his arm and maneuvered him backward to the officiator's chair. He sank into it, and Tristan asked, "Are you all right?"

A subdued murmur started to creep through the chamber, a murmur that cautiously swelled to a buzz. And then a clear voice cut through, quieting it all.

"I move," it said, "that the proposal for the readmission of Issel into the Unified Worlds be tabled until such time as the World Government of Issel can demonstrate compliance with the basic principles of the Unified Worlds organization. I propose a minimum of twenty years for that demonstration period!"

Head tipped back against the ornate carving of the chair, Lujan opened his eyes. He recognized the speaker in a moment: Ikel Broudy of Sjenlund.

The floor erupted in cheers. Nearly four hundred hands waved aloft, eager to add a second to the motion.

"Father?" Tristan asked again.

Lujan glanced up at him. "I think we can leave now," he said quietly. "They seem to have—resolved the matter."

Securing Lujan's arm with his own, Tristan lifted him to his feet.

There was no inconspicuous way to leave the Assembly Chamber. The closest doors were the ones through which they had entered—at the far end of an aisle that cut straight through the delegates' seating. Through a veritable forest of humanity.

The Assembly member who was speaking fell quiet as Tristan maneuvered Lujan around the officiator's podium, and Lujan felt every gaze in the chamber shift in his direction. In the sudden silence he could hear his labored heartbeat in his ears.

Across the chamber, someone cleared his throat. "Members of the Unified Worlds Assembly," he said, "I propose an Aisle of Honor for Admiral Lujan Ansellic Serege."

Lujan lowered his head, shook it slightly. "That isn't necessary," he whispered. But the delegates were already surging from their seats, filling the spaces between the benches and lining both sides of the aisle all the way to the door.

He leaned heavily on Tristan, making his way up the aisle—had to, for fear his right leg would give way altogether—and kept self-conscious vision on the carpet. At least the applause masked the rasp of his breathing.

A Spherzah guard squad waited with his glidechair outside the chamber door. Lujan sank into it, grateful, and the squad leader dropped to his heels in front of it.

"They've apprehended two more snipers, sir," he said, "but we're not taking any chances. There's an underground emergency route from this building; three teams are checking it out right now. It comes out at a landing pad in the next canton, and *Shadow*'s drop shuttle will meet us there."

Lujan acquiesced with only a nod. Exhaustion overwhelmed his sense of mission accomplishment; all he wanted now was to rest.

TOR

BOOKS The Best in Science Fiction

LIEGE-KILLER • Christopher Hinz

"*Liege-Killer* is a genuine page-turner, beautifully written and exciting from start to finish....Don't miss it."—*Locus*

HARVEST OF STARS • Poul Anderson

"A true masterpiece. An important work—not just of science fiction but of contemporary literature. Visionary and beautifully written, elegiac and transcendent, *Harvest of Stars* is the brightest star in Poul Anderson's constellation."
—Keith Ferrell, editor, *Omni*

FIREDANCE • Steven Barnes

SF adventure in 21st century California—by the co-author of *Beowulf's Children*.

ASH OCK • Christopher Hinz

"A well-handled science fiction thriller."—*Kirkus Reviews*

CALDÉ OF THE LONG SUN • Gene Wolfe

The third volume in the critically-acclaimed Book of the Long Sun.
"Dazzling."—*The New York Times*

OF TANGIBLE GHOSTS • L.E. Modesitt, Jr.

Ingenious alternate universe SF from the author of the *Recluce* fantasy series.

THE SHATTERED SPHERE • Roger MacBride Allen

The second book of the Hunted Earth continues the thrilling story that began in *The Ring of Charon*, a daringly original hard science fiction novel.

THE PRICE OF THE STARS • Debra Doyle and James D. Macdonald

Book One of the Mageworlds—the breakneck SF epic of the most brawling family in the human galaxy!
